*Many of these titles are also available as abridged and unabridged audiobooks.
Order the full range of Horus Heresy novels and audiobooks from*
www.blacklibrary.com

Nick Kyme

VULKAN LIVES

Unto the anvil

BLACK LIBRARY

A BLACK LIBRARY PUBLICATION

Hardback edition first published in 2013.
This edition published in 2013 by
Black Library,
Games Workshop Ltd.,
Willow Road,
Nottingham, NG7 2WS, UK.

10 9 8 7 6 5 4 3 2 1

Cover illustration by Neil Roberts.

A CIP record for this book is available from the British Library.

UK ISBN: 978 1 84970 512 7
US ISBN: 978 1 84970 513 4

See Black Library on the internet at

www.blacklibrary.com

Find out more about Games Workshop
and the world of Warhammer 40,000 at

www.games-workshop.com

Printed and bound by CPI Group (UK) Ltd, Croydon, CR0 4YY

THE HORUS HERESY®
It is a time of legend.

The galaxy is in flames. The Emperor's glorious vision for humanity is in ruins. His favoured son, Horus, has turned from his father's light and embraced Chaos.

His armies, the mighty and redoubtable Space Marines, are locked in a brutal civil war. Once, these ultimate warriors fought side by side as brothers, protecting the galaxy and bringing mankind back into the Emperor's light.
Now they are divided.

Some remain loyal to the Emperor, whilst others have sided with the Warmaster. Pre-eminent amongst them, the leaders of their thousands-strong Legions are the primarchs. Magnificent, superhuman beings, they are the crowning achievement of the Emperor's genetic science. Thrust into battle against one another, victory is uncertain for either side.

Worlds are burning. At Isstvan V, Horus dealt a vicious blow and three loyal Legions were all but destroyed. War was begun, a conflict that will engulf all mankind in fire. Treachery and betrayal have usurped honour and nobility. Assassins lurk in every shadow. Armies are gathering.
All must choose a side or die.

Horus musters his armada, Terra itself the object of his wrath. Seated upon the Golden Throne, the Emperor waits for his wayward son to return. But his true enemy is Chaos, a primordial force that seeks to enslave mankind to its capricious whims.

The screams of the innocent, the pleas of the righteous resound to the cruel laughter of Dark Gods. Suffering and damnation await all should the Emperor fail and the war be lost.

The age of knowledge and enlightenment has ended.
The Age of Darkness has begun.

~ DRAMATIS PERSONAE ~

The XVIII Legion 'Salamanders'

VULKAN	Primarch, the Lord of the Drakes
ARTELLUS NUMEON	Pyre Captain, and Vulkan's equerry
LEODRAKK	Pyre Guard
SKATAR'VAR	Pyre Guard
VARRUN	Pyre Guard
GANNE	Pyre Guard
IGATARON	Pyre Guard
ATANARIUS	Pyre Guard
NEMETOR	Captain, 15th Company Reconnaissance
K'GOSI	Captain, Pyroclast of the 21st Company
SHEN'RA	Techmarine

The VIII Legion 'Night Lords'

KONRAD CURZE	Primarch, the 'Night Haunter'

The X Legion 'Iron Hands'

FERRUS MANUS	Primarch, the Gorgon
DOMADUS	Battle-brother and unofficial quartermaster
VERUD PERGELLEN	Legionary sniper

The XIX Legion 'Raven Guard'

CORVUS CORAX — Primarch, the Ravenlord

HRIAK — Librarian, Codicier

AVUS — Battle-brother

The XVII Legion 'Word Bearers'

EREBUS — Dark Apostle, disgraced First Chaplain

VALDREKK ELIAS — Dark Apostle, sworn to the service of Erebus

BARTHUSA NAREK — Huntsman, former legionary Vigilator

Non-Legion personnel

SERIPH — Remembrancer

VERACE — Remembrancer

CAEREN SEBATON — Frontier archaeologist

From scorched earth…

'VULKAN LIVES.'

Two words. Two grating words. They closed around me like a rusty trap, snaring me with their savage teeth. So many dead… No, slain. And yet…

Vulkan.

Lives.

I felt each one reverberate inside my skull like a triphammer striking a tuning fork, pressing at my temples, every syllable pulsing headache-red. They were little more than a mocking whisper, these two simple words, mocking me because I survived when I should have died. Because I lived, they did not.

Surprise, awe, or perhaps it was the simple desire not to be heard that made the speaker craft his words so quietly. In any case, the voice that gave utterance to them was confident and full of undeniable charisma.

I knew its cadence, its timbre, as familiarly as I knew my own. I recognised the voice of my gaoler. And I, too, rasped as I declared it to him.

'Horus…'

For all my brother's obvious and demonstrative puissance, even in his voice, I could barely speak. It was as if I'd been buried for a long time and my throat was hoarse from swallowing too much dirt. I had yet to open my eyes, for the lids were leaden and stung as if they'd been washed out with neat promethium.

Promethium.

The word brought back a sense memory, the image of a battlefield swathed in smog and redolent of death. Blood saturated the air. It soaked the black sand underfoot. Smoke clung to banners edged in fire. In fragments, I recalled a battle unlike any other that I or my Legion had ever fought. Such vast forces, such strength of arms, almost elemental in their fury. Brothers killed brothers, a death toll in the tens of thousands. Maybe more.

I saw Ferrus die, even though I wasn't present at his murder, but in my mind I saw it. We had a bond, he and I, forged in more than fraternal blood. We were too alike not to.

This was Isstvan V that I saw. A black, benighted world swarmed by a sea of legionaries bent on mutual destruction. Battle tanks by the hundreds, Titans roaming the horizon in murderous packs, drop-ships flooding the sky and choking it with their death-smoke and their engine fumes.

Chaos. Utter, unimaginable chaos.

That word had a different meaning now.

Further snatches of the massacre returned to me. I saw a hillside, a company of battle tanks at the summit. Their cannons were aimed low, firing off ordnance into our ranks and punishing us against the anvil.

Armour cracked. Fire rained. Bodies broke.

I charged with the Pyre Guard, but they soon lost pace with me as my anger overtook my capacity for reason. I hit the tanks on my own at first, like a hammer. With my hands I tore into the line of armour, battered it, roaring my defiance at a sky drenched crimson.

As my sons caught up to my wrath, light and fire arrived in the wake of my assault. It tore open the sky in a great strip of blinding magnesium white. Those nearby shut their eyes to it, but I saw the missiles hit. I watched the detonation and beheld the fire as it spread across the world like a boiling ocean.

Then there was darkness… for a time, until I remembered waking, but dazed. My war-plate was burned. I had been thrown from the battle. Alone, I staggered to my feet and saw a fallen son.

It was Nemetor.

Like an infant I cradled him, raising *Dawnbringer* aloft and crying out my anguish for all the good it would do. Because no matter how much you wish for it, the dead do not come back. Not really. And if they do, if by some fell craft you can restore them, they are forever changed. Revenants. Only a god can bring back the dead and return them to the living, and we had all been told that gods did not exist. I would come to understand the great folly and undeniable truth of that in the time that followed.

My enemies reached me in a flood, stabbing with knives and bludgeoning with clubs. Some were midnight-clad, others wrapped in iron. I killed almost three score before they took Nemetor from my arms. And as I knelt there, bruised and bleeding, a shadow fell across me.

I asked, *'Why, brother?'*

And these next words were freshest in my memory, because of what Curze said as he loomed over me.

'Because you're the one who's here.'

It wasn't the answer I was expecting. My question had a much wider meaning than what Curze took it to be. Perhaps there was no answer, for isn't it inevitable that one day a son will rebel against his father and desire to succeed him, even if that succession meant committing patricide?

Though my eyes were gummed with blood, my helmet gone, I swore I saw Curze smiling as he looked down on me as at one of his slaves. The bastard. Even now, I believe he found it amusing. All the horror, the dirty shame of treachery and how it stuck to all of our skins. We primarchs, we who were supposed to be the best of all men, turned out to be the very worst.

Konrad had always enjoyed irony like that. It brought us all down to his level.

'You are full of surprises.'

At first I thought it was Curze again – my sense of time and space was colliding but not connecting, making it hard to focus properly – but he never said that to me at Isstvan; he never said anything else after that moment.

No, it was Horus speaking. That cultured tonality, that deep basso which had made this treachery possible. Only he could have done it. I just didn't know why. Not yet.

I opened my eyes at last and saw before me the patrician countenance of a once noble man. Some would call him a demigod, I suppose. Perhaps we all were in our different ways, but then gods were supposed to be superstition honoured by lesser, credulous men.

And yet here we all were. Giants, warrior-kings, superhuman in every aspect. One of us even had wings: beautiful, white, angelic wings. Looking back now, I cannot fathom why no one looked at Sanguinius and wondered if he were really a god.

'Lupercal,' I began, but Horus cut me off with a mirthless laugh.

'Oh, Vulkan, you really were badly beaten.'

He was armoured in black, a suit I had only seen him wearing once before and which bore no resemblance to either the Luna Wolves of his origin, or the Sons of Horus that he led afterwards. As much as he wore it, the black also bled off him in waves like it wasn't armour at all but some dark anima enclosing him. I had felt it before, caught some inkling of the man he was becoming, but to my shame did nothing to prevent it. An eye glowered in the midriff, blazing and orange like Nocturne's sun but without the honest heat of natural fire.

He gripped my chin with a taloned power fist, and I felt the claws pinch.

'What do you want with me? To kill me, like you killed my sons? Where is this place you have me imprisoned?'

As my eyes adjusted, healing through the gifts my exceptional father gave me, I saw only darkness. It reminded me of the shadow Curze cast over me when I was at his mercy on the plains of Isstvan.

'You are right about one thing,' Horus said, his voice changing as I grew more lucid, becoming gradually sharper and more rigid, 'you *are* a prisoner. A very dangerous one, I think. As to my purpose,' he laughed again, 'I honestly don't know yet.'

I blinked, once, twice, and the face before me transformed into another, one I could scarcely believe.

'Roboute?'

My brother, the primarch of the XIII Legion Ultramarines, had drawn a gladius. It looked ceremonial, never blooded.

'Is that who you see?' Guilliman asked, eyes narrowing before he slid the blade into my bare flesh.

Only then did I realise that I was unarmoured, and sense the fetters around my wrists, ankles and neck. The gladius bit deep, burning at first but then growing colder around the wound. It was sunk into my chest, all the way to the hilt.

My eyes widened. 'What... what... is this?'

Breath knifed through my lungs, bubbling up through the blood rising in my throat, making me gurgle.

He laughed. 'It's a sword, Vulkan.'

I gritted my teeth, anger clamping my mouth shut.

His voice changed again as Guilliman leaned in close and I could no longer see his face, but felt his charnel breath upon my cheek.

'Oh, I think I am going to like this, brother. You definitely won't, but I will.'

He hissed as if savouring the thought of whatever tortures he was already concocting, and it put me in mind of soft, chiropteran wings. My jaw hardened as I discovered the true identity of my tormentor, his name escaping through my clenched teeth like a curse.

'Curze.'

Persona non grata…

A FIGURE ARMOURED in crimson stumbled into the chamber as if through a cut in a veil, a literal knife-thrust that parted realities and allowed him to escape into blessed darkness.

Valdrekk Elias had been waiting in the sanctum, waiting for days for his master's return. It was foreseen, his humbling at the Warmaster's hands. It was known that Horus would challenge the Pantheon and it was known that his own father would forsake him. A martyr's cause was not for him, however. He was destined for greater and everlasting glory.

So it had been told to Elias, and so he had waited.

Now he cradled a wretched figure in his arms, torn and broken, savaged by the very warriors who were meant to be his allies.

'Blessed master, you are injured…' Elias's voice trembled, in fear, in shame, in anger. There was blood all over the floor. Rivulets of dark red ran into sigils marked upon the iron tiles, casting off an eldritch glow as each engraving was filled with blood.

Elias muttered to keep the lambent glow from growing into something he could not control. He doubted his master would be of any use at that moment. The chamber was a holy sanctum;

blood should not be spilled there idly.

Head bowed, facing the floor, his master was shaking and mewling in pain. No... it wasn't pain.

It was laughter.

Elias turned him over and saw the ruin of Erebus's face, white eyes staring from a skull wrapped in blood-soaked meat. His red-rimmed teeth chattered in a lipless mouth, clacking together in a rictus grin before parting as he breathed.

Elias looked at him aghast. 'What has been done to you?'

Erebus tried and failed to answer, spitting up a gobbet of crimson.

Disciple lifted master, carried him in both arms despite the weight of his war-plate, holding his partly insensate form across his body.

Parting with a blast of escaping pressure and the whirr of concealed servos, the sanctum doors opened into a corridor. The apothecarion was close.

'A lesson...' Erebus croaked finally, gurgling his words through blood.

Elias paused. Blood was dripping with a steady *plinking* rhythm as it struck the deck plates underfoot. He leaned in, the stink of copper growing more intense as he closed. 'Yes?'

'A lesson... for you.'

Erebus was delirious, and barely conscious. Whatever had been done to him had almost killed him. *Whoever* had done it had almost killed him.

'Speak it, master,' Elias whispered with all the fervour and devotion of a fanatic.

Erebus might have lost favour in some quarters, with his father certainly, but he still had supporters. They were few, but they were also ardent. The Dark Apostle's voice shrank to a whisper. Even for one with Elias's enhanced hearing, words were difficult to discern.

'*Sharpen ours, blunt theirs...*'

'Master? I don't know what you are saying. Tell me, what must I do?'

With a strength belied by his frail condition, Erebus seized Elias by the throat. His eyes, those ever-staring lidless orbs of pure hate, glared. It was like he was peering into Elias's tainted soul, searching it for any vestige of falsehood.

'The weapons...' he gasped, louder, angry. He laughed again, as if this were a truth he had only just realised, before spitting up more blood.

Elias's gaze went to the athame clutched in his master's claw-like hand. It was only because the fingers were bionic that he still held the ritual knife at all.

'Weapons?' Elias asked.

'We can win the war. They are all... that matters.' He sagged, the Dark Apostle's passionate fire finally usurped by his injuries. 'Must have them or deny them to our...' Erebus trailed off, falling into unconsciousness.

Elias was without compass. He didn't know what to do, but trusted in the divine will of the Pantheon to guide him. Quickly, he took Erebus to the apothecarion and as soon as the Dark Apostle was on the slab and in the tender care of his chirurgeons, Elias opened a vox-channel.

'Narek.'

The voice that answered was harsh and grating.

'*Brother.*'

Elias knew that the athame was powerful. He was not some novice unschooled in the art of the warp. He knew full well what it could do. He possessed his own, a mere simulacrum of the one in Erebus's clutches, as did his lesser apostles. But he had always wondered if other such artefacts existed in the universe. Other 'weapons', he now supposed.

Elias smiled at the thought of obtaining one, of the power he might hold with it.

'*Brother,*' Narek repeated when Elias didn't answer straight away. Elias's smile turned into a broad grin that didn't reach his eyes. 'Ready your warriors. We have much work to do.'

CHAPTER ONE

Disciples

*'The struggles of warring gods are oft fought not between them-
selves, but through their disciples.'*
– Sicero, ancient Terran philosopher

TRAORIS WAS DESCRIBED by some as a *blessed* world. Blessed by whom
or what was open to interpretation. The facts that were known
were simply these. In the year 898 of the 30th millennium of the
Imperial calendar, a being came to Traoris who was known as the
Golden King.

Hailed as a liberator, he banished the dark cults that ruled before
his coming. He slew them with sword and storm, an army of knights
at his command that were both magnificent and terrifying. The cabal
of sorcerer-lords that the Golden King vanquished had enslaved the
Traorans, a people who had not known peace or freedom for many
centuries, their ancestors having ventured from Old Earth long ago.
Alone, isolated during the time of Old Night, Traoris fell victim to
a primordial evil. Sin made the minds of weaker men eager vessels
for this darkness and only glorious light would remove it.

And so it was that the Golden King banished darkness, preaching freedom and enlightenment. He touched this world with his mere presence. He *blessed* it.

Many years passed, and between the Golden King's departure and the recolonisation that followed, Traoris was slowly transformed. Gone were the bastions of the sorcerer-lords, great factories and mills rising in their stead. Industry came to Traoris and its people.

Eight cities stood upon its grey earth, built upon the ruins of the old, their tenements teeming with workers. Anwey, Umra, Ixon, Vorr, Lotan, Kren, Orll and Ranos – they were islands of civilisation, divided by many kilometres of inhospitable ash desert and storm-lashed lightning fields, raised up where seams of ore coveted by Mars were in their greatest concentrations.

Yes, Traoris was described by some as a blessed world. But not by any who lived there.

THOUGH SHE KNEW in her heart it was futile, Alantea ran. It was raining hard, and had been ever since the ships of ebony and crimson had been spotted in the sky over Ranos. Underfoot, the rain-lashed street was slick. She had fallen twice already and her knee throbbed dangerously with the past impacts.

Alantea had been working a manufactorum shift, so was only wearing green-grey overalls and a thin cotton shirt darkened from white to grey by manual labour. A plastek coat kept out the worst of the rain, but parted as she ran. Her hair was drenched and hung down in front of her face in blonde clumps, obscuring her vision in the dark.

Phosphor lamps hissed and spat as the raindrops touched them. Shadows clawed away from the dingy light, revealing square structures of grey granite beneath them. The whole city was grey, from the fog that oozed from the foundry stacks to the stone slabs under Alantea's feet. Ranos was dark iron, it was industry and strength, it was an engine that ran on muscle and blood.

It was also her home.

The phosphor lamps glared like beacons, hurting Alantea's eyes. But she welcomed them, because they would lead her to the square.

If she could just reach Cardinal Square…

Heavy footfalls drummed behind her, a noisy refrain against the frenzied beating of her heart, and as she turned down a side street she dared to glance back.

A shadow. Just a shadow, that's all she really saw.

But she'd seen these shadows tear old Yulli apart, gut her dutiful overseer like he was swine and leave his steaming entrails on the ground for him to look upon as he died. The others had died soon after. Throaty barks, accompanied by harsh muzzle flashes from thick, black guns, had ripped them apart. Nothing was left, not even bodies. The manufactorum floor a bloodbath; its various machineries destroyed.

Alantea had bolted for the gate to the yard. She'd considered taking one of the hauler trucks, until one of the half-tracks exploded, chewed up by a heavy cannon. So instead she ran. Now they chased her, those shadows. Never fast nor urgent, but always just a few steps away.

Fear was in the air that night. Talk was rife amongst the workers that men had been found and arrested in the culverts. Rumours abounded of strange doings, of ritual suicides and other 'acts'. The clavigers had apparently found a missing girl with the men, or at least her remains. But what was worse was that the men were just ordinary citizens, workers of Ranos just like her.

So when the manufactorum was hit, paranoia and terror were already infecting its workers. The panic had been terrifying. But a different kind of fear seized Alantea now, one fuelled by the desperate desire to escape it and the belief that something far worse than death waited for her if she didn't.

This district of the city was a warren, full of avenues crowded over with dirty tenement blocks that shouldered up against warehouses and silos. Alleyways and conduits gave way to labyrinthine side streets where even the rats lost their bearings. Except she couldn't lose them, not her shadows. They had the scent of prey.

Ducking around a corner, Alantea sank to her haunches as she tried to catch a breath. It was tempting to believe she was safe now, or to give up and relinquish the chase. The city was quiet, overly so, and she feared then that she was the last surviving inhabitant, that Ranos was extinct but for her tiny life spark. She'd seen no sign of the clavigers, no dramatic call to arms from the shield-wardens. No response at all. What enemy force in all existence could achieve such a feat of absolute subjugation with barely any resistance?

A harsh, grating voice speaking in a language she didn't understand got Alantea to her feet. She guessed he was talking to the others. The thought of a noose tightening ever so slightly around her pale, slender neck sprang unbidden into her mind. They were closer than before, Alantea knew it instinctively. She thought of her father, and the slow, cancerous death that awaited him. She remembered better days, still poor, but tempered with happiness when her father had been whole. He needed medicine; without it… A few more precious moments with her father was all she wanted. In the end, that's all anyone ever really wants, just a little longer. But it was never enough. It was part of the human condition, to want to live, and when faced with our mortal end men rail against it to further that desire. It galvanised Alantea now. Cardinal Square wasn't far. Another hundred metres, maybe fewer.

Dredging up whatever stamina she had left, Alantea ran.

Even with her injured knee she covered the last few metres steadily and at pace.

Bursting into Cardinal Square, gasping for breath, she saw *him*.

Rendered in gold – holding aloft a sceptre of command that would later be given to the Lord Excavator General of Traoris, patron of Ranos and the other seven worker-cities – he looked magnificent. He had come to her world, set foot in this very spot after the liberation, after the Traorans had been freed. He had spoken and all had tried to listen. Alantea was not born then. She had neither seen the one they came to know as the Golden King, nor heard his speech during the triumph, but sitting upon her father's shoulders as he remembered back to what his father and his father before that told him of the liberation, she had felt the Golden King's power and benevolence.

Something had changed since that day with her father. Standing in Cardinal Square now, she no longer felt that reassurance. It was as if something had arisen to challenge it and was even now worming away at all it represented. She could not say why. Perhaps it was instinct, that unfathomable intuition that only the female of the species possessed. All she knew was that a different blessing had fallen upon Ranos, one that felt far from benevolent, and its nexus was focused on the square.

Five points ran off from the square – though to call it such was a colloquial misnomer for it was actually pentagonal – including the one where Alantea was standing. At each of the other four she saw an armoured form blocking her escape. Phantoms at first, shadows, they advanced slowly out of the darkness. Edged in silver phosphor light their movements seemed almost syncopated and inhuman.

Turning back, realising her mistake, Alantea didn't know she'd been stabbed until the feeling left her legs and she collapsed. Strong, armoured hands caught her before she fell and she looked up into the face of her rescuer. He was handsome, despite the strange script gilding his cheekbones and the exposed areas of his scalp that hurt Alantea's eyes to look at. His black hair was short, shorn close to the scalp, and ended in a sharp widow's peak over his forehead.

His eyes were pitying, but it was a cold pity, one usually reserved for the culling of cattle no longer fit for the herd.

Alantea whispered, using up a good measure of her courage to speak, 'Let me go.'

The armoured warrior, clad in wine-red plate, festooned with chains and scroll work, slowly shook his head.

'Now, now, my dear,' he said, soothing, but seizing Alantea's arms when she struggled, 'that's quite enough of that.' He caressed her cheek with a long metal nail he wore on one of his gauntlets, drawing a thin line of tiny bloody jewels across her skin.

Whimpering like the animal he regarded her as, Alantea tried to answer, but the warrior shushed her, holding the bloodstained finger up to his slightly curved lips. Exhausted, unaware of the internal trauma her body was experiencing as a result of the knife wound, Alantea was powerless to prevent her head from lolling back. Vision fogging, she saw the Golden King, upside down and lashed by the rain.

As it ran across his face and down his cheeks, it looked as if he were crying. In her delirium she wondered what could have upset him so, what could have instilled in a being such as he such profound remorse.

Chains were being looped around the statue by the other warriors that had entered the square. They heaved, a single gargantuan effort, and brought the Golden King down amid the dirt and the blood.

'Don't struggle, you're bleeding...' the warrior holding her told Alantea benevolently, before his tone grew darker, 'and we must not waste a single drop.'

THEY WERE IN DEEP, as far down into the catacombs as it was possible to go. The steady thrum of rock-cutters and the heavy bang of blasting charges was a constant and insistent drone and could be heard in the ruins above. It had been a battlefield, or part of one, frozen in time at the point of victory by order of the ruler of this world. The last bastion of anti-Imperial resistance destroyed by a storm of psychic lightning. Nothing had changed since the fortress had fallen.

The ruins had been left as they were all those years ago. Untouched. They were a reminder of a glorious past, a place of commemoration and veneration.

Sebaton had violated the sanctity of that, besmirched it with hanging phosphor lamps, industry-grade digging servitors and the cluster of spades, shovels, cutters and excavation kit now strewn about the place. It played little on his conscience. Reality was, his conscience was so blighted already that such minor sacrilege would barely register.

Archaeology was not his strong suit, yet he could play the role, adopt the persona of Caeren Sebaton as needed. He knew they were close. He could feel it, just as he could feel the slowly deepening inevitability of what would follow their discovery and where, ultimately, it would lead him.

Dust thronged the air, making it hard to see in the dirt and the darkness even with the lamps. Surrounded by the reliquary of a time long past, Sebaton began to feel old. He looked up at the cavernous opening above, at the wide cleft of tunnel through which they had bored down to reach the catacombs, at the ramp down which they had ferried their equipment, and felt the desperate urge to climb. He wanted to be in the light, a keeper of shadows and lies no more. He resisted, his pragmatism far outweighing his whimsy, and asked, 'How much farther, Varteh?'

The ex-Lucifer Black glanced up from the dig site where a pair of servitors were chewing up rock with their manifold tools, a tech-adept looking on.

'We're close.'

He spoke through a crackly short-gain vox-link, patched from a unit in his rebreather and received by the ear-bud attached to Sebaton's own mask. This far down, this much dust, both men would have choked to death by now. The rest of Varteh's team wore them too. Two men, ostensibly for security, flanked the dig perimeter.

Both had lascarbines slung casually over their shoulders. Varteh carried a fat, military-grade autopistol in a holster on his left hip. He also had a long flensing knife strapped to his right boot.

All three men wore simple desert tan fatigues, bleached almost white by the dust, and cracked-leather jackets over plain grey vests. Varteh also wore a grey cowl that covered his ears and came up just over his chin. Sebaton could just make out his eyes through his goggles. They were hard; for Lucifer Blacks, even those who no longer served in the Army, were hard men.

Sebaton knew this from experience.

He was similarly attired, but wore a long damson-red duster coat with black tanker boots that went halfway up his shins. Sebaton's fatigues were deep tan, pleated at the edges like an equestrian's. He only carried one visible weapon, a snub-nose flechette pistol that fired tiny razor-edged discs and sat snugly in a shoulder holster concealed by his coat.

Glancing again at the opening that led out of the catacombs, Sebaton beckoned Varteh over.

His tone was insistent. 'How long, Varteh?'

'You expecting trouble?' Varteh jerked his chin at the opening. Falling rain sparkled in the light. 'Nothing is coming after us, is it? I can only protect you if you tell me what it is you need protection from.'

Sebaton met the ex-Lucifer's gaze, and smiled warmly. 'Anything I'm hiding is for your benefit, believe me, Varteh.'

Varteh frowned.

'Something amiss with that?' asked Sebaton.

'Not at all. But ever since we met I've been wondering something about you. When I was with the Army, I travelled,' he said. 'Met a lot of men from a lot of different regiments, lot of different places. Until I made your acquaintance, I thought my knowledge of accents was fairly broad but I can't place yours. It's unique and yet also familiar. Not really one accent, but several. Therefore I'm wondering, where is it from?'

Sebaton's smile faded. 'A bit of here, a bit of there. Does it matter? You're being well paid for your services. And I thought Lucifer Blacks were meant to obey and not ask questions.'

Now it was Varteh's turn to smile.

'I did, that's why I'm in this shit hole with you.' Varteh let it go. 'Fair enough. We all have our secrets, I suppose. Yours, I suspect, are many.'

'It's because you're a shrewd man that I hired you, Varteh.' Sebaton looked back up at the opening.

Varteh took a step towards him and whispered, 'What's coming, Sebaton? What is this all about?'

Sebaton was staring. 'What it's always been about, Varteh. Weapons.' He twisted the small ornate ring he wore on one finger, before returning his gaze to the ex-Lucifer. 'Keep digging.'

CHAPTER TWO
Remembrance

'What we do defines us. Our deeds are like shadows and depending on whether we run into or from the sun, they either lie behind us or before us.'
                                    – ancient Terran philosopher, unknown

Kharaatan, during the Great Crusade

SMOKE HUNG OVER Khar-tann City in a dark pall. It seemed to stick to its towers and battlements, drenching them in an oily gloom.

Fifteen hours of bombardment. Its shields had taken quite a battering. Parts of the city were demolished, but its main gates, its core walls and its defenders were still intact. Defiant. It was the first of nine major cities on One-Five-Four Six, or Kharaatan, as the natives called it.

Regarding the shadows that haunted its walls, its people unmoving as they watched the massive force sent to quell them, Numeon hoped the other cities would be easier to crack. He stood just over eight kilometres away on a rough escarpment of dolomitic limestone with three of his closest brothers. The Salamanders stood apart from the rest of the Imperial officers, who were farther back, camped halfway down a ridge that descended into a wide, low basin where their forces gathered.

'It's quiet,' hissed Nemetor, as if to speak any louder would shatter the calm before the coming storm and pre-empt their attack.

'Wouldn't you be, facing off against the Legion?' said Leodrakk. He looked up, craning his neck and pointing the snout of his dragon's helm to the sky. 'Two Legions,' he corrected, though he could see no sign of their cousins.

Both warriors were Salamanders, yet could not be less alike. Nemetor was softly spoken and wore the emerald-green of the Legion, his iconography that of the 15th Company with a white drake head on his left shoulder guard. He was broad, with a thick neck and shortish, stout legs. Even out of his war-plate, he was formidable. It was partly the reason he was also known as 'Tank'.

'Perhaps they're thinking about giving up, Tank,' offered Atanarius, watching the city's movements through a pair of magnoculars.

Like Leodrakk, he was armoured in the trappings of the Pyre Guard, a suit of plate fashioned in a draconian aspect with a reptilian battle-helm and scalloped greaves, pauldrons and cuirass. It was permanently blackened from Promethean ritual, and branding marks scored the metal in the Salamanders' oaths of moment. Both warriors were taller than Nemetor, but lost ground in terms of sheer bulk.

'Is that what your eyes tell you, Atanarius?' Numeon asked in a deep voice. He turned, the fire-red crest jutting from the crown of his battle-helm marking him out as their captain. He was also the primarch's equerry, and that made him unique. Even through his retinal lenses, his gaze was penetrating.

Over the Phatra plain where Khar-tann City presided, night was starting to fall. Like hot embers in a fire, Numeon's eyes blazed in the pre-dark. All of the Salamanders' eyes did. It was a part of their heritage, like the onyx black of their skin and the self-sacrificial mindset of their Promethean creed.

'Even through the scopes, it's hard to be certain of anything they are telling me, Pyre Captain.' Atanarius lowered the magnoculars, returning them to his equipment belt, before facing Numeon. 'I can detect very little movement. If they were planning on trying to repel our forces, then whatever measures they mean to use to do it are already in place.'

'Eight thousand fighting men, plus twice that number again in civilians, some of whom may have been levied to bolster the troops,' said Leodrakk. 'Nothing they can do will prevent us knocking down their gate and cleaning house.' He sounded belligerent as ever. A hot vein of magma ran through his skin and bone, as was often remarked by his brothers.

Nemetor cocked his head. 'I thought you were planning on burning down their house, not cleaning it, brother?'

Leodrakk glared, cracking his knuckles inside his gauntlets.

'Temper, Leo,' Atanarius warned, before turning to Nemetor, 'but don't think your familiarity with the Pyre Guard allows you to disrespect us, Nemetor. Even from a captain, that won't be tolerated.'

Nemetor inclined his head to apologise.

'If you are finished goading one another then please attend.' Numeon nodded down the ridge where several Army officers were slogging uphill. 'I believe we are about to get some news.'

Numeon opened up a vox-link in his battle-helm.

'Skatar'var.'

A crackling voice answered immediately.

'Summon Lord Vulkan,' said Numeon. 'The Army and Titan legio are ready to march.'

He cut the link, knowing the order was given, so would be carried out.

Below in the desert basin, the Legion waited. A sea of emerald-green, six thousand warriors stood ready to bring a city to its knees. Beyond them, four full regiments of tanks, including super-heavies,

a squadron of Infernus-pattern Predators and enough Mastodons
to transport every legionary on the ground. Behind the infantry
loomed a trio of Warhound Titans from Legio Ignis, nicknamed
the 'Fire Kings'. Traditionally, Warhounds fought alone, but this
particular pack was seldom parted.

Khar-tann City was formidable, its armed forces devoted, but it could
not outlast this. There was something unsettling about the silence and
the way the Khar-tans had given in wholly to alien subjugation.

Numeon snarled, feeling the old familiar call to war. It filled his
vox-grille with the reek of ash and cinder from his heavy exhala-
tions. In the end, their resistance mattered not.

'It's time to make them burn.'

VULKAN KNEELED, HEAD down, inside a cell of obsidian and black
metal. What little light penetrated the darkness was from the forge-
heat of irons and brands, the warm glow of embers surrounding a
pit of coals.

The air was hot, stifling. Seriph was wearing a rebreather, and put
questions to the primarch through a vox-coder attached to her belt.
It made her otherwise mellifluous voice tinny and marred with static.

'And so you were raised a blacksmith's son?' she asked, wiping
away another bead of sweat from her brow, dark patches showing
under the arms of her robes and down her back. The remembrancer
took a moment to sip from a flask she wore at her hip. Without it,
dehydration and acute heatstroke would have occurred in minutes.
She wanted longer with the Lord of the Drakes, and if this was the
only way then so be it.

'Is that so hard to believe?' Vulkan answered as the sound and
smell of burning flesh – his flesh – filled the chamber. 'And he was
a *blacksmiter* and a metal-shaper, a craftsman of consummate skill
that I greatly admired.'

A human, augmented to be able to perform his duty and live to do so again, withdrew a burning brand from the primarch's skin.

'Noted,' said Seriph, scratching with her stylus on the data-slate in her other hand. 'It just seems like a humble origin for a lord of Space Marines.'

The remembrancer was sweltering now, having endured a full twenty-one minutes in the primarch's chambers, a feat none before her had matched without expiring from the heat.

'Should I have had a more regal upbringing then?'

The brander picked up a fresh iron, examining the hooked end and imagining the shape of the mark it would make.

'No, I didn't mean that,' said Seriph, wincing as Vulkan's flesh burned anew, sizzling like meat in a cook-pan. 'I just assumed all the primarchs came from warlike, vaunted beginnings. Either that or born as orphans on death worlds.'

'Nocturne *is* a death world and hardly civilised. But our origins were all very different. I wonder sometimes how we all came back to our father's service as warriors and generals, but here we stand at the forefront of the Great Crusade doing just that.'

Seriph frowned, then wiped her brow with the sleeve of her robe.

'What else could you have been?'

'Tyrants, murderers... architects. It was only fate that made us leaders, and I am still unsure as to how our genetic heritage predisposed us to that calling.'

'And which would you have been, then?'

Vulkan smiled, though it did little to warm his diabolic voice.

'A farmer, I think.'

'You would take your blacksmiter's anvil and turn a sword into a ploughshare, is that it?'

'Overly poetic, but yes that's it.'

Seriph paused. Either she was gasping in the heat or drawing some conclusions.

'You don't seem like the others.'

'And you know my brothers, do you, Remembrancer Seriph?'
There was mild reproach in Vulkan's tone, just enough to intimidate.

It flustered the remembrancer and she looked on the verge of collapse. 'No, of course not. I have just heard–'

'A wise chronicler does not believe all she hears, Seriph.' For the
first time since the interview began, Vulkan raised his head. 'Tell
me,' he said, his voice deepening, 'what do you see in my eyes?'

They blazed like the calderas of a volcano.

'F… fire…'

At last she wilted. Vulkan rushed forwards and caught her so that
she didn't fall.

At the same moment a crack opened in the darkness and Skatar'var
stepped through it into the branding chamber.

'My lord,' said the Pyre Guard.

Skatar'var was one of two brothers that were now part of the primarch's inner circle. Like his sibling, he was haughty and proud. A
warrior-king of Hesiod, he had learned nobility from his biological
father and honed it in the Legion.

The warrior bowed his head a fraction, before realising what he
was seeing. 'Another one unequal to the task?'

A large draconian horn arched from his back, attached to the
power generator of his armour. He had 'won' the trophy when he
had slain Loktaral, one of the deep drakes, and joined his brother
at Vulkan's side. Leodrakk, his hot-tempered younger sibling, bore
the other horn. They had killed the beast together.

'She was strong, and lasted longer than the others. I will speak
with her again,' said Vulkan, cradling the woman and passing her
over to Skatar'var like he would an infant to its parent. 'I assume
you come to tell me the Army is ready.'

Skatar'var looked down at the woman like she was a piece of unfamiliar equipment, before answering his primarch. 'Aye, the Legio
Ignis too.'

Vulkan nodded.

'Very well. Remove her from here and make sure she stays with the medicaes. I have one more oath to take before we can make war on Khar-tann City.'

'Yes, lord.'

Skatar'var took the woman and his leave.

In the darkness, Vulkan turned back to his brander. The primarch's onyx-black body was like a muscled slab of granite. Almost every part of his exposed skin was marked. They represented deeds, battles, lives taken and spared. Some even went as far back as Nocturne, before he was reunited with the Outlander. Without exception, Vulkan remembered each and every one in precise detail.

It was ritual, a part of the Promethean creed which was born upon Nocturne many years ago. Method and tradition were important to Vulkan; his teachings to his sons were predicated on these very tenets.

'So comes the moment, so the brand is burned,' he said, kneeling as he lowered his head again. 'Prepare me for war.'

In the shuddering confines of the Mastodon, the hololithic image of Commander Arvek phased in and out of resolution.

'Once the core wall is breached, we can roll right into Khar-tann and demolish it,' the Army officer declared, smacking a fist against his open palm for emphasis. Even through the built-in vox-unit, he sounded imperious. He hailed from Vodis, a world of austere military households that could trace their lineage back to the first ancient kings of Terra.

The audio was as bad as the visual, but the commander's meaning was clear enough.

'Negative,' said Vulkan firmly. 'Breach the wall, then withdraw.'

Arvek tried to mask his surprise. 'With respect, lord primarch, we can crush them with minimal casualties. I was led to believe–'

Vulkan cut him off. 'To our ranks, commander, not theirs. There are over fifteen thousand civilians in Khar-tann. I've read your collateral damage estimates – they are conservative at best and even that forecast is unacceptable. Make a hole for the Legion, and we will subdue the native soldiery with the minimum loss of civilian life. Consider that an order.'

Arvek saluted sharply, the medals and laurels on his crisp blue uniform jangling as he moved.

Vulkan nodded to him, and switched the link.

The grainy, semi-monochrome image of the tank commander hazed out and was replaced with that of Princeps Lokja. The Titan officer was festooned with mind impulse cables, linking his cerebral cortex to the violent anima of his war machine. Already deep into the mind-link, his brow was furrowed, his curled black moustaches raised in a snarl of concentration.

'*Lord Vulkan*,' Lokja acknowledged in the cultured accent of Attila.

'Commander Arvek is going to make a hole in the core wall for the Legion. I need the Fire Kings to shepherd them in. Threat response only, do not engage the city's soldiery.'

'*Understood*,' said Lokja, a blink relaying the orders to his moderati sitting below him in the Warhound's cockpit.

The princeps cut the feed and the interior of the rumbling Mastodon went dark.

Their eyes ablaze in the hold, seven Pyre Guard awaited their lord and master's next words.

'Soon as the gate is down and Arvek has withdrawn, Fifteenth go in as first recon,' said Vulkan. 'We follow swiftly, supported by the rest of the Firedrakes.'

Numeon nodded curtly, turning as he opened up a channel to Nemetor.

Vulkan then added, 'We will lead the spearhead, fighting in pairs, dispersed formation. Suggestions?'

Varrun stroked his chin, smoothing his ash-grey beard. As the oldest amongst the order, he was often allowed to speak first. 'One point of ingress, we'll be attracting a lot of fire.'

'We've taken worse,' said Leodrakk. His eyes flared with fierce pride. 'The honour of securing the breach should fall to us, and with the primarch leading us they don't have nearly enough guns on that wall.'

A chorus of nods and muttered agreement went round the warriors.

'I'd recommend storm shields in the first breach team,' said Ganne, nodding to Igataron, who sat unmoving at the edge of the group. Both were assault specialists: the former outwardly pugnacious, the latter silent, but ferociously aggressive.

Varrun chuckled. 'I thought the objective was to minimise civilian casualties.'

Ganne's slab jaw tightened as he sent a crackle of energy down the haft of his thunder hammer, but he didn't bite.

'Skatar'var and I will go in as second wave,' suggested Leodrakk, ignoring his bantering brothers.

'Side by side, brother,' said Skatar'var and the two locked gauntlets, hand to forearm.

'That leaves you and I,' Atanarius said to Varrun.

'Hold the breach, leave it clear for the Legion,' said Varrun. 'We'll keep the gate open for the Drakes.'

Ganne bared his teeth. 'Rearguard obviously plays to your strengths, Varrun.'

Varrun bared his teeth back.

Inwardly, Vulkan smiled. They were hungry, ready for war. Pyre Guard were not like other Salamanders; they had more fire, more fury. Like the volcanoes of ancient Nocturne, the great jagged chains of the Dragonspike and Mount Deathfire, they were perpetually on the brink of eruption. Even the Pyroclasts weren't as volatile.

Pyre Guard were *chosen* warriors, those that displayed a level of self-sacrifice and self-sufficiency that exceeded all others. Like the *saburai* of old Nihon, they were fighters foremost, who could ally as a unit or function expertly on their own. They were also leaders, and each of the Pyre Guard commanded a Chapter of the Legion in addition to their duties as the primarch's inner circle warriors. All were Terran-born but still displayed the physical traits of onyx-black skin and red eyes, an irreversible reaction to the unique radiation of Nocturne combined with the genetic heritage of their primarch, which every Salamander, regardless of origin, possessed.

'Skatar'var,' said Vulkan. 'How is Seriph?'

'The remembrancer?' he asked, initially wrong-footed by the request. 'She lives.'

'Good,' said Vulkan. He addressed them all. 'You are my finest drakes, my most trusted advisors. Our father fashioned us as crusaders, to bring fire and light to the darkest reaches of the galaxy. Our task is to protect mankind, shield humanity. It's important that the Remembrancer Order sees this. Our appearance is…'

'Monstrous, my lord,' ventured Leodrakk, eyes blazing through his helm lenses.

Vulkan nodded. 'We come to Kharaatan as liberators, not conquerors. We cannot forge civilisations out of rubble, out of sundered flesh and bone.'

'And our cousins, will they hold to that also?' a voice asked from the shadows.

All eyes turned to Igataron, whose gaze was fixed on the primarch.

'If they do not,' Vulkan promised, 'my brother and I will have *words.*'

Numeon ended his vox exchange with Captain Nemetor. 'Fifteenth are advancing,' he announced, as he turned back to face his brothers.

Vulkan nodded. 'Commander Arvek will be making contact in less than a minute. Helms on, prepare for immediate embarkation. When the ramp opens we will be ready to advance.'

In clanking unison the Pyre Guard obeyed.

Igataron and Ganne moved to the front, shields up, as Leodrakk and Skatar'var unhitched their power mauls and went in just behind them. Vulkan was next, Numeon at his side clutching the staff of his halberd. Varrun and Atanarius were last; the former holding his power axe high up the short haft near its double-edged blade, the latter unsheathing a power sword to kiss the naked blade.

All seven warriors carried bolters. Save for Varrun, who was an exceptional marksman, they seldom used them. Every one of their weapons was forged by its bearer, every one could spit fire like the drakes of old.

'Eye-to-eye,' snarled Numeon, reciting the Pyre Guard's war mantra.

'Tooth-to-tooth,' the rest replied, including Vulkan.

Now they were forged and ready.

The hololith transmitter crackled into life, displaying a head and torso rendering of Commander Arvek.

'You have your breach, my Lord Primarch. Withdrawing now.'

Through his retinal lenses, Vulkan saw Arvek's tank formations pushing away from Khar-tann's core wall. Each engine was rendered as an icon – the display was awash with their signatures. Behind them came the Rhino armoured transports of the 15th and behind that were the Mastodons.

'Any losses?' asked Vulkan.

'None. We met zero resistance. Even when we closed to fifty metres they did not fire on us.'

A tremor of unease entered Vulkan's mind, but he concealed it at once.

'Relay to Captain Nemetor,' he said to Numeon through the vox-feed as he cut the link to Arvek.

'Something wrong, my lord?' asked Numeon.

'I expected some form of counter-attack.'

'Perhaps they've decided to capitulate after all,' suggested Atanarius.

'Then why not open the gates?' countered Varrun.

'A trap?' growled Leodrakk, prompting a nod of agreement from his sibling Skatar'var.

Vulkan's mood darkened, his unease evident in his silence.

Either way, once Nemetor was inside the core wall they would find out.

CAPTAIN NEMETOR HAD already removed his war-helm as he met Vulkan at the breach point in the core wall. The broad-shouldered warrior looked uneasy, and a fine sheen of sweat glistened on his forehead.

All lights inside the city were doused; roads, battlements and interior buildings snuffed out by darkness. The only source of illumination came from scattered fires left by the earlier bombardment, but even in this gloom evidence of Commander Arvek's armoured assault could be seen everywhere.

Bodies of the Khar-tann soldiery were twisted amidst the rubble of the shattered core wall, which had collapsed in on itself from the severe shelling. Several watch towers had fallen into the city itself, lying broken in heaps of rockcrete and plasteel. Corpses lingered here too, already polluting the air around them with the stench of putrefaction. The entire city was rank with it, and stank of death.

Beyond the core wall and the flattened gate, burst inwards by a demolisher shell, there was a long esplanade. From the positions of exploded sandbags and mangled tank traps, Vulkan imagined the Khar-tans might have been staging a second defence line here. In several places he noticed the burned-out shells of pillboxes designed to create choke points and funnel an invading enemy into a kill zone. Punctuating the line of pillboxes were much larger bunkers, solid-form and permanent additions to the city's defences. Smoke still drooled from the vision slits of some of the bunkers, telltale evidence of a rapid and aggressive clearance.

Of the inhabitants of Khar-tann, there was no sign.

'Do you see that?' asked Numeon, nodding to where the primarch had been looking.

'Yes.' Vulkan's earlier sense of unease grew further.

'A tank bombardment doesn't do that. It flattens bunkers, it doesn't cleanse and burn them. A strike team has already been here.'

Vulkan took in the scene of carnage, tried to look beyond the obvious wreckage and mortal destruction. Past the esplanade, the concentration of buildings thickened from initially military to civilian. He saw warehouses, manufactorums, vendors, commercia… homes. Through a gap in the narrow city streets he caught a glimpse of something swinging gently in the breeze.

Nemetor saluted as Vulkan reached him, the sharp clank of his fist striking his left breast enough to get the primarch's attention. Behind him, the Pyre Guard were spreading out. Strict orders had been given that the rest of the Legion should stand down and wait outside.

'Captain,' said Vulkan.

Nemetor was shaken, though it was hard to tell from what. 'You need to see this, my lord.'

Vulkan spoke over his shoulder to Numeon. The Pyre Guard were to secure the area immediately beyond the breach but advance no further. Then he nodded to Nemetor, and the captain led them both on.

AT THE HEART of Khar-tann City they found the bulk of the dead. Soldiers in barrack houses, gutted and flensed; pyres of still-burning bodies, impossible to identify from their charred remains, filling the air with greasy smoke; city officials impaled on spikes; civilians hanging by their necks, swinging to and fro in the breeze.

'They slaughtered them,' said Nemetor as he surveyed the carnage. Four Salamanders accompanied him, and despite the fact they were wearing their battle-helms they looked just as uneasy as their captain.

Vulkan unclenched his teeth.

'Where are the rest of your company?'

'Dispersed amongst the ruins, trying to find survivors.'

'There'll be none,' Vulkan told him. 'Recall them. We are not needed here. The people of Khar-tann are beyond our help.' His gaze settled on a bloody symbol daubed on the wall of a scholam. The primarch's jaw hardened.

'When did they even make planetfall?' asked Nemetor, following Vulkan's line of sight.

'I don't know.'

He didn't speak the language, but he recognised the cursive script, the sharp edges to the graffiti.

It was Nostraman.

BACK UP ON the escarpment, Vulkan was alone but for the distant roar of the flames below.

Khar-tann burned. It burned with the fire of a thousand flame gauntlets, Vulkan having set his Pyroclasts the task of turning the city to ash. He wanted no such monument to slaughter to stand any longer than was strictly necessary. Its very existence had disturbed the Army cohorts especially, and even the legionaries treated it warily.

Vulkan waited patiently, listening to the vox-channel he had just opened. It took several seconds of softly crackling static before Vulkan got an answer. When he did, it sounded like the person on the other end of the link was smiling.

'Brother.'

Despite himself, Vulkan couldn't disguise his anger. 'What have you done, Curze?'

'*Freed you from dirtying your hands. We arrived early, while you were still marshalling your tanks and Titans.*'

'My orders were to take the city as bloodlessly as possible.'

'*I don't follow your orders, brother. Besides, it's better this way.*'

'Better for whom? You've slaughtered an entire city – men, women, children all dead. It's a butchery worthy of Angron's Legion in there!'

'*Don't confuse me with our hot-headed sibling, though I believe you would run him close at this precise moment. Are you angry with me?*'

Vulkan clenched his fists, biting back a retort.

'Where are you, Curze? Where are you hiding?'

'*I am close by. We will be reunited soon enough.*' Konrad Curze paused, his playful tone ebbed. '*You and I know this was never going to be a bloodless compliance. One-Five-Four Six is a war world, and no warrior I have ever fought has given up without first shedding a little blood.*'

'A little? You practically exsanguinated the entire populace.'

'And what do you think that would do to their fighting spirit?'

Vulkan turned sharply at the sound of Curze's voice. Not through the vox any more – he was here. The Night Haunter was a few paces behind him, standing in the shadows at the edge of the flickering firelight.

'You are either bold or foolish, meeting me out here like this,' Vulkan warned, the combination of the flames and his drake-like armour enshrouding him in a volatile aspect. Even the carcass of the great drake Kesare, slung over his right shoulder, seemed animate. His forge hammer was within easy reach but he didn't so much as glance at the weapon.

'Why, what are you going to do?' Curze stepped out of the shadows.

He went without a helmet, the light hitting his features in such a way that where the darkness pooled it made him appear gaunt, almost skeletal. Nostramo, his birthplace – unless one counted the laboratory where he, like all of his siblings, was first created – had been a lightless world. This fact was obvious in the chalk-like pallor of its inhabitants, and Curze was no exception to that. One onyx-skinned, the other alabaster; both primarchs were a study in chiaroscuro.

In stark contrast to Vulkan's fiery eyes, Curze's were like thin ovals of jet staring through strands of lank, black hair that hung down across his face. Where Vulkan wore a firedrake hide as his mantle, Curze had a cloak of ragged crimson. One brother had a reptilian appearance in his scaled war-plate of oceanic green, clad with rare quartz; the other was armoured in midnight-blue, inscribed with sigils of death and mortality.

Vulkan kept his voice level, neutral. 'Are you trying to goad me, Curze? Do you want this to escalate?'

'That sounded like a threat.' Curze smiled thinly. 'Was it a threat, brother? Am I a rough blade to be tempered at your righteous anvil? Do you also think yourself my better and my teacher, then?'

Vulkan ignored him, instead gesturing to the inferno that had been Khar-tann City. 'Look at what your deeds have wrought.'

'Ha! *What my deeds have wrought?* Vulkan, you sound like a poet, and a poor one at that.' Curze grew serious. 'I've broken this world for you, brother. By culling the city you're now putting to the torch, I've spared us a wealth of blood. What do you think this world's rebels will do when they see and hear what we've done to one of their major cities?' Defying Vulkan's palpable anger, Curze took a step closer with every emphasised word. 'They will *cower*, and *shrink*, and *weep*...' When the two were face to face, he snarled the last part through a barricade of teeth, '*Begging* for mercy.' He stepped back, opening his arms. 'And you can give it to them, that is my gift.'

Vulkan shook his head. 'Terror is your *gift*. They were women and children, Curze. Innocents.'

Curze sneered, bitterly. 'No one is innocent.'

'You came from the gutters, brother, but our father has raised you up. Stop acting like the murderous swine you inherited on Nostramo.'

'Raised me, did he? Brought me up from the darkness and into the light? We are killers, Vulkan. All of us. Don't try and convince me we are noble men, for we are not. My eyes have just opened before yours, that's all.'

Curze turned and walked away, back down the ridge. 'Fear, Vulkan,' he called, disappearing into the shadows, 'that's the only thing they understand. You all need to learn that.'

Vulkan did not reply. His body was trembling. Looking down, he saw his forge hammer gripped in both hands. He hadn't even realised he'd picked it up. He gasped, exhaling to relieve the tension, and fought his body. When he was calm again, he turned towards the inferno. The flames were rising now, touching the sky with tendrils of coiling black smoke. It reminded him of Ibsen, and the jungles they had set ablaze there.

How many more worlds must burn before this is over?

He stood in silence, just watching, and stayed like that for several minutes until a quiet voice from behind the primarch disturbed his reverie.

'Lord Vulkan?'

It was the remembrancer, Seriph.

'Your equerry said you'd be up here.'

'Did he also tell you I did not wish to be disturbed?'

Seriph bowed her head slightly. 'He was too preoccupied to stop me.'

Vulkan turned his back on her. 'I'm not in the mood for further questions now.'

'Sincere apologies, my lord. I had hoped to continue our–'

Vulkan's head snapped around savagely. 'I said not now!'

She shrank back, her eyes alive with fear.

Curze's last words came back to him, almost mocking, but Vulkan was powerless. He glared, eyes burning hot with fury. This was the monster, this was the image he was trying so hard to conceal from the remembrancers. His hearts pulsed, and his chest heaved up and down like a giant bellows. Curze was right – he was a killer. That was the purpose for which he had been bred.

His anger at what his brother had done, the memory of those bodies, the children… It was overwhelming, so consuming Vulkan hissed his next command and filled the air with the smell of ash and cinder.

'*Leave. Me. Alone.*'

Seriph fled down the ridge.

Vulkan didn't bother to watch her go. Instead he watched the burning ruins of Khar-tann.

'It will all end in fire when the galaxy burns,' he said, a heavy melancholy settling upon him. 'And all of us will light the torch.'

PAIN AWAITED ME when I awoke. I was no stranger to it, for I was a warrior born, a primarch. And it took a primarch to know how to really hurt another.

Curze must have been well schooled, for my body was alive with pain. It brought me back from a torpor of unconsciousness into a world of nerve-shredding, white-hot agony. Even I, Vulkan, who have stood in the mouth of a volcano, who have endured the nucleonic, cleansing fire of a missile strike and lived. Even for me, this… *hurt.*

I screamed, opening my eyes. Through vision drenched arterial red I saw a cell no larger than the hold of a gunship. It was black with circular walls, metal-forged and without any door or gate that I could see.

First calming the urgent pulse of blood drumming through my hearts, I then slowed my breathing. Shock and severe injury were retarding my efforts to control my body, but my will was stronger, and I regained some semblance of function.

I blinked, banishing the red rime of clotted blood that had crusted over my iris like a dirty lens. Aching bones and limbs protested, but I managed to rise. It was as if a Titan's foot was resting on my back.

I took a faltering step but staggered, falling painfully on one knee. I hadn't walked in a while, I had no idea how long. The cell was abjectly dark despite my enhanced eyesight, and I had lost all sense of time.

Rising to my feet again, I trembled, but stayed upright. Waiting like that for a few moments – it could have been an hour, it was difficult to gauge – the tremors ebbed and then ceased entirely as my strength gradually returned. I got three more steps before the shackles binding me to the wall yanked me back. I scowled, looking down at the chains fettered around my wrists and ankles as if seeing them for the first time. Another was fastened around my neck, attached to a collar. I pulled at one experimentally, assessing resistance. It did not yield. Even with two hands, I couldn't break the chain.

'You're wasting your time,' a familiar voice uttered from the darkness, making me quickly turn.

'Show yourself,' I demanded. My throat was sore from the sharp air in this place, and my voice lacked conviction because of it.

Even so, a face loomed out of the shadows at my command. It was pale, framed by closely cropped black hair, with sunken cheeks and cold, glassy eyes. Sharks have eyes like that – dead eyes. But it was a man, not a shark at all. It was my brother. One I barely recognised.

'Pleased to see me?' asked Ferrus Manus, in gravel-raw tones.

'What? How is this poss–' I began before the blade slipped into my side. As white fire exploded in my flesh, I realised that my gaolers were here too, waiting silently in the dark. They had brought a great many swords with them. I heard them slip from scabbards before they sank into my body.

Before I blacked out, the charnel stink of Curze's breath washed over me, and as I fell again I caught a last glimpse of my cellmate.

Those same dead eyes staring, Ferrus lifted his chin.

Around his neck was a bloody scar, partly clotted with his primarch blood. I knew the wound, I had inflicted several during my time as a warlord. It was from decapitation.

'As you can see,' he answered, 'it's not possible.'

And my world was swallowed by darkness.

CHAPTER THREE
Discovery

'What is true faith? Is it belief in the absence of empirical truth?
No. Faith is a manifestation of will, it is the fealty-price given in
the presence of actual godhood and the only protection from its
divine wrath. That is true faith.'

– spoken during a meeting of the Lodge
by a Chaplain of the XVII Legion

SEBATON TOOK A deep breath of clean, outside air. Confinement inside the catacombs had begun to manifest as mild claustrophobia and with the night air cooling his skin, he let the relief from being out of the hole wash over him. His heart was hammering so hard, he felt the need to put a hand over his chest just to quieten it. Fear of enclosed spaces wasn't something he had suffered from before but the sense of creeping dread, that intangible belief that something – or someone – was tracking him like a bloodhound, had unsettled him more than he cared to admit.

'Get a damn grip,' he chided.

Despite his promises to the contrary, he was right back where he didn't want to be. He hoped after the last time that they would have left him alone. He had dared believe he was free, but he would never truly be free, not from them. And so, here he was.

Darkness had fallen completely over the ruins and rain was trickling from bruise-purple clouds above, pattering on the canvas awning of his tent.

They had made camp on a rocky promontory overlooking the dig site. The ruins were behind Sebaton, about twenty metres down, reachable via a slightly inclined slope. The other side of the promontory dropped away into a sheer-sided cliff, below which was a short expanse of grey scrub wasteland that was slowly being eroded by the creeping pipework and industry of Ranos.

It was also the pain that had driven him out. Sebaton had felt it like an ache at the back of his skull, an itch behind his teeth that refused to be scratched, a bitter taste under his tongue that made him feel sick. It hurt to simply *be* in the hole. The closer they came, the harder it got to be down there. Sebaton wasn't sure if that boded well or ill for his endeavour. His *employers* had been detailed about the object of this excavation, providing everything he needed to recognise it, as well as what it did, how it worked and what he was expected to do with it once he had it. This was the worst thing, not the digging, but what came next – his mission.

It had grown colder above the dig site and Sebaton nursed a cup of cooling recaff in one hand in a vain attempt to warm up, kneading his right temple with the other. It didn't help; he was still cold, and the migraine still lingered.

'Are you all right?'

Varteh had followed him and was approaching up the slope, pistol loose in the holster, moving with that same soldierly confidence he always had. Sebaton stopped massaging his head, allowing his hand to stray to the pistol he wore, but immediately berated himself.

Got you jumping at shadows, he told himself. *When did you become so paranoid?*

Who are you kidding, you've always been this paranoid. Comes with the territory.

'Fine,' Sebaton lied, taking a sip of the brackish caffeine. He grimaced at the taste.

'Sorry,' said Varteh, reaching him at the summit of the ridge. 'My brewing skills aren't as honed as my ability to kill people.'

'I'm hoping you won't need to employ the latter.'

The ex-Lucifer poured himself a cup, but didn't answer.

'It's hot, at least,' said Sebaton, turning to face the city as Varteh joined him. 'Well… warm.'

They *chinked* their cups together.

'What are we drinking to?' asked Varteh.

'Getting out of here.'

The ex-Lucifer's expression suggested he thought Sebaton meant more than just Ranos. He took a rolled up stick of lho-leaf from his jacket pocket, offering one to Sebaton, who refused.

'No, thank you. My mind feels overstimulated as it is.'

'Keeps me sharp,' said Varteh. 'Funny what you miss when you're out.'

Sebaton turned to see the soldier's profile. 'Out?'

'Service, the Army.'

Ah, thought Sebaton, *out…*

Now it was Varteh's turn to ask, as he picked up on the change in mood, 'Something wrong?'

'Freedom, Varteh. You're talking about freedom.'

'Not everyone desires it. And I was thrown out, remember? For some, routine is an anchor that keeps them grounded, stops them from drifting. I've met plenty of soldiers who think like that. They can't function without it. Downtime is like hell for men like that.'

'Indeed,' said Sebaton, taking in the sight of labyrinthine industrial works, manufactorums and hab-blocks, 'I believe you.' Tiny pinpricks of flickering light emanating from drum fires, cook stands

and furnaces illuminated the otherwise drab vista. Sebaton imagined the hordes of indentured workers clustered around them for
warmth. It had been months organising this dig, finding the correct
site and then the excavation itself. Now, with the object of his visit
so close, Sebaton was more than ready to leave.

Varteh thumbed over his shoulder. 'So, why here? I know you
won't give me details and I honestly don't care if you're doing this
for profit or prestige, but this place is just rubble. There's no tomb
here, no Gyptian sarcophagus waiting for us to open it. Does it even
have a name?'

He wasn't wrong. Even with the benefit of looking down on the
ruins from above, it resembled nothing of the fortress it had once
been. Now it was a rotting shell of overhanging beams, like spears
of broken limbs jutting from the burned-out husks of long forgotten halls. For many years the people of Ranos, and even Traoris,
had been in thrall to the masters of this fortress and the seven
others dotted around the planet. This one had been the last, its
octagonal border barely visible. Eight, eight-sided fortresses. Even
that word was a misnomer. Some had referred to them by another
name – temples.

Yes, this place had a name but I won't speak it. Not here, not to you.

'Something happened here,' said Sebaton instead, 'something
important, and a part of it was left behind.'

'This "weapon" you mentioned?'

'No, not that,' said Sebaton, momentarily distracted, regretting
even saying that much. He paused. 'Does it seem overly quiet to
you?'

Deep in the heart of Ranos, the tiny lights were going out.

Overhead the thrum of heavy turbine engines invaded the silence.
They were distant enough that neither man reached for his sidearm,
but close enough that Sebaton went to grab a scope from inside the
tent.

'Landers,' said Varteh, not needing the benefit of the scope to realise what the engines belonged to.

'I count three, cutting through the cloud layer,' Sebaton replied, scope pressed against his right eye. 'Definitely a landing party.'

'Of what?'

'No idea,' he lied again, shutting the telescopic lens and putting it in his pocket.

They were bulky, heavily armed gunships. The kind used by deadly warriors. He'd met them before, and not enjoyed the experience.

'I'd like to know what they're doing here,' said Varteh.

'No, you wouldn't.'

Varteh laughed mirthlessly.

'Perhaps you're right. I'll go and kick our adept up the arse. See if we can move things up a notch.'

'Good idea.'

Varteh jogged back down the slope, one hand on his holster to keep it steady.

Sebaton lost the gunships a few seconds later as they disappeared below benighted rows of smoke stacks and silos. He swore under his breath.

'I suppose it was too much to ask that *they* didn't show up.'

The cup in his hands grew hot, much hotter than the tepid caffeine within. As he looked down into its brownish depths, he frowned.

'Oh,' said Sebaton, 'it's you.'

CHAPTER FOUR

Sons of our fathers

'Of all men else I have avoided thee.
But get thee back. My soul is too much charged
With blood of thine already.'

— From 'Masbeth' by the dramaturge Kristof Mylowe

'DO YOU REMEMBER how I found you, alone on the ash plains? I thought you were a miracle, or some devil cast back from the earth to plague us. But you were just a child, an infant. Something so small, so vulnerable, surrounded by so much death. I thought you were dead, burned black from the crash. The sand inside the crater you made had turned to glass... But the fire never touched you, didn't even leave a mark. You barely cried, and it wasn't from pain or discomfort. You just didn't want to be alone, Vulkan.'

'I remember.'

I smelled smoke and leather, metal and sweat.

'Wake up, son,' said a man, and in my half-conscious state I thought I recognised him.

I was back in the forge. I was home.

'Father?'

Smoke cleared, darkness parted, I blinked and there he was before me. Like it was yesterday.

N'bel.

Face tanned by the Nocturnean sun, hands calloused from metal working, skin that felt rough in my grasp, N'bel was every inch the craftsman. He had the broad shoulders of a blacksmiter, the fuller tucked in his belt providing further unneeded proof of his profession. A coarse overall of dark, heavy fabric was overlaid by a smock of leather. His arms were bare, scarred and tanned like his face, bound with torcs, thick with brawn and ropes of sinew. This was a man who made a living out of honest toil and muscle. He had taught me everything I knew, or at least, everything I cared to remember.

'You are alive...'

He nodded.

Longing ached in my chest, my eyes tearful. Around me was the workshop, smelling of ash, warmed by fire. Somewhere close by, an anvil chimed out a steady rhythm, the beat of a blacksmiter's drum, one whose tune I knew very well. It was pure and good, this place. A stone hearth sat in one corner of the room, where a pot of broth bubbled dulcetly above a quietly crackling fire. Here was the earth. Here, I was in my element.

'I have missed you, father.'

Tears stained my cheeks. I tasted salt and cinder when they touched my lips as I embraced N'bel, a lost son returning home. Despite his brawn and bulk, he was like a child in my arms. We parted as a frown crept upon my face at our sudden reunion.

'How? What about the war? Is it...?'

Something was clouding my mind, preventing me from seeing clearly. I shook my head but the fog was not here, it was within.

'All that matters is you are back, my son.'

He clapped me on the arm and I felt the warmth of a father's respect and admiration spread through me like a balm, washing away all the guilt and the blood.

For so long, I had wanted to come back. After the Crusade was over, and the war was done; in my heart, I knew I would return to Nocturne and live in peace. A hammer can sunder – in my hands it was an incredibly effective weapon – but it was also a tool to craft. I had destroyed populations, razed entire cities in the name of conquest; now I wanted permanence, to fulfil a desire to build, not break.

I helped build this place; not only this forge, but also this city in which I knew it resided, and the other six sanctuary cities besides. Nocturne had ever been a tribal society, the earth upon which it sat, but its trade and lifeblood was also its doom, as the hot and volatile world demonstrated during every Trial of Fire.

N'bel's eyes were staring, not with paternal joy at being reunited with his son, but in fear.

I held him by the shoulders, firmly, but not so hard that I would hurt him.

'Father, what is it? What's wrong?'

'All that matters is you are back...' he repeated, and nodded behind me.

I followed his gaze to the door of the forge. It was ajar and the night-time sounds of Nocturne drifted inside on a warm breeze. I could smell the heat of the desert, taste the acid-tang of the Acerbian Sea and also something else.

I released N'bel, turning to the door. 'What has happened?'

Nearby was the rack of tools my father used on the anvil. I picked up a branding iron shaped like a spear. It was an odd choice; there were several hammers, but for some reason I chose the iron.

'You weren't alone,' breathed my father, his strong blacksmiter's voice fading to a whimper, 'when you came back.'

I snarled, advancing on the door, the haft of the branding iron gripped tight in my hand.

'Father, what has happened?'

N'bel was lost to fear, and a sudden coldness swept through the forge, turning my blood to ice.

In the days before the Outlander, we Nocturneans had fought war-bands of dusk-wraiths for our freedom and safety. They were raiders, pirates and slavers. I later came to know them as the eldar, an alien species that had particularly blighted my world, but also countless others.

I had wanted peace, a chance to build, but now I saw that fate would not release me – the galaxy wanted a warrior. My other father was calling and he would not be denied.

'Stay in the forge,' I told N'bel and went outside.

The night was coal-black, and a vast pall of pyroclastic cloud moved slowly across the horizon like a dark phantom. All the lights were out. Every home, every forge and furnace was dead.

I had stepped out onto a platform of iron and steel. Gone were the tribal dwellings of my formative years, gone were the simple forges of my forebears. With the coming of the Outlander, and the arrival of the nascent Imperium, Nocturne had changed. Vast mining engines, furnaces and manufactorums replaced the old forges now. Where once there had been humble dwellings, now there were great conurbations of habitation domes, relay stations and vox-towers. The earth-shaman and metal-shapers, even the blacksmiters had given way to seismologists, geologists and manufactorum masters. Our trade had not changed, but our culture had. It needed to. For Nocturne was a capricious world, ever on the brink of destruction.

She was venting now, Mount Deathfire, in all her fiery glory. Pyroclastic cloud obscured most of my view, scudding across the invisible void shield suspended above me. The generators, one for each major city, were another gift from the Imperium. The one above me shimmered violently as pieces of debris flung from the volcano struck it. Fire was raining from the sky, cascading in waves and exploding into sparks as it met the resistance of the void shield.

It was beautiful to behold, nature's fury viewed in panorama like this. When I finally lowered my gaze from the heavens, that sense of awe and beauty left me. In its place was the coldness I had felt in the forge.

'You,' I uttered like a curse as I saw the lone figure with his back to me. He was sitting down, shoulders hunched over something. Dark hair cascaded over his back. He wore a smock of sackcloth. In one hand he carried a knife. Its edge was serrated and in the darkness I thought it had a blacker sheen around its toothed blade.

He was at odds with this place. I knew it in my heart, but also saw it in his anachronistic clothing.

He hadn't heard me, so I stepped closer, my grip tightening around the branding iron.

The dark figure was sawing, I could hear the rasp of his knife shearing through something. At first I thought it was wood, fuel for the furnace, but then I remembered the blade and the black sheen around the edge. A basket lay off to one side within easy reach. Every time he finished making a cut, he threw something into it.

'What are you doing?' Even as I asked the question, I knew the answer. *'What are you doing?'* I asked again. Rage took hold of me, and I raised the branding iron above my head like a spear.

The black sheen around the blade... It was blood.

No lights, no forge fires – the city was dead, and he had killed it.

'Turn, curse you!'

He stopped at the sound of his name. Sat up straight, knife held out casually to one side.

'Murdering scum!'

I pulled back my spear, aiming for his back, where I knew the iron would punch through into his heart. Even primarchs can die. Ferrus had died. He was the first of us, the first I was certain of, anyway. Even primarchs can die...

'Vulkan, no.'

The voice came from behind me, compelling me to obey.

At first I thought it was N'bel, venturing out of the forge to see what was going on, but I was wrong. I turned, and standing before me, in the same robes he had been wearing on Ibsen, was the remembrancer Verace.

'Vulkan, he is your brother and I forbid it.'

My grip tightened on the spear. 'But he murdered them.'

'Do not kill him, Vulkan.'

Who was this human to tell me my business, to give me orders? He was nothing to me, a memory from the Great Crusade, a–

No, that wasn't right. I shook my head, trying to banish the fog, but it wasn't out here with me, it was within.

Verace was no remembrancer. He was a cloak, a mask to hide something greater.

Very few mortals could behold the Emperor's true form and live. Even his voice was lethal. So he wore masks, erected facades that he might move around the galaxy without leaving deathly awe in his wake. I was his son, and as such able to withstand much more than any mortal man ever could, but even I had not seen my father's true face. He was at once a warrior, a poet, a scientist and a vagabond, and yet he was also none of these things. They were, all of them, merely camouflage to conceal his true nature. And the costume my father chose to wear now was that of an ageing remembrancer.

'My son, you must not kill him.'

'He has earned his fate,' I spat belligerently, not wishing to defy my father but at the same time unable to let the murderer go unpunished.

'Vulkan, please do not kill him.'

'Father!'

I felt a hand grip my shoulder, cold and vice-like. The spear was no longer clenched in my fist, its absence like smoke escaping through my grasping fingers.

'Brother…' said Curze as he rammed the spear into my back and I saw it punch through my chest a second later.

The world was fading again. I clutched at the iron impaling me, slumping to my knees as Curze let me go.

Verace was gone and left no trace of his parting; so, too, was my brother, though it was the lack of his presence rather than his actual disappearance that I noticed.

Above me, the void shield flickered once and died. Fire rained down, the skies were burning with it. Powerless, dying, I closed my eyes and let the conflagration take me.

THE REEK OF smoke and ash greeted me as I came round. For a moment I believed I was still on Nocturne, trapped in some infernal cycle from which there was no escape, destined to relive my imagined death at the hands of Curze, my brother, and now my captor, again and again.

But when the cell and not N'bel's forge came into focus around me, I realised I was truly awake and that my return home had just been a nightmare. Feverish sweat lathered my body; it was the first thing I noticed after the smell of the forge dissipated. Darkness reigned, as ever, and steam coiled from my oil-black skin as the heat of my body reacted to the cold. Honour scars stood out, my oaths of moment, etched into flesh and thrown into relief by a harsh light emanating from above. For a moment I thought I saw a marking I didn't recognise, but lost it in the shadows.

The second thing I noticed was that I was not alone, and this took my mind off the mark. Though the nightmare had left me, my ghastly cellmate had not.

Ferrus was watching from the shadows, his dead eyes twinkling like opals.

'You are dead, brother,' I said to him, rising. 'And I am truly sorry for that.'

'Why?' asked Ferrus, the gruesome neck wound adding more gravel to an already rasping cadence. 'Do you blame yourself, brother?'

It sounded almost like an accusation, so much so that it made me turn to regard him. He was truly a spectre, a shade, a withered version of what Ferrus Manus had once been, clad in my dead brother's armour.

'Where are we?' I asked, ignoring my dead brother's question.

'Where do you think we are?'

'Isstvan.'

Ferrus nodded. 'We never left, either of us.'

'Do not pretend to be him,' I said.

Ferrus opened his arms, looked around as if searching for answers. 'Am I not? Is it easy to assuage your guilt if you make yourself believe I am not some aspect of him? Do you know where my body is now? It lies headless on a desert of black sand, slowly putrefying in its bloodstained armour. I don't recall any of the statues erected in my honour bearing such an image.'

I was tiring of this cajoling. It was beneath me, it was beneath Ferrus, and I felt like I was besmirching his memory by the very act of listening to it.

'What are you, creature? For you are not Ferrus Manus.'

He laughed. It was an unpleasant sound, like the cawing of a crow. 'I thought I was your brother. Is that not how you addressed me? Am I so easily forgotten, now I am dead?'

Ferrus, or the thing that wore his skin and armour like a man wears a cloak, feigned disappointment.

I was unconvinced.

'Ferrus was a noble warrior, a good and honest man. He was steel and he was iron, and I will never forget him. Ever.'

'Yet you let me die.'

Guilt was more painful than any blade, and as it pierced my weary heart I staggered at first, but then righted myself.

'There was nothing I could do. Nothing either of us could do.'

'"Either of us"?' he asked, a look of belated revelation crossing his face. 'Ah, you mean Corax. You want him to share in your guilt?' His face brightened, as if enlightened, before it grew abruptly dark, prompting Ferrus to slowly shake his head. 'No. You own this, Vulkan. This was your mistake. *You* let me down, not Corax.'

I turned away, even as the spectre's words cut me without showing any visible trace of the wounds they'd inflicted. 'You are not real, brother. You're just a figment of my imagination, a remnant of conscience...'

'Guilt! I am your guilt made manifest, Vulkan. You can't escape me because I live in *you*.'

Trying not to listen, I started to examine the cell. It was circular, the metal used in its construction thick and impenetrable to my fists alone. But it was made in sections, and each of those was betrayed by a welding line that yielded a shallow lip. Fifty metres straight up. I couldn't jump that distance, but I might be able to climb it. As my lucidity returned, so too did my capacity to plan and strategise. I put those gifts to work on my escape.

An oubliette is a hole, a dungeon in which people are thrown and forgotten about. This was what Curze had done. He had left me in a hole, beaten me, cut me and assumed I would break, that my mind would shatter and I would be forever lost.

Curze was not Nocturnean. Nostramans did not possess our pride, our determination, our endurance.

'Despair' was not a word we recognised, nor was 'submission'.

Purpose providing me with newfound strength, I seized my chains. The iron felt rough against the palms of my hands as my grip tightened. Muscles bunched in my neck, hardened over my shoulders and back. Threads of sinew stood out on my blacksmiter's chest, cord thick and straining against the chains. And as I pulled, the links began to stretch and open, slowly yielding to my might. With a supreme effort, as much will as it was strength, I wrenched the chains apart and broke them. Each and every one, until their fragments lay scattered upon the cell floor.

Ferrus sneered - I could almost hear his lip curling. 'So, you are free of those chains. So what? You are *weak*, Vulkan. And because you are weak, you will fail. Just as you failed me, just as you failed your Legion.'

I stopped for a moment, and bowed my head to remember the fallen.

Nemetor, cradled in my arms... He had been the last.

'I did not fail *you*, brother.'

Pressing a hand against the cell wall, I felt for imperfections in the metal, the smallest handhold I could exploit.

The voice behind me interrupted my planning.

'Do you want to know how I died, brother?'

I did not turn this time, for I had no wish to see the thing that had somehow crept inside my thoughts and was trying to unman me.

My reply was caustic. 'You are not my brother. Now, shut up!'

Ferrus's voice grew lower, more sinister. 'Do you want to know what I realised at the very moment of my death?'

I paused, and cursed myself inwardly for doing it.

'I bested him, you know. Fulgrim, I mean.'

Now I turned. I couldn't help it. Deep down, a part of me must have suspected this, otherwise how could this apparition speak to me of it? 'He was your slayer?'

Ferrus nodded slowly, as a smile crept up over his lips like a spider crawling across a weed.

'He was.'

'You hated him, didn't you? For his betrayal, for the bond of friendship he broke.'

'We were once very close.'

I felt the weight of the chains anew, their paltry fragments dragging me down like an anchor into the abyssal deep of an ocean. Darkness lingered here in this trench of the mind, all-consuming and endless. I knew that I was succumbing to something – that my will, not my strength, was being tested, and I wondered again at the nature of the darkness in this place that I could not see through it. That I was blind like any mortal man would be.

'Yes – you are, brother,' said Ferrus, causing me to start when I realised he had read my thought and turned it to his own ends. 'Blind, I mean. Blinded to truth, by so-called enlightenment.' Ferrus's smile reached his eyes, and it was hideous to behold. All light was drawn to them, devoured by those deadened orbs as a black hole devours a sun. 'You know of what I speak.'

'You said you defeated him.' I felt a weight upon my back, pressing me down to my haunches.

'I did. I had him at my mercy, but Fulgrim,' said Ferrus, whilst shaking his head, 'was not all he appeared to be. You know of what I speak,' he repeated, and my mind was cast back to when I saw Horus for that second time, when I felt the nature of the power he had cloaked himself with. I could not put a name to it, to this presence, this primordial fear, but knew that Ferrus spoke of the same thing.

He leaned back to expose the neck wound. 'He cut off my head, slew me in cold blood and left my Legion shattered. You failed me, Vulkan. I needed you at my side, and you failed me. I asked you–' Ferrus grew angry, '–no, I *begged* you to follow me, to stand by my side!'

I stood, the weight leaving me, the chains losing their power to drag me down into the dirt, into this dark hollow with only an apparition and my eventual madness to keep me company.

'You lie,' I told the spectre. 'Ferrus Manus would not beg. Not even for that.'

I turned back to the wall, took hold as my fingers pressed into the metal, and began to climb.

'You will fail!' Ferrus raged below me. 'You are weak, Vulkan! Weak! You'll perish in this place and no one will ever know your fate. Unmourned, your statue will be shrouded. Your Legion will diminish and die, lost like the others. Unspoken of, unwanted, a cautionary tale for those that remain behind to spit on your unworthy ashes. Nocturne will burn.'

One hand over the other, I kept on climbing.

'Shut up, brother.'

Ferrus had never been this talkative before; I wondered why in my subconscious he was now. It was guilt, and the slow erosion of my resolve, that provided his words. They were my words, my fear.

'I am starting to understand, Curze,' I muttered, finding all the imperfections in the metal with my fingertips, rising like a feline predator from my prison.

I slipped, fell a half-metre, my knuckles scraping against the wall, but managed to grip where one of the weld points jutted almost imperceptibly in a shallow lip of metal. No one berated me or willed my death. I glanced down.

Ferrus was gone. For now at least.

Making sure of my grip, I set my mind to the task ahead.

Above me, with every painstaking metre I climbed, the oval of light that cast down into my cell widened.

Once I neared the end of the shaft, no more than two metres from the summit, I stopped and waited. Listened.

Two voices, low and grating, emanated from above. The rough tonality came from vox-grilles. Curze had positioned two guards to watch my cell. I briefly wondered if they were amongst the legionaries who had stabbed me so grievously before. I could still feel the presence of the blades as they pierced my body, but it was a phantom pain and no scars marred my skin other than those rendered by the branding iron.

During the Great Crusade, there were few occasions I could remember when the VIII and XVIII Legions had fought together on campaign. Kharaatan was the last time, and that hadn't ended well for me or Curze. Whatever bonds of loyalty I felt towards him, whatever fraternal love and respect I might have borne for him, ended on Kharaatan. What he did there… What he made me do…

I shuddered, and one of the guards laughed in such a way as to suggest the nature of their discussion: death and torture, and how they had meted it out to those weaker and smaller than them. Murderers, rapists, thieves, the children of Nostramo came from spoiled stock.

I felt my anger boil, but kept my fury in check. This needed to be swift, silent.

From the resonance of their footfalls against the metal floor, I gauged each legionary's position relative to the opening of the shaft. One was close by – bored, as he shifted around often. The other was farther away, perhaps a few metres between each warrior. Neither of them was watching the opening. I suspected they thought I was dead or dying. Certainly, they had plunged enough steel in me to see it done.

I am a primarch, and we do not die easily… or well, I reminded myself, thinking of poor Ferrus. And for a moment, I felt his presence again below me, but he did not stir or speak.

I eased out of the shaft.

Two guards, midnight-clad in their legionary colours. Night Lords both. One had his back to me. Moving silently I slipped my hand around his gorget, smothering his vox-grille with my palm, and twisted.

The other saw me too late, a little farther down the corridor. He saw my eyes first – he saw them when I chose to open them after I killed his comrade. Two fiery orbs, burning vengefully in the darkness. Shadows were the province of the VIII but they were not the only Legion who could dwell in darkness. Balanced on the edge of the shaft, dropping the body of the first guard to land with a dull metal-hitting-metal *thunk*, I pounced.

The second guard was raising his bolter. It must have felt like gravity had exerted itself fourfold over his muscles; every movement glacially slow in the face of a primarch's concerted attack. He aimed for my chest, going for the centre mass as instinct would have urged him to. I carried the guard down as I landed upon him, my fingers clamping around his trigger hand and mashing it into the stock of his bolter so he – and it – would never fire again.

He hit the ground, grunting as my sheer weight and power dented his chest plate and cracked the fused ribcage beneath. I masked his scream with my hand, crushing the vox-grille, breaking teeth. Blood geysered up through his ruined war-helm, splashing hot and wet against my face. I kept squeezing, immune to the guard's panic.

Then it stopped, and silence followed.

Still straddling the dead guard's body, I looked up and tried to get my bearings.

A long corridor stretched out in front of me: bare metal, faintly lit, nondescript. I could be anywhere on Isstvan. I remembered little of my abduction from the battlefield. What happened between when Curze appeared and my waking in the cell might never return.

A sense of enclosure as I touched the metal wall on my left made me suspect I was underground. Perhaps Horus had ordered the construction of tunnels beneath the surface. I wondered if there were cells for Corax and Ferrus too. I dismissed the idea almost as soon as it was formed. Horus did not take prisoners of war, it wasn't in his nature – though I had much cause to question exactly what his nature was over these last few months. This was Curze's doing.

I knew then he hadn't forgiven me for Kharaatan, for what I did to him.

My brother was a petty-minded, shallow creature; this was his way of evening things up between us.

Taking the bodies of the guards, one by one, I threw them down into the pit. I suspected much of this place was deserted – after all, Curze had left me here to die – and no one would hear the crash of their broken bodies when they hit the ground, but a pair of dead Night Lords out in the open would arouse alarm immediately. A few seconds gained might be the difference between my escape and continued incarceration.

With the guards dispatched, I padded gently to the end of the corridor, slowing as I reached the junction and listening intently for sounds of disturbance.

Nothing.

Peering around the corner, I saw another passageway, empty like the one I was just leaving.

The peace didn't last. After a few minutes, I was halfway down the next corridor when a door slid open along the right-hand side and a legionary stepped out.

Acting with greater alacrity than his dead brothers festering in the pit, he opened up a comm-channel and sounded an alarm.

'Vulkan lives!' He sounded afraid, and the irony of that fact gave me a cruel satisfaction as I ran at him. I took a glancing hit from a hurried snap shot, before I smashed the flat of my palm against his chest. It was a heart strike, which, if delivered with enough force, can kill instantly. His primary organ collapsed – so, too, the secondary back-up. The legionary crumpled and I left him for dead, racing into the chamber from where he'd come as the sirens started screaming.

Again, I was confronted with more bare metal. No weapons, no supplies, nothing. It was spartan to the point of being deserted. Except I heard them coming for me above the wailing alarms. Some were shouting in that ugly, guttural language of their home world;

others hurried in silence, the drum of their booted feet betraying their urgency and panic.

I crossed the room, rushing through the only other exit, and found another corridor. It was shorter than the previous one but just as barren, yet I had begun to feel a familiarity for this place. Around the next junction I almost charged into a pair of guards who were coming the other way. I killed them both swiftly, lethal damage inflicted in less than the time it took for me to blink. I stole one of their chainblades – it was the only weapon I could take and use effectively – wondering how I would escape, trying to formulate some kind of plan.

I needed to find somewhere to stop and think, adapt to the changing situation.

I went up.

The ceiling duct was tight against my body, and I had to discard the weapon I had only just procured, but by replacing the overhead grate I could temporarily mask my point of egress.

It stank in the vent, of blood, of sweat, and I wondered where exactly it was ferrying air from and to. Crawling on my belly, using my elbows and toes for propulsion, I reached another grate that looked down onto a room below.

Banks of monitors surrounding a much larger screen showing a schematic of the prison marked it as a security station. Unaugmented human serfs were in attendance, speaking into vox-units, desperately trying to find me. No legionaries were visible. They were hunting, attempting to establish a trap.

These men and women were not warriors, but they were allied with my enemies.

If I were to escape, none could live.

Quietly removing the grate, I slid through the opening head first and dropped down amongst them. A woman, her face daubed in Nostraman tattoos, cried out and I backhanded her across the chamber. Going for his sidearm, one of the male operators tried to draw down on me but I was faster. Much faster. I killed him, too. In fewer than three seconds, all six human operators were dead. I made it quick, as painless as I could, but failing to salve my conscience in the process.

The schematic on the screen showed only a portion of the underground complex. Again, I was struck with a sense of familiarity concerning the layout and wondered how massive this prison actually was. The other monitors showed pict-feed images of the search teams, linked up to retinal lenses. Data inloaded from the legionaries' battle-helms ran across the screens. Heart monitors on every Night Lord thrummed agitatedly below the feed from each helmcorder, graphic equalisers slaved to their voice patterns rose and fell as they breathed and hissed orders.

I ignored the pict-feeds, focusing on the half-map instead and committing it to memory.

Two doors led out of the security chamber. I took the one that, according to the schemata, led to an upper level. I had no idea how far down beneath the Isstvan surface I was, or what would be greeting me when I got there, but there was no other course for me to take.

Another corridor faced me, at the end of which was a cross-junction. Halfway down, I paused and shook my head to clear it.

'Where am I?' I breathed, not recognising this junction from the schematic. I had an eidetic memory – this should not have been happening. I considered going back but the risk was too great. By entering the ducts above I had gained only a few seconds against my pursuers. I had to move on. And fast.

Reaching the junction, I paused again. Two more corridors stretched away from me, the destination of each concealed in darkness. A faint breeze, detected by the tiny hairs on my bare skin, flowed from the right. I was about to take that branch when I saw a shadow seemingly emerge out of the darkness.

Gaunt, grinning, I recognised the cadaverous features of my brother.

'Ferrus…'

Placing a finger mockingly to his lips, he beckoned me to follow him into the shadows.

I knew I could not trust my own mind. By manifesting this apparition, here and in my cell, it had already betrayed me.

Weak, he mouthed as I paused before the threshold to the right-hand branch. *So weak.*

I took the left branch, trusting my instincts over my mind, and as I turned I saw another figure. Incorporeal, a wraith in form and features, it wore gossamer-thin robes that appeared to float as if they were suspended in water. Its eyes were almond-shaped and the runes crafted about its person were eldritch and alien. The eldar flickered once as if captured on a bad pict-cording and disappeared.

My brother or my enemy; it was not much of a choice. I felt the jaws of the rusty trap closing around me again, their teeth pinching my flesh.

I raced down the left branch, finding its terminus was a bulkhead. It was the first of its kind I had seen since my escape, more robust and inviolable than the doors I had passed through so far. Metres thick, triple bolted, I wasn't able to just rip it from its hinges.

Pressing my hand against the metal, acutely aware of the shouts of my pursuers getting closer, I felt coldness. Then the light glaring from the bulkhead's inbuilt access panel went from red to green.

Klaxons sounded as the amber strobes above the door kicked in; I noticed the black-and-yellow chevrons delineating it.

Backing away, too late, far too late, realising now where I was and why this place was so familiar to me, I watched as a jagged crack formed diagonally in the bulkhead and its two halves slid apart to reveal a second emergency door.

The coldness intensified. Tendrils of it touched my skin, freezing me. Knowing it was pointless to run, I waited as the second door split just like the first. Invisible force shields collapsed and I was wrenched up off my feet as the pressure inside the corridor began venting outwards, taking me with it.

I was not on Isstvan. I had never been on Isstvan.

It was a ship, Curze's ship.

The emergency door opened and I had a few seconds to behold the void of deepspace before I was wrenched out.

CHAPTER FIVE
Blood begets blood

VALDREKK ELIAS CROUCHED at the bottom of the shaft. Masked by shadows, he surveyed the dig site.

'What were they looking for?' asked one of the Word Bearers in the hole with him. His name was Jadrekk, a loyal if unimaginative warrior. He was pacing the edges of the site, bolter locked across his chest.

'Whatever it was, they found it,' Elias replied.

Tools lay strewn about the subterranean chamber, and doused phosphor lamps were still suspended from cables bolted into the cave roof. A cup of recaff sat next to an upturned stool and there were scuff marks in the dust made by the hurried passage of booted feet.

In the middle of the chamber – some kind of reliquary if the presence of bones and skulls was any guide – the flagstones had been upheaved. They were cracked apart, blackened at the edges and not by the action of any digging tool. Through careful excavation, through the use of micro-trenchers and the application of debris-thinners to gently extract extraneous layers of dirt and granite, a crater had been revealed. And in its core, half a metre down, was a void.

Elias leaned into the hole cut into the crater, exploring the unusual cleft in the rock where the fortune hunters, or whatever they were, had been digging.

'And it was removed from here,' he added, standing and dusting off his armour.

Amaresh dipped his horned helmet towards the mess surrounding the crater.

'I'd say they left in a hurry.'

He knelt down to touch the cup of recaff.

'And not that long ago, either.'

'Agreed,' said Elias, activating the arcane-looking flask attached to his belt.

'*I have their trail,*' Narek reported without having to be asked.

'How many?'

'*Not enough.*'

'Don't kill them all, Narek. Not until we know what they took from the catacombs and why.'

'*I can't swear to that.*'

Narek ended the communion, allowing Elias to appreciate the primitive architecture of the room. Though much of it had been destroyed, collapsing in on itself as entropy was exerted upon stone and steel, he could still discern the eight-sided structure, the weave and weft of the arcane in its construction. Primitive, centuries old, he felt the latent power in this temple. It was nothing but a shadow, the artefact that had been taken from the crater having destroyed it and robbed it of its potency long ago.

Elias felt the distant touch of the Pantheon on this place and knew that whatever secret it held was worth discovering for himself.

'Come,' he told the other two. As he ascended the ramp back to the surface, Elias looked up at the light coming down through the opening and the raindrops caught in its shaft, sparkling like stars. It reminded him of the constellations in the night sky, and how they were changing.

'Brothers,' Elias said, 'I sense there is more to do here than taint the False Emperor's sacred earth.' He smiled. 'A revelation is near.'

Above the pit into the catacombs, Deriok was waiting. He had four other legionaries with him. The rest of the landing party were at large in the city; two were hunting with Narek, the others were silencing comm-stations, killing any resistance and otherwise keeping the Word Bearers' presence in Ranos concealed. There were seven more cities, and in addition to Ranos, their populations might be needed too. For most important of all Elias's acolytes' duties here was the procurement of sacrifices.

'Eight disciples, one for each of the eight points,' said Elias, emerging into the light.

Like the statue in Cardinal Square, these ruins were a monument to the Emperor's dominance and former presence on this world. The potency of the effigy that the natives had erected was nothing compared to this place, however. That had been easy to taint. The Emperor had unleashed his power upon the old temple that had once stood here, and reduced it to rubble. He had broken the strength trapped in its walls and overthrown it. He had literally *touched* it with his godhood, and like a fingerprint it remained still. Indelible, enduring.

Here, in Ranos, did the Emperor's power manifest and here, in Ranos, at the very site of Imperial victory, would Elias taint that power and corrupt it to the will of the Pantheon. It would take time and patience. Most of all it would take blood. As the first stage of the ritual began, he tried not to be distracted with thoughts of what had been hidden in the catacombs, forcing his mind to the matter in hand, but the mystery of it intrigued him.

'Gather,' he said to the other seven, the acolytes forming a circle

of eight with their master. Ritual daggers glistened in fists of red
ceramite. Seized in each zealot's other hand was a mortal.

'Blood begets blood,' Elias uttered. He barely saw them as people
any more. The men and women at his brothers' mercy were just a
simple means to an end. 'Let the galaxy drown in it,' he concluded
and slashed the throat of the woman he was holding, spilling her
blood to profane the earth.

They would need more. Much more. But the harvest of Ranos
had yielded a plentiful crop. And as he listened to the plaintive
cries of the cattle his warriors had herded, Elias smiled and said to
Amaresh, 'Bring forth the others.'

VARTEH'S SENSE OF direction was good, but even the ex-Lucifer Black
was struggling to keep his bearings in the warren of Ranos City.

'Are we lost, Varteh?' Sebaton glanced over his shoulder and saw
his worried expression mirrored by the thin-looking man behind
him.

Gollach, the tech-adept, had railed against leaving the servitors
behind but Sebaton knew the predators that were hunting them
– he suspected Varteh did too – and ended Gollach's argument at
the muzzle of his pistol. The cyborgs would only slow them down.
Deployed this way, they might actually prove useful, obfuscating
the trail and thus gaining the others vital time on their pursuers.

'Not yet,' Varteh replied. He battle-signed to the man alongside
him. A mercenary – not ex-Army, but as he peeled off into the shadows in response to the ex-Lucifer's command, he was obviously well
versed in a soldier's argot.

The other hired gun stayed at the back, behind Gollach. Sebaton
knew the mercenaries' names, but they were as inconsequential as
the mud under his feet, now that he had what he'd come for. Even
wrapped up in cloth, centuries beneath the earth, it felt warm under
his arm and emitted a very faint resonance that slightly pained him.

As soon as Sebaton realised that they had been compromised, they had fled. His masters would have to wait to learn of his discovery. So far away, in all respects not merely space, there was nothing they could do to aid him anyway. Besides, he knew what he had to do.

Duugan, one of Varteh's men, a lean-muscled pugilist with a handle-bar moustache and neck tattoos, had spotted the hunters. He was good, a sniper by trade, but caught only the barest glimpse of the warriors converging on their position. They moved after that. Quick and fast.

It was Duugan who had peeled off from the main group, running point and scouting ahead to make sure they weren't being encircled.

Trio, so named for the bionics that replaced three of the fingers on his right hand, brought up the rear. He was clean-shaven, and thinner-faced than Duugan, previous profession unknown. He was also the group's pilot, but then Sebaton had that covered if needed.

'How close, Trio?' Varteh said into the vox. They'd ditched the rebreathers, Varteh and his men switching them for throat mics and comm-beads. Up here on the surface, they didn't need the masks. They'd only hamper their senses and ability to communicate. Sebaton had removed his too, but kept it in case it proved useful later.

'Haven't seen anything in the last eleven minutes, sir. Must've slipped them.'

'We haven't,' said Sebaton. 'They are closing on us.'

Varteh's grim expression hardly inspired confidence. 'I know.'

It wasn't a sprint, the streets were too crowded and labyrinthine for that, but the sense of urgency made their flight seem faster. Every shadow held the promise of danger, every doorway or tunnel a freshly imagined terror. Even swaying cables and hanging strips of plastek became potential enemies, transformed by fear and the dark.

Though Sebaton did not necessarily consider himself a brave man, certainly not in the same way as a soldier, he was also not so suspicious that he jumped at shadows, but the quiet, rising tension was testing his fortitude.

It had nearly broken Gollach.

The thin, hunchbacked man was fading, unable to keep the pace. He was used to his workshop, comfortable with his machines and the isolation of that existence. In this life, physical exercise had been confined to scripting doctrine-wafers or light mechanical maintenance. A crook in his spine had developed as a result of constantly stooping over some engine or device. A bad decision – or decisions – along the line had thrust him into Varteh's employ and turned him into a man so desperate that he had no choice but to step beyond the wreckage of his old life to try and build a new one. Clearly he hadn't envisaged that part of that would involve running for his life in a strange city, on a world he did not know, from an enemy he could not see.

He kept grabbing his chest, so much so that Sebaton slowed down in case he suddenly expired.

Don't be stupid. Just let him fall back, maybe buy some more time... Throne! When did I become this callous?

All of his life, or rather *lives*, Sebaton had done what was necessary to survive. He took what he needed from people and discarded the rest. There was remorse at first, some nightmares even, but that all faded in time and he had become aware of a void developing within him, a slow hollowing-out of his soul. Not literally his soul, of course – as such things were real and could happen – but rather a moral degradation which he didn't know how to reverse. He had become nothing more than a tool, used at someone else's bidding. No different to a hammer or a wrench, except more subtle and less obvious. Some would describe him as a weapon.

It was a little late for redemption now, but Sebaton slowed down anyway and urged Gollach to move faster.

'Why are we running?' Gollach asked, trying to keep his voice from trembling. 'I thought this was an archaeological dig. Only of interest to scholars, you said. Who could be after us?'

Sebaton tried to be reassuring. 'It would not help if I told you. But you have to keep running.' He looked over to Varteh, who was getting farther ahead and seemed distracted by his vox.

'How much further to the ship?' Sebaton asked, though he knew the answer to that.

Varteh didn't answer straight away. Something was distracting him.

Sebaton grew insistent. 'Varteh, the ship?' He was close to abandoning these men and this pretence to strike for the vessel on his own when Varteh answered.

'Can't reach Duugan on the vox,' he said.

'Meaning?' Although Sebaton already knew the answer to that as well.

'Either something is baffling the signal, or he's dead.'

'*Oh fugging hell...*' Gollach murmured, stumbling. Sebaton caught his elbow, and righted him so he didn't fall.

Varteh dropped back, less sure of pushing ahead so aggressively now Duugan was off-vox. 'Those landers you saw in the sky,' he asked Sebaton. 'Is this them? Are they looking for that thing too?' He nodded to the cloth-wrapped bundle under Sebaton's left arm.

'Not sure.'

That was a lie, but as he didn't know who the ones in the landers were or what they wanted, there seemed no point in saying anything further.

'Who are they, Sebaton? Duugan said they were massive, armoured to the gunwales. Are we running from what I think we're running from?'

Sebaton didn't see the point in lying further. These men in his service had earned some truth.

'They're Legiones Astartes.'

Varteh ruefully shook his head. 'Fugging Space Marines? You whoreson. How long have you known?'

'Ever since we arrived, it was a possibility they would follow after us.'

'A *possibility*? What the hell is that supposed to mean?'

Sebaton was genuinely contrite. 'I am sorry, Varteh. You don't deserve this.'

'I should shoot you in the leg right now, leave you and that–' he gestured to the cloth bundle again, '–and make my getaway with Trio and Gollach.'

'It won't help.'

'It'll make me feel better, you fugging twist!' He calmed down, compartmentalising his fear to a place where it couldn't inhibit his ability to survive. 'That thing you're carrying, it's important isn't it?'

Sebaton nodded. 'More than you know, and more than I could ever tell you.'

'Who are you, Sebaton? I mean *really*?'

Sebaton shook his head, his rueful expression saying more about his troubled mind than any words ever could.

'Truthfully, Varteh, I don't know any more.'

The ex-Lucifer sucked his teeth, having reached an important decision. He stopped running. Sebaton slowed in turn and the others caught up.

'Time to catch a breath, Gollach,' he told the man, who seemed both glad and alarmed that they didn't have to run any more. He sat down.

'Are we safe?' he asked in a breathless wheeze, glancing nervously over his shoulder.

'We've lost them,' Varteh lied, the truth of what he was really doing showing in his eyes and the slight, almost imperceptible shake of the head to Trio that Gollach would never see. He turned to Sebaton. 'You go on ahead, switch with Duugan.'

Sebaton nodded, and felt his admiration and respect for the ex-Lucifer grow, while his own self-loathing redoubled.

'I think the Army misses you greatly.'

'Oh, I doubt that. Just another pair of boots.'

They didn't shake hands, nothing so trite as that, but a look passed between them and in it Sebaton found some hope that he could be a better man than he was. Perhaps he could be more than a weapon.

'He's going?' asked Gollach, getting agitated again. 'Where? He's no soldier. Why is he going? I want to go with him.' He got to his feet.

Gollach was exhausted, and would only slow Sebaton down. Like an airship struggling for loft, Sebaton needed to drop some ballast. Only in this case, it was the men he had hired.

Holding Gollach by the shoulders, Sebaton spoke clearly and calmly.

'*Stay here with Varteh. He'll keep you safe.*'

A sort of blankness came over Gollach's face and he nodded once before sitting back down.

Varteh didn't look surprised. Sebaton knew the ex-Lucifer had suspected that he was a psyker for a while.

'You need to go,' he said. Trio was already breaking out a pair of heavy calibre cannons from a case he'd been hauling all the way from the dig site. With the exception of the servitors that they had since abandoned, it was about all they did take with them. Sebaton counted three weapons in total. Duugan wouldn't need his.

'You want one?' Varteh asked. 'Might come in handy.'

It wouldn't, not against *them*.

'Keep it. It'll only slow me down.'

'Is it worth it?' Varteh asked. 'What we took from the hole.'

'Worth all of mankind.'

Sebaton ran.

✠ ✠ ✠

THOUGH IT WAS hard to tell from his dour demeanour, Narek relished the hunt. He used to be reconnaissance, a Vigilator, until an injury impeded his scouting abilities and saw him fall behind the others in his unit. He'd given up the squad soon after that, and rejoined the Legion proper as part of Elias's Chapter.

It was on Isstvan V that he had been wounded. In command of a stealth unit, sent to sabotage Legion forces loyal to the Emperor before the attack began and their betrayal was revealed, his unit met some enemy Scouts who saw at once what they were doing. They killed the fledgeling Raven Guard, but at the cost of Narek's entire squad and his left leg. A bolt shell had shattered it. He'd finished placing the charges, crawling over the bodies of his dead comrades to do so, and found his way back from the dropsite before the firestorm began.

Bionics replaced his bones and his burned-up muscle and flesh, but he wasn't the same. That battle had left a mark on Narek that went beyond mere injury. It made him morose, prone to angry self-recrimination, even self-doubt, but he served because he was a soldier and that's what soldiers did – they followed orders.

Elias needed a huntsman, so Narek took up the post, but never divulged how he really felt about what happened on Isstvan. It sat poorly with him, but he understood its necessity and believed in their cause, perhaps less blindly than some of his brothers.

Catching prey was the only time when his mind felt occupied enough that none of his other concerns mattered. Everything else faded back to grey when Narek was on the hunt.

Using the servitors as decoys was smart. The cyborgs went down quickly, without much fight, but the distraction absorbed precious minutes. Narek had let Dagon do it, content to look on before scouring the area for further signs. He sent Haruk on ahead to close the trap he had so artfully set for his prey.

Narek was looking down on them now as he crouched on a

rooftop, obscured by steam venting from ceiling ducts and the shadows of the night. All lights were out in Ranos; the rest of the brothers had seen to that. Only this small act was left to carry out now.

A three-man hunting party. Were he younger, and without the bionic, Narek would have done it alone. As he was, he needed the others.

'*A last stand.*' Dagon was on the opposite rooftop, about twenty metres away. Ranos was heavily industrialised, providing an abundance of hiding places from which the Word Bearers could observe their prey.

Below them were two armed men, hunkered down in cover, nervously eyeing the dark. A third man sat apart from the others, unarmed, not a fighter.

'Another distraction,' Narek answered Dagon through the vox. 'One is missing.'

'*Haruk will gut him like the other one he found.*'

Such a bloodthirsty warrior was Dagon, perhaps better suited to the VIII than the XVII. But he killed clean and didn't linger over his prey like some in the XVII were prone to do. Still, Narek knew he wasn't wrong. Haruk would have silenced the scout. That left these three scalps to him and Dagon.

'Elias wants that one alive. He has something of value to us.'

'*Does Haruk know that?*'

'He will if he kills him, Elias will make certain of it.'

'*Then let's make this quick and not keep the Dark Apostle waiting.*'

Narek cut the vox-link. He unhitched the sniper rifle slung across his back and brought it up into position. This was a singular weapon. A Brontos-pattern rifle was heavy and difficult to wield, but its heft was backed up with sheer stopping power. It took specially crafted bolt-rounds, with an added impeller in the rifle stock to offset the reduced range with a boost of pneumatic propulsion.

A racking handle allowed for manual reload, but that was only useful in an emergency. Narek liked to keep his targets at distance and make use of the weapon's automatic chambering function.

Pressing his right eye to the scope, he adjusted the targeter until its crosshairs lined up squarely over the head of the man on the right. The rifle stock was cold against his cheek, and he felt the roughness of the grooves he'd made in it to celebrate each of his long-range kills. There were many.

Narek muttered an oath, then, waiting three seconds to control his breathing, he fired.

SEBATON PAUSED WHEN he heard the shot. His breath caught in his chest and he had to make a concerted effort to exhale. He was no stranger to gunfire, but the quietude in the city was so absolute, the avenues and buildings so deserted, that the sudden presence of violent noise alarmed him.

He'd taken a similar route to the one Varteh had been leading them down, only more circuitous. Deliberate detours had taken him further off the main streets, embedded him deeper into the warren. Arriving on Traoris from off-world with Varteh and the others, there had been no time to reconnoitre properly. Besides, the mission was supposed to have been relatively simple. Find the relic, leave and catch an atmospheric craft from the nearest space port, heading corewards. This side of the rift it wouldn't be easy, but it was straightforward. The other 'task' made it slightly more complex, but Sebaton was a pragmatist, so first things first. He had studied maps of his location, but it was no substitute for seeing, getting a *feel*.

Deep in the heart of Ranos the habs were more like hives, clustered together in dirty colonies. There were warehouses, silos, smoke stacks and manufactorums, all pressing for space, all suffocating on top of and next to one another. But here he was anonymous. Here, he was nothing more than a rat and he hoped that, like all vermin, his passage through Ranos would go largely unnoticed. It would take him longer to reach the shipyard but at least he would reduce the risk of meeting up with whatever had ended Duugan, for the scout was certainly dead.

So too, Varteh and Trio. He hadn't heard screams, even from Gollach, but the men were gone.

On reflection, Sebaton thought it might have been two shots, fired in such perfect unison that the first masked the second. Neither was silenced, which meant his pursuers had discarded stealth in favour of intimidation. They wanted him to know they were closing and that they had him in their trap.

It was working. As he ran, Sebaton tried to gauge the distance from which the shot or shots had been taken, but panic was affecting his mental acuity. His legs were burning, lactic acid setting fire to his joints, and his chest ached. Leaden fear was adding to the strain on his body, and even though he regarded himself as fit and strong, the constant changes of direction were becoming taxing. He wanted to stop, get a breather and his bearings, but survival instinct wouldn't let him. *Stop now, die now.*

There was no help here, Sebaton knew that. He was alone, although he sensed the presence of something lurking in the stacked domiciles and manufactorums he had passed. Like standing next to a recently dug grave, death lingered about this place and was given form by a palpable sense of outrage and violation that had left a stain on everything around it at the point of life's ending.

Eyes fixed ahead, he ignored the barren shells of buildings that were not quite empty, fearful that a side glance might reveal to him some revenant of that lingering death. But like a corpse bloated by putrefaction, an old memory rose to the surface of Sebaton's mind.

He had been a child, no more than eight years standard, in his first life, long before the war. A boy had died in his township, trawling in one of the drainage basins that bled out of Anatol Hive. The boy had waded in too deeply, got snagged on a piece of debris hidden by the murk of the water and been dragged to his drowning as the machine processors that kept the basin churning activated, creating an artificial current.

Though the town's men had dredged the water, no body was ever found.

It was several months later that Sebaton had gone to the basin to see if there was treasure left to salvage in the water, excited by the dark reputation of the place. Standing at the plascrete bank, all he found was sorrow and an abiding sense of rage. When he walked into the drainage basin, ankle-deep in the water, he saw something small and pale lurking beneath the surface. It filled him with such disquiet that he bolted and never returned, only later swearing that he felt something scrape at his skin and finding five tiny weals left in his flesh afterwards. The wounds never healed. Life to life, he carried them like the growing burden on his conscience, a reminder of his encounter.

The memory had come unbidden, and Sebaton wondered if its resurfacing was a symptom of what was being done to Ranos or had been stirred up by the presence of the artefact wrapped in cloth under his arm.

Staying on the street and in the open suddenly felt unwise. The back of his neck itched, and though he didn't really want to enter any of the buildings that seemed to slowly close about him, Sebaton had no desire to be next in the hunters' crosshairs either.

He saw a warehouse, its gate ajar, and headed for it.

As he ducked inside the building, the darkness cloaking Sebaton intensified. He stayed still, allowing time for his vision to adjust. After a few minutes, an expansive storage yard stretched out in front of him. Above, crisscrossing gantries and beams put him in mind of a spider's web as the moonlight streaming through an upper window hit them. The irony of that was not lost on Sebaton. For he was trapped, his arachnid predator looming close and preparing to pounce.

Staying low, Sebaton ran across the store yard floor into a cluster of packing crates, drums and pipes. He'd seen no door or gate other than the one he had entered by, so he assumed that the exit was somewhere within this maze. He nervously twisted the ring on his finger, pausing at every junction, trying to tell the difference between sounds that were real and imagined.

Halfway down a corridor, flanked on both sides by a rack of heavy pipes that were secured by metal cabling, Sebaton realised he wasn't alone. An infinitesimal movement, the minuscule shifting of metal as pressure was applied to it had given the hunter away. Most ordinary men would have missed it or dismissed it as cargo settling in its container, but Sebaton was not an ordinary man.

Sebaton stopped and reversed direction, just as something large and heavy thundered down behind him. An instant later massive metallic footfalls clanged in his wake as Sebaton sprinted down the corridor. Spinning around as he reached the end of the corridor, just past the stacked pipes, he uttered a single word.

'*Stop!*'

His voice resonated, like it was two voices, one overlaid upon the other, rooting his pursuer to the spot. For the first time, Sebaton got a good look at who was hunting him. He didn't like what he saw, not remotely.

Clad in crimson and black, the legionary's war-plate was engraved with scripture. One of Lorgar's zealots, then. Sebaton had no wish to be taken by this man. He knew enough about how the Word Bearers tortured and killed their prisoners – that even death was not the end of it, but rather the beginning of an eternal torment that threw their immortal soul into jeopardy – to be certain he had to escape.

It was a struggle to hold him. The legionary's will was immense, straining constantly against Sebaton's psychic command as a rabid hound does against the leash. Sebaton's forehead was already layered in sweat. His temples throbbed painfully with the effort of maintaining the mental strength needed to harness this monster. But he only needed a few seconds. He briefly considered using his flechette pistol, but his other weapon was easier to use and fit for the task. He lashed out with his ring and a bright beam of energy lanced from the digi-laser concealed within, severing the cable securing the pipes and sending them crashing down on his pursuer.

Sebaton didn't wait to see what happened next. He heard the clash of metal against metal, the grunt of the Word Bearer. He knew it wouldn't kill the legionary but it might give him a few seconds to get away. He ran in the opposite direction, barrelling round another junction and straight through a door just beyond it. Confronted by a stairwell, Sebaton only paused long enough to see how far it went up, then took the steps three at a time. Still dizzy from using his psychic ability, he stumbled and hit the wall hard. The impact jolted his arm and he lost his grip on the cloth bundle, snatching at the air and turning just enough to see it bounce down the stairs and into the darkness.

He cursed loudly but couldn't go back. There was no time. Glanding a measure of additional adrenaline into his system, he pushed forwards, trying to put as much distance between himself and the Word Bearer as he could.

Head pounding, the extra adrenaline making his heart thump like a cannonade, Sebaton emerged onto an upper floor. It was much more open than the one below, and he suspected it was there for overspill when the lower part of the warehouse got full. There were few places to hide but he noticed a room at the back of the spartan chamber that was partitioned off. An overseer's office, he assumed. A row of windows to Sebaton's left looked like they might open easily. If he could reach one, he could scale the roof, drop down in a side alley and–

Who am I kidding, thought Sebaton, *this is the end of the game.*

From downstairs he heard a crash as the legionary pulled himself from the wreckage of the pipes. Thundering up the stairwell, a battered-looking Word Bearer burst through the door spitting fury and taking most of the wall with him.

'No more running,' he said, advancing with the slow finality of a predator who knew he had caught his prey.

Backing up, Sebaton considered his options. Go for the window and he'd be quickly brought down. He was too weak to stop the legionary psychically for a second time and the digi-weapon in his ring was still charging. Even at full strength, Sebaton doubted it would trouble power armour. The flechette pistol was even worse at cutting ceramite and adamantium. He was starting to wish he had packed something a little more serious when the Word Bearer spoke again.

'It will be slow,' he said.

Light flashed off the blade of a flensing knife clutched in the legionary's left hand, an unspoken promise of pain to come.

Nowhere left to turn…

Something whipped by Sebaton's ear, like an arrow loosed from a bow, only much, much faster.

The legionary stumbled as if struck. It took Sebaton half a second to realise that he actually had been. A burst of dark liquid and bone had exploded from the legionary's neck. Feebly, the Word Bearer reached up with his hand to try and staunch the wound. A second impact hit him in the chest, fast and hard like the first. It tore open his armoured ribcage and put him on his knees, where he wavered for a few seconds before collapsing onto his side.

Someone else was in the room with Sebaton and they had just killed a Space Marine with the same ease it takes to swat a fly.

Equally disturbing was that he had failed to detect their presence. He turned around and saw a hulking figure blocking him.

Sebaton backed up. Too late, he realised a second figure had crept up behind him. The blow came swift and hard, with blackness following close behind it.

CHAPTER SIX

From ice to fire

'Let me make something clear – death isn't personal. It isn't. It doesn't happen to you, it happens to everyone else left behind after you're gone. That's the truth about death. Death's easy. It's life that's hard.'

– Lonn Varteh, ex-Lucifer Black

KINETIC THUNDER VIBRATED the air. A storm raged around us. Fire and smoke billowed overhead. A body spiralled through this fog, pinwheeling wildly until arcing downwards to the battlefield where it was lost amongst a host of others. Reeling, struggling to comprehend the sheer depth of this betrayal, I looked upon a sea of ruin...

My sons, carved open upon the dark sands of Isstvan V.

Lifeblood ran in rivers, turning the earth underfoot into a viscous sludge.

It was carnage: armour plate ripped apart, peeled back like a metal rind, exposing fragile flesh beneath; retinal lenses shot out, the head beneath broken and oozing; stray limbs strewn like a butcher's leavings; a ribcage, split open and wet with crimson. Death screams strangled the breeze, almost as loud as the threats of vengeance.

We were under heavy bombardment. Ordnance struck the ground around the Legion, shaking my very bones. Somewhere in the distance, on a black hill, Perturabo was shelling us. His tanks glowered down ferally, snouts aimed squarely at our ranks.

Impact bursts dug instant craters in the black earth, driving thick dust clouds into the air and spitting up plumes of rock. Flung bodies joined the flying dirt, half entangled in razor-wire, their limbs limp and broken. Emerald-green war-plate turned dark and red, the blood of my sons spilled to satisfy a traitor's ambition and measure a warsmith's guns.

I ran, cleaving fury and a righteous sense of retribution to my pounding chest. Not even blood would slake my desire for revenge. Nothing could balance the scales of this perfidious act. I wanted the Iron Lord's head, and then I'd take Horus's next.

Time slowed, the ground beneath my boots thickened into a quagmire and I was suddenly waist-deep in sucking earth and bodies.

The storm abated, and slowly the sound of thunder lessened until it was a drumming on the inside of my skull. Growing fainter, the sound rose in pitch until it was reduced to the slow *plink* of liquid hitting metal. I awoke. The black desert where my Legion's soul fought a losing battle for its body was no more. Isstvan V was gone.

I heard my breath rattling through my chest, trembling in the aftermath of a nightmare. I grimaced, hurting. My senses were still over-attuned, unable to properly regulate the information being fed into my brain. Sweat and melting ice were rolling off my body. Beads of liquid hit the ground beneath me, not as loud as ordnance any more but still over-pronounced. Pitted steel and mesh felt rough to my touch. A faint heat warmed my fingertips, but burned at first. It was like being born anew, my mind and my body not quite in concert with one another.

A tightness clenched my muscles until I rose up from my knees and flexed, cracking a veneer of void-frost encasing my body. Like a serpent with an old skin, I shed it. Underneath the onyx-black of my body, my flesh was burning as if some profound biological trauma had spurred my physiology into sudden and urgent action.

I tried to recall what had happened to me, but my memory was fragmented. Only pieces of it were connected, the rest adrift in my shattered psyche. I remembered running, the adrenaline rush from my escape attempt. I had climbed from the pit where I'd been cast down. Blood was on my hands, both legionary and mortal. An impression of the tunnels came back. I remembered the sense of rising, the familiarity in form and structure of the bonded cage around me. I knew the hand that had fashioned this elegant prison. In its bowels I had seen a dead man, rendered in my mind's eye. First my sibling, now also my tormentor; he was the expression of my guilt incarnate. And like a lake mist banished by the heat of a rising sun, my occluded memory cleared. Through the parting haze, I remembered something else too, an alien figure, one revealed to me in aetheric snatches, reminiscent of a bad pict-feed.

A last, final revelation dawned. It visited my mind like a hammer, smashing the hope I'd harboured into dust. I was aboard a ship, a great space-faring vessel. Cold reality asserted itself with that knowledge. I was not on Isstvan. I was no longer on earth of any kind. I was in Curze's element now and there would be no escaping from it.

A chamber slowly came into focus around me, the frost that encrusted my eyelids cracking as I opened them to see it. This was not the same cell as before. It was much larger, not an oubliette but an octagonal shaft hundreds of metres up and down. No chains; my wrists and ankles were free of any fetters. A circular platform surrounded me instead, not much wider than the span of my feet. Here was the pitted metal I had felt upon waking and the mesh through which I now saw the dull orange glow from where the heat was emanating. Surrounding the platform were my new chains – a gulf, many metres across and a fathomless drop into a scorched black abyss. And at the edges of this prison without walls, this cage without bars, was a thin gantry of steel.

A dull throb invaded my senses, which were slowly returning to normal. Far below, a turbine was whipping currents of hot air up the shaft, foul with the stench of engine wash. In one corner, looking on as I assessed the manner of the trap ensnaring me, was the apparition of my dead brother.

'You look ill, Vulkan,' said Ferrus, the shadows in the chamber pooling in his cadaverous features. 'You're burning up.'

I didn't answer. As I reasserted control over my senses, I did the same for my body. My skin was cooling, the intense heat I had previously felt now abating. I smelled cinder and ash like before. An itch on my back irritated, as if a brand had been seared in my flesh. I couldn't see it but managed to touch the edges of the mark with my fingers, navigating past countless others that I knew as intimately as my own face. This one, however, was unfamiliar and the very fact of its existence terrified me. For what else had I forgotten?

Like a shadow creeping across a lone traveller on a desolate road, I felt another presence in the chamber. As I realised who it was, the chill of the void came back anew.

Like Ferrus, he sat in darkness. But he didn't just inhabit the dark, he was a part of it, he moulded it and made it his mantle.

'Curze.' I didn't have the strength to force any real vitriol into my voice.

'I am here, brother.'

His tone was almost soothing. Did he regret this insanity?

'I have been watching you, Vulkan. You are a fascinating subject.'

No. This was another facet to his game. As my eyes adjusted, I picked out my brother's form, hunched and squatting like a bat at the edge of the gantry. Curze rested his chin upon his fist, his eyes unblinking as they regarded me.

It was the first time I had seen him since waking to this nightmare. 'You joined with Horus.'

'What gave me away? Was it the murdering of your Legion?'

'My Legion…' My voice wavered. I had no knowledge of what had become of my sons.

'Destroyed, Vulkan. They're all dead. You have no Legion.'

I wanted to kill him. I imagined making the impossible leap and wrapping my hands around Curze's throat, squeezing until all life had left his eyes. As my fists clenched of their own volition, as my jaw locked tight, I saw the smile on my brother's face and knew then the lie in his words.

'No. No, they're not. They live.'

Curze gave an amused snort.

'Yes. They are still alive. At least, I think they are. Much diminished, though. And without you to guide them… Well, I fear for them, Vulkan. These are trying times. Our fealty has been besmirched. Our father lied to us. He lied to you. Cleave to His side or cleave open His side, those are the only roads for us now. Which one do you think the Salamanders will choose, brother? After all, you are such a pragmatic race. Honour or survival.' Curze sucked his teeth. He was mocking me. 'Difficult.'

'What have you done?'

'You sound anguished, brother.'

My teeth clenched, as the image of cradling Nemetor in my arms returned.

'What have you done?'

The Night Haunter leaned forwards, and the light from the lume-strips above struck the lineaments of his face, describing them in white.

'We killed you,' he grinned, eyes mad with glee as he remembered the slaughter. 'Cut you down like swine. I swear, the surprise on your face was priceless.'

'We were brothers. We *are* brothers, still. Horus has gone mad.' I shook my head, the anger bleeding away like the ice melting off my body. 'Why?'

'Because we were sold a false dream, by a false god. We were lied to and–' Curze's faked solemnity collapsed into sarcastic laughter. 'I'm sorry, brother. I tried to maintain the facade as long as I could. I don't care about any of that, I really don't. You know, there is a cancer in some men. I've seen it. Rapists, murderers, thieves – Nostramo was overrun with them. Even when you try to stamp it out, like a disease it returns. If you'd seen what I've seen…'

For a moment, my brother's gaze went to a distant place as if he were remembering, before his attention came back to me.

'Some men are just evil, Vulkan. There is no *why*, it just *is*. Gluttony, sloth, lust, I am intimately acquainted with the sins of man. Which one do you think we were guilty of? Pride? Wrath? Was it greed that drove our father's urge to reconquer the galaxy in his name and call it liberation? Terra just wasn't enough.'

'I see your sin, Curze. It's envy.'

'No, it isn't. It's the burden of knowing the future and being rendered powerless to do anything about it. I am cursed, brother. And so I must sin.'

'And this is your justification for throwing the galaxy into turmoil? You follow a madman.'

Curze snarled, 'I follow no one! And it was not so long ago, Horus was your brother. Are you so quick to turn your back on him? Did father make you more loyal than he or I? Are you his noble scion, Vulkan?'

I had seen Horus before he rebelled. After the Crusade had begun and we were thrown across the galaxy, twice I had met with him. I loved Horus, I looked up to him. I had planned to show my loyalty in the form of a gift, a weapon to befit his status as Warmaster. After I learned of his heroism at Ullanor, I forged a hammer. It was my finest work, craft I have not surpassed since. But I never gave it to him. Our second meeting did not go well. I sensed something of what Curze had mentioned, the 'evil' in some men that cannot be explained, that cannot be reasoned with or excised. Even though I could not answer then why I had withheld this boon, I did so because of the disquiet he stirred in me. I had not thought on it until that moment, and the revelation of it chilled me.

'You betrayed us,' I said to Curze. 'Ferrus is dead.' Although I could not help glance at his decaying corpse, grinning at me from the shadows.

Curze gave a wry smile. 'Is he?' Tapping the side of his head, he added, 'Not in your broken mind, I think. Who is it you think you're talking to in the darkness?'

So, he *was* watching me. And listening. All the time. I wondered what he hoped to learn.

'You are a traitor,' I told him. 'Roboute will not stand by and allow this.'

'Always Guilliman, isn't it? What is so lordly about that war-accountant? At least Russ or Jonson have passion. Roboute fights battles with an abacus.'

'He is rival enough to defeat Horus. His Legion will–'

'Roboute is gone! That officious little snipe is done. Don't cling to him for rescue. Dorn won't help you either. He's too busy being the Emperor's groundskeeper, hiding behind the palace walls. The Wolf is too busy cutting off heads as our father's executioner, while the Lion holds on to his secrets, and has no special fondness for you. Who else will come? Not Ferrus, certainly. Nor Corax either. Even as we speak, I suspect he flees for Deliverance. Sanguinius?' Curze laughed cruelly. 'The angel is more cursed than I. The Khan? He does not wish to be found. So who is left? No one, Vulkan. None of them will come. You are simply not that important. You are alone.'

'I'm not the one who fears isolation, Konrad.'

Curze didn't bite. He had waited for this meeting between us, planned every word and barb. He sighed.

'It doesn't matter why, Vulkan. All that matters is the here and now, what happens next.'

'And what does happen next?' I felt no fear or trepidation, only pity for him.

'You lasted longer than I expected, I will grant you that,' Curze said. 'I greatly underestimated *you*.'

I tried to hide my ignorance behind a mask of defiance. Curze liked to talk. He was no proselytiser like Lorgar, nor was he prone to giving speeches like Horus, but he knew how to use words and liked how the right ones induced fear and uncertainty. Of all my brothers, Curze knew the mind and how to turn it upon its owner. To him, psychology was a ready blade as damaging as any knife or gun.

I said, 'I am still your prisoner.'

'Yes, and in that you also surpassed all my expectations.'

Again, I had no idea of his meaning but kept the fact of that hidden. I felt his blade, probing for weakness, searching for a chink in my mental armour. He could break my body, kill me if he wished to. But for some reason, he had kept me alive. I just didn't know why.

Curze smiled, the shape of his upturned mouth reminiscent of a hooked dagger.

'Eleven dead, six of those were mortals.' A slight shake of the head betrayed his sense of admiration at the gruesome deed. 'The way you swatted that wench...' Curze whistled then bared his teeth in the light. Their points shone like arrowheads. Curze's unguarded pleasure revolted me. 'She broke like a reed, Vulkan. A *reed*.' He gave a rueful laugh. 'And here was I thinking Corax's claims of your strength merely boasts. Because... you *are* strong, aren't you, brother? You must be to do what you did.'

'Murder a woman? What strength does that require?' I scowled. 'Slaying the weak and helpless is something only you laud, you coward.'

'Bloody-minded determination? The single-minded purpose needed to escape from an impossible prison? I'd call that strength.'

'It's not your prison, though. Is it?' I said.

Curze nodded. 'Very astute of you. You craftsmen do know how to recognise each other's work, don't you? It amazes me how you do it, how you can tell one rivet from another.'

He was taunting me again, trying to belittle me. It was petty and Curze knew it, but he did it anyway because it amused him and somehow reduced me in his eyes.

'No, this prison is not mine,' he admitted at last. 'I've neither the patience nor the inclination. I had another build it for me.' He looked around the chamber, and I followed his gaze, noticing the ornate flourishes, the way that function met artistry. Engraved upon the eight walls was a gruesome display, celebrating torture and pain. Agonies described in metal greeted my eyes and I looked away.

'Beautiful,' said Curze. 'I can't say I appreciate art, but I know what I like. And this... this, I *like*. Our brother was never really given enough credit for his aesthetic eye.'

It was a pantomime, all of this, a dark performance more in keeping with Fulgrim than the self-proclaimed Night Haunter. I suspected Curze was doing it deliberately, savouring every moment.

Then Curze turned his cold eyes back upon me. 'It was always you that was hailed as the craftsman, Vulkan. But Perturabo is just as skilled. Maybe even more so.'

'What do you want with me, Konrad?'

'You intrigue me. When I said you'd shown strength, I wasn't referring to you killing that serf...'

He let it hang like that, waiting for a response. I had none to give, so kept my silence.

Curze's eyes narrowed, like little slivers of jet. 'Are you really *that* ignorant? Did our father create you to be blind as well as blunt?'

'I have sight enough to see what you are.'

My brother laughed, unimpressed at my attempted goading. 'Indeed. But then, I already know what I am. I am at peace with it. I've accepted it. You, on the other hand...' He gave a slight shake of the head, pursing his pale lips. 'I don't think you've ever been wholly comfortable in your armour.'

He was right, but I wasn't about to give my gaoler the satisfaction of knowing that.

'I am my father's son.'

'Which father?'

I gritted my teeth, tired of Curze's obvious mind games. 'Both of them.'

'Tell me, brother,' he said, changing tack, 'how well do you remember One-Five-Four Six? I believe you called it Kharaatan.'

I didn't know what Curze's purpose was in asking me this, but my eyes locked to his and didn't waver.

'I remember it very well, as I know you must do also.'

'Was it when we fought together during the Crusade? Yes, I believe it was.'

'Thankfully.'

The dagger smile returned to Curze's face. 'You didn't enjoy that war, did you?'

'What is there to enjoy about war?'

'Death? You are a bringer of death, a warrior, a merciless killer that–'

'No, Curze. You are mistaken. You're the merciless one, you're the sadist. I never realised it before Kharaatan. Fear and terror are not a warrior's weapons, they are a coward's. And I pity you, Curze. I pity you because you have spent so long languishing in the gutter amongst the filth that you've forgotten what it's like to be in the light. I doubt you can even see it through all that self-loathing.'

'You're still blind, Vulkan. It's you who has forgotten, and don't realise you're down here in the gutter with the rest of us, murdering and killing. It's in your blood. The pedestal you have built for yourself is not so lofty. I know what lies beneath that noble veneer. I've seen the monster inside, the one you tried so hard to hide from that remembrancer. What was her name again?'

My jaw tensed.

Curze betrayed no emotion. 'Seriph.' He smiled indulgently. 'Yes, that was it.'

'So what now?' I asked, tiring of his game. 'More torture? More pain?'

'Yes,' Curze answered frankly, 'much more. You have yet to feel the extent of it, of what I have planned. You are, in many ways, the perfect victim.'

'So kill me, then, and be done with it, or is part of my torture listening to you?'

'I do not think I will kill you this time,' said Curze. 'We've tried ice.' He stepped back, coalescing with the darkness. 'Now let's try fire.'

From below, I heard a low rumbling. It trembled the metal platform I was standing on. In seconds it grew into a deafening roar, and brought with it a terrible heat.

I realised then the nature of the prison I was in.

It was a furnace.

Curze was gone, and I was left alone with only the shattered memory of my grim brother for company.

I could hear the fire rising, feel it prickling my skin. Soon those needles would become knives, scraping back my flesh. I was born from fire on a brutal, volcanic world. Magma was my blood, onyx was my skin. But I was not impervious to flame. Not like this. Smoke billowed upwards in a vast and dirty cloud, engulfing me.

Through it, as the conflagration followed and turned the air into a vibrating haze, as my screams rang out with the scorching of my body, I saw Ferrus.

He was burning too. The skin of his ghoulish face melted to reveal iron beneath. The silver of his arms, so miraculous, so magnificent and enigmatic, ran like mercury and merged with the soup of his flesh and blood. Bone blackened and cracked, until only a rictus skull mask remained. And as the fire took me, I saw the skull's mouth move in a last silent condemnation.

Weak, said the fire-wreathed skull of Ferrus Manus.

And then it was laughing as we burned, laughing to our ending and damnation.

CHAPTER SEVEN
We are not alone...

'In this age of darkness, only one thing is certain. Each of us, without exception, must choose a side.'
— Malcador the Sigillite

HARUK HAD BEEN dead several minutes. Almost twenty by Narek's reckoning. He was lying on his side, one arm flung out, still clutching his ritual knife, the other pinned beneath the dead weight of his body. His partially helmeted head lay askew. It had almost been forcibly removed.

He had received two fatal wounds. The first, a bolt-round through the neck, had ripped open Haruk's jugular and exposed his carotid artery. It had also removed a portion of his lower jaw and vox-grille with it, but had not killed him immediately. The second, to the torso, had caved in most of his chest and destroyed eighty per cent of his internal organs when the mass-reactive shell had exploded on impact. From this, Haruk had died instantly.

Narek had found the wreckage of the body on the upper floor of a warehouse, slowly growing cold in a pool of blood. Kneeling down by his dead brother, he felt no grief for Haruk. The Word Bearer was a true bastard amongst bastards, who liked to make sport of his prey. His predilection had been his undoing this time. Kill quietly, kill quickly – this was Narek's way. A toy was a thing to be played with, and toys were best left to children. An enemy was not a toy, he was a threat to your life until his was ended. But Haruk was a sadist. So many of Narek's kin were turning this way. A change had come upon them, and it was not just manifest in the vestigial horns that were more than mere affectation for a war-helm, it was soul-deep and irreversible. This did not sit well with Narek, for he had once believed that the Emperor was a god and served this deity with a true zealot's fervour. When the Legion erected the cathedrals on Monarchia, he had wept. It was beautiful, glorious. All of that was gone now and an older Pantheon had resurfaced to usurp the supposed pretender.

So, the sight of his slain brother did not hurt him. But, as Haruk was of the Word, Narek would perform the rites over the corpse as required.

Swathed in darkness, he muttered the necessary incantations that would put Haruk's soul in service to the Pantheon. Now he would become the sport, a plaything of the Neverborn. Narek almost felt them in his veins, pulsing beneath his skin, and in the staccato beating of his twin hearts. They clung to this place, and their grip was ever tightening as Lorgar wrote his song of murder.

Elias had spoken of it one night, when the sky seemed blacker than pitch and the two of them had shared a drink between comrades, if not friends. This was the primarch's symphony, and it had unleashed a Ruinstorm of such terrible intensity that the very galaxy was cleft in twain by it.

Lifting his hand from Haruk's corpse, Narek concluded the rites, but felt the hunger of what dwelled in unreality pressing against the gossamer-thin veil of the mortal realm. A barrier can only stretch so much, and this one was near to splitting. Soon two worlds would meet; soon the galaxy would indeed burn.

Lorgar had foretold it in his writings. He had foreseen it in visions, and who was Narek to oppose that?

'I am but a soldier, who clings to his duty and the bonds he once swore to his brothers,' he whispered, and felt the weight of melancholy wrap around him like a cloak.

Dagon, returning from below, interrupted him.

'He chased the mortal up here. But the place is empty. No sign of his killers.'

Dagon was waiting by the ruin of the stairwell, near to where Haruk had met his end.

Narek cast his gaze about the room, a panorama that began and ended with the body beside him.

'Oh, there are many, brother. I can see two distinct tread patterns in the dust. They were already in here when Haruk followed the human.'

'Doing what?'

'Watching. They were using this place as a vantage point to observe our movements.'

'How could they know we were here?' A hint of agitation in Dagon's voice betrayed his sense of unease at hearing this news.

'How else? They've been tracking and following us.'

'A counter-attack? I understood there were no enemy assets in this region.'

'There aren't. None that we know of, anyway.' Narek regarded the ruin of Haruk's body, the silenced rounds that had ended him so precisely. 'I don't think it's a counter-attack. They don't have the numbers. This was quiet, a hunter's kill. They want to stay covert, whoever they are. And they took the human with them also.'

'Why?'

'That's an extremely good question.'

'So what now? This changes things.'

Narek looked off into the middle distance. 'Perhaps…' He needed to consult Elias.

Narek activated the warp-flask. A foul sulphur stench fogged the air through his rebreather as communion was achieved quickly. Another sign of the veil thinning – the enhanced warp-flasks were proving more reliable than vox-comms.

'*Do you have him?*' asked Elias.

A simulacrum of the Dark Apostle was rendered in violet grainy light emanating from the neck of the flask like a vapour. On the other end of communion, Narek knew his image would also be rendered to Elias in this way.

'No. Someone else took him.'

'*Someone else?*'

Elias was still at the ritual site. In the background, Narek could hear the human sacrifices mewling as they awaited their fate. Elias would bleed the entire city if he had to. The cults too.

'Yes.'

'*What about Haruk?*'

'He's dead. I am crouched by his recently ventilated corpse.'

'*Should I be concerned, Narek?*'

'Too soon to tell.'

'*What is that supposed to mean?*'

'It means someone tracked us to Traoris and has shadowed our movements all the way to Ranos,' Narek said levelly.

'*Who tracked us?*'

'I have a theory. Too early to be sure yet.'

'*I'm sending reinforcements.*'

'Not necessary.'

'*They're coming anyway.*'

'I want to find out exactly what we're dealing with first. Dagon and I move faster alone.'

'*I doubt Haruk would agree with that.*'

'Haruk is dead. He won't be agreeing with anything any more.'

'*Humour doesn't suit you, Narek. Stay where you are. Wait for the others.*'

Elias ended the communion, leaving the huntsmen alone again.

'So, we wait?' asked Dagon.

'No,' Narek replied, and got to his feet. 'Search everywhere. Leave nothing untouched. I want to know everything, every scrap of information this warehouse can yield. We are not alone in Ranos, Dagon. Our former brothers-in-arms are here with us.'

Dagon scoffed. 'To what end?'

'What else? What would you or I do if we were them? They want vengeance. They mean to kill us.'

SEBATON'S HEAD POUNDED like he'd drunk too much *svod* and had woken to a particularly brutal hangover. He was unbound, slumped on a chair, head down. Wincing slightly, but not moving to touch it, he could feel the contusion on the side of his head where something had hit him hard. No, not some*thing*, some*one*.

The encounter in the warehouse came back to him in all its life-threatening glory.

He should be dead right now, or at the mercy of a ritual knife. Instead he was here, wherever *here* was. He listened, feigning unconsciousness and trying to get a sense of exactly what level of trouble he was in. Harsh machine noise surrounded him. At first he thought he might have been taken to a manufactorum, but if he was still in Ranos that was unlikely, as, from what he'd seen, the city was effectively dead. A low background hum underneath the machine noise put him in mind of a generator, adding weight to a theory about the nature of his captors, if not their identity.

Sebaton put together what he knew. Varteh and the others were almost certainly dead. This meant he was alone. A Legion faction, possibly more than one, was on Traoris. They had found the dig site and had sent scouts to hunt him down and take what he had exhumed from the catacombs. This meant they had some knowledge of what it was, or at the very least realised that it was important enough to divert significant resources to obtain it. At least two others, enemies of the Word Bearer sent to kill or capture him, had intervened and he was now in their custody. What happened next depended on what else Sebaton could discover about his captors' motives. With that in mind, he stayed still and listened hard.

Half-heard mutterings; the crackle and static of a vox-feed suggested an exchange between at least two people. As Sebaton tried to home in on the conversation and discern some meaning, two others started talking. Obviously standing much closer, their words were easy to understand.

'He doesn't look like much,' said the first speaker, his tone rough with a slight growl adding to its bite. The voice was male, and very deep.

'That traitor seemed to think he was worth the effort of killing,' answered another. His voice had a resonance that was almost mechanical, as if re-vocalised and amplified through vox-augmentation.

'And on that evidence we should take him?' asked the first. 'We have more urgent concerns.'

'Agreed,' said the second, before a third voice chimed in.

'I would know why the Word Bearers want this man.' This one was older, rasping. 'He is more than he seems, and I don't think he's from Traoris, either.'

There was a pause, and Sebaton heard the dulcet whirr of servos connected to a warrior's gorget as he shook his head.

Then the first said, 'We're wasting time. What does it matter if he's not a native?'

The third continued. 'Not sure. But the Word Bearers want him, which means we should deny them that. As to their purpose, I also mean to find that out, and *he* is the answer.'

The conversation paused again, but for longer this time. Sebaton felt his raw nerves bite, and his heart trembled.

'You're fooling no one,' the older one rasped in his ear. It was as if the speaker were standing right next to him, until Sebaton realised the words were spoken directly into his mind.

'You have uncovered no secrets. Your intent is as obvious to me as that costume you are wearing. Now... awake!'

Sebaton opened his eyes, realising that any further attempts at subterfuge would likely only get him hurt or worse. His vision was blurred, probably from the concussion. He was staring at his feet and a grubby floor underfoot. When he tried to move, to lift his head and rub his eyes, he felt the press of cold metal against his skull.

'I know you know what this is,' said the first voice, Sebaton catching the barest glimpse of dirty, emerald-green leg greaves. 'And what it can do. No tricks.'

Sebaton nodded. The bolter was pressed so tightly to the side of his head that the muzzle would leave an angry red ring in his skin.

He was inside, still in Ranos as he'd suspected. He had been taken from the warehouse, though. The air was musty and reeked of ink. It was a large room; it had to be to accommodate the heavy machinery hinted at in the shadows at its periphery. He noticed a sheaf of parchment on the floor, trapped beneath one leg of the chair where he was sitting, but couldn't read what was on it. Stacks of this parchment were piled up in three corners of the room. A printing press, then.

'May I raise my head?' he asked, spreading his arms in a gesture of compliance. He still had his digital weapon, that was something. But the contents of the cloth bundle he had risked and lost four men's lives to obtain were no longer in his possession. His captors might have it, although he suspected not. If they were looking for it then why bother to interrogate him? Why bother to pull him from the warehouse and bring him here? That gave Sebaton an advantage – he knew they wanted him alive. How long that situation lasted would likely depend on what he said and did next, and what they could find out.

The pressure against the side of Sebaton's head eased as the gun was withdrawn. He looked up, gingerly touching the abrasion left behind. Three warriors surrounded him. Two in front, another just visible in his peripheral vision around the side. One more waited farther back, observing.

They were huge, hulking men, clad in full armour that growled as they moved, with the gears and servos engineered into it. It was power armour. Sebaton had escaped one legionary, only to be caught by at least four others.

Now his head was up, he got a good look at his closest aggressor.

The legionary wore emerald-green armour, tarnished by wear and battle-damage. He also noticed rasping marks where the bearer had tried to shave off pieces of rust that had colonised the edges. It was ornate, a battered antique now, with artistic flourishes wrought into the metal that seemed at odds with a warrior's wargear. He still had his helmet on; a cage of ivory fangs framed the jaw and snout. Behind the red retinal lenses the warrior's eyes burned. A pelt, or perhaps a hide, hung raggedly from his shoulders. Even this had seen more than its fair share of battle.

He was one of the XVIII. A Salamander. No wonder he looked rough.

'How many of you are there?' Sebaton asked him, without thinking.

The Salamander seized him by the chin. The edges of his gauntlets were warm and pinched Sebaton's flesh.

'No questions will come from your mouth, only answers.' Behind the oval eye-pieces of his helmet, his eyes burned brighter as if reacting to his sudden anger. 'Understand?'

Sebaton nodded and was released.

'Who are you?' the Salamander asked, stepping back.

'Caeren Sebaton.'

'And what is your purpose here?'

'Archaeology. I came to excavate relics.'

'Alone?'

'No, I had a team.'

Another of the three, armoured in black, muttered, 'The pair of servitors Pergellen found.'

Like the Salamander, he also looked ragged. His armour was broken, held together by field repairs and, Sebaton suspected, sheer will. He was hard to focus on, blending well with the shadows, and although a lumen strip buzzed and crackled overhead, the warrior's power armour reflected no light.

XIX Legion. Raven Guard.

This one also gave off an aura. Like knew like. Sebaton realised this was the psyker that had addressed him earlier.

The Salamander nodded to his brother-in-arms.

'There were four men also,' offered Sebaton, hoping his unprompted show of cooperation would improve his chances of survival. He had to get away from here, double back somehow and retrieve what he had taken from the catacombs. 'Dead too.'

'You know the manner of what is hunting you?' asked the Salamander.

'I do.'

'Then you'll also know how much danger you are in.'

'Painfully so, yes.'

'What do you know about why the Word Bearers are here?'

'Nothing.'

The Salamander turned. The Raven Guard slowly shook his head, prompting his flame-eyed comrade to bear down on Sebaton again.

'Don't lie to me.'

'It's the truth. I have no idea what they want, or you for that matter.'

That was bold. A little foolish, too.

'Well,' said the Salamander, unhitching the clasps around his helmet, 'that's easy to answer,' he added, removing it and revealing a face as black as jet with two burning orbs for eyes. Even the pict-captures as part of his data inload had not prepared Sebaton for this, and he balked.

'I want to know *everything* you know,' the Salamander said. 'And I want to know it... right now.'

Something had happened to these warriors, something that had changed them deeply.

'Who are you? What are you even doing here?'

'I warned you once not to ask questions.' Somewhat forebodingly, the Salamander stepped back and gestured to his comrade.

'Hriak...'

Without seemingly moving, the psyker was upon him. Close up, Sebaton could see that he wore a tattered grey cloak over his power armour and had a fetish of avian bones attached to the conical snout of his helmet. Definitely one of the Raven Guard. Several of the Legions wore black but a closer look had confirmed it. Legionary psyker, known as a Librarian. They were supposed to have been forbidden in the Legions, but evidently circumstances had forced that particular edict into repeal. In the Raven Guard's outstretched hand, Sebaton could see a thunder-head of dark lightning. It was raging, the force of a storm held in his palm.

Incredible. The sheer will required for that level of mastery...

When Sebaton realised that it was about to be unleashed on him, he flinched, but a steel-fingered hand held him fast. It was a bionic

– he could hear the machine parts grinding as they flexed and bit hard into his shoulder.

'Take it easy, I'm not a threat,' said Sebaton.

'We know,' uttered the warrior behind him, the one who spoke with the strange machine-like cant.

'If you were,' said the Salamander, 'you'd already be dead. And should you prove to be after Hriak has *scryed* you, I'll have Domadus pull out your spine.'

Sebaton didn't doubt it. Domadus was X Legion, Iron Hands. They weren't known for their compassion. His presence raised further questions. All three legionaries came from forces that had been nearly destroyed on Isstvan V. Yet here they were, together, allied to some common cause.

Sebaton suspected that it might be the desire for revenge.

'We got off to a poor start, I think,' he said. 'There's no need for any of this.'

'Your demands fall on deaf ears,' Hriak rasped. It sounded like some old injury was marring his speech, but Sebaton couldn't see what because the warrior was wearing his helmet. His voice put Sebaton in mind of a cold wind rustling through dry leaves, of a dead and desolate winter, and bones lying under the snow.

A moment later and the lightning touched against Sebaton's forehead.

Fire, cold and terrible, burned him. It hollowed Sebaton out, tendrils of flame worming into him, slowly unpicking the mental barriers he had erected to protect himself from incursion. Deeper it went, spreading out, searching. His mind was a labyrinth, but this was a Legion psyker and he moved swiftly through the contours of it on feathered wings.

He thought of the drowned boy, his pale face lurking under the water.

Hriak's voice penetrated the memory, a distant echo on the

horizon that filled the sky with the promise of rain.

'He's hiding something…'

Sebaton was standing at the edge of the drainage basin, a hook and net in his hand, ready to scavenge. He rooted himself to that spot, like an anchor in time, and replayed it over and over. Stepping into the water, feeling the brush of fingernails against his naked skin. The burn as they gripped. The five red weals left behind, a hand grasping, entreating another child to come down into the water and join the rest of the damned.

Lightning split the sky, dark and forbidding. Standing ankle-deep in the murky water, Sebaton sheltered his eyes, but the storm continued to rage behind them.

'Do not resist…' bellowed the thunder.

Sebaton held on, just as the drowned boy clung to his ankle.

He groaned, 'Let me go,' his voice that of a child's and an adult's at the same time as two realities collided.

'Please…'

'Let him go.' The voice was distant at first, recalling Sebaton from the brink of unconsciousness. The pain abated, his eyes opened again, but the sense of violation remained.

The Librarian, Hriak, was standing in front of him. The dark lightning had gone from his hand.

He hissed, 'He's a psyker, Leodrakk.'

So that was the Salamander's name then, Sebaton assumed.

'What did you find, Hriak?' asked Domadus.

'Despite trying to obfuscate it with some childhood trauma, he is not who he claims to be. He found something in some ruins, in a sector of the city far from here. But I don't think he has it any more.'

Leodrakk changed places with Hriak to continue the interrogation.

'Those traitors are here for a dark purpose. For some reason, they were also looking for you. Now,' he said, raising his bolter so Sebaton was staring down its ugly, black maw, 'I will ask you one final time. Who are you and what are you doing in Ranos?'

Sebaton realised then that the situation he was in was much more grave than it had first appeared. He hadn't been rescued, he had simply traded one potential captor for another. These warriors were loyal servants of the Emperor, but something had broken inside them. They were verging on desperate, even fatalistic. Wounded, and not only physically. They were the kind of scars that would never heal, like the five tiny marks on Sebaton's leg.

Sebaton sagged in the chair, but looked the Salamander in the eye.

'I am Caeren Sebaton. I am an archaeologist, and I came here to excavate relics.'

'No more lies or I'll kill you here. Now,' Leodrakk warned, priming his bolter. 'We didn't survive the betrayal of Isstvan with a great deal of patience. Speak truthfully!'

Leodrakk's hand was suddenly around Sebaton's throat and lifting him out of the chair. As the ground fell away beneath him, Sebaton felt his larynx being slowly crushed.

'*I can't... speak... with your hand... around my throat,*' he croaked, feet dangling in mid-air.

Snarling, Leodrakk threw the man down. Sebaton sprawled, bouncing hard off his right shoulder but landing with some grace on all fours. Scurrying backwards into a corner of the room, he thought about using the ring, but the three warriors had him cornered.

He saw Domadus properly for the first time. The Iron Hand was heavily cybernetic. Most of his left side had been reconstructed, the mechanism of his body visible through the gaps in his black armour. His throat and lower jaw were completely augmetic, and puckered scar-tissue ringed the area around where his left eye should have been, but where instead a red lens flashed as it refocused on its target.

Mag-locking his bolter to his thigh, Leodrakk advanced on

Sebaton. They were in pain, all of these warriors, and like anyone in that position they wanted to lash out.

'I'll crush the truth out of you.'

A fourth figure stepped into the light, the one whom Sebaton had seen observing from the shadows. 'Stop.'

Leodrakk faced the legionary angrily. 'It's under control.'

Now Leodrakk had turned, Sebaton saw the chunk of bone tusk jutting from his armoured hide. It was split, little more than a stump.

The legionary who had interrupted was a Salamander too, and wore fine-crafted armour like his comrade's, but had his helmet clamped to his thigh. His hair was cut into a red crest that perfectly bisected his scalp. A scar throbbed under his right eye, but he wasn't blind in it, nor did it ruin his noble countenance.

'No, you lost control when you nearly choked him, brother.' He gestured to the door. 'Shen'ra is outside. Something tripped the sentries.'

Leodrakk suddenly looked concerned.

'Both guns?'

'Sensors, Tarantula sentries. Everything.'

'How far out?'

'First marker.'

Sebaton had no idea what they were talking about, but it sounded serious.

Leodrakk's anger returned with interest. 'All the more reason to put this one in the fire.'

'I hope he's speaking metaphorically,' said Sebaton.

'He is,' said the other Salamander, but Leodrakk didn't give that impression at all.

'We make him talk. Tell us everything he knows,' he snarled, clutching the grip of his sidearm.

'By force-feeding him your bolter?'

'If necessary!'

'Out,' the other Salamander said, flatly.

'What?'

'You heard me, Leo. You'll kill him if you stay in this room. I can see it in your eyes.'

Leodrakk's eyes were burning with the heat of a firestorm. His knuckles cracked and for a few seconds he stood his ground before capitulating.

'Apologies, captain. I forget myself.'

'Yes, you do, Leo. Now leave us.'

Leodrakk did as ordered, prompting Domadus to guard the door behind him.

After watching his brother go, the other Salamander crouched down at Sebaton's eye level.

'You seem a little more civilised than your companions,' said Sebaton without a trace of belief.

'I am not,' the other Salamander assured him. His voice was deep, cultured. It shared some commonalities with Leodrakk but possessed the authority of true command. 'As you can see,' he gestured to his visage, 'I am a monster. Much worse than Leodrakk. He is more temperate than I.'

'What about your psyker?' Sebaton nodded to the Raven Guard, who had folded his arms and taken to watching quietly from a distance. Sebaton still detected some latent psychic activity, like a mental polygraph gauging his every response.

The Salamander looked askance at the other legionary.

'No, his manners are worse than my own. Given his own way, you'd be dribbling the last dregs of your sanity into your lap right about now.'

'I would prefer to avoid that.'

'That's up to you. We are now being hunted, just like you are. Our time here is finite before we're discovered. Our enemy's scouts have already tripped the first of our alarms. So, you can appreciate I would prefer this to be concluded quickly. My name is Artellus Numeon, and I lead this group. The lives of the men in it are my responsibility, which is why Leodrakk would not have killed you without my say so. It's also why Hriak hasn't cored out your head like a piece of fruit. I, however, answer to no one in this place and I *will* kill you in the next four seconds unless you give me a reason not to.'

Sebaton's head still hurt from the psychic probe and between this maniac and the psyker preparing to eviscerate him mentally, he was running short of options.

Just like Nurth all over again. Stepping out of that airlock, he'd thought that was an end to it but they brought him back. Again. To do *this.*

I am a spy, not an assassin. And as for the mission… Well, that would require something incredibly special.

Sebaton knew he really had no choice. Trust this Numeon, or die here. But then would that really be so bad? Even if he did, would that really be an end to it? He suspected not.

'We were excavating, that much is true. We found something. An artefact. It's very old, very powerful, and your enemies want it.'

Numeon exchanged a glance with the others.

'What kind of artefact?'

'A weapon. Like a spear.'

'*Like* a spear?'

'To call it thusly would be overly prosaic, but it's the closest word I can think of that still accurately describes it. It's smaller, more like a spearhead with a short shaft.' Sebaton indicated the approximate size with his hands.

'Why were you looking for it? What is so important about this spear that the Word Bearers sent hunters after you to get it?'

Sebaton sighed. 'May I at least sit down?'

Numeon backed off and nodded to the chair.

'Before I tell you,' said Sebaton, once he was seated, 'there is something else you should know first. My name isn't Caeren Sebaton. It's John Grammaticus.'

CHAPTER EIGHT
Shattered

'When brother fights brother, it is called rivalry. When brother kills brother, it is called succession.'
— Valdrekk Elias

EIGHTEEN DEAD BODIES cluttered the street below.

Fifteen of those bodies were Traoran, and were wearing black and red robes over their urban attire. Narek barely noticed them, but the three warriors clad in power armour that joined the cultists in death sent a tremor of consternation across his jawline.

The quiet hunt was over. Despite Narek's misgivings, Elias had gathered his dogs from sects around the city and unleashed them without thought or knowledge of what fate he had consigned them to. Cultists were everywhere within Ranos. They had paved the way for the Legion's arrival, softened the prey before the kill. It was a task well suited to their limited talents.

Against legionaries, however, they had come up drastically short.

One of the humans had tripped a hidden wire alarm, unleashing a chain of explosives embedded in the road. Flash bangs went off simultaneously, filling the narrow street that was crowded by buildings either side with light and smoke. A secondary group of incendiaries went live three seconds later, front and back of the patrol, effectively bracketing them into a kill box. In the last short minute that remained of their lives, the cultists panicked and the legionaries fell back on training, forming a defensive perimeter in the middle of the street. The saboteurs had factored this reaction into their trap as a pair of auto-slaved sentries cycled up.

Muzzle flash had cut into the smoke as heavy fire chugged relentlessly from the pair of Tarantula mounts secreted at either end of the street. The concealment of the guns was effective, as was the entire trap. Even Narek hadn't seen the wire or the sentries and wondered privately if he was actually losing his edge.

Disorientated, some of their dead already lying broken before them, the cultists were ripped apart in seconds. Narek's brothers didn't last much longer. Power armour was staunch protection but even it couldn't hold up against enfilading fire at close range from a pair of autocannons.

The end result was bloody and quick.

Narek and Dagon survived by virtue of the fact that they were above the metal storm, maintaining overwatch from a rooftop. Narek had been about to make contact with his brothers when the trap was sprung and death was unleashed.

As he looked down on the carnage, Narek scowled.

'Beliah, Zephial, Namaah, all dead. Haruk also. Tell me, brother,' he said, turning to Dagon, who had just returned from street level, 'who must I kill to avenge them?'

'The trap was good,' Dagon replied. 'Very good. Even on the ground, I would have had difficulty seeing the wire.'

'Frag-belt?' asked Narek.

Dagon nodded. 'And some heavier explosives too. Armour-breaking.'

That would be the secondary burst they had seen and felt from the rooftop.

'Naturally. And the sentry guns?'

The two tripod-mounted Tarantulas were spewing smoke. Tiny sparks erupted sporadically around the gimbal joint that linked the tripod mount to the gun stock. Narek had disabled them, but not before they had shredded Beliah, Zephial and Namaah.

'Slaved to an automatic firing routine, based on motion detection,' said Dagon.

'So they had no intention of staying to watch the bloodshed.'

'No, but I found this.'

In Dagon's open palm was a small metallic device. It was disc-shaped and a red light in its centre winked rapidly.

A sensor.

Narek took it, examining the device in his hand.

'They might be few but they are certainly well equipped.' He glanced back down at the street. 'And have a talent for disruption.'

'Saboteurs?' Dagon asked.

'Definitely. The broken Legions have turned to guerrilla tactics to prosecute their war.'

'They might just be a vanguard. How can you be certain?'

Narek's eyes returned to regard the sensor.

'Because it's what I'd do.' He paused, turning the sensor disc over in his hand as if scrutinising it would reveal his enemy's secrets. Narek surveyed the urban skyline, paying close attention to the nearest buildings.

'What is it?' asked Dagon.

Narek's gaze lingered on the shadow of a cooling tower in the distance.

'Nothing,' he said. 'Watch the street, I have to tell Elias what we've found.'

Dagon nodded and headed back down.

When he was alone again, Narek activated the warp-flask. After a few seconds, Elias's warp-form materialised. He was cleansing his ritual knife, preparing it for the next kill.

'You interrupt me with good news, I hope. Sacrificing an entire city is painstaking and I have a lot of work to do yet before we're done.'

'Your reinforcements are all dead.'

'A little profligate, don't you think? Those were the only warriors close to your location.'

'It wasn't my decision to send them.'

Elias's tone grew suddenly barbed. *'Remember who you're talking to, Narek.'*

A vein in the hunter's neck throbbed but he held back his anger.

'You are my master, Dark Apostle.'

'I gave you purpose, huntsman. Don't forget that.'

'It is a worthy one. I will not.'

'What of the cults? They should have risen up by now. Use them. The city is in my thrall.'

'The mortals are dead too.'

Elias looked displeased, but kept his agitation checked.

'What happened? I thought you were just tracking the human.'

'We were. But that "someone else" I mentioned decided to get in our way.' His gaze went back to the cooling tower. 'One of your worshippers sprung a trap our enemy had laid for us. They're of the Legions.'

'You're certain of it?'

'Yes.'

'You've seen them?'

'No, but every sign points to our former cousins. No human kills Beliah, Zephial and Namaah like that. It just doesn't happen. Not to them. Even I didn't see the tripwire.'

Elias sneered. *'You're losing your edge.'*

'That is possible, I suppose.'

'*There are no Legion forces concentrated in this region of space. It's precisely why Lord Erebus sent us here. We were supposed to be undisturbed. Who are they?*'

'Remnants, I think. Survivors banded together and performing their own operations.'

'*Dregs from Isstvan?*' Elias sounded nonplussed.

'I believe so, yes. I want to take a closer look to be sure.'

Elias paused, as if weighing up the import of that.

'*Nothing can prevent what we're doing here, Narek. The outcome of the war could hinge on the cosmological shift we effect here.*'

'It's fortunate that I am not empty-handed, then.'

'*You have what they took from the catacombs?*'

Narek held it up in his other hand.

'It's a spear. At least the tip of one.'

Elias's eyes seemed to brighten. '*Sharpen ours, blunt theirs…*'

Narek frowned, confused.

'*Bring it to me at the ritual site,*' said Elias. '*The rest of our brethren are returning with fresh mortals to blood, and I would examine it before they arrive.*'

'What should I do about the Legionary infiltrators? They still have the human we were tracking.'

'*They are of no consequence for the moment. Bring me the weapon, Narek. We will run down these broken wretches later.*' Elias smiled with self-indulgent malice. '*We will make them wish they had died on the plains of Isstvan with the rest of their kin.*'

'Of course.' Narek was about to sever their connection when Elias interrupted him.

'*What's it like?*' he asked.

Narek turned the spear over in his hand. It was short, the spearhead not much larger than a combat knife in terms of its length and width, with a broken shaft that was roughly half that. To look upon it, it was unremarkable, a perfect mineral fossil fashioned into a single spear-like fork. Grey, almost metallically smooth, with a sharp edge. But when Narek held it, he could feel the thrum of power contained within and see the flash of energy coursing continually along its length as the light touched it.

'Godlike...'

Communion ended and Narek was left alone with his thoughts. It did not anger him that three of his brothers were lying dead in the street below him; to call it anger was too simple a word for his emotional state at that moment. Even the death of Haruk, who he despised personally, required response. It was more like an itch, a sense of something unfinished, an imbalance to redress.

He decided he would not return with the spear straight away. It went against orders, but it was duty that motivated Narek, not the whims of the Dark Apostle. First and foremost, he owed something to his brothers. Besides, he wanted to see the face of his enemy.

Unsheathing his gladius and putting the spear in the empty scabbard, Narek opened a vox-feed to Dagon.

'I tire of this rooftop, brother.'

'What do you suggest?'

'Beliah, Zephial, Namaah and Haruk are slain. We should honour the dead.'

'I'm listening.'

'Let's go hunting.'

NUMEON LOOKED UNIMPRESSED.

'Is that name supposed to mean something to me?'

'No, it isn't,' said Grammaticus. 'Not to you. But what I am doing here should.'

'And what is that, exactly?'

'I think I know why the Word Bearers are here, and why you're here too.'

Domadus twitched, his hand straying to a bolt pistol holstered next to his right hip before a shake of Numeon's head stood him down.

'Keep talking,' said the Salamander.

'Are we in danger here?' Grammaticus asked. 'Your... *friend* seemed agitated when he left.'

'Immense danger, but I told you to keep talking,' said Numeon. 'What do you know?'

Grammaticus dragged his attention back, trying not to imagine what could present immense danger to a Space Marine, and said, 'I think they are defiling this place. I think the Emperor came here long ago, and they are tainting that with their craft.'

Numeon came closer, until Grammaticus could smell the ash on his breath.

'And what *craft* is that, John Grammaticus?'

'Am I right?'

Numeon narrowed his eyes. 'What craft?'

'You know of what I speak. You want to stop them, don't you? You are no longer Legion, that much is obvious from your battered weapons and armour. I doubt there are more than twenty of you. I saw your landers. How many can they carry? Enough for a ground war?'

'Ninety men at capacity,' Numeon replied, 'but their holds were sparsely occupied when we made planetfall, you're right about that.'

Numeon stooped to grab the scrap of parchment still wedged underneath the chair leg.

'We are here to disrupt their efforts but have no plans to fight a war.' He showed Grammaticus the paper. It was a propaganda poster, one denouncing the rule of the Imperium and citing Horus as the true Emperor of the galaxy. 'Rebellion was festering here long before the Word Bearers came. We must prevent them from tainting it further.'

So Traoris was in the thrall of the enemy. But revolt was very different to willing service to the Primordial Annihilator. Grammaticus imagined secret cults, formed over years of Imperial rule, slowly chipping away at the foundations of society, and their sudden and terrifying rise when Horus defied his father's will and embraced an old evil.

'Rebellion is one thing,' said Numeon. 'Conversion to the dark power Horus now serves is another. I don't understand it fully but I have seen some of what it can do. Turn men into monsters, and twist once noble hearts to baser instincts. Every world liberated during the Great Crusade is facing a battle for its soul. Traoris teeters on the brink of an abyss. I am here to ensure it doesn't fall in.'

'That seems a difficult aspiration.'

'And yet, here we are.'

Grammaticus was emphatic. 'I *need* that spear.'

'Even if I wanted to, there's no going back for it now.'

'Have you considered that you could serve a greater purpose?'

'And help you?'

'Yes.'

'And why, John Grammaticus, would I do that?'

'Because what I'm doing here concerns your primarch.'

'What did you just say?' Numeon's eyes narrowed.

'Vulkan.'

The Salamander bunched his fists. 'I know the name of my primarch. Explain yourself.'

'The spear I found is not a spear as such. It's a fulgurite, a fork of lightning crystallised in rock.'

'I also know what a fulgurite is,' said Numeon. 'Tell me now what this has to do with Vulkan.'

Grammaticus licked his lips. 'Do you believe that your primarch is dead?'

Numeon did not hesitate. Something akin to hope flickered in his eyes. 'No.'

'He lives, Numeon. Vulkan lives.'

'How do you know this? Where is your proof?'

'You said you believed he was alive.'

Numeon's patience was ebbing and he snarled, 'There is a difference between belief and fact. Why would you say this if you have no evidence?'

'Because it is true, and because I am giving you my word.'

'Which is worth what?'

Grammaticus held up his hand, as if surrendering.

'Please. You asked for the truth and I am giving it to you.'

'You would say anything to save yourself.'

'True, but I am not lying to you. Have your psyker scry me again if you like – you will see I don't speak falsely.'

Numeon looked like he was considering that, when he asked, 'What does this spear have to do with Vulkan?'

'I honestly don't know. It is tied to his fate somehow. I was merely tasked with coming here to retrieve it.'

That was a lie; at least part of it was, but Grammaticus knew his masters had given him all he needed to shield his mind.

Numeon frowned. 'Tasked by whom?'

'It's difficult to explain.'

Domadus's vox crackled and Grammaticus caught the murmured intonation of a voice on the other end of it.

'Try,' said Numeon and was about to say more when Domadus approached him.

'Pergellen is back with Shen'ra and wants to see you.'

Numeon nodded in return. 'Say *nothing* of this to anyone else.'

Domadus nodded. 'And what of *him*?' he asked, drawing a short-bladed sword from his belt. Grammaticus didn't like the cold look in the Iron Hand's eye. 'I could silence him now. It would end his seditious talk. He also knows our whereabouts, some of our strength.'

'I'm not sure yet if it is seditious…' Numeon paused, thinking. 'Besides, he knows nothing, not about us anyway.'

'He would complicate our mission,' said Domadus.

'It's a risk I'm prepared to take. He knows something, Domadus. I want to know it too.' He turned towards the Raven Guard.

'I will watch him,' said Hriak, unfolding his arms slowly like he was unfurling his wings.

'Domadus,' Numeon added.

'No one gets in or out unless it's with your say so.'

'No, I was going to say, don't let Hriak hollow the human out. I want his mind intact for questioning later.'

'You wound me deeply,' uttered the Raven Guard.

Numeon frowned. 'Was that sarcasm, Hriak? You sounded almost as warm as Domadus.'

The Iron Hand laughed loudly and stepped aside.

Numeon nodded to them both, turned his back and left the room.

'I felt safer when I was on my own,' Grammaticus said with half-hearted humour, glancing from the stoic figure of the Iron Hand to the menacing spectre of the Raven Guard.

Hriak didn't share Grammaticus's humour and glared back at him through the slits of his battle-helm.

'You were,' he rasped.

After a short walk through an access corridor and the old manu-factorum bunk room, Numeon arrived at the printer's abandoned refectorum. It was a largely barren space, tiled grey underfoot and with a few benches and tables upturned at the room's edges. A short skirmish had unfolded here, the loyal citizens of Ranos ulti-mately on the losing side. Amidst the spilt food stains, there were also patches of blood.

In the middle of it all, waiting for the Salamander, stood Pergellen.

The Iron Hand was lean-faced, his eyes concealed behind a steel visor with a single retinal band across its surface. The lights were out in the refectorum, making the visor glow lambently in the darkness. Pergellen's only other bionic was his left hand, which ground noisily as he used it to grip Numeon's wrist. His hair was black like jet, and cut close to his scalp in the same manner as his deceased lord and father's had been.

Over his shoulder on a strap Pergellen had a long-barrelled sniper rifle. It was his deadly aim that had killed the Word Bearer in the warehouse, although from such close range that wasn't exactly a challenge. He'd wanted to use the warehouse as his nest from which to keep a lookout, but hopes for that were ruined as soon as the human had burst in.

'You looked troubled, Artellus,' he said to Numeon.

'It's nothing.' Numeon smiled to cover the concern that had obviously crept over his face, and returned Pergellen's grip in formal but comradely greeting. 'I'm glad to see you back. Where's Shen'ra?'

'In the yard with the others,' he said flatly.

Pergellen was a serious soul, rarely given to humour. But he had also saved Numeon's and Leodrakk's lives on the plains of Isstvan V. So few of the Morlocks had escaped, so very few of the Clan Avernii left to continue its great and noble legacy.

When the shells were falling and the full horror of the betrayal revealed, it was Pergellen who had fought his way back to the dropships when others were losing their minds at the death of Ferrus Manus. It was Pergellen who had dragged Domadus's unconscious form across the black sand, and he who had kept open a path to the transport. Many didn't make it.

He and Leodrakk would have died on that field were it not for Pergellen. Their brothers in the Pyre Guard might well all be dead, but Numeon clung to the hope that they were not, just as he believed that Vulkan, too, still lived.

If what the human had said was the truth, then perhaps... He dismissed the thought at once, knowing it was foolish to place his hope in such a man.

Instead he asked, 'How many days were we on that drop-ship, Pergellen?'

It was often where their conversations went at some point.

'Fifty-one days, eight hours and four minutes,' the Iron Hand replied.

They had been a mess of disparate units and Legions back then. Not all had survived the escape. Some were simply too badly wounded or had been dead when they were dragged aboard. Of the forty-seven legionaries that took flight on that vessel, only twenty-six survived.

They lived long enough to be reunited with the *Fire Ark*, a strike cruiser that had escaped the carnage – one of the few. It had not done so unscathed. Many of the crew were killed during that desperate flight. Wounded, weary, they had levelled what guns they had on the drop-ship emerging from that self-same chaos, not realising they were friends, not foes.

There were no legionaries aboard, not one. Every single able-bodied warrior that could don war-plate had been sent to bring the disgraced Warmaster to heel. It was extravagant, Numeon realised in retrospect – a means of showing force to force and hoping the latter balked in the face of the former. How wrong they were. It didn't seem like extravagance now; instead, it smacked of ignorant sacrifice. And how Horus had prepared his altar for their willing offering. The blades of his traitors were sharp indeed on that slab of Isstvan V.

Since finding the *Fire Ark* and the brave but depleted crew aboard, they had lost three more legionaries. Numeon had allied them together, given them back some semblance of purpose. But it did not come without risk, and a vein of fatalism was growing in this company. He had expected it of the Iron Hands, but they bore the loss of their primarch with a quiet and steely determination that did the Medusans much credit. No, it was the Nocturneans, the sons of Vulkan, that suffered most. Of all the Salamanders, only Numeon *believed*. In his heart, he knew that his father had survived. The rest, despite his impassioned arguments, were not so convinced, and fought for vengeance instead of hope and a desire to serve.

Numeon knew these men were broken. Bereft of leadership, they would have destroyed one another, and with no way to return to their Legions they were cut adrift and aimless.

Yes, Pergellen had saved his life, but Numeon had to believe he could save this shattered Legion too.

'What did you learn?' he asked the scout.

'Nothing good. Shen'ra's sensors were tripped by a small patrol. I shadowed it for a while before the sentries cut them all down. It will certainly alert the enemy to our presence here.'

'We knew the Word Bearers would find us eventually. What else?'

'In addition to their legionaries, which I believe are significant in number, they also have many cultists. Seeds were sown here long before we arrived on the Word Bearers' heels. The cults control most of Ranos now, and more Stormbirds are coming in from other parts of the city to reinforce the legionaries already on the ground. They are mustering close to this district. Too many for us to engage.'

Numeon cursed under his breath, '*Vulkan's merciful wrath...*' He did not want to abort the mission, but it wasn't too late to signal to the *Fire Ark* waiting in high orbit. If they moved now, they could reach the gunships and their cruiser, but what then?

'There was something else, too,' Pergellen said, arresting Numeon from his thoughts.

Numeon narrowed his eyes. 'More good news?'

'Someone was watching.'

'They saw you?'

'Not us. They were watching their allies get gunned down by the sentries.'

'Friendlies?'

'No, I don't think so. They disabled the Tarantulas. Shen'ra and I left shortly after that. I think they may have caught our trail from the warehouse and followed us.'

'So, in all likelihood, they are coming here.'

'Yes.'

Numeon's face darkened. They had spent some time choosing a secure location to act as a base of operations. This district was mostly deserted. The gunships were far away, well outside the habitable zone. It was believed that at the edge of the city they would remain largely unnoticed by the enemy until they chose to act. Much of their plan hinged upon this assumption.

'Any sign of their cleric?' Numeon asked.

Pergellen shook his head. 'No.'

The Salamander grew stern. 'We've seen this before, brother. We failed at Viralis...' As he spoke the name of this world, an image of corpse-filled streets, bodies defiled and mutilated in service to dark powers, came back to him. The traitors had left something else behind, too. The few survivors had been greatly *changed*, human no longer. They had become... *things*. Monsters, sleeved in flesh, that had crawled into mortal vessels and hollowed them out from within. The people of Viralis, an entire colony, were people no longer. Something else had taken their place, wearing them as a man might wear a suit.

'We were too late for them,' Numeon said, grimly.

'We are not too late for Traoris,' said Pergellen. 'The cleric will die, but without the element of surprise we will need to draw him out. We won't fail, Numeon.'

'Ever since Isstvan. Since Vulkan...' Numeon faltered.

Pergellen gripped his shoulder.

'You told me you believe he still lives, Numeon. Don't abandon your faith in that belief.'

'I haven't, even if I am the only one. I wish bitterly, though, that there was some sign, anything to give us hope.' Again, he reminded himself that he could not trust the prisoner. 'I have never felt this before... this... *doubt* that I feel now.'

'I have lost my progenitor. His body lies headless amongst a field of our dead. *You* give me hope now. I follow you as my captain. You gave us all a purpose beyond vengeful fatalism. If you must believe in something, believe in that.'

Numeon smiled – wearily, but honestly. 'I do. I hold to it. How many times I wished I had died on Isstvan Five with my brothers and instead ended up here, trying to make sense of this madness, trying to do something that still matters.'

'*This*, here, now – this matters.'

Numeon nodded, finding strength.

The Iron Hand released his grip as the need for it faded.

'I assume we are not staying here,' he said.

Numeon shook his head. 'This place is compromised. We're moving.'

'Will you inform the *Fire Ark*?'

'No. It's possible atmospheric communication could be intercepted. Then the zealots really will know where to come and kill us.'

'Then I'll summon our quartermaster to come and break down our gear.'

'Thank you, brother. Tell Domadus I'll be in the vehicle yard.'

'What's to be done with the human?'

'He comes with us. He's keeping secrets.'

'Couldn't Hriak prise his mind open and wrench them out?'

Numeon shrugged. 'If we wanted him dead, I dare say he could. He's watching him now.'

'And do we not? Want the human dead, I mean. He's a liability and will slow us down.'

Numeon shook his head. 'You are a cold breed, you Iron Hands.'

'I saved your life, didn't I?'

Now the Salamander laughed, though Pergellen wasn't making a joke. 'You did, yes. I want to speak to the human again. He knows something. Besides, the cleric wants him. We might be able to use that.'

'So he's not a prisoner at all then,' said Pergellen, 'he's bait. And you say I'm cold.'

Numeon replied without humour. 'I'm pragmatic, brother. And I will do *anything* to kill this Word Bearers cleric.'

'Even if it means our lives and the life of this man?'

'Yes, even that. I would sacrifice all of it to stop them, to prevent another Viralis.'

'And *that*, Artellus, is why I saved you.'

The two warriors parted, the Iron Hand headed for the printing works where they were holding the prisoner.

As Numeon returned to the vehicle yard, he tried to remain focused on his address to the other legionaries, but two words kept repeating in his mind. He barely dared to hope they were true. *Vulkan lives.*

CHAPTER NINE
Honouring the dead

'Day after day, day after day,
We stuck, nor breath nor motion;
As idle as a painted ship
Upon a painted ocean.'

– From 'The Rhym of the Ancyent Starfarer' by the bard Colwrit

TWENTY-THREE LEGIONARIES comprised Numeon's company, himself included. It was barely more than two squads. The majority were Salamanders, mainly line warriors with a few Pyroclasts, as well as himself and Leodrakk from the Pyre Guard. A pair of battle-brothers and Codicier Hriak represented the Ravens. And of the Iron Hands Legion, there were only Domadus and Pergellen. Ever since the evacuation from the Isstvan killing fields, there had been no contact with any other Legion force.

Their vessel, the *Fire Ark*, had been badly damaged in the exodus from Isstvan V. Some weapon systems were still functional, though these were insufficient to last long against a fully operational ship of the same calibre. Life support, power for lighting on certain decks, the engines and warp drive still worked, albeit at a reduced and unreliable capacity. Communications were another matter, however. Shipboard vox worked well enough but long-distance augurs and the sensorium arrays were beyond repair and use. Even ship-to-surface vox was extremely patchy. Captain Halder had achieved the near-impossible in effecting a successful escape, but they had limped on ever since and knew nothing of the greater war. Or even if there was a greater war. For all they knew, everyone was dead and Horus had won.

Numeon refused to believe that. Just as he refused to believe that Vulkan had died along with Lord Manus. He hadn't seen the primarch fall, but the news from their fellow survivors who had was as compelling as it was grim. They fought on, hoping that others did too.

In the vehicle yard, his broken company were currently stood down.

Some were sitting on storage crates, checking weapons, aligning targeters or reloading. He recognised Daka'rai, K'gosi and Uzak huddled around a fire. The three Salamanders weren't keeping warm, they were speaking oaths and blackening their gauntlets in the flames to seal each pact. More than ever, the different legionaries fell back on their native rituals and customs to give them resolve and purpose.

Others were less clandestine and spent their downtime making battlefield repairs on armour, or testing and refocusing retinal lens resolution, or running biometrics. One legionary, a Salamander called Helon, was performing field surgery on one of the Ravens who'd been injured when a gunship had crash-landed during planetfall. The gunship was no longer operable, but Shaka would live. Helon was not a trained Apothecary, but in the absence of such a specialist he had adapted.

The Raven's rookery brother, Avus, was squatted atop an iron gantry that overlooked the yard, keeping watch. Hriak was nowhere to be seen, but Numeon knew that the Librarian would be close by if he were needed.

Leodrakk had been waiting for Numeon to appear, and left his guarded conversation with Kronor to go and speak with him.

'Pyre Captain,' he said, crafting a small bow. 'How fares our prisoner?'

'He lives, no thanks to you.'

Leodrakk had removed his battle-helm. It was sitting in the crook of his arm, so Numeon saw him lower his eyes at the mild reprimand from his captain.

'You have heard Pergellen's news,' he offered, changing the subject.

'I have.'

Leodrakk smiled coldly. 'I wished for this moment. We will finally get our deserved revenge.'

'We're leaving, Leo.'

'What?'

'We can't stay here, not now our enemies have learned of us.'

'What does it change? Let them come. We shall be waiting.' He clenched his fist in emphasis.

'No, brother. We won't be. They have many times our numbers. This place is hardly a fortress. We could not hold it against an army, and besides, we did not come here to die a vainglorious death.'

Leodrakk stepped forwards, prompting Numeon to do the same until their breastplates almost touched.

'Yes, brother?' asked Numeon levelly, breathing in the scent of hot ash drifting from Leodrakk's mouth.

For a moment Leodrakk looked as if he were about to say or do something foolish. Numeon had to remind himself that Pyre Guard were not like other Salamanders. They were forged of a fierce, independent spirit; it was how Vulkan had shaped them.

'I have Ska's blood on my hands,' Leodrakk whispered, but backed down. '*Literally*, brother.'

In the face of his brother's grief, Numeon relented. He gripped Leo's shoulder guard as Pergellen had done for him.

'I know, Leo. I was there.'

Numeon glanced down at the vambrace and gauntlet on Leodrakk's left arm and hand. It was still stained with Skatar'var's blood.

'Then tell me what else other than revenge are we fighting for?'

'A greater purpose.'

'What purpose? To kill a cleric, and achieve what?'

'No, not just that. I am talking about the Eighteenth, the Legion.'

'There is no Legion, Artellus.' Leodrakk gestured agitatedly behind him. 'We are all that remains.'

Numeon saw the anger and doubt in Leodrakk's eyes. He'd seen it mirrored in his own many times since their escape. Something else filled them now, though. Hope.

'Vulkan lives,' Numeon said.

Sighing ruefully, Leodrakk shook his head. A little mirthless laugh passed his lips.

'This again. He is dead, Numeon. He died on Isstvan like Ferrus Manus. Vulkan is gone.'

Numeon's eyes narrowed with certainty. '*He lives.*'

'How do you know?'

'I feel it,' said Numeon, tapping two fingers against his left breast, 'in here.'

'I want it to be true, brother. I want it more than anything, but he's dead. So is Ska, so are all of them. We are the only Salamanders that now live and I would rather die in vainglory, killing our betrayers and those that murdered our kin in cold blood, than wither away and run like cowards.'

Leodrakk walked away. Numeon let him go, having no argument

with which to recall him. Belief and the desperate testimony of an already proven liar were no grounds to convince anyone of proof of life.

'Not like him to lose his temper,' said Domadus, having just come from where they had been keeping the prisoner. He came into step beside Numeon. Numeon looked at him askance. 'Are you sure you're Tenth Legion?'

'My overly augmeticised appearance suggests otherwise?'

'Your sarcasm does.'

'We all have our coping mechanisms, brother-captain.'

'Seems Leodrakk's is rage,' Numeon murmured, watching the other Salamander storm out of the vehicle yard and into the city street beyond.

'He would not be alone.'

'Aye, a fact of which I am all too aware, Domadus.'

'Then let us put these warriors to purpose. Pergellen informs me we're striking camp.'

Numeon nodded. 'Yes, the Word Bearers know we are here and are coming. We need to be gone when they arrive.'

'Ah,' said Domadus, realising, 'and hence the stoking of Leodrakk's ire.'

'Indeed.'

'How long?'

'Ten minutes. Pergellen thinks he and Shen were followed. I won't take chances.'

'It will have to be light arms only then. Spare ammunition, grenades, anything that can be carried easily. We'll need some fire-power, though.'

'Take the heavy bolter – suspensors should make it light enough to bear at speed.'

'To be honest with you, captain, I hadn't considered leaving it behind. Besides, it will make an excellent mess of those traitors.'

Numeon allowed himself a wry smile as he caught the flash of amusement in Domadus's eyes.

'Aye, that it will, quartermaster. Det-cord everything else. No weapon we leave behind will fall into enemy hands.'

'Or we could cache the spares close by,' Domadus suggested. 'An ammo dump could prove useful against numbers. Strike and fade, resupply then repeat?'

'A valid tactic, but no. It'll take too long. Disable anything extraneous.'

'Very well.' The quartermaster nodded his understanding. 'You want me to pass the word to the others?'

'No, I will do it.'

Numeon mounted a storage crate. Some of the other legionaries were already turning towards him when he began.

'Gather...' Numeon's powerful voice carried across the vehicle yard with strength and authority, demanding attention. The legionaries drew in to listen. 'Brothers, the Word Bearers are amassing a large force in this part of the city. Needless to say, we are not equipped to engage such a force. If they discover this location we'll be overrun, so we're moving out. Immediately.'

Numeon's announcement provoked mutterings from some quarters, but none gainsaid him.

'Domadus will redeploy weapons and kit. No heavies unless it's suspensored. Only what can be carried. Rifles, pistols, blades, grenades. Anything else, leave behind. Our mission is unchanged. Killing the enemy cleric is our primary. Secondary is to cause as much damage as possible then egress off-world.' He raised his fist. 'For the blood of our fallen.'

'We remember them and their sacrifice,' twenty-one legionaries replied, mirroring Numeon's salute.

'And vengeance for Lord Manus,' muttered Domadus, slamming his gauntlet against his breastplate. 'You'll need to talk to Shen'ra.'

He gestured to the back of the vehicle yard.

Numeon looked at the Iron Hand as he was climbing down. 'Is there a problem?'

'Not yet. But there will be.' said Domadus, before heading in the opposite direction to carry out his orders. 'As his commanding officer, he's less likely to hit you,'

Numeon exhaled a long, calming breath.

'Vulkan grant me strength,' he muttered, and went over to the Techmarine.

Shen'ra was stooped over a long, rectangular packing crate inspecting the contents as Numeon approached. The box was gunmetal grey and Munitorum-stamped. Like his brothers, he wore emerald-green battle-plate but his right shoulder guard was red and carried the icon of the Cog Mechanicum to show his allegiance to Mars. He had no helmet; the left hemisphere of his skull had a plate bolted to it which interfered with the armour sync-up, and he was bald-headed. Over his left shoulder hung the stump of a servo-arm that had been wrecked during the massacre. Some of the tools in the lower branch still functioned, however, so he had yet to dismantle it.

Shen'ra still felt the pain of its loss. It woke him sometimes during meditation, together with the after-image of a dark dream. He was beset by phantoms, the memory of his cleft servo-limb and the remembrance of dead brothers killed in front of his eyes.

'Do you know what's in this crate?' Shen'ra asked as Numeon came to stand behind him.

'A tracked weapons mount.'

Shen'ra straightened up and ran his hand over the barrel of the cannon contained within.

'It's a half-tracked, up-armoured, Rapier semi-automated heavy weapons platform with onboard targeting systems and power generators.' He half glanced at Numeon over his shoulder. 'This one carries a laser destroyer array. It is one of the single most devastating mobile weapons in the entire Legiones Astartes arsenal. We have it at our disposal, and you want me to leave it behind?'

The Techmarine turned to meet Numeon's gaze, his armour's servos growling in mechanised empathy with their wearer.

Shen'ra was a Nocturnean, native to the Sanctuary City of Themis. He was a giant; broad-shouldered and a head taller than Numeon. But the captain of the Pyre Guard was undaunted as he looked up at the Techmarine.

'We're striking camp. Anything larger than a bolter stays behind, and in no fit repair. Our enemies won't be able to use our own weapons against us.'

'Look around, Numeon.' Shen'ra gestured to the vehicle yard.

Every warrior was being strapped up with grenade bandoliers, their belt pouches rammed with spare clips. They looked determined, well armed, but they were few, and a ragged few at that.

Shen'ra spoke in an undertone. 'This is no Legion, and according to Pergellen that is what faces us.'

'I know you're not suggesting we abandon this world,' said Numeon, his tone dangerous.

'I'm insulted you'd even mention it,' Shen'ra replied.

'Apologies, Techmarine.'

'I can have the Rapier assembled and armed in under thirteen minutes. Let me take it with us. The half-track can easily match our ground speed and we'll need its killing power if we're to have any chance of achieving our mission.'

'Ranos is a labyrinth, Shen. What if it gets snared in wreckage? Speed it might have, but there are places we can go where a weapons mount cannot.'

'Let that be my concern. If we have to leave it then so be it. I'll wreck the weapon myself, and we'll have lost nothing. What we scavenged from that drop-ship is all we have, Numeon.'

'Each other, Shen, *that* is all we have.'

'Agreed,' said the Techmarine. 'All the more reason to bolster that with a track-mounted cannon.'

Numeon shook his head at Shen'ra. Between Leodrakk's petulance and the Techmarine's tenacity, he wondered which would get him killed first.

'You have ten minutes,' he said, and went to assist Domadus in coordinating the rest of the breakdown.

'THEY ARE LEAVING,' Dagon hissed over the vox.

Narek had the vehicle yard under surveillance through his scope. As suspected, remnants of the three Legions they had helped decimate on Isstvan V had been responsible for the deaths of four of his brothers.

A reinforced gate separated the vehicle yard from the street. It was roofless but walled. Beyond it there was an outer yard, a tarmac apron upon which traffic could be logged in and out. It too was walled, but peaked around waist height and crested by a wire mesh that wouldn't stop an arrow, let alone a mass-reactive shell.

He'd just seen a Salamander slam through the gate. He looked unhappy.

'Tempers are fraying,' he muttered to himself, before answering Dagon, 'Someone must have spotted us at the ambush site and guessed we'd follow.' Narek remembered the cooling tower, and the sense of someone watching. Now he knew his instincts hadn't been lying. Perhaps he was not as blunt as he first thought.

'*Do we engage?*' Dagon asked.

'Not yet. I'll advance, get a closer look. You stay high and maintain overwatch.'

Narek reattached the scope to his rifle, slung it over his shoulder and began to move. Just before entering the street, he cast a quick glance at the smoke stack where Dagon was positioned far above him and then headed out.

Crouched low, Narek moved quickly and stuck to the shadows. The enemy might have sentries, or the one that had seen them earlier might be watching. Having gained a distance of two hundred metres up the street, he ducked into a side alley and from there a domicile, breaking in quietly through a back door.

There were bodies inside. Dried blood painted the walls, dark and shiny. The lights were out, smashed. Furniture was upturned. An elderly man and a young woman had been cut open. Viscera glistened in the ambient light flooding in from outside through a smashed window, the blinds designed to shroud it bent and broken.

A marking was described in the blood. The octed – a star with eight points.

Elias had ensured that the cults were well secreted until their calling came. Narek could see the look of surprise and horror still etched on the young woman's face. The older man wore a death grimace. Heart attack, he presumed.

Staying low, Narek advanced to the broken window. Vantage was good. Nothing in the way of line of sight. He had an uninterrupted trajectory to the vehicle yard. Cover in the room was satisfactory too. He pulled over a section of the broken blind to further conceal his presence. Then he crouched on one knee, bracing the muzzle of his rifle on the window lip, and aimed down the scope. The errant Salamander slipped straight into his crosshairs.

He reopened the vox-link.

'In position.'

'Orders?'

'Four kills for four kills. Wait until they make egress out onto the street, then I'll give the signal.'

'Confirmed.'

Dagon cut the link.

Now all they had to do was wait.

☩ ☩ ☩

THE SHOT, WHEN it came, was muffled by the explosion from the det-cord.

At first it appeared as if the medic had slipped, but for the geyser of blood erupting from his ruined gorget.

The Salamander crumpled to his knees, gurgling and frothing through his vox-grille, the warrior nearest to him reaching for his comrade's flailing arm and simultaneously alerting the others to the attack.

Grammaticus felt a strong pressure against his back as the psyker, Hriak, pushed him to the ground.

The assertion that time moved slowly during a crisis was actually true. It was the way that the brain managed to order and cope with the ensuing trauma, enabling the body to react as quickly as it could to protect itself from harm.

In the glacially slow seconds that elapsed between Grammaticus being upright and then taking stock of his new situation, several things happened at once.

Numeon shouted the order to grab cover, pointing to the low wall surrounding the tarmac apron where the company had assembled. A data-slate on which he'd been reviewing a secondary base location was mag-locked to his thigh plate, whilst the other hand reached for a sidearm holstered at his belt.

Domadus went into a brace position, slowly turning his heavy cannon so it faced outwards towards the street and the buildings beyond.

Pergellen had been on point with the Techmarine. Both stayed down, the former scanning the darkened city for suppressed muzzle flash; the latter putting his back against the wall and lighting up a control panel on his gauntlet. The two were exchanging curt responses but, deafened by the shouting and the strange, almost subterranean filter his brain was putting on his hearing, Grammaticus could discern none of it.

He hit the ground a fraction later than the shot Salamander. The legionary dropped hard, like a felled tree, spitting blood, a pool of which was expanding from the shattered artery in his neck.

'S-t-a-y... d-o-w-n...'

Hriak shouted at him, the pysker's words slowed by sensory distortion.

As soon as he felt the earth beneath his hands and elbows, time resumed at its normal pace for Grammaticus.

'Don't move from here,' said Hriak, drawing a weapon as he moved up to support his brothers. Grammaticus watched him, followed him all the way to the low wall where another Salamander was hunkered down.

The Salamander popped up, bolter flaring in an effort to provide covering fire. A second shot pinned him as he rose, jerking his aim and piercing his chest. He fell back, perforated and unmoving.

More shouting, this time from Numeon to Leodrakk, who was edging closer to the end of the wall, shaping like he was going to attempt a dash across the street into deeper cover and then seek out their attackers from there.

'Hold!' Numeon bellowed at him, his voice tinny and urgent through his vox-grille.

Domadus was still scanning, the concentric scoping rings in his bionic eye whirring as they focused and refocused on different targets.

The Salamanders medic was being dragged away by two other legionaries when a third shot came from the darkness. It pitched one of the Raven Guard over, spinning him with the force of entry, ripping a death shriek from his lips.

'Stay down,' called Hriak, putting out his hand, telling Grammaticus not to move.

'No arguments from me,' muttered Grammaticus, and threw himself flat.

✠ ✠ ✠

'Glint of metal. I see him, on the rooftop. Thirty degrees east. Range, eighty metres.'

Pergellen's assessment came through Numeon's vox.

There were seven metres between them, and Numeon saw the scout was dirtying up his scope, trying to hide the tells that had exposed the enemy sniper.

'Difficult to get line of sight in this warren. We'll come around, take his blind side.'

'Wait,' warned Pergellen. He glanced at the three dead legionaries, now alone and bleeding out in the open. *'Trajectories suggest two firing positions.'*

'Two gunmen,' Numeon replied grimly.

Pergellen nodded.

'Permission to return fire,' shouted Domadus. He was standing against a pillar just inside the vehicle apron, heavy bolter primed for auto-fire.

'Negative. You'll be cut down before you can engage the trigger.'

'We can't stay pinned like this,' snapped Leodrakk, six metres from Numeon on the opposite end of the wall.

'I have the other one in my sights now,' Pergellen returned, scope pressed against his eye. He relayed coordinates, turning again so his back was facing the wall, and began to prep his rifle.

Numeon peeked above cover to gauge the snipers' relative positions but was forced back when a bolt shell clipped the wall.

Breathing hard, furious at their impotence to do anything, he opened up the vox.

'Hriak.'

The Librarian shook his head. *'They're too far away, and without a target I can see, there's little I can actually do.'*

Numeon snarled. 'Damn it.'

He noticed Shen'ra working at the panel on his gauntlet, his haptic implants making the data connection between the Techmarine and his Rapier.

'*Get me a precise vector for both targets,*' he voxed.

Leodrakk overheard and called to Pergellen.

'If I draw them out, can you track them?'

The scout nodded, ditching the rifle but keeping the scope.

Realising what his brother was about to do, Numeon shouted, 'Leo, no!' and began to move just as Leodrakk stood up with bolter ready.

GRAMMATICUS HAD HIS head down as instructed, facing the Techmarine and the scout.

He heard Numeon shout his brother's name, felt the tremor of motion as both rose to their feet.

Two shots followed in rapid succession, a carbon copy of the ones that heralded the deaths of Varteh and Trio.

A half-second later, he read the following words on the Techmarine's lips, '*Engage forty-seven point six by eighty-three. Strafe.*'

The churn of servos activating cut the tension as the Techmarine's tracked cannon cycled up. A burst of incandescent light from its weapon array was pre-empted by a hot flare of pain and the searing white magnesium flash that accompanied being shot.

Grammaticus knew he was hit even before he felt the blood seeping through his clothes, and the chill as his frail human body was torn open.

THE CITYSCAPE ERUPTED in a series of explosions as domiciles, manufactorums and other structures were ripped apart by the Rapier's laser destroyer mount. Debris cascaded in chunks like heavy hail from shattered facades, ruptured pillars and thoroughly gutted interiors.

Emitting a high-pitched, staccato drone, the laser destroyer stabbed a continuous barrage of beams into the area designated by its operator. It didn't stop until the Rapier powered off for emergency cool-down.

Dust clouds were still dissipating, the odd section of debris belatedly collapsing onto the street below by the time Numeon and the others surfaced from cover.

Helon, Uzak and Shaka were all dead, their bodies littering the apron outside the vehicle yard.

Domadus stomped forwards through the narrow gap between the outer wall sections. His bionic eye was still scanning, exothermic and motion detection.

'There's nothing out there. No visible threats.'

Pergellen agreed, snapping his scope back onto his rifle, but adopting overwatch all the same.

'Keep eyes on, both of you,' said Numeon, going over to help Leodrakk to his feet.

Numeon had tackled him to the ground when he'd tried to bait the shooters, sending them both sprawling.

Leodrakk had a mark down the flank of his battle-plate where something had scored a shallow groove into the metal.

'Ricochet,' he said, grunting as he got up with Numeon's assistance. 'Lucky.'

'Luckier than them,' said Numeon, and as he turned to gesture to their dead comrades he noticed the prone form of John Grammaticus.

The human was lying with his face to one side, clenched in a mask of pain. He clutched his side, his hand and most of his arm drenched in blood.

Numeon scowled, realising where the errant shell had deviated.

'Damn it.'

NAREK YANKED DAGON clear of the rubble. It looked as if several storeys had collapsed on top of him whilst the sniper was making his escape.

'I warned you not to linger,' Narek told him, letting go so that

Dagon could dust off his armour and cough the grit up out of his lungs. His helmet was wrecked, dented by a stone slab or a girder. Both retinal lenses were smashed, Dagon had a deep gash above his left eye where the impact had pushed inwards, and the vox-unit was in pieces. Taking a last look at the snarling, daemonic visage on the faceplate, Dagon discarded his helmet.

His true face, Narek decided as Dagon looked at him, was entirely more disturbing.

The brow, nose and cheekbones were raised, the skin in between sunken as if drawn in by age. It had a slightly coppery tinge, but not like metal – more like oil, and the colour changed subtly depending on how the light struck it. Most disturbing of all, though, were the two bony nubs either side of Dagon's forehead. In their infancy right now, Narek knew they would only grow, the longer Dagon was in Elias's presence.

Here, on Traoris, in Ranos, he felt the shifting of reality. It trembled, affecting him on an internal level, like maggots writhing beneath his skin.

Narek betrayed none of this to Dagon, who smiled, revealing two rows of tiny fangs instead of teeth.

'Four kills, you said.'

Narek checked the load in his rifle before slinging it back over his armoured shoulder.

'I counted a tally of three,' he replied.

'The human was caught by a stray.'

'You should have killed the legionary as instructed.'

'He shifted.'

'Then compensate,' said Narek, and headed out of the wreckage.

'He was ripped open, brother. No human could survive his injuries. Four for four.'

'No, Dagon. We scratched three. Even if the human dies, it's blood for blood. Legionary for legionary.'

Dagon nodded and followed his mentor back through demolished streets.

'We'll be back for the fourth,' Narek called over his shoulder. 'And then we'll take the rest.'

CHAPTER TEN
Burning flesh

'We have all burned. Down in the fire pits, or from the brander's iron in the solitorium, we have all touched the fire. It leaves scars, even for us. We carry them proudly, with honour. But the scars we took that day on that battlefield, we bear only with shame and regret. They are a memorial in flesh, a physical reminder of everything we have lost, a burn even we fire-born cannot endure without pain.'

— Artellus Numeon, Captain of the Pyre Guard

I LIVED.

Despite the fire, I had, against the odds, survived. I remembered the furnace, or at least fragments of what it had done to me. I remembered my skin blistering, the stench of burning fat, the smoke from cooking meat filling my eyes as the vitreous humour boiled within them.

Scorched black, rendered to ash, I was nothing but dust. A shadow without form, not unlike my gaoler-brother's favoured aspect.

And yet...

I lived.

The furnace was gone. Ferrus was gone. All was darkness and cold.

I remembered that I was on a ship, somewhere in deep space. I remembered the prison that my iron-hearted sibling had made for me, a cage strong enough to hold a primarch.

I was still weak. My limbs felt heavy and my hearts were beating furiously in my chest as some act of enhanced physiology worked to keep me alive. Perhaps I had healed, some regenerative gift I didn't know I possessed. More likely, the furnace was not real, nor my ordeal in it. I had been seeing the grim corpse-visage of my dead brother, after all. Who knew what traumas my mind had endured?

For a moment I considered the possibility that all of this was fabrication, that I was lying on Isstvan V, wounded and in a sus-an membrane coma. Or that I had been recovered and my body laboured to revive itself in some clinical apothecarion chamber, my mind struggling to catch up with it.

All of this, I dismissed. My abduction was real. Curze was real. This place, this prison that Perturabo had made for me, was real. There was no waking up from a nightmare – this *was* the nightmare. I was living it. Every tortured breath.

But it was hard to think, to reason. Ferrus's very presence and everything I had seen or not seen made me question myself. It was harrowing enough to have flesh and bone rent, split and cleaved, but what was truly terrifying was the slow erosion of sensibility, of self and the trust in my capacity to tell reality from fantasy. How can you defend yourself against your own mind, what your senses tell you? There was no armour for that, no shield or protection save strength of will and the ability to reason.

I didn't try to rise. I didn't voice my defiance or anger. I merely breathed and let the coolness of my darkling cell wash over me. I tried to recall everything I knew of my gaoler, everything I could accurately remember.

And then, closing my eyes, I allowed myself to dream.

✠ ✠ ✠

Kharaatan, during the Great Crusade

UNWASHED, MALNOURISHED, the soldiery of Khartor City were a sorry sight. Like an ant horde, dressed in carapaces of dirty red, they filed from the open city gates with their arms held above their heads in surrender.

The wall guard had come first, escorting their captains and officers. Then the first line troopers from the courtyard, and the second barricaders, the tower sentries, the inner barracks troopers, the reserves, the militia. They piled their weapons in the city square as instructed by the loudhailers of Commander Arvek's black-jacketed discipline masters. By the time the city had been emptied of its warriors, the surrendered materiel reached into a mighty black pyre.

Civilians came next.

Women pressed infants to their chests, wide-eyed men tramped in solemn procession, too afraid to cry or wail, too broken to do anything beyond stare into the rising dawn that crept across the sand dunes like a patient predator. Canines, cattle led by farmers, labourers, fabricators of every stripe, vendors, clerks, scribes and children. They vacated Khartor, their home and solace, in a great and sullen exodus.

Vodisian tanks flanked battalions of Utrich fusiliers and Navite hunters, crisp in their Imperial Army uniforms. Even Commander Arvek himself leaned from the cupola of his Stormsword to watch the throng of natives tramp past. Several stopped at the feet of their oppressors, pleading for mercy until the discipline masters moved them along. Others balked in the shadow of Princeps Lokja's Fire Kings, believing them gods rendered in iron. When aggression and intimidation could not move them, these poor individuals had to be carried by teams of orderlies from the medicae. There was little else to use these surgeons and hospitallers for – the Imperial force had ended the conflict unscathed. And this was despite the presence of xenos amongst the dirty hordes.

It was a fact that both pleased and irritated the Lord of the Drakes greatly.

'He was right,' Vulkan muttered, watching Khartor City from a distance as it gradually emptied.

'My lord?' asked Numeon, standing beside his primarch in the muster fields. Nearby, on a plain of earth flattened by Imperial pioneers, the Salamanders were re-embarking their Stormbirds for immediate redeployment. Compliance was over. The Imperium had won.

'Bloodless, he said,' Vulkan replied, surveying the human masses as they left the city.

On the walls of this last bastion, cannon embrasures lay empty, watch towers stood like impotent sentinels and only shadows manned the battlements. One by one, soldier and civilian alike, the entire populace of Khartor submitted to the will of the Imperium.

Numeon frowned. 'Was it not?'

For the first time in almost an hour, Vulkan turned his fiery gaze on his equerry. Numeon did not so much as flinch. Even his heartbeat did not betray him.

'You are a brutal warrior, Artellus,' said the primarch.

'I am as you need me to be, my lord.' He bowed his head just a little, showing deference.

'Indeed. All of the vaunted Pyre Guard are without equal in the Eighteenth. Like the deep drakes, you are savage and fierce, sharp of claw and tooth.' Vulkan nodded to the blade affixed to his equerry's back. It had yet to be bloodied on this campaign and judging by the utter capitulation of the Khar-tans, it would remain unsullied. 'But would you slaughter an entire city, soldier and civilian alike, just to send a message and spare further bloodshed?'

'I...' There was no right answer, and Numeon knew it.

'The scales are in Curze's favour. Blood for blood. Yet, I am left with a cloud of compromise and guilt over my conscience.'

Numeon looked down as if the earth at his feet could provide an answer. 'I feel it too, my lord, but what is there to be done?' He spared a glance at the rest of the Pyre Guard, who were waiting solemnly for their captain and primarch a little way back, separate from the Legion.

Vulkan looked over to where one army was met by another as several of Commander Arvek's battalions joined up with swathes of Munitorum staff to receive the natives and accept their surrender. The Army troopers did it with their lasguns held ready; the Munitorum officers greeted them with mnemo-quills and data-slates instead.

'I don't know yet, but had I realised how deep Curze's malady went, I would not have agreed to this compliance.'

Numeon regarded Vulkan. 'His malady? You think the primarch ill?'

'In a manner of speaking, yes. A sickness, and a most insidious one. The darkness of his home on Nostramo – I think he never really left it.'

'You could take these grievances to Lord Horus or Lord Dorn.'

Vulkan nodded. 'I have always valued the counsel of my elder brothers. One is close to the Crusade, the other to Terra. Between them, they will know what to do.'

'You still sound troubled, my lord.'

'I am, Artellus. Very much so. None of us wants another sanction, another empty pillar in the great investiary, another brother's name excised from all record. It is shame enough to bear the grief for two. I have no wish to add to it, but what choice do I have?'

Numeon's reply was muted, for he knew how it grieved Vulkan to speak ill of his brothers, even one such as Curze. 'None at all.'

Nestling in a shallow desert basin by the muster field, the Munitorum had assembled an armada of transportation vessels. Gunmetal grey, stamped with the Departmento sigil and attended by a flock of overseers, guards, codifiers and quartermasters, the ships were being prepped for immediate atmospheric embarkation. Unlike the Stormbirds, these vessels were not bound for fields of war. Not all of them, not yet.

They were vast, cyclopean things, far larger than the legionary drop-ships or the tank transporters utilised by the Army. Designated for recolonisation, Army recruitment and, in some instances, potential Legion candidacy, the fate of every Khar-tan man, woman and child would depend on how wholly they embraced their new masters. Certainly, none would return to Kharaatan again; only the manner of their departure and their onward destination were in question.

After several hours of slowly denuding the city of its occupants, two camps had begun to form comprised of Khartor's citizens: those who had fought alongside the xenos willingly and those who had fought against them. Establishing the guilt or innocence of either was taxing the Munitorum staff in the extreme, and herds of people were amassing in a sort of limbo between both whilst a more thorough assessment could be made. Pleas were made, bribes ignored under the watchful eye of Munitorum overseers, but one by one they were codified and hustled aboard ships.

It was tight. Between the sheer number of bodies, the pre-fab Munitorum herding stations, tanks and landers, there was little room to move or breathe. Processing was taking too long, but still more were fed into the codifying engine of the Departmento. Hundreds became thousands. Choke points began to form. Unrest developed, put down by vigilant discipline masters. Order held. Just.

Within the gaggle of Imperial servants, the Order of Remembrancers was also represented. Cataloguing, picting, scribing; some rendered the scene in art that would later be confiscated, others took personal testimony of the liberated where they could – this too would be redacted. No images or reports of the Crusade escaped into the wider Imperium without first being sanctioned. Capturing glory, the gravitas of the moment, that was the purpose of the remembrancers. Nothing more. Vulkan saw Seriph amongst the throng, carefully staying out of the way behind a squad of Utrich fusiliers.

Following his primarch's eye, Numeon asked, 'Isn't that your human biographer, my lord?'

'We parted poorly when we last met. Another effect of Curze's presence on me, I am ashamed to admit. I will redress that.' Vulkan started off towards the Munitorum encampment. Despite the cramped conditions, none stood in his way. 'Have the Legion ready to depart when I return,' he called to his equerry, who saluted behind him. 'I wish to linger here no longer than is necessary.'

'Yes, my lord,' Numeon replied, and in a lower voice added, 'You will find no argument here.'

Numeon's gaze strayed from his primarch to the edge of the camps where a squad of Night Lords looked on. Wisely, they had chosen to pitch their landers far from the Salamanders' muster field and were represented by a token force yet to join the others. There was no sign of Lord Curze.

The VIII legionaries mingled with the Munitorum officers, who gave every one of them a wide berth. This was also wise. Even with their skull-faced helmets concealing their expressions, Numeon could tell that the Night Lords were enjoying this petty act of intimidation. More than once, a legionary deliberately strayed needlessly close to the path of a busy clerk or scribe, forcing the poor individual to alter his course lest he be harassed or called to account under the glare of retinal lenses. The others not involved in these 'games' muttered snidely with one another at the obvious sport.

'They're goading us,' said Varrun, appearing quietly at Numeon's side with the rest of the Pyre Guard.

'Our primarch,' said Atanarius, noble chin lifted in the face of the VIII, 'how does he fare?'

Numeon answered honestly, 'The same as us. The Kharaatan compliance has left a bitter taste.'

'They revel in it,' offered Ganne, only half holding back a snarl.

'I would see the smirks wiped off their faces,' said Leodrakk, prompting a slow nod and muttered agreement from his brother, Skatar'var.

'Aye,' Varrun agreed. 'In the duelling cages, I would measure their true worth as warriors.'

Only Igataron said nothing, silently glowering at the Night Lords.

'They are still our brothers-in-arms,' Numeon reminded them. 'Our allies. Their cloth is not so different from ours.'

'It is of a darker hue,' snarled Ganne. 'We all saw the slain in Khartann City.'

Numeon gestured to the human rebels being herded slowly into the Munitorum's pens.

'And here, the very much alive citizens of Khartor. It is a fact difficult to ignore.'

No one spoke, but the heat of anger was palpable between them and directed at the VIII Legion.

The Night Lords were not just there to cajole, however. Their legionaries ringed a third, much smaller encampment. This one was a prison of enclosed ceramite, warded by no fewer than three Librarians. It surrounded the xenos overlords who had enslaved this world.

Khartor had been the greatest of Kharaatan's cities, its planetary capital. And it was here, when the Imperium returned with flame and retribution, that the aliens had chosen to make their lair. A coven of twelve had subverted the will of Kharaatan, a cautionary tale of the dangers of xenos collusion. Xenographers codified them: eldar. Long-limbed, almond-eyed and smouldering with arrogant fury, the XVIII knew this race well. They were not unlike the creatures they had fought on Ibsen, or the raiders that had once plagued

Nocturne for centuries before the coming of Vulkan. The Pyre Guard
were Terrans by birth, they had not experienced the terrors inflicted
on their primarch's home world, but shared his ire at the aliens in
spite of that.

The natives of Kharaatan had worshipped these witch-breeds as
gods, and would pay a price for that idolatry.

'What persuasion could the xenos have used to press an entire
population into service?' Numeon wondered aloud.

'Psychic subversion,' said Varrun. 'A trick to bend weak minds,
favoured by the witch. How many worlds have we seen undone,
thusly?'

Grunts of agreement from the other Pyre Guard met this procla-
mation from the veteran.

'I can think of one very recent in the memory,' uttered Ganne.

'The tribes of Ibsen were victims, not cohorts,' Numeon corrected
him.

'But how to choose which from which amongst this sorry lot?'
said Varrun, smoothing his ashen beard as if contemplating that
very conundrum.

Army troopers and Munitorum staff were thronging the camps
now as the citizens of Khartor were steadily divided. A sea of desert-
tan fatigues and grey Departmento-issue uniforms swept between
the Salamanders and the Night Lords, parting them. The legionaries could still see one another, as they towered above the humans,
their upper torsos, shoulders and heads still visible.

Numeon had seen and heard enough.

'Get to the ships and finish the muster. All shall be in readiness
for the primarch's return.'

The Pyre Guard were moving out when Numeon saw a flicker
of activity in the third camp enclosing the xenos. He was half-
turned when he noticed the flash of light in his peripheral vision,
harsh against the setting sun, that described the Night Lords in

monochrome. Suddenly, they were moving. Someone cried out
and fell, his voice too deep and vox-augmented to be human.

Another flash came swiftly. Lightning. And not a cloud in the sky.

'The psykers!' snapped Leodrakk.

A muzzle flare erupted, the deep, staccato report of a bolter echoing across the muster field and the encampments at the same time.
It traced a line through the masses, shredding blood and bone,
sundering flesh as the hail of shells reacted.

A second flare was born, chasing the quarry of the first. Then a
third and a fourth.

Numeon saw their prey, just as he saw the numerous Vodisian
troopers and Munitorum clerks destroyed as they fell beneath the
guns, collateral damage to the Night Lords' efforts at recapture.

The eldar were loose.

Somehow, they had slipped the psychic noose put about their
necks by the VIII Legion Librarians and were now running amok.

In the face of this unexpected carnage, panic swiftly followed. In
seconds, the close confines of the camps became a crush.

Khar-tans fled, leaping over the barriers intended to funnel them
towards their new lives, only to be gunned down as discipline masters shouted orders to open fire. Others fought, tearing at their new
oppressors with bare hands and teeth. Cudgels and shock mauls
were unsheathed. Some wept, the terror for them not yet over.
Many were trampled in the stampede, taking Imperial servants with
them. One clerk, slow to realise what was happening, disappeared
in a surging mass of shrieking Khar-tans. A trooper was knocked
aside accidentally, crushed against a ship's hull. Blood fountained
up its grey flank in an arterial spray.

'Into the crowd!' Numeon bellowed, leading the others in to
restore order.

Behind them, the rest of the Legion had begun to move.

'*Brother?*' It was Nemetor, hailing Numeon over the vox-link.

'Breach the Munitorum's cordon,' Numeon shouted. 'Get their pilots to move those ships. Tell them if they don't, their precious mortal cargo will be crushed to death.' He cut the link, letting Nemetor get to work.

The Pyre Guard formed up quickly into a spear shape, piercing the morass of bodies the Munitorum and Army seemed adamant would not spill out onto the desert.

'Break your ranks,' Numeon snarled at a Vodisian lieutenant, yanking the young officer off his feet.

His brothers did the same, ripping out the herding pens the Munitorum had put in place and relieving the pressure on the deadly crush that had begun to form.

'Arvek,' Numeon voxed, grunting as a Khar-tan man was floored as he bounced off the Pyre Guard's war-plate. Leodrakk hauled him to his feet, sending him on his way. 'Tell your men to break ranks.'

The Vodisian commander sounded fraught when he replied. '*Negative. We have the situation contained. None of these rebels will get past our cordon.*'

'That is the problem, commander. Kharaatan native and Imperial servant alike are being crushed in this chaos. Break your ranks.'

Upon seeing the commotion, Arvek had brought his armoured companies together, plugging gaps in the Munitorum's encampments, closing off escape, herding the frightened natives back onto themselves.

Officials farther back, confused by the commotion at first, had not realised what was happening and had continued to feed more natives into the grind. By the time they had taken stock of the situation, hundreds more had added to the pressure. Fearing for their lives when the crowd had realised their fate and their potential salvation, the Munitorum clerks had sealed the natives in behind a wall of tracked steel.

'*They will escape,*' Arvek countered, voice echoing in the confines of his Stormsword.

'And will you unleash your guns next if they try to scale your hull?' Numeon batted a discipline master aside with the back of his hand.

Together, the Pyre Guard had made a small vent. Their brothers in the XVIII were now working hard to widen it. People began to spill free – exhausted, bleeding, halfway dead. The presence of the Salamanders kept them rooted, however. None were willing to transgress and attempt escape with the red-eyed devils watching them.

But deeper into the camp, people were dying, smashed against the armoured prows of Vodisian tanks.

'*I will do what is necessary to maintain security.*' Arvek cut the feed.

'Bastard...' Numeon swore. A *discussion* with the commander would have to come later.

'It'll be a massacre...' said Varrun.

Numeon eyed the static Vodisian armour that had now engaged loudhailers and search lamps as additional deterrents. People staggered back into one another, blinded and deafened. Arvek was employing riot control tactics where the rioters had no room to back down.

'We need to move that armour.'

Through the thickening mob, it might as well have been leagues away.

Then Numeon saw the primarch, towering above the madness.

Realising the danger presented by the tanks, Vulkan had raced towards them. Not slowing, he shoulder-barged Arvek's Stormsword at full pelt and began to push.

Grimacing with effort, booted feet digging trenches in the earth, he heaved the super-heavy back. Its sheer bulk dwarfed the primarch, the veins cording in Vulkan's neck as he exercised his prodigious strength. Even Arvek dared not defy the will of a primarch and could only look on as Vulkan hauled the Stormsword's dead weight across the sand. He roared, body trembling as he forced a gap wide enough for the trapped masses to escape.

Without waiting to recover, Vulkan was moving again, fleeing Khar-tans flowing around him in a flood of mortal desperation. The primarch barged his way through them towards the escaped xenos, using his size and presence to make a path. He had yet to draw a weapon, instead focusing on cutting off the eldar as they sought to run into the desert.

No, Numeon realised as the Pyre Guard waded through the sea of bodies, still fighting to reassert some order; he was going for Seriph. Several of the remembrancers were already wounded, possibly dead. Abandoned by the Utrich fusiliers, they clung to each other, striving not to be dragged into the chaos, holding close to ride out the sudden storm.

Yelling Nostraman curses, the Night Lords closed on the xenos from behind, firing off their bolters indiscriminately in the hope of hitting an eldar.

Five of the witches were already down, one with a still-churning chainblade embedded in its chest. Another two threw up a kine-shield of verdigrised light to absorb the chasing bolt-rounds.

A hot shell grazed Vulkan's cheek, searing it as he was caught in the crossfire. Reaching the remembrancers, putting himself between them and the Night Lords' heedless fury, he raised his gauntlet.

Thanks in part to the VIII legionaries' bloody efforts but also because of the breach left by Arvek's forcibly reversed Stormsword, the area around the eldar had cleared. Staring down a primarch of the Emperor did not seem to give the xenos pause, but before they could cast their lightning arcs, Vulkan unleashed a storm of his own.

An inferno burst from his outstretched hand, the in-built flame units in his gauntlet reacting to their master's touch. What began as a plume of flame expanded quickly into a conflagration of super-hot promethium. The eldar were caught by it and engulfed, their bodies rendered in heat-hazed, brownish silhouettes as they shook inside the blaze. No kine-shield could save them; their robes and armour burned as one, fused to flesh until all was reduced to ash and charred bone.

Vulkan relented. The fire died and so too the riot, which was now being wrestled under control.

A single eldar witch remained, her face blackened by soot, her silver hair singed and burned. She looked up at the Lord of the Drakes, eyes watering, rage telegraphed in the tightness of her lips and the angle of her brow. The faltering kine-shield that had spared her life crackled and disappeared into ether.

She was not much older than a child, a witchling. Teeth clenched, fighting the grief at the death of her coven, the eldar offered up her wrists in surrender.

Numeon and the others had just breached the crowds, which were now slowly dissipating into the wider desert and being mopped up diligently by Nemetor and the rest of the Legion. In the wake of the fleeing civilians, the true cost of the eldar's escape attempt was revealed.

Men, women, children; Khar-tans and Imperials alike, lay dead. Crushed. Blood ran in red rivulets across the sand, the death toll in the hundreds.

Amongst them a solitary figure was conspicuous, crowded by a clutch of battered remembrancers unwilling to let anyone close, desperate to defend her unmoving body.

Vulkan saw her last of all, the shock of this discovery turning to anger on his noble face. His eyes blazed, embers flickered to infernos.

The eldar child raised her hands higher, defiance turning into fear upon her alien features.

Numeon held the others back, warning them with a look not to intervene.

Glaring down at her, Vulkan raised his fist...

Don't do it...

...and turned the air into fire.

The eldar child's screams didn't last. They merged with the roar of the flames, turning into one horrific cacophony of sound. When it was over and the last xenos was a smoking husk of burned meat, Vulkan looked up and met the gaze of the Night Lords.

The legionaries had stopped short when the flame-storm began. They stood and watched the primarch of the Salamanders at the edge of the scorched earth he had made. Then, without uttering a word, they turned and went to retrieve their wounded.

Ganne muttered something and made to go after them.

Numeon barred his path, his gauntlet clanking against Ganne's breastplate. 'No, go to the primarch,' he said to all of them. 'See him away from this place.'

Ganne backed down and the Pyre Guard went to their lord.

Only Numeon stayed behind, opening a channel over the vox to Nemetor.

'Prepare the primarch's transport. We're coming in,' he said, and cut the link.

VULKAN WAS STANDING over the lifeless body of Seriph. A stray bolt-round had grazed her side. It had been enough to kill her. There was a lot of blood – her robes were sodden with it; so, too, were the robes of the other remembrancers who had tried to save her.

Despite the primarch's presence, his obvious threat, the other remembrancers did not shrink away from Seriph's side.

An elderly man with rheumy eyes and wizened features gazed up at the Lord of the Drakes.

'We'll see her back to the ships,' he said.

Vulkan opened his mouth to say something, but could find no words to express his feelings. Instead, he nodded before replacing his helmet, but found it could not hide his shame as well as it could his face. Turning, he became aware of his warriors gathering next to him.

'The Legion awaits you, my lord,' said Varrun humbly, and gave a slight bow of his head.

About to respond, Vulkan stopped short when he felt someone watching him from afar. Looking around, he caught sight of a dark and distant shadow out on the dunes. A second later and his helmet vox crackled to life.

'*See brother, I knew you had it in you. A cold-hearted killer, just like me.*'

Vulkan replied, 'I am nothing like you', and severed the link, yet the stench of burning alien flesh remained.

CHAPTER ELEVEN
Mortal pillars

'To be more than human is; at the same time, to be less than human. Within us is the capacity for greatness. We are warriors, but we must also be saviours. Our ultimate goal is self-obsoletion, for when our task is successful and peace, not war, reigns in the galaxy, our usefulness will be ended and with it us too.'

– Vulkan, from the *Trials of Fire*

THE DREAM ENDED and I shuddered myself awake.

Curze's last words on the outskirts of Khartor had unsettled me and forced me to look within myself for evidence of the monster he claimed me to be. They echoed in my skull like old bones, unearthed from an old grave thought long forgotten.

The past will always come back. It never truly stays dead.

The first thing I realised upon opening my eyes was that this was not my cell.

The chamber was small, and yet expansive at the same time. Its walls were white, glowing, smooth like bone. I heard voices within them, and as I strained my eyes saw tiny circuits of light rushing like shoals of minnows with the river's flow.

There was no smell, no taste. As I moved, rising to my feet, I made
no sound. I could detect no air and yet I still breathed, my lungs
functioning as they always had. Evidence of my previous tortures
could not be seen, my body as unblemished and bereft of scars as
when I had first arrived on Nocturne.

'What is this place?' My voice echoed as I asked the question of
the figure standing opposite me.

Its face was hooded, and the rest of its body draped in robes, but
I could tell immediately that it wasn't human. Too tall, too slight. I
knew an eldar when I saw one. This one was a farseer.

'Nowhere of consequence, a meeting place is all,' he said in a low,
mellifluous voice.

'You speak Gothic?' I asked, though he had just given me the
answer to that question.

The eldar nodded.

He wore black, with strange sigils and eldritch runes stitched into
the slightly iridescent cloth. A weeping eye, a pyramid, a pair of
bisected squares rendered into an angular figure of eight – I could
not read them but suspected they were symbols of the farseer's
power and even origin. Though his face was concealed by the
hood, and perhaps an even more effective and unnatural concealment, the edges of his aquiline features were suggested where the
shadows lessened.

In his right hand, which was hidden beneath a black glove, he
clutched a staff. Like the runes described on his robes, the figure's
staff was fashioned from the same strange bone-like material forming the chamber. Its peak was a simple eye and teardrop design.

I believed that this too was a glamour, in the same way that the
eldar had masked his true appearance from me.

'You are dreaming, Vulkan,' he said, not stepping towards me,
not moving at all, not even breathing. 'That isn't air you are taking

into your lungs. That isn't light making your pupils retract. You are not really here.'

'Who are you?' I demand, angry at being manipulated by this psychic passenger.

'It doesn't matter. None of this is real, but what is very real is what I am about to impart to you. The very fact you have not chosen to attack me suggests I chose wisely.'

'You make it sound like you've tried this before,' I said.

'Not I, one of my kindred. Despite my warning not to, he proceeded anyway.' There was resignation in the eldar's voice, changing its melodic tone into something approaching regret. 'It went poorly, I'm afraid, and so we are here. You and I.'

My eyes narrowed, the words of the alien coiling in my mind, unfathomable and deliberately obscure.

'Are you a spirit, a wraith followed me from Kharaatan?'

I sensed the ghost of a smile in my strange companion's reply.

'Something like that, but not from Kharaatan. Ulthwé.'

'What? Why am I here?'

'It's not important, Vulkan. What is important are my words, and the matter of earth.'

'The matter of earth?'

'Yes. It is tied inextricably to your fate. You see, I needed to speak to you. While you were still able to heed me, before you were lost.'

'Lost? I am already lost. A prisoner aboard my brother's ship, at least...' I looked down at my bare feet, 'I *think* I am.'

'Are your thoughts so confused already?'

Looking up again, the eldar had drawn closer to me. His eyes, oval and lambent with power, bored into me.

'I saw you, didn't I?' I asked. 'On the ship, before I realised where I was.'

'I tried to make contact before, but your mind was reeling, overcome with rage and a desire for freedom. You were also not long recovered.'

'Recovered from what?'

'As I say, it is the matter of earth upon which I must speak to you.'

'You're making no sense, *creature.*'

'This might be the only chance I get to contact you. After this, I may not be able to return. You must *live*, Vulkan,' the alien told me, 'you must live, but stand alone as a gatekeeper. You are the only one who can perform this duty. You alone are the hope.'

I frowned as the words spilling from this alien's lips made less and less sense to me. I shook my head, believing it to be another trick of my gaoler, albeit an extremely elaborate one.

'My duty? A gatekeeper? This is meaningless.' As a cloud creeps over the sun, my face darkened and I made fists of my hands.

Sensing anger, the farseer retreated back into the light.

'It is not a trick. I speak the truth, Vulkan.'

I grabbed for him, trying to snatch the edge of his robes and shake this illusion to dust, but there was nothing to hold on to.

'When the time comes...' uttered the eldar, his voice and form becoming one with the light as the entire chamber brightened like a sun, 'you will know what you must do.'

Falling to my knees, I roared, 'Get out of my head!'

Pressing the palms of my hands against my temples, I tried in vain to push the interloper out and return myself to reality.

'No more,' I cried, shutting my eyes to the light as it burned them. 'No more!'

'NO MORE...' I WHISPERED.

The light had gone. The chamber, the alien, everything. Gone.

Reality reasserted itself, and, as I opened my eyes again, for real this time, I saw it was made of dirty stone and dark iron.

I was standing, the chains around my wrists taut as they took my weight. On my forearm a fresh mark was branded into my flesh. Like the others I had noticed, I couldn't place its origin. The mystery of it would have to wait. Cruciform, I stared out into a different prison. Not the bottomless oubliette from before or even the furnace where Curze had tried to burn me to ash as I had burned the eldar on Kharaatan. This place was new, and yet entirely old.

A long hall stretched in front of me. Embedded in either flanking wall were mechanisms of an esoteric design – great gears and cogs fashioned alongside smaller and more intricate servos. Antiquity met modernity and became a fusion of genius so prevalent in the tech-craft of old Firenza.

Perturabo's work. I knew it instantly.

Flagstones had been laid along the floor. They were grimy and slick. I suspected that whatever this room's intended purpose was, Curze had thoroughly tested it before my incarceration. The stone was but a veneer, a grubby falsehood to give this hole a darker, more medieval atmosphere. Sconces set into alcoves along the flanking walls flickered with the torches within. To the naked eye they appeared to be wood, but this too was a lie. They were springs and clockwork, just like every other half-shrouded machine in this dungeon.

The change in surroundings was not the only thing that differed about this particular cell.

Unlike before, this time I was not alone.

At the opposite end of the long hall, huddled together and barred from me by a screen of dirty armourglass, were human captives.

In the gloom I saw Army uniforms, civilian trappings. Men and women both. I was not Curze's only prisoner in this place and as an unpleasant sensation arose in my gut, a voice uttered beside me, 'You can see them, but they cannot see you.'

I scowled. 'Aren't you supposed to be dead?'

Ferrus chuckled – it was an ugly sound – his ghoulish eyes fixed on the other prisoners.

He extended a bony finger; part of his gauntlet had rusted. Even the miraculous living metal that once coated his arms and hands had sloughed away.

'Their fate,' he croaked, jabbing the skeletal digit in the direction of the human prisoners, 'lies in your hands.'

A dull *clunk* of metal heard from somewhere deep within the chamber's unseen artifice heralded the first motion of the machinery embedded in the walls. One of the larger gears creaked, overcoming inertia, and started to move. Others followed, their teeth interlocking, an engine noisily cranking into life before my eyes.

With the action of the gears, the servos started up, too. Pistons exerted pressure as they expanded pneumatically with an unseen hiss of compressed air. Vents opened, momentum built. The exposed clockwork churned and finally there came a louder, heavier *clank* of metal as some mechanism I could not see disengaged.

Immediately, a savage strain was placed upon my arms as the chains retracted violently into recesses in the walls on either side of me.

I grunted in pain, but my eyes snapped forwards when I heard the cry of terror from the other cell. The prisoners were looking up. Some of the men had got to their feet as the ceiling came down at them. Too heavy for them to bear, the brave men who had stood up were quickly crushed to their knees.

A child screamed. *A child. In here.*

Above the ceiling line, hidden from the eyes of the other prisoners but clear to me through the dirty glassaic, was an immense weight. And as the chains pulled at my arms, I realised to what they were both attached.

Despite the agony it caused, I heaved and pulled the chains back in.

In the other cell, the ceiling stopped falling.

'As I said,' uttered Ferrus, 'their fate lies in your hands. Quite literally, brother.'

I held on, the muscles in my neck, back, shoulders and arms screaming at me to let go. My teeth were locked together in a grimace of defiance. Sweat drenched my body and trickled through the channels of my bunched muscles.

I screamed and the people who neither saw nor heard me screamed as well. My grip was slipping; the ceiling and the weight bearing down to crush the others was slipping too.

More of the prisoners got to their feet and tried to push back. Their efforts were utterly futile, no strength they possessed would prevail. Through the red rime clouding my vision as capillaries burst in my now bloodshot eyes, I saw those too weak or injured to stand wailing at their fate. Others trembled or clung to each other in the desperate need not to die alone.

One sat by himself. He was calm, accepting of his inevitable death. Though it was hard to tell, I thought I recognised him. I could not be certain but he resembled the remembrancer, Verace. And it appeared as if he were looking at me.

The terrible strain came on anew as the machine exerted even greater pressure.

Legs braced, arms locked, I closed my eyes and held on.

I stayed like that for hours, or so it seemed, my world a prison of constant pain and the plaintive mewling of the men and women I knew I could not save.

When finally it came, the silence was both sweet and bitter.

I was screaming, spitting defiance, half delirious from what I'd been forced to endure.

'I will not yield,' I roared. 'I will never yield to you, Curze! Show yourself, stop hiding behind your victims.'

'Surrender, Vulkan,' Ferrus answered. 'Let go. You can achieve nothing here. There is no victory to be had. Let go.'

'Not while there is still strength...'

I stopped, realising that I was the only one screaming. The

prisoners in the other cell, their voices were silent. Opening my eyes, I saw what had ended their pleas. Through the glass a solid slab of dark iron had filled the cell completely.

I sagged against my bonds, arms upright, my legs buckling beneath me as the last of my strength ebbed from my body.

'Where are they?' I asked the apparition beside me, despite the fact I knew he was only a figment of my imagination.

'Look...' said Ferrus, a rictus grin enhancing his ghastly features. With each fresh visitation he was becoming more emaciated, more skeletal, as if decaying in my mind's eye.

Gears churning again, the iron slab slowly rose. It had but to creep a few centimetres before I saw the visceral red that adhered to its underside. Strands of it clung to the deadly weight, stretching and splitting as gravity exerted itself. Fragments of bone and biological matter came unstuck with the resonance fed through the slab by the machine lifting it. They splashed into a lagoon of guts and blood covering the cell floor.

As the chains slackened, my arms fell too, and I with them onto the ground, my face landing hard in the dirt.

Ferrus chuckled, his voice a little reminiscent of Curze, before he sank back into the shadows and left me to my failure and guilt.

CHAPTER TWELVE

Fulgurite

THE EXCAVATION SITE had become a pit for ritual sacrifice. A fresh crop of less than willing supplicants brought from the other districts of Ranos surrounded it on their knees, staring into blood-soaked darkness.

As soon as he had first descended into the pit, Elias had felt the significance of this place. A temple to the Pantheon, raised on blessed stone, fashioned into the holy octed.

Eight walls for the eightfold path; eight temple cities erected around the globe.

'Eight times eight,' muttered the Dark Apostle, revelling in the divine provenance of it all.

Elias looked down upon his fell works from a pulpit wrought from piled stone. Black robes entwined with the scripture of his lord and primarch overlaid his war-plate, and he had removed his battle-helm so all could see the mark of the faithful upon his patrician face.

Sixty-four men and women knelt before and below him, their faces pressed to the earth. Some wept or shook, others did nothing but stare as if they had perceived their ending and knew there was no averting it.

Behind them, clad in crimson war-plate, were the legionaries of the XVII. They had borne the Word, and the Word was *sacrifice*.

Not their blood, but the blood of Ranos and all Traoris when Elias's ritual was fulfilled.

He muttered incantations, invoking the Pantheon, entreating the Neverborn, guiding them with the bright soul-fires of the cattle he was about to harvest. The Word ran thick and heady from his mouth, uttered in ancient Colchisian, every syllable an affirmation to Chaos.

As the eighth verse began and the shaking supplicants trembled in ever greater fear and fervour, spittle flecking from their lips, tears of blood streaming down their cheeks, limbs jerking in spastic tremors, the legionaries took up the chant. As one they unsheathed their blades, one each for the souls about to be cast unto the aether.

Below them, the abyssal shaft yawned. Above, the sky crackled with hellish energy. A metaphysical event was taking place, a cosmological alteration that had much in common with the Ruinstorm, albeit on a much smaller level. Darkness clung to this place, tendrils of it were returning as the ritual advanced in potency. They had only to extinguish the remaining light to bring the night forth.

Here was the Emperor's power, Elias reminded himself. Here, *he*, Valdrekk Elias, would see it broken and supplanted. The fabric of reality was diminishing, like a film of skin stretched over a skeleton too large for it. Patches of it were thinning, allowing the light – and what was drawn to that light – to peer through.

As he spoke, he reached up with his dagger, his words echoing below through his disciples, and could almost *touch* the beyond...

It had visited Dagon, Amaresh, Argel Tal... Even Narek possessed some measure of its influence, regardless of his denial. Now, Elias would receive its boon for loyal and faithful servitude. It was his due. Erebus had promised it.

The eighth verse drew to a close and Elias brought his gaze

downwards towards the pit and the mewling creature clenched firmly in his grasp.

Eight times eight blades were touched to eight times eight throats. The cut was made in unison, the robed disciples acting on their master's signal as the last words were spoken and sacrificial blood was released, for the glory and sustenance of the Pantheon.

NAREK SAW THE storm several kilometres out. He and Dagon were travelling apart, so if one was discovered the other could better effect escape or counter-attack.

It troubled him, the storm. Narek could see it even above the tallest smoke stacks, billowing in clouds of eldritch lightning. He hoped that Elias knew what he was doing. As he picked his way through the deserted streets, he could imagine Dagon's beseechments and zealous babbling. He was spared that trial on account of the fact that, without his battle-helm, Dagon was no longer linked to him by vox.

'We were once warriors,' he said to the lonely wind, swearing there were voices trapped in it. 'When did we become fanatics?' Phantom pain in his missing leg throbbed and he clutched the bionic that had replaced it, feeling only cold metal and the touch of flesh no longer.

His lip was curling with displeasure when he felt something warming his side. His retinal display had triggered no alarms concerning his suit's efficacy, so Narek assumed that it was undamaged. When he looked down, he found that the source of the heat was his scabbard. For a moment he forgot that he had replaced his gladius, and wondered what the object was that glowed faintly within it.

The fulgurite. The lightning spear.

Narek stopped, gazing in sudden wonder at the sublime artefact in his possession. He hesitated to draw it, and found his hand trembling as he reached to do so.

'*Godlike…*' he whispered, repeating the same word he had used to describe it to Elias.

Finding his resolve, he clutched the haft of the spear and was about to draw it when Dagon's voice interrupted him.

'Brother,' Dagon called to him, 'why have you stopped? Are you injured?'

Narek released the haft at once, only half turning towards Dagon and clutching his leg.

'Old wounds, slowing an old soldier,' he lied.

Dagon approached, only a few metres away when he had called out, and gestured towards the storm. 'I can feel it, brother.'

Narek's eyes narrowed behind his faceplate. 'Feel what?'

'The touch of the Neverborn, the whispered promise of the Pantheon...'

Narek recalled the voices and realised they were no trick of the wind. Elias was literally *reshaping* reality, bending it to his will in his attempt to fashion something akin to a gate. Narek wondered briefly if, when that gate was opened, what was on the other side would recognise friend from food.

'You are more gifted than I, Dagon,' he replied, though he felt the ripple of the warp's presence under his flesh, just as he always had. It was an itch, a reminder of what they had all given up in pursuit of so-called 'truth'.

Dagon clapped Narek on the shoulder, drawing an unseen snarl from the veteran huntsman.

'We shall all be beneficiaries of the Gods' boons when this night is done,' he smiled and walked on ahead. 'I will take point, brother. Rest your leg, knowing your spirit will soon be nourished.'

My spirit is likely to be nourishment, not nourished, thought Narek.

Glancing at the spear one more time, he waited for Dagon to be lost from sight and followed in silence. The warmth at his side did not abate, but throbbed, reminding him of his every doubt.

✠ ✠ ✠

THEIR NUMBERS HAD swelled since they had first made planetfall. Almost a hundred legionaries and twice that amount in simpering cultists were arrayed before the great ritual pit where Elias sermonised and proselytised. His bombastic doggerel did little to move Narek, who had been last to join the gathering, having followed on behind Dagon, who had already taken his place with the devout.

Offered robe and cowl by a mortal wearing a graven mask and attired in the same priestly vestments, Narek found his place amongst the throng. He watched in mute fascination and revulsion as Elias preached his dogma from on high, standing aloft like a deacon of old Colchis. Narek thought him a petty demagogue, bereft of honour or true purpose. He was Erebus's puppet, but then Narek supposed that only made him Elias's hound.

A life given for a life spared, he reminded himself, and barely noticed the humans with their throats slit, cascading into the dark abattoir that awaited their flesh. Their souls… Well, that was another matter.

Many more cattle trembled in their pens, awaiting execution by Elias's 'divine' hand. The efforts of the other legionaries had yielded a ripe harvest. Narek could smell the mortals' fear, just as he could detect the Dark Apostle's greed and ambition. Both sickened him.

On Monarchia, they had erected monuments, great citadels of worship. It was worthy endeavour – it was refulgent and glorious. This was grubby and base. The XVII had sunk low, squirming on their bellies, not much better than the vermin they preyed upon. Yet, he could not deny the sense of power. They all felt it, the warriors of the Legion, the cultists, the other humans in their thrall. It was potent and it was also imminent.

The ritual ended. Elias descended from his pulpit, a prophet to his devoted following, his communion with the Gods over for now.

'Narek,' Elias said, his eyes finding the huntsman in the throng, warriors parting with muttered benediction as he approached him through the crowd. 'Do you have it?' he asked, eyes still bright from the borrowed power he had siphoned through the ritual.

Narek nodded, fighting a sudden reluctance to relinquish his hold upon the spear.

'Come,' Elias beckoned, keen to be away from the others when presented with his prize.

A small encampment had been established in close vicinity to the pit; tents, a shrine at which to worship, flesh-pens to harness the cattle. Elias had deemed it necessary to erect a commune. Narek joined him inside one of the tents. After dismissing a pair of hooded cultists, they were alone.

'It smacks of more permanence than I thought was needed for this,' said Narek, indicating the encampment.

'Blood begets blood, brother, but much must be spilled in order to taint this place.'

'And is there enough, amongst your cattle and your slaves?'

Elias scowled, unused to being questioned by his disciples in such a manner.

'What concern has that ever been of yours, Narek? You are a soldier, are you not? A warrior-zealot, devoted to the Word. *I* am the Word in this place, so your fealty is to me. Is it not?'

The mood had soured quickly, Elias brought down from his euphoria to the canker of mistrust and doubt.

'I serve you as always, Dark Apostle.' Wisely, Narek bowed.

A small dark bowl at the back of the canvas chamber was put there for Elias's ablutions after spilling sacrificial blood. He went over to it now and began cleansing his hands so that he could begin the next octed circle unsullied by the previous one.

He didn't have an accurate count, but Narek estimated several hundred mortals awaiting slaughter in the pens. Hemmed in by sharp stakes and spools of razor-wire, they reminded the huntsman of wide-eyed swine fearful of the culling to come.

'Pure, it must be pure, Narek,' Elias muttered, his back to the huntsman. 'Now,' he added, fastidiously cleaning his fingertips, fingers, palms and knuckles, 'I would see the weapon.'

Shaking off his hands, drying them on a cloth, Elias turned with hands open and ready to receive.

Narek gave a second's pause, not so much to make the Dark Apostle concerned but enough to realise he resented giving up the spear. Fluidly, he drew it from his scabbard and watched Elias's eyes widen at the sight of it.

'Godlike,' he breathed – *that word again* – 'you were not exaggerating.'

Narek placed it reverently in Elias's hands, where he could examine it more closely.

'So this is what they withdrew from the ruins?' He exhaled, his craving for the power contained within this shard self-evident. 'I can sense its strength.'

'It is divine...' murmured Narek, briefly forgetting where he was and who he was with.

Elias looked up sharply. 'The *Pantheon* is divine – this is but a means through which to manifest their beneficence. I must profane it, curb its strength to my own ends.'

'*Your* ends?' asked Narek when Elias had returned his gaze to the spear again.

'Indeed.'

So, that was it. The Dark Apostle meant to try and yoke the spear's captured power for himself, either as a way to enhance his standing with Lord Erebus or perhaps even to usurp him. Elias *was* certainly ambitious, but that was bold even for him.

'Are you intending to harness it then?' Narek asked, choosing to leave his suspicions unspoken.

Elias regarded him sternly again.

'You are... overcurious, Narek.' His eyes narrowed. 'Is something amiss?'

'I...' Narek began. 'It *is* divine, this thing.' He gestured to the spear, eyes drawn to its fulgurant glow which even now threw back the shadows inside the tent. 'Does it not make you...'

Elias had not lowered his gaze, and listened intently to his huntsman.

'Make me what, Narek?'

'*Question*.' He barely whispered it, for fear that to speak it aloud was part of some blasphemy.

'You have doubts?'

'I am merely seeing what is in front of my eyes. Here, in your hands, lies a piece of the Emperor's will. It is lightning, cast from His fingertips and forged into a weapon.'

Elias was nodding. 'Indeed it is a weapon, one I mean to wield. I see now that was Lord Erebus's plan for us all along.'

'When we raised those cathedrals to His honour and glory, all the years we spent extolling His holy church and divine right to rule mankind, did you think we served the needs of a false prophet?' Narek asked. 'I am talking about faith, Elias.'

'*He* has denied it, denied our worship and faith. *He* spits on us, and in so doing are the *true* gods of the universe revealed unto us. And your words border dangerously close to sedition, not revelation.'

'The revelation is before us, brother. The Gal Vorbak, they are men no longer–'

'They ascend!'

'No! They merely harbour sustenance for the monsters dwelling within and wearing their flesh.'

'I would welcome such a union, to be so blessed. This here,' he brandished the spear like he was considering stabbing it into Narek's heart, 'is my path to that glory.'

'I see only damnation, but I am bound to it, as are you. And don't threaten me with sedition. Your words smack more thickly of betrayal than mine.'

Elias, realising he had revealed too much of his ambition, backed down.

'It is… a *suggestion*, nothing more than that.'

'To do what, exactly?'

'Elevate us, you and I, Narek,' he said, his voice low enough to be mistaken for a conspiratorial whisper. 'Erebus spoke of it. Weapons to win the war. This is clearly what he meant, and it obviously has power. I merely need to harness it.'

'You can do that?'

Elias mistook Narek's incredulity for eagerness.

'Yes, brother,' he hissed. 'You will be restored, better than you were before. I…' He smiled a viper's smile. 'I will have what I've always sought, a patron in the Pantheon.'

Smile widening into a feral grin, he waited for Narek to see this vision as he did.

He was to be disappointed.

'You invite destruction upon yourself, Elias.'

And like the viper that is suddenly threatened and prepares to fight back, Elias recoiled. 'Remember the debt you owe to me, Narek,' he warned, appealing to the huntsman's sense of honour.

'Like I say, I am bound to this fate as I am bound to you. Do not worry, I have no urge to enhance my own standing. I merely wish to fight and die in this war. But by turning a blind eye, my debt is paid in full. Are we in agreement?' Narek held out his hand for Elias to take it.

Instead, the Dark Apostle merely nodded.

'Good,' said Narek. 'Once this is done, you and I will part company, our alliance ended.'

'Agreed,' said Elias, 'which leaves from now until then.'

'The shattered legionaries have amassed to disrupt our plans here. The human with them is very likely dead, shot by Dagon's deflected bullet, so they'll be coming, one way or another.'

'You need men?' asked Elias.

'All hand-picked by me. No hoods.' He referred to the cultists. 'Legion only. Seven will suffice.'

'Including yourself, an auspicious number.'

'Not really. I need twenty others, two more squads. Whoever you can spare from the rituals. That's how many I will need to stop them. And by stop them, I mean kill every one of our enemies.'

Elias smirked at him, as if amused by his soldier's rhetoric, and turned away dismissively.

'Take what you need from the ranks, including your seven. Get it done.'

'This is my last hunt, Elias,' Narek warned.

'I really think it might be, brother,' Elias replied, but when he turned around he was alone.

Narek had gone.

CHAPTER THIRTEEN
Ritual

THE WHITE-TILED FLOOR was steadily turning to grey with the accreted grime of neglect. It was also covered in blood. They had moved him from the factory to an infirmary. Presumably, it had been used to tend the injuries of machine workers sustained through accident or misadventure. It was a modest size, and modestly stocked. A work bench served as an operating table. The drug cabinet had been raided, but there were bandages and gauze left behind.

Shen'ra was using them to try and staunch the bleeding.

The man, Grammaticus, if that identity was to be believed, had fared poorly during the rapid relocation to this secondary hideout. Despite Leodrakk's protestations and even Domadus's murmured counsel that to put him out of his misery was not only the logical thing to do but also the most humane, Numeon had insisted Grammaticus be taken with them.

Helon, Uzak and Shaka had come as well. Their bodies, anyway.

Leodrakk would not leave them, nor would Avus, who had shouldered the burden of his Legion brother all the way from the printing house. The Raven Guard had refused all offers of help, even from

Hriak, who was a distant figure to Avus, anyway. Helon and Uzak had many volunteers to bear them and were dragged hurriedly between two of the fire-born.

Numeon had carried the human, allowing Pergellen to lead the company in his stead.

'I am not Helon, I am no Apothecary,' Shen'ra griped, up to his vambraces in gore.

'Nor was Helon, brother,' said Numeon, looking askance at the pyre his brothers had erected outside on the factory floor. 'He adapted, as we all must.'

'Life signs are beyond faint. He barely draws breath,' said the Techmarine. 'If he were a servitor, I would see his parts rendered down for scrap. That is what remains now.'

'But he is flesh,' insisted Numeon. 'And I would see him restored if it is within your considerable abilities, brother.'

'Faint praise will not alter the course of events here,' Shen'ra reminded the captain.

'Just do your best,' said Numeon and left the Techmarine to grumble in peace.

Leodrakk was waiting outside.

'He fades?' he asked.

'Was it etched upon my face?'

'Actually, yes. Coupled with the fact that when he went in there, the human was almost cut in half by that deflected shell.'

'Prognosis is bleak,' muttered Numeon, starting to walk. 'Even if Helon had lived…' His eyes strayed to the pyre. 'I doubt we would have had any better chance of saving the human.'

'Is it wise?' asked Leodrakk, following his captain's gaze. 'The smoke may signal to our enemies.'

'We aren't staying for long,' said Numeon, 'and, besides, there are fires burning throughout the city. How could they tell one from another?'

Leodrakk agreed, before his expression darkened.

'May I speak my mind?' he asked, walking in lockstep with his captain.

'I suspect you would anyway.'

Leodrakk didn't bite, his thoughts were elsewhere. At a belated nod from Numeon, he gave voice to them.

'Is he really that important? The human – this *Grammaticus*, or so he claims.'

'I would dearly like the answer to that question, but unless he pulls through I fear we will never have it.'

'I don't understand, why does this mortal possess such meaning to you?'

'I don't know. I feel something...' Numeon pressed his hand to his stomach, 'in my gut. An instinct.'

'A belief?' Leodrakk assumed.

Numeon met his questioning look with one of determination. 'Yes. The same belief. That Vulkan lives and this man, however insignificant, seems to know something of that.'

Leodrakk scowled. 'What?'

'He told me Vulkan is alive.'

'Where? On Isstvan?' Something as dangerous as hope affected Leodrakk's tone.

'He didn't say. Or at least, I have not had a chance to ask him yet.'

The other Salamander's mood rapidly soured. 'And when did he say this?'

'During interrogation, after you left.'

'You cannot believe this,' he scoffed, disbelief obvious on his face.

Numeon remained sincere. 'I do,' he said, with certainty.

Leodrakk was unconvinced. 'An act of desperation, brother.'

'I thought so too, at first, and dismissed it, but I went over his saying it again and again. I can tell a lie from truth, Leo. Humans in the presence of legionaries tend not to be very good at it.'

'Then he is a rare breed, this Grammaticus. He's probably had training. It doesn't make what he said true.'

'Then why say it? Why *that*, specifically? I went over it in my head and could find no legitimate reason for the nature of this lie. A dozen other stories would have been more effective for any other legionary, but he chose *specifically* to tell me this, as if he knew it was what I, and only I, would want to hear.'

'Then there is your answer. He's a psyker. Even we can be read by telepaths. Evidently he's a powerful one.'

'Hriak was there throughout. If my thoughts were being read, he would have known. So I ask, how?'

'I don't know. But does it matter? I know you haven't forgotten what happened at the dropsite – our brothers were lost. The only survivors are those warriors who boarded ships. I saw Vulkan engulfed in conflagration. It killed Ska, and it most likely killed the rest of our kin too. This mortal knows he is in trouble. Likely he is from one of the cults, a defector or a supplicant. He wanted to spare his life. He would've said anything to keep us from silencing him.'

'Is that what we are now? Murderers?'

'We're warriors, Artellus. You and I, peerless amongst them. But we are not a Legion, not any more, and we do what we must to survive, for our own protection.'

'But to what end,' Numeon urged him, 'if there is no hope?'

'To the only end left to us, brother. *Vengeance.*'

'No. I have to believe there is more than that. I *do* believe it.'

Leodrakk smiled, but his mood was melancholy.

'You always were the most devoted of us. I think that's why he made you captain, Artellus. It's your spirit. It never falters.'

Further debate would have to wait for another time. They had reached the edge of the pyre where the rest of the company, barring Hriak, Pergellen and Shen'ra, had gathered in a broken circle.

Numeon was left alone to ponder Leodrakk's parting words as the other Salamander took his place in another part of the circle. But he was unconvinced by any of the arguments he had heard, and hoped the human would survive, so he could understand the full truth of what Grammaticus knew. With K'gosi igniting a torch with the dulled fire of his flame gauntlet, thoughts turned to the imminent cremation.

Not only Uzak and Helon, but Shaka also lay in silent repose at the summit of the pyre. All would burn, die the warrior's death. For the sons of Corax, tradition demanded they be divested of all trappings and left for the birds to pick clean, but tradition was in short supply and fire was readily available. An even compromise was reached, so all three would become ash together.

As K'gosi knelt down to light the base of the pyre, he began to incant words of Promethean ritual as described by Vulkan in the earliest days and adopted from the first tribal kings of Nocturne. This recitation spoke of ending and the return to the earth, of the circle of fire and the belief of all Nocturne-born Salamanders in resurrection and reincarnation.

The mood was sombre, heads were bowed throughout, helmets clasped under arms, the eyes of the sons of Vulkan burning with sober intensity.

As the fire grew, quickly burning through pallet stacks, wooden beams and broken furniture the company had scavenged for the rite, so too did K'gosi's voice grow louder and more vehement. The final verses were spoken by the throng and interspersed with words spoken by Avus alone, of the raven taking flight and the great sky death that was the sacred right of all Corax's sons.

The blaze swallowed the warriors swiftly, burning hungrily through the gaps in their armour, made all the more intense by the measure of promethium dousing the pyre before it was lit. This was a sacrifice – it would mean K'gosi and the other Pyroclasts would have to share the remaining ammunition, but all deemed it a worthy cause.

Until the moment when the ritual was ended, Domadus stood

apart from the circle and looked on stoically. When there began talk of bonds deeper than blood, forged through mutual suffering and the shared desire for retribution, then he rejoined them.

The pyre shifted and cracked, fell apart under the weight of the armour at its summit and the wood slowly disintegrating beneath. A few seconds later it collapsed in a flurry of scattered sparks, the flames flickering dulcetly as a narrow pall of smoke rose into the air above. Ash was falling, and it covered all the legionaries on the factory floor in a fine, grey veneer like a funerary shroud.

'And so it is done,' intoned K'gosi and a moment of silent reflection prevailed.

It was broken by Shen'ra emerging from the infirmary. The Techmarine looked less like he had been operating and more like he had been in battle. Both, in fact, were true.

From his place in the circle, Numeon turned, his eyes intense and pressing for an answer.

Shen'ra gave him one, solemnly.

'He's dead. The human didn't make it.'

THE LOW THWOMP of turbine engines on minimum rotation provided a balm to Narek's troubled thoughts. He was crouching in the troop hold of a Thunderhawk, leaning from one of its open side hatches and surveying Ranos through a pair of magnoculars. Two other gunships followed behind, similarly quietened.

'Any sign?' grated Amaresh. The Word Bearer sat with his long flensing blade in his lap, sharpening the edge.

He was a beast, Amaresh, literally, with those horns sprouting from his skull and through his battle-helm. One of the touched. An *Unburdened* in the making.

'Many,' Narek replied, lowering the scopes to signal to Dagon, who was leaning out the opposite side of the transport, looking through his rifle's targeter.

The other hunter slowly shook his head.

'Any of our quarry?' Amaresh pressed, annoyed at Narek's little games.

'I have their trail. It won't be long now.' He voxed fresh coordinates to their pilot and there was a slight change in engine pitch as the Thunderhawk shifted course.

Narek had taken the gunship along with the men.

Amaresh, Narlech, Vogel and Saarsk were all brutal warriors, bladesmen every one of them. Some had fought in the pits with the XII, locked swords with the likes of Kargos and Delvarus. That left Dagon, Melach and Infrik as snipers, along with himself. Infrik had cut out his own tongue, convinced it was babbling dark secrets to him in the night hours and during battle; whereas Melach found speech difficult with the growth of skin colonising his neck, slowly hardening to a brownish carapace, so said little.

The rest, those following in the other two gunships, were less significant to Narek's plans.

He knew that they were unbalanced individuals, the seven he had chosen, but mental stability wasn't amongst his criteria for selecting them. He wanted killers, specifically warriors who had slain other legionaries. The tally between this particular group was in the hundreds. That made them uniquely suitable for this mission.

With the exception of Dagon, whom he could tolerate, Narek hated every one of these bastards. Elias had cultivated a crop of dishonourable, wretched legionaries. Gone were days of righteous purpose and holy service. This slow mutation into devilry and aberration was all that was left now.

Narek meant to extricate himself from that as soon as he was done with this mission. Never once, not even when his leg was in bloody tatters, had he reneged on an oath. That was not about to change now.

As he hung on to the guide rail inside the hold, leaning out a little farther and allowing the wind whipping past to buffet him and howl around his battle-helm, he found that he missed the presence of the fulgurite and wondered just how the Dark Apostle would subvert its power.

Where once there was warmth at his side, a reminder of the existence of the divine, now there was only cold. Narek could feel it creeping further into his body, attaching its talons around his soul. And yet, so far he had resisted damnation.

Something on the darkened skyline got his attention and he quickly went back to the scopes for a better look.

'There,' he said, pointing.

Vogel got up and went to stand beside him. 'I don't see it.'

'Look closer.'

Vogel's eyes narrowed. One was not like the other. It was a fiery slit in an otherwise black retina, blind to one world but not the other.

'A plume of smoke? There are fires burning everywhere in this city.'

'It's them,' Narek assured him, opening up the vox again to converse with their pilot. 'Saarsk,' he said, 'find us a place to land nearby.'

'Why don't we simply strafe their new stronghold,' suggested Narlech, 'then rake through the rubble to finish them?'

Narek shook his head. 'No. I want to be sure they're all present. Besides, ramping up our engines to attack speed would alert them to our presence. They have a weapon mount that took out two buildings. It would have no difficulty shooting us down, and then we would be the ones being searched for amongst the wreckage. We set down near here,' he decided. 'Go in slow and quiet on foot.'

Narlech muttered his agreement. Vogel sat back down.

'It matters not to me,' uttered Amaresh, who had not ceased sharpening his ritual blade since they had taken off. 'So long as we get to cut them open and spill their fears at their feet, a feast for the Pantheon.'

Dagon snarled in pleasure at the thought. The others, too, all revelled in this idea.

Only Narek looked away, out into the dark, and wondered what would await them when they arrived.

NUMEON SAT IN silence next to the slowly dying embers of the pyre. Tendrils of smoke were coiling from inside the armoured husks of his former brothers. He wondered how long it would be before it was him lying amongst the flames, burning and ending.

He was alone and the manufactorum floor was dark, barring the glow that remained in the ashes and charred pieces of wood. Only pausing to lay their dead to rest, the others were getting ready to move.

News of the human's death had done little to affect the company. Most were in private agreement with Leodrakk. Now, this man, this John Grammaticus, would be left behind like the rest. And his secrets would die with him.

Numeon clasped an icon of a small hammer in his fist. It was partly fire-blackened, and the piece of chain that had once attached it to a suit of armour was broken.

'I still have hope. I still believe you live...' he said to the shadows. His eyes then strayed to the fire that filled the air around him with its crackling, reminding him of the day they had been wrested apart.

CHAPTER FOURTEEN
Misgivings

'I can scarcely imagine what inspired Horus to this madness. In truth, the very fact of it frightens me. For if even the best of us can falter, what does that mean for the rest? Lord Manus will lead us in. Seven Legions against his four. Horus will regret this rebellion.'

— Vulkan, Primarch of the Salamanders

Isstvan V

NO ONE HAD seen Vulkan since he had returned from the meeting with his brothers aboard the *Ferrum*. Upon re-docking with the *Fireforge*, the primarch of the Salamanders had removed himself to his private chambers without a word of explanation.

Artellus Numeon had expected a briefing, even an address. Something. The ways of his primarch were as inscrutable as the very earth he was bound to. Numeon dearly wished that he could read Vulkan now, and wondered what had transpired aboard the *Ferrum* that had vexed the primarch to such a degree. Less than an hour from planetfall, a veritable armada of Legion drop-ships berthed aboard the flagship vessel preparing to pierce Isstvan V's upper atmosphere, it perturbed the Pyre Captain greatly that his liege lord had absented himself.

Walking hurriedly down the shadowed corridors of the *Fireforge*, Numeon had yet to encounter a single soul. Vulkan had dismissed his chamber guards, all serfs and even his brander. So when the doors to Vulkan's solitorium appeared through the soot-choked darkness of the ship's lowest hold, barring the enginarium decks, Numeon did not know what to expect.

Though sealed, the entrance to Vulkan's private chamber was not locked. Flickering lumen-torches cast a reddish haze over the doors, which parted at Numeon's approach, revealing a deeper shadow within.

Crossing the threshold into the room, Numeon tried to still his thundering heartbeat as the reek of cinder and ash enshrouded him. Like the corridors outside, the solitorium was dark, but abjectly so. Numeon felt Vulkan's presence before he saw him, as a man feels the presence of a monster when he is let into its cage.

The door sealed shut behind, and the dark became absolute.

'Come...' uttered a deep, abyssal voice.

It came from the centre of the room, a circular vault made from obsidian. Around the edges, Numeon heard the crackle of coals, the embers within their brazier-troughs casting off a faint glow. In this wan light he discerned the shape of a large kneeling figure, its head bowed so that its chin was leaning on its fist.

Even in the utter darkness of the branding chamber, Vulkan was resplendent. Clad in his full panoply of war, a sublime suit of power armour forged by his own hand, the Lord of the Drakes was immense. Studded with quartz, rubies and gems of every hue that had been dredged from the Nocturnean earth, the primarch's battle gear flashed with captured fire. On one shoulder guard he wore a massive drake skull, whereas the other was affixed with the jade-coloured hide of a second beast. Without his helmet, Vulkan's glabrous scalp shimmered in the lambent forge-light.

As he stepped farther into the chamber, Numeon caught his reflection in the obsidian's black surface, wreathed in mirrored flame. Like his lord, he was wearing his full battle-plate. A long drake-hide mantle cascaded from his shoulders and a snarling war-helm sat in the crook of his arm. In his other hand, he clasped the haft of his glaive. The volkite weapon attached just below the blade was chromed and ready-charged.

'You seem anxious, Pyre Captain,' Vulkan breathed, intensifying the fuliginous pall around him.

'Orbital bombardment is due to commence in less than an hour, my lord.'

'And you request my presence on the muster deck.'

Breathing slowly and deeply, Vulkan released another heavy exhalation, renewing the volcanic stench cloying the air. Such strength and savagery clothed in armour and flesh, Numeon could almost believe that beneath the onyx-black skin Vulkan *was* a drake, a beast of primordial myth trapped in a man-shaped vessel of bone and blood.

'I have prepared the Legion. They are oathed to the moment and await your order,' Numeon said, unable to hide his agitation.

Vulkan sensed it at once.

'Speak freely, Artellus. I won't have secrets between us.'

Numeon cleared his throat, and came a step closer into the light.

'What are you doing here?'

'Ah.' Vulkan smiled. Numeon caught it in the change in his voice, 'That's better.'

The hide of Kesare hanging from Vulkan's armoured shoulder unfurled as he stood, giving it the illusion of reanimation. Kesare had been a monstrous beast, one of the deep drakes. Vulkan had slain him as part of a contest against another warrior, a stranger to Nocturne, one who had called himself the Outlander. It was only later revealed that this strange visitor was in fact the Emperor of Mankind, a being of such immense power and wisdom as to defy definition.

Everything had changed that day. Truths kept from Vulkan had been revealed; his destiny and purpose. His father had come, his creator in the truest sense, and Vulkan had been cast unto the stars where he was reunited with his intended Legion.

Numeon had rejoiced at the primarch's return. Lost on such a remote and volatile world, Vulkan had nonetheless been amongst the first of the Emperor's sons to be found. Even so, the Salamanders had suffered in the Great Crusade before that, as a desire to prove their worth almost resulted in their extinction.

'You think this is a poor time for self-reflection,' said Vulkan.

It wasn't a question, but Numeon gave the only answer he could.

'Yes. You are needed. We are on the brink of war, about to engage warriors in battle that we have fought beside – warriors we once considered allies.'

'And this troubles you, Artellus?'

'Greatly.'

'It should, but do not let that rush you into ill-considered action.'

'No, of course,' Numeon answered, himself now bowing in response to Vulkan's chastening remarks.

'Raise your head, captain. Did I not teach you to meet me eye to eye?'

Numeon lifted his chin.

'I remember, my lord. You remade us, alloyed us even as we looked into the very abyss of self-annihilation. Without you, we would not have survived.'

Before Vulkan, like all the Legions, the Salamanders had hailed from Terra. The very fact that there were so few Terran Salamanders left alive was testament to how close the XVIII had come to destruction. Being reunited with their primarch had saved them, and with the hardy people of Nocturne already students of Vulkan's teachings, it was not long before the Salamanders saw their numbers swell again.

Numeon was a Terran by birth, like all the Pyre Guard. They were the few, the chosen, and they remembered well the disaster that had very nearly befallen them. How easily their legacy could have ended short like the others of whom no one now spoke.

'I saved you because in you I saw a great potential. My father knew I was the perfect son to temper this Legion and forge it strong again. So then, be assured that there is no better time to reflect than when we strike our oaths and brand them into flesh before battle, Artellus. Temperance in the face of war is not only prudent, it also saves lives. To my mind, it is a practice my brother Ferrus would benefit from greatly.'

Vulkan's gaze was suddenly far away, as if remembering.

Numeon frowned. 'Did all not go well aboard the *Ferrum*? I understand a plan of attack was being devised.'

'It was.' Vulkan returned his gaze to the Pyre Captain. To Numeon, he looked almost regretful.

Vulkan went on. 'The Gorgon has always been volatile, but the words he spoke against Fulgrim aboard the *Ferrum* were embittered and wrathful. Like the magma which churns below the surface of both our worlds, Ferrus is on the brink of violent eruption.'

'His anger is justified,' Numeon asserted. 'Former allies or not, this rebellion must be stopped.'

'Yes, it must. But I fear Ferrus's choler bodes ill for what is to come,' said Vulkan. 'He isn't thinking clearly and acts rashly, out of anger. Corvus felt it too, I am certain, but the Ravenlord conceals his emotions as carefully as his presence. He said nothing of his own misgivings during our brother's impassioned briefing.' Vulkan sighed, a weariness affecting him. 'To rush in against a foe like Horus... It smacks of madness and rage.'

Numeon's brow furrowed. 'Madness?'

Vulkan slowly shook his head. 'To even think of Horus as an enemy seems like insanity. Rebellion, it is said. And not the Sons of Horus alone, but three other formerly loyal Legions as well. I apologise for my candour, Artellus – you should not have to shoulder these burdens. They are mine to bear alone, but what other word is there for it, except madness?'

Numeon was at a loss to answer at first. It would not be long before the bombardment began and the Legion embarked on drop-craft for an immediate, aggressive ground deployment. If it was madness they had come too far to turn back from it now.

'I can think of no other word. Yet what else can we do but follow Lord Ferrus into battle? Here is where we will end it. Seven Legions against his four. Horus will be brought to heel and made to answer for his sedition.'

Vulkan laughed, but it was a sad sound, bereft of humour.

'You remind me of Ferrus. Such belligerence.'

'How else do we meet our enemies but thusly?' Numeon asked.

Vulkan considered that, before lowering his gaze again.

'Do you see this?' he said, gesturing to a hammer cradled in his gauntleted grasp. The primarch did not grip the weapon, rather he allowed it to rest, his fingers barely wrapped around the haft and neck.

'Magnificent,' said Numeon, confused as to his lord's meaning.

The warhammer had an immense double-head. Each head was based on three square wedges, rotated at angles to produce an almost flanged finish. Bisected by a long metal haft, crosshatched at the handle and ending in a gem-studded pommel, the weapon's killing end looked weighty, but Vulkan held it like it was nothing. Ostensibly it was a master-crafted and much upgraded thunder hammer, possessing both a power generator at the top of the haft and another device Numeon did not recognise just below it.

'It rivals *Thunderhead*,' Vulkan told him, gently turning the

hammer around in his loose grip. 'It wasn't intended as a replace-
ment. It was meant as a gift. And even now, as we follow in the
wake of my brother's tempest, I am struck by the import of the decision in holding on to it.'

'A gift,' said Numeon, fighting the sense of unease growing within
him, 'for whom?'

'You have always served loyally and faithfully as my equerry,
Artellus. I trust your counsel. I would have it now.'

Numeon thumped his fist against his breastplate in crisp salute.
'You honour me, my lord. I am yours to command.'

Vulkan's eyes narrowed, the fire burning inside them reduced to
hot, red slits as if measuring his equerry and deeming him worthy
of what he was about to say next.

'What I tell you now, I have told no one before this moment.'

'I understand.'

'No,' said Vulkan sadly, 'you don't. Not yet. After Ullanor, I began
forging a weapon to honour Horus's achievement and our father
making him Warmaster. This,' he said, now holding the hammer in
a firm grip and raising it aloft in one hand, 'is *Dawnbringer*. It was
meant as my gift to my brother.'

'But you chose not to give it to him. Why, my lord?'

Vulkan lowered the weapon, regarding the exquisite craftsman-
ship of his labours before going on.

'That is what vexes me, Artellus. Horus and I spoke privately only
twice after he replaced our father at the head of the Crusade.'

'I remember, my lord. After Kharaatan, you consulted both Lord
Dorn and Lord Horus.'

'Yes. Konrad's... *behaviour* concerned me greatly and I was in need
of guidance. At the time, the forging of *Dawnbringer* was unfinished.
I wanted the gift to be a surprise, a token of our brotherhood and
my respect, so I said nothing of it.'

'I am still unclear as to why this is on your mind now, my lord.'

'Because when the hammer was finished, I spoke to Horus for the second time. His advancement to Warmaster had placed a great strain on his time and attentions, so I wanted to arrange a meeting when I could present my gift to him.' Vulkan paused, his expression darkening as he recalled the exchange.

'My lord?' said Numeon, as the same cloud cast its shadow over him too.

Vulkan kept his eyes down as he remembered, and did not raise them as he concluded his account.

'Horus was much changed from the brother I knew, and had looked up to. Even across our hololithic link, I felt it... A presence that had not been there before.'

'What kind of presence?'

'It is difficult to describe. He seemed... *distracted*, and at first I thought it was merely matters of the Great Crusade that preoccupied him, but as our conversation went on, I realised it was something else.'

'Do you think he was planning this rebellion even then?'

'Perhaps. Now, I wonder if it was always in my brother's heart and simply had to be teased out of him for it to flourish and bloom. Either way, I knew there was a canker within Horus that had not been there before, a shadow upon his soul like a cancer. And it was growing, Numeon, the host embracing this parasite in front of my eyes. I do not possess the prescience of Sanguinius, nor the mental acumen of Guilliman or the psychic gifts of Magnus, but I know my instincts, and they were screaming at me in that moment. *Horus has fallen*, they were saying to me. In some way, he had slipped and the pit had taken him. Even though I could not put meaning or evidence to any of this, it unsettled me. So I decided not to tell him of the gift I had fashioned, instead keeping it for myself. And it concerns me still,' he said to Numeon, looking up again. 'Because the same misgivings I had that day, I feel now. They warn me to be cautious, to heed the disquiet in my soul.'

'I will be ever vigilant,' said Numeon, though he didn't yet know for what.

Vulkan nodded. 'Be mindful, Artellus. On the dark sands of Isstvan far below, we face a foe unlike any other. But it *is* an enemy, and one we can afford to give no quarter. Whatever bonds of loyalty you may once have felt to these warriors, forget them. They are traitors now, led by a warrior I no longer recognise as my brother. Do you believe we are right in this, and that our cause is a just one?'

Despite the bitter taste that the other Legions' treachery had left in his mouth, Numeon had never been more certain of anything.

'I am sure of it. Whatever sickness has come upon our old allies, we will burn it to ash.'

'Then we are as one. Thank you, Artellus.'

'I did nothing, my lord.'

'You heeded me when my mind was troubled. You did more than you realised.' Vulkan gave a feral smile, his misgivings transformed and reforged into purpose. 'Eye-to-eye, Pyre Captain.'

'Tooth-to-tooth, my lord.'

'The bombardment is soon?' Vulkan asked.

'Imminent,' said Numeon, reassured and galvanised by Vulkan's revivified demeanour. He realised, as Vulkan attached *Dawnbringer* to his belt, that it wasn't weakness he had seen in his primarch, but humanity. It was the genuine concern that his brothers had fallen to darkness, and the emergence of the resolve he would need to fight them. He *should* doubt the justness of this fight, and he *should* stop to consider the consequences of it. Only by doing so could a warrior be sure that he drew bolter and blade in good cause and against a true enemy.

This, Numeon realised, was Vulkan's teaching.

Morality, conscience, humanity, these were not flaws; they were strengths.

'Take me to the muster deck,' said Vulkan, donning his war-helm. 'When we make planetfall, I would look my brother in the eye and ask him why he did this, before he's taken to Terra in chains.'

CHAPTER FIFTEEN
The dread feast

'If music is nourishment for the soul, what then of screaming?'
— *Konrad Curze, the 'Night Haunter'*

AFTER THE SHAME of my defeat, I became lost for a time. Curze did not visit me, Ferrus's malignant presence was conspicuous by its absence, and I even started to miss the shade of my dead brother. There was only the stench of the dead, rising over the hours and days to a noisome fume that filled my senses with the stink of failure.

Ferrus had been right; I *was* weak. I could not save the mortals from their fate, I could not beat Perturabo's death trap. Curze had changed tactics. I had no idea why. Instead of trying to punish my body, he had decided to punish my conscience.

The effects were enervating.

Cut adrift amongst my fractured thoughts, I sat unmoving in the darkness of my cell and in that moment I am not too proud to admit that, for the first time, I truly knew what it was to despair.

Suns rose and fell, stars were born and died again. The cosmos shifted

around me, and after a while time ceased to have meaning. I was as a
statue of onyx, my arms hanging by my sides, my forehead touching
the ground. Arch-backed, too wounded to do anything but breathe, I
felt the slow atrophy of my limbs and the hunger in my chest. Vigour
was leaving me, as steam flees cooling metal, and I welcomed it.

To die would be a mercy.

A legionary can live for many days without sustenance. His
physiology is enhanced to such a degree that he can be practically
starved and still march, fight and kill. Our father made His sons
even stronger still, but I knew, as a man who knows he is dying of
cancer, that I was not myself. My humours were out of balance;
the many woundings Curze had subjected me to, the mental tortures, were beginning to take their toll. At my lowest ebb, when
even my will was fading, I slipped into blessed oblivion and let it
take me in.

My peace was not to last.

A sound like a distant stream trickling next to my ear brought me to
my senses. I realised as I opened my eyes that I was still in the deathly
chamber, but that now it was filling with water. It chilled my face,
lapping up against my cheek. Lips parched, tongue leathern, I tried
to drink but found the water brackish and metallic tasting. My guts
churned, hunger gnawing, threatening to devour me from within.
Too weak to stand, to even lift my body, I could only watch, and
see the open sluices at the base of the walls admitting this languid
torrent.

I saw the spark of electricity a moment later and had only a few
seconds of realisation before the shock hit and I was jerked off the
ground in a bone-wrenching spasm. My wretched frame, emaciated
from lack of food and water, groaned; my muscles, partially atro-
phied from lack of use, burned. My throat, dry as desert ash, could
barely muster a scream.

✠ ✠ ✠

'VULKAN...'

As if I were trapped in a deep well, my saviour calling down to me from above, I heard my name.

'Vulkan...' it repeated, only this time the voice was clearer. I was reaching for the light, kicking hard to breach the surface and end my submergence.

'Vulkan, you must eat.'

As my eyelids snapped open, I discovered that I must have passed out, and had regained consciousness in a different part of the ship.

I was sitting down; my hands and feet were bound.

Opposite me, sitting across a broad banquet table, my dead brother grimaced at me.

'Take your fill,' he said, hollow eye sockets gesturing to the feast arrayed before us. 'You must eat.'

We were sitting in a long gallery. Ornate candelabras, steeped in dust, provided a flickering luminescence. Above us, silver chandeliers swayed lightly on a stagnant breeze. Gossamer-thin strands conjoined them like the webs of some ancient and long dead arachnid. Similarly, the feast itself was swathed in a fine and farinaceous veneer of grey-white.

I smelled meat, but here and there the scent was somehow wrong, as if some of it were spoiled or raw. There were fruits and bread that both bore the suggestion of mould despite their ostensible freshness. Carafes of wine littered the table in abundance but in some the grapes were bad, the vintage corked and unpalatable.

Despite the decaying feast, I salivated at the prospect and struggled impotently against my bonds to taste it.

'Eat, Vulkan,' Ferrus urged. 'You are wasting away, brother.'

I tried to speak, but my throat was so raw I barely managed to croak.

'Speak up,' said Ferrus, his lipless mouth champing open and shut, the darkness of his tongueless mouth gaping and black but

somehow still able to form words. With a skeletal hand, he made
an expansive, sweeping gesture. 'We all want to hear what you've
got to say.'

Until that moment, I had not noticed the other guests.

Seventeen men and women sat around the banquet table. Like
the other prisoners Curze had shown me, these humans were both
Army and Imperial citizenry. I even saw some remembrancers
amongst the host, and one who bore a resemblance to Verace. Of
all the guests, he was the only one who seemed calm and unaffected
by it all. It could not be the remembrancer, of course, for Verace was
not a man in the strictest sense. He was merely a mantle, thrown
about the shoulders of a being who wore it like a cloak.

Skin stretched across their bones like thin parchment, lips were
drawn back over their gums, eyes hooded with dark rings of fatigue
– the mortals were evidently being starved too.

Unlike me, though, they were not bound.

Instead, I noticed their hands had been removed at the wrist.
Impaled in the cauterised stumps were long, jagged knives and
trident-pronged forks. A few of the humans had managed to spear
hunks of meat or carve into wedges of bread but could not bring
these victuals to their mouths, the length of their concomitant uten-
sils preventing them.

This great feast was laid out before them and they could only
watch as it decayed and festered whilst they starved.

Ferrus got my attention by raising a goblet.

'Should I toast, brother? It seems in order, before this greedy rab-
ble devours everything.'

Again, I tried to speak, but my throat felt as if it had been scoured
raw by razor blades and all I achieved was an aggravated rasp. I
clenched and unclenched my fists, straining weakly against my
bonds. I stamped my feet, feeling the bone bruise and crack.

'To you, dear Vulkan,' said Ferrus, raising the goblet to his lips and draining it. Dark red wine cascaded down his throat, through the ruin of his neck and out again via the cracks in his ribcage where his armour and flesh had begun to crumble away with the onset of decay.

As if bemused, Ferrus looked around at the other diners.

'Perhaps they are waiting for you, brother?' he suggested. 'They have yet to consume a single morsel.'

The bindings around my wrists were beginning to bite into skin now. I ignored the pain, my jaw locked in anger and my entire body trembling.

'F... e...' I croaked. 'F... e... e...'

Ferrus turned his head as if trying to listen, but his ears had shrunk into nubs of rotten flesh.

'Speak up, Vulkan. Let's all hear what you have to say.'

'F... e... e... d. Feed. *Feed! Feed each other!*'

I roared and struggled but still couldn't break free.

Slowly, certainly, Ferrus shook his head.

'No, Vulkan. I'm sorry, but they cannot hear you.' He pointed a bony digit at one thrashing individual, a dried rivulet of blood having crusted from his ear and down the side of his head.

Deaf.

As the poor man turned to face me, I noticed the milky consistency of his iris.

Blind too.

Only smell, touch and taste remained. So cruel to be so close to what the body craves and the mind imagines, only for it to be denied.

'The greedy cannot listen, *won't* listen,' said Ferrus. 'Nor can you make them. Humankind's greed will eventually destroy it, Vulkan. By aiding them you are only prolonging the inevitable.'

I stopped listening and ignored my dead brother's babbling mouth. Instead, I roared. I cursed Curze's name until I no longer had voice to speak it.

And then I sat there, a king at his dread feast as his guests slowly starved and died.

My constitution, however weak, kept me going. Curze knew I would survive longer than the humans and when the final one breathed his last, I was alone.

I wept as the candles bled down to nubs and the accumulated dust snuffed them out as well as the chandeliers above me, throwing the hall into darkness.

'Curze…' I sobbed.

'Curze!' With greater vigour this time, my anger lending me much-needed strength.

'Curze!' I shouted it, bellowing at the shadows. 'Curze, you coward. Come out! Finish me if you can. Even like this, I will not yield.'

A slow sigh made me start, so close that I knew it came from the seat next to me.

'I am here, brother,' said Curze, seated by my side. 'I have always been here, watching, waiting.'

'Waiting for what?' I hissed, the effort to speak after my outburst taxing me.

'To see what happens next.'

'Cut my bonds and find out, brother…'

Curze laughed. 'Still fierce, eh, Vulkan? The monster within isn't cowed quite yet, is he?'

I growled, 'Kill me or fight me, just get it over with.'

Curze shook his head.

'I didn't want you to beg. I *don't* want you to beg. I would not have you brought low like that. You are better than that, Vulkan. Better than me at least. Or so you think.'

'I'm not begging, I'm giving you a choice. One way or the other, you *will* have to kill me. As a dog or as your equal.'

'Equal?' Curze snapped in a sudden burst of apoplexy. 'Are we peers then, you and I? Are we princes of the universe, bonded by common cause and blood?'

'We are warriors and still brothers, despite how far you have fallen.'

'I have fallen nowhere. My perch is as lofty as it ever was. *You*. You are the one who is brought down from grace. Not so noble in the shadows, are you? Tell me, Vulkan, now you inhabit the gutters as I do, what do you see in the black mirror before you? Are we all our father's sons, or are some of us just a little better than the others? Do you think he made all twenty of us believing we each would have a purpose beyond making his favourites shine that little bit brighter?'

'Envy? Is that still it? Is that why I am here?'

'No, Vulkan. You are here for my amusement. I cannot be jealous of someone who is only as great or weak as I am.'

'Cut me loose, face me without these games, and we shall see who is weak.'

'I would slay you where you stand, brother. Have you seen yourself, lately? You aren't looking so formidable.'

'Then what is the purpose of all this madness and death? If you want to kill me, just do it. Get it over with. Why won't you just–'

Shadow-fast, Curze snapped the fork off one of the dead human's wrists and rammed it deep into my chest.

I felt it pierce the breastbone, the dirty metal driven into my heart to impale it. Crouching over me, Curze proceeded to drag the blunt implement up through my ribcage, tearing through the chest and neck as I jetted blood across his breastplate in arterial black.

'I tried,' he told me, snarling through his anger as the fork reached my chin and blackness began to intrude at the edge of my vision. 'I cut off your head, pierced your heart, crushed your skull, impaled every major organ in your body. I even burned and dismembered you. You came back, brother. *Every. Single. Time.* You cannot die.'

Aghast, mind reeling with my brother's confession, I died.

Curze had done as I asked, as I begged, and killed me.

CHAPTER SIXTEEN
Burned

THOUGH THE SPEARHEAD felt light in his grasp and cold to the touch, Elias knew the weight of the moment and the weapon's part in it before him.

He had returned to the pulpit, choosing to be divested of his armour and coming to his altar of sacrifice wearing only his priestly vestments.

Eight fresh supplicants stood ready around the pit, including the one waiting on his knees before Elias on the stone pulpit. Behind them, seven of the Dark Apostle's most devout disciples loomed. These men and women were not the sacrificial lambs of Ranos – they were adherents to the cult, true believers. They had given themselves willingly, to become part of the Pantheon's great weft and weave. Not a one amongst them quavered or wept; they merely prayed, and it gave Elias's heart such joy to hear it.

'Reveal your devotion!' he cried to the eight, prompting the cultists to disrobe and expose their carved flesh.

Skin profaned with dark and fell sigils was revealed from under crimson cloth. Using ritual blades, the cultists had marked themselves with a serpent that uncoiled across all of their bodies. Elias's supplicant was the eighth and his chest bore the serpent's head, described in his own partially clotted blood.

'It is good,' he muttered, becoming lost in reverie.

Hell would come to Traoris and he would be its gatekeeper, admitting it into the mortal plane.

Chanting the names of the Neverborn, Elias began the ritual. He felt the thrum of power in the spearhead, saw its fulgurant glow between raptures and knew that this was the tool of *his* elevation. Not Erebus, not even Lorgar, but he would be the one.

Valdrekk Elias would receive what he had always craved. Ascension.

Beseeching the daemons of the aether to hear him, praying for them to be attracted to the spear's psychic resonance, he felt the heat from the blade begin to intensify. At first it was just uncomfortable, a necessary forbearance to yield the greater prize, but then it became painful. Looking down at the weapon in his grasp, Elias realised it was aflame and his skin with it.

He uttered the cursed verses faster, prompting his disciples to chant with ever greater vigour. Still it burned.

The glow was so bright that it lit up the sacrificial site, chasing back the shadows that had been slowly creeping from the old ruins like spilled ink. They seemed to recoil, as did the supplicants, smoke rising from their mutilated bodies.

One woman cried out, and Elias almost faltered in his well-practiced dogma before a Word Bearer held her steady. Others were showing signs of displeasure too, writhing and coughing as their forms were devoured by cleansing flame. It spread, the burning light, crawling inexorably over the disciples.

The names of the Neverborn, so crucial to the ritual, slipped from Elias's memory. The agony in his arm was such that he clutched it. Rendered down to blackened flesh, he balked at his sudden disfigurement and realised that harnessing the power of the spearhead was beyond him. Like a horse that has slipped its reins, it was wild. But it was also vengeful.

'Kill them!' Elias cried, with more fear than he intended, but it was too late.

Unfettered, the power contained within the fulgurite broke free of its shackles and coursed out in a flood. It sprang from Elias, a storm seeking to earth itself in a lightning rod.

It found seven.

Sinking to their knees, their ritual daggers now forgotten, the disciples died quickly and in agony. Their battle-plate was no protection.

Furcas clutched at his throat, a death scream issuing from his mouth in a plume of smoke. Dolmaroth, his hands held up to his head, became fused in a solid mass of flesh and metal. Imarek managed to wrench off his helmet before he died, but took half of his face with it as it stuck to the inside. Eligor shuddered and melted like wax through the vents in his armour. The others fell in similar fashion, prompting the Word Bearers watching from behind them to recoil for fear of sharing their brothers' fate.

The supplicants were already charred meat and bone before the first disciple fell, and they were blasted to ash by an unfurling wave of fire.

Realising his peril, teeth clenched with the pain of his arm, Elias rammed the spearhead into the stone dais of his pulpit and fell back as the fire returned.

The Dark Apostle bounced off one step then another, tumbling into a wretched heap.

Of his pulpit, only a jagged spur of burned rock remained, with the still-glowing spearhead lodged within it.

Breathing hard, acutely aware of the trauma his body had suffered, Elias screamed. Not in pain, but in anger and frustration. He had expected ascension, revelation, not to be thwarted.

Jadrekk was the first of his followers to reach him.

'Dark Apostle...' he began, but shrank back at the sight of Elias's wounds.

His arm was completely burned, all the way from his shoulder to his fingertips. The bones had fused, a crooked and malformed limb in place of what was there before.

'My armour,' snapped Elias, standing up unaided, snarling at any attempts at assistance. 'Bring me my armour.'

Jadrekk obeyed and hurried off into the camp.

Elias didn't notice. Instead, he glared at the spearhead still embedded in the rock. His gaze went from it to the legionaries, then his flock of cultists and finally the remaining citizens of Ranos.

'Round them all up,' he said to his warriors, burning with shame and fury. 'I want them executed. No knives, no rituals, just kill them.'

Elias turned away, his ruined limb clutched close to his chest as the pronouncement was met first with stunned silence, then fear, as the mortals realised what they were fated for. Shouts and grunts for order competed with wailing protestation and begging.

Elias sneered at the sound. It disgusted him, as did the fact he would now have to go to Erebus and plead for his life.

'And someone bring me that spear,' he said, almost as an afterthought, before staggering back to his tent.

CHAPTER SEVENTEEN
The face in the blood

WHEN HE BLINKED, a thin crust of dried blood parted and flaked away off his eyelid.

His back hurt from an hour spent lying in the cold and on this slab. Vaguely aware of remembered pain down his side, he reached over to explore the injury but found only reknit skin and bone.

'Not again...' groaned Grammaticus, and heaved himself up.

He was sitting on a makeshift operating table in some kind of infirmary. So they had moved him then. At least that boded well, he supposed. The lights were out, but a glow was coming through a portal window in the door from a much larger room beyond the infirmary. Despite the gloom, Grammaticus could see that there was blood everywhere. The reek of it was heady and unpleasant. In particular it spattered a grimy-looking side bar where a selection of rough tools and ripped bandages lay discarded. Not a surgeon's work, then. He found no stitches, but he was still badly bruised despite his new sleeve of flesh.

Slau Dha, you wretched alien bastard...

A metal bowl close to hand, filled with his blood and draped with the half-cut leavings of the butcher's bandages, caught Grammaticus's attention. The liquid was perfectly still and unusually reflective. As it shimmered, he realised what was happening and fought the urge to kick over the bowl and upend its contents onto the floor. It wouldn't help. If he didn't *flect* they would just find another way to make contact. It would go badly for him if he refused.

So instead he leaned over and waited for the face to appear.

He'd been expecting Gahet, as before, but instead the haughty yet severe features of the autarch started to resolve instead. For a fleeting moment, Grammaticus thought Slau Dha had somehow 'heard' his earlier remarks. But he was mistaken, as he also was about the identity of the face in the blood.

'You are not Slau Dha,' he said to the eldar regarding him from across time and space.

'An astute observation, John Grammaticus.'

'Humour? You surprise me. I didn't think your kind possessed it.'

'*My kind*? Are you really so jaded, John Grammaticus?'

'I am the herald of destruction for my entire race,' answered Grammaticus. 'Jaded doesn't even begin to cover it.'

The eldar didn't respond to his sarcasm. He was male, dark hair scraped back over his forehead to reveal an inked rune on the skin. Only his face and shoulders were visible and described in red monochrome, the rest lost beyond the edges of the bowl.

'Seems you know my name,' said Grammaticus. 'What's yours? Are you another agent of the Cabal?'

'Your *association* is how we have come to be in communion, John Grammaticus. And my name is unimportant.'

'Not to me it isn't. I like to know who my handlers are before they jerk my strings.'

The eldar pursed his lips. 'Hmm. I detect some bitterness in your tone.'

'How astute of you,' Grammaticus mocked. 'Now, what do you want?'

'The question is, John, what do you want?'

'Who are you?'

'I am not with the Cabal, and I know that you wish to extricate yourself from their "strings", yes?'

Grammaticus didn't answer.

'Why are you here, John Grammaticus?' the eldar went on. 'What is your purpose?'

'You seem knowledgeable, more so than me at least. Why don't *you* tell me?'

'Very well. You are seeking a fragment of power, weaponised in the form of a fulgurite spear. Your mission also concerns the primarch, Vulkan. I too am concerned with him as well as the matter of earth. I came to you because I need your help, and you are in a unique position to give it.'

'And what makes you think I would be willing to exchange one puppeteer for another?'

'You want to be released. I can give that to you, or at least show you how to release yourself. You are… long-lived, are you not?'

'I suspect you already know the answer to that, too. Although, I think you've got me confused with a friend of mine. I would say I have had many lives rather than one that is especially long.'

'Yes, of course. You perpetuals are all different, and not all human in the strictest sense either.'

'You are referring to the Emperor?'

'You met him once, didn't you?'

'Yes, briefly.' Grammaticus did not know who this being was, but whatever his other claims, he was certainly powerful to be able to contact him in this way and knew a great deal of the greater stakes at play in the war. Long ago, during the Unification Wars when he had been part of the Caucasian Levies, Grammaticus had learned to be wary of those who possessed more knowledge than himself. When in such circumstances, he found it best to say little and listen intently.

The eldar went on. 'Many years ago, wasn't it? Several lifetimes, in fact.'

Grammaticus nodded.

'No,' said the eldar flatly. 'I do not mean him, I refer to Vulkan. He also cannot die as such, but you already knew that, didn't you? As you and I speak, he is in terrible danger. I need your help to save him, if you are willing?'

'If I am willing?' Grammaticus scoffed. 'Do you even know why I am here, what I've been charged to do? So you are giving me a choice then, assuming I believe all I have been told?'

'I am certain you know I speak with veracity, just as I am certain you will take up this cause.'

'Then why ask, if it's predetermined?'

'Politeness, illusion of free will. Invent whatever rationale you choose, it does not matter.'

'You say choice, but it still feels like manipulation. For argument's sake though, tell me what you want me to do.'

'Place your hands against the conduit,' the eldar instructed.

Grammaticus was about to ask him what he meant by 'the conduit' when he guessed it was the bowl, so did as asked.

'Now prepare yourself,' said the eldar, not needing to be told that Grammaticus had done as requested.

'Why?'

'Because this will hurt.'

CHAPTER EIGHTEEN

Dropsite

'When the traitor's hand strikes, it strikes with the strength of a Legion.'

– Warmaster Horus, after the Isstvan V massacre

Isstvan V

CLOUDS ROILED ACROSS the sky, presaging a storm to come. They were a mix of deep red and umber, turned that way by the planetary bombardment unleashed from warships at anchor in the upper atmosphere, and so thick they clung to the vessels ploughing through them at speed in billowing streamers.

Thrusters blazing, the combined loyalist force led by Ferrus Manus surged through the fog, bent on retribution. The Gorgon's drop-pod joined thousands of others, just as Vulkan's Stormbird flew at the spear-tip of a vast flock of vessels.

Seconds after the first drop-ship pierced the cloud layer, batteries of emplaced guns erupted across metres of earthworks dug along the Urgall Depression. Flak fire filled the sky like upwards-pouring rain, chewing through wing and fuselage, detonating arrow-headed cocoons of metal and spilling their lethal payloads into the air.

It barely dented the assault, and when the Imperial loyalists finally made planetfall, over forty thousand legionaries tramped out upon the scorched earth.

NUMEON SAT MAG-HARNESSED in the Stormbird, trying to track the unfolding carnage. His battle-helm was firmly clamped and he cycled through the various force commanders in his retinal display as the ship bucked and shuddered with its evasive actions.

A close impact prompted a rapid course correction, and he felt the sudden exertion of gravity as they pitched. Unperturbed, the captain of the Pyre Guard kept working through the Salamanders officers, committing their positions and statuses to his eidetic memory.

Heka'tan, 14th Company Fire-born...

Gravius, Fifth Company Fire-born...

K'gosi, 21st Company Pyroclasts...

Usabius, 33rd Company Fire-born...

Krysan, 40th Company Infernus...

Nemetor, 15th Company Reconnaissance ...

Ral'stan, First Company Firedrakes...

Gaur'ach, Fourth Cohort Contemptors...

Chapter Masters, lieutenant commanders, company captains.

It went on.

More than a hundred names and faces scrolled across Numeon's vision as he sought to follow the ever-shifting engagement. Thus far, they had only lost a dozen ships and eight drop-pods. In his mind's eye, formations adapted, battle plans subtly altered, all to accommodate the violent landscape that was steadily unfolding above and below.

The Stormbird they rode in was a Warhawk IV. It could carry up to sixty legionaries and also had some capacity for transporting armour. During the apex of the Great Crusade, the Stormbird

had been as ubiquitous as the stars in the night sky but its favour
was fading. This one was an antique, having been usurped by the
smaller and more agile Thunderhawk. Numeon liked the solid-
ity of the Warhawk IV, just as he liked the fact he was harboured
alongside fifty Pyroclasts, led by Lieutenant Vort'an. With chain
face-masks that hung below the eye slits of their battle-helms and
long surcoats of drake scale, they cut a stern figure in the hold.
Unlike assault troopers of the line, Pyroclasts each wore a pair of
flame gauntlets, slaved to a reservoir of promethium contained in
canisters attached to their armour's generator. Few warriors were
as unyielding, as vengeful. In the old Gothic, their name literally meant 'break with fire'. On the Isstvan killing fields, that was
exactly what they would do.

Numeon could feel their hunger; the flame troopers were eager
for battle.

In contrast, the Pyre Guard were still and calm like their lord.
Vulkan's eyes were closed, the retinal lenses of his helmet extinguished, as he meditated on what was to come. Numeon was
reminded of their conversation aboard the *Fireforge* just moments
before they had gone to the muster deck and the primarch had
addressed his warriors. His words were brief but poignant. They
spoke of brotherhood and loyalty, they also referenced betrayal
and a fight the Legion had not seen the equal of since the earliest days of its formation. They would be entering a caldera in the
midst of violent eruption, and none amongst them would emerge
from that unscathed.

Alert sirens screamed into activity, strobing the inside of the dingy
hold in amber light.

'*One minute to planetfall,*' the pilot's voice issued through the
vox.

Of their initial complement, only fifteen ships and eleven drop-
pods would not make the surface intact. Nigh-on full Legion

strength would be levelled against Horus and his rebels.

The Salamanders would hit along the left flank, the Raven Guard the right and Ferrus Manus with his Morlocks dead centre.

In Numeon's retinal display, the roll call of Salamanders officers was replaced by a data-feed from the other two Legions which he relayed at once to Vulkan.

'Nineteenth and Tenth confirm assault vectors and imminent planetfall,' Numeon said.

'Any word from the other four Legions?' asked the primarch.

He referred to the Word Bearers, Iron Warriors, Alpha Legion and Night Lords. Since Kharaatan, relations with the VIII had been strained, but Numeon would rather have them fighting with, and not against, them.

These Legions, led by their primarchs, would form a second wave to relieve those making first planetfall. According to their last communications, which were well before the commencement of planetary bombardment, the other Legion fleets were inbound. Without them, the scales were evenly balanced between Horus and the loyalists. With them, it would be a massacre for the errant Warmaster and his rebels.

'None, my lord.'

Any response to that from Vulkan was cut off as a second alert sounded, higher pitched than the first.

Thirty seconds.

'Prepare yourselves,' the primarch growled, opening his eyes at last.

Across the hold, power weapons energised, bolter slides were racked and igniters at the mouths of flame gauntlets lit up in *whoosh-ing* unison.

Screaming retro-thrusters kicked in, jolting the Stormbird hard. Mag-harnesses disengaged but the legionaries stayed steady, locked to the floor with their boots.

'Eye-to-eye!' Vulkan shouted as the ship touched down, hard and hot.

'Tooth-to-tooth,' the Salamanders roared as one, as the embarkation ramp opened to admit them onto Isstvan.

CHAPTER NINETEEN
Trench warfare

'Say what you like about the Fourteenth Legion. They are mean, ugly bastards but tenacious. There's no one else I'd rather have by my side in a war of attrition, and almost anyone else I'd rather have against me.'
— Ferrus Manus, after the compliance of One-Five-Four Four

Isstvan V

BLACK SAND CRATERED by ordnance made for uncertain footing. As the vast armies of the three loyal primarchs ran from the holds of ships or emerged through the dissipating pressure cloud of blooming drop-pods, several legionaries faltered and slipped.

Sustained bolter fire met them upon planetfall, and hundreds amongst the first landers were cut down before any kind of beachhead could be established. Fire was met with fire, the drumming staccato of thousands of weapons discharged in unison, their muzzle flashes merging into a vast and unending roar of flame. Dense spreads of missiles whined overhead to accompany the salvo, streaking white contrails from their rockets. Sections of earthworks erupted in bright explosions that threw plumes of dirt and armoured men into the air. Las bursts lit up the swiftly following darkness, spearing through tanks and Dreadnoughts that loomed behind the foremost ranks of enemy defenders, only for return fire to spit back in reply. Flamers choked the air with smoke and the stink of burning flesh, as yet more esoteric weapons pulsed and shrieked.

It was a cacophony of death, but the song had barely begun its first verse.

The right flank was swollen with warriors of the XVIII.

Salamanders teemed out of their transports, quickly coming into formation and advancing with purpose. The black sand underfoot was eclipsed from sight, as a green sea overwhelmed and overran it. Vexilliaries held aloft banners, attempting to impose some order on the emerging battalions.

Methodical, dogged, the XVIII Legion found its shape and swarmed across the dark dunes.

At the forefront of this avenging wave was Vulkan, and to his flanks the Firedrakes. Lumbering from the metal spearheads of drop-pods, the Terminators amassed in two large battalions. They were dauntless, dominant, but not the most implacable warriors in the Salamanders' arsenal.

Contemptors, striding through the smoke, laid claim to that honour. Great, towering war engines, the Dreadnoughts jerked with the savage recoil of graviton guns and autocannon. Not stopping to see the carnage wreaked, they slowly tramped after the rushing companies of legionaries in small cohorts, attack horns blaring. The discordant noise simulated the war cries of the deep drakes and was pumped through vox-emitters to boost its volume.

Disgorged by Thunderhawk transporters, Spartans, Predator-Infernus and Vindicators disembarked at combat speed, tracks rolling. The battle tanks rode at the back of the line with a steep ridge behind them, anchoring the dropsite with their armoured might.

Three spearheads were driven at the traitor's heart, two black and one green, all determined to bring down the fortress squatting at the summit of the Urgall Hills that overlooked the expansive depression.

In seconds the shifting sand became as glass, vitrified by the heat of tens of thousands of weapons, and cracked underfoot.

The percussive *thud* of mortars sounded overhead. Moments later and a line of explosions stitched the right flank, green bodies borne aloft on clouds of dark earth and smoke. Answering it, the plosive exhalation of a tracked-mounted siege gun. Part of the embankment was ripped up by the massive cannon shell, the mortar battery destroyed with it.

On the opposite side, a spit of flame from an Infernus lashed across an enemy squad lurking in a clutch of foxholes with grenades primed. The small explosives cooked off before they could be thrown, their fury turned upon their wielders, who were blasted apart. From an upper echelon, a lonely missile streaked across the smoke-choked field and cracked against the Infernus's hull. Its turret split, a second flame burst already building as its side sponsons chattered and its tracks clanked. The tank went up in a loud ball of flame, killing a swathe of legionaries advancing beside it and staggering a second vehicle in its squadron.

All of this Numeon perceived in his peripheral vision and the frantic data inload from his retinal display. They all did.

'To the ridge line,' Vulkan shouted above the clamour, 'and gain the higher ground!'

Withering fire hailed down on them from above, chugging from bunkers and murder-slits cut into the earth. Larger fortifications had been constructed farther up the bank, where it grew steep and was plugged with iron spikes meant for the disembowelling of tanks. In front of that was the first trench line, shouldered with sandbags and supported by jagged revetments, crowned with spools of razor-wire.

Shells pranging off his armour, the primarch took up the van-guard position, whilst his chasing Pyre Guard tried to keep pace. Numeon had no desire to see Vulkan's back and would prefer to be his primarch's shield than his rearguard. Roaring them to greater effort, he urged his six brothers to charge faster. They had yet to be measured against this battle's fury, save for enduring its guns, and Numeon would have it that they close with their enemies before they were but smears on the black sand.

Behind the Pyre Guard, the stoic advance of the Pyroclasts struggled to keep up as they laid down sheets of burning promethium in front and to the flanks. The Terminator-armoured Firedrakes were also slipping back, unable to compete with the primarch's speed, and Numeon began to see that there was a realistic danger of becoming estranged from the rest of the Legion.

But rather than suggest caution, he called in support to fill the gap instead.

'Captain Nemetor,' he rasped into his vox-feed, hoarse from shouting commands.

Above, the steady cascade of fire went on without cessation.

Two seconds of whispering static lapsed before Numeon got an answer.

'Commander...'

'Lord Vulkan makes for the ridge line intent on clearing these trenches in advance of our tardy brother Legions' arrival. I would see him reinforced.'

'Understood.'

Adding their strength to the spearhead the primarch was forging, the 15th Company reconnaissance took up fresh position. Their charge line would take them in alongside the Pyre Guard, able to maintain pace where the bulkier Firedrakes and Pyroclasts could not.

Numeon opened up a different channel. 'Captain K'gosi, burn us a path to that first trench line. I want it aflame before we break it open.'

'*Much closer and you'll be the ones lit up and aflame,*' replied K'gosi, but gave the order.

'Fire above!' hollered Numeon, prompting the Pyre Guard and Nemetor's company to crouch, still running, as a wave of flame streaked overhead and spilled into the edges of the first trench-works. The trammelling revetments burned, their spikes reduced to molten slag along with the razor-wire.

Ahead of the charging legionaries, Vulkan finally drew his sword. It shone in the visceral light that had stained the clouds above, a tongue of flame whipping down its edge. As if sensing that his Legion was losing him, he slowed but a fraction as the fire-blackened lip of the outermost trench drew close.

Hunkered within the partially sundered defences, the legionaries of the Death Guard brought guns to bear.

'Into the fires of battle,' Vulkan cried as a second flame-salvo spat from the advancing Pyroclasts. 'Unto the anvil of war!' he concluded, caught in the backwash of the flame storm but barrelling through it and into the trench.

Vulkan's words still ringing in his ears and echoing from his own mouth, Numeon saw a Death Guard section leader rise up to challenge the Lord of Drakes. A hefty power maul crackled lightning in the formidable warrior's left hand.

Vulkan split him in two before the blow could fall and smashed through the still-flailing corpse into his next opponent. Three more Death Guard warriors met similar fates before the Pyre Guard charged into the trench alongside their lord.

The XIV Legion were hardy fighters – the Salamanders had fought alongside them at Ibsen, but those days were gone and now allies had turned into enemies.

The flame storm and the ferocity of Vulkan's attack had scattered the defenders but they were rallying quickly and now counter-attacked from three separate channels. Although the trench network was wide enough for three legionaries to stand abreast, the fighting was thick and fierce. A glaive swing took the head off one legionary, the dirty-white Maximus-pattern helmet spinning away into the churned up dust and smoke. More advanced through the gloom and Numeon angled his glaive to unleash a focused beam from his volkite, cutting through the traitor ranks.

For a few seconds his tunnel section was clear. Above him, the battle still sounded. Under his feet, the earth shook with every Titan salvo. But it had dulled and become almost a step removed as a strange sense of muted submersion fell upon Numeon. It gave the Pyre Captain opportunity to gauge the status of his brothers.

Atanarius was advancing down the right-hand channel, reaping limbs and cleaving bodies with his double-handed power sword, as deadly as any of Dorn's praetorians. Varrun followed a few paces behind the swordsman, laying down covering fire with his bolter. Igataron and Ganne went down the left spoke, storm shields locked in an impenetrable wedge, thunder hammers swinging. Leodrakk and Skatar'var stayed close to Numeon, the three of them holding the breach.

'Such death...' breathed Skatar'var, horrified at the slaughter.

'Not ours, brother,' Leodrakk reassured him.

Numeon envied a bond such as theirs, one he had never known himself, but now was not the time for such thoughts.

As the Death Guard poured in more troops from other parts of the trench-works, the eerie solemnity broke and battle resumed.

'Should we follow?' asked Leodrakk, gesturing to where Vulkan stormed up the middle trench.

Wilting before his charge, the defenders sensibly chose to hang back and harry the primarch with a welter of bolter fire. Meeting it head on, the primarch shrugged off the shell damage as the brass casings broke apart against his near-inviolable armour.

Shouting a fresh challenge, Vulkan threw himself into them.

Numeon shook his head in answer to Leodrakk.

'We hold here and keep the breach open.'

To the left and right, the others were already in a staggered retreat. With the initial shock and awe of the assault now spent, the Death Guard were showing signs of recovery and the mettle Numeon knew they had in abundance. Droves of them came down from the upper slopes, filing into the trenches with sterner weapons than bolters.

Ganne took the burst from a plasma gun against his storm shield and he staggered, until Igataron hauled him up off one knee. Atanarius looked hard-pressed as he swung in a wide arc to avoid being overwhelmed. Varrun was falling back and urged his brother to do the same as the swordsman finally deigned to yield. Only Vulkan was undaunted and released a burst of flame from his gauntlet to cleanse the middle channel for a few seconds.

Reading the relative positions of their forces on his retinal display, Numeon ordered the others to regroup and rejoin the primarch. In their wake came Nemetor and the 15th, who had held on for further support just outside the trench. Coming up behind them were the Pyroclasts, surging left and right as the reconnaissance company pushed up the middle and went after the Pyre Guard, where heavier resistance was amassing.

Behind a flak-board palisade, a gun crew hurried to bring a mounted Tarantula to bear.

Leaping the barricade, Atanarius ran the first gunner through. A second drew a knife, but Atanarius blocked that and punched the legionary so hard that it cracked his faceplate. A third he decapitated, hacking around in a circle that ended in a downwards thrust to finish the warrior he had only stunned. It was over quickly, the cannon and its crew silenced before they could act. Igataron and Ganne repulsed a second squad who were moving in to an enfilading position from a narrow trench tributary spilling off the main course. Taking a flurry of snap shots against their storm shields, they then rushed the warriors and broke them with their thunder hammers.

The victories were bloody, but small and insignificant when compared to the larger conflict.

Across the entire Urgall Depression, hundreds of battles between legionaries were being fought. Some were company-strong, others were squads or even individuals. There was no scheme to it, just masses of warriors trying to kill one another. Most of the loyalist troops had moved on from the dropsite and were engaging Horus's rebels at the foot of his fortifications, but a few still occupied this beachhead. Scattered groups of traitors had spilled out as far as the dropsite but were quickly destroyed by the troops holding it. These were skirmishes, though, and nothing compared to the greater battle.

Death Guard forces were spilling out of their tunnels now, and roamed down the slopes, bolters chattering. One of the reconnaissance company, pausing to sight down a sniper rifle, took a lucky shell in the neck and crashed back into a trench. Apothecaries moving amongst the Legion army were already hard-pressed, and the lone sniper was lost in the morass before help could reach him.

Knowing his men were taking fire, Nemetor had his company rise up to meet the counter-attacking Death Guard and the lower hillside was instantly swamped with clashing, armoured bodies. Close combat and short-range firefights erupted in their hundreds and the ridge practically undulated with their furious ebb and flow.

Tramping over the scorched remains of the Death Guard brought down in the inferno from Vulkan's gauntlet, Numeon and his brothers kept to the middle trench and soon found themselves reunited with their primarch.

In a brief moment's respite, Vulkan stared to his left in the direction of a distant battle where the Morlocks fought and died.

'Ferrus drives hard up the centre,' he said as Numeon drew to his side. The Pyre Captain had followed his primarch's gaze but could not discern Lord Manus amongst the embattled warriors.

'It is as I feared, Artellus,' Vulkan went on, lost briefly in remembrance. 'He acts without thought or concern.'

Varrun gave Numeon a questioning look.

'It is a private matter,' he hissed curtly, making clear that was an end to it.

'I would not have him fight alone,' said Vulkan, 'but nor should we give up what we have bled to obtain. Have K'gosi maintain position here. The Pyroclasts will hold the breach and this section of the trench. Relief is coming and we must be ready to clear the way for it when it does.'

Numeon gave a quick nod and saw it done. He also saw Nemetor and the 15th still driving up the ridge, becoming stretched. By now, the bulk of the Firedrakes were deep inside the trenches and coming up in support.

'Nemetor,' voxed Numeon, 'you are pulling your company out of position. Regroup and return to the command battalion. Firedrakes are inbound.'

Nemetor was quick to reply. *'The Death Guard are on the run. Have switched to short-scopes and blades. If we pursue now we can destroy them so they can't regroup.'*

'Denied, captain. Pull your forces back.'

'I can press the advantage, brother.'

Nemetor had ever been a fierce warrior. He drove his troops hard, leading by example, and smashed into the fleeing first defenders with irresistible momentum. Short-scoped, the legionary sniper rifle was deadly and incredibly powerful. It was a credit to Nemetor's company that they could adapt their tactics so fluidly in the face of opportunity. At short or long range, the Reconnaissance Marines excelled, but if they kept pushing it would get them all killed or overrun.

Numeon was about to give the captain a direct order to fall back and regroup when he saw something in the distance that made the words catch in his throat.

Rolling down the slope was a dirty cloud, too thick and too low to be fog. It spilled into the myriad trench-works, funnelled by the conduits of hewn earth.

And it was fast. In seconds it had cleared the no-man's-land between the previous trench and the next bank of fortifications and was hurtling at Nemetor and his warriors. It overtook the Death Guard first, who adjusted respirators before the miasma hit as if they knew it was coming.

Which, Numeon realised, they did. The retreat was a feint, a trap, and Nemetor's company were in it.

'Gas!' cried Numeon, but by then it was too late. Though the other legionaries switched their respirators to maximum filtration, Nemetor and the bulk of his company were engulfed before they could act. Still chasing down the retreating warriors, they suddenly found themselves enveloped by a poison cloud and surrounded by rapidly regrouping Death Guard.

The Legion armoury was vast, and not all of its weapons were as obvious as a bolter or as noble as a sword. There were those who wielded devices of much more insidious potency – the slow and agonising ones, the weapons that forever scarred both the bearer and the victim. They did not discriminate and made no allowance for even the strongest armour. From the vaunted champion to the lowliest mortal, they were the great levellers and their works were terrible to behold.

Numeon saw them now and swore an oath that he would kill the one that had unleashed such terror on another legionary.

Whatever contagion the Death Guard had used, it was potent. Moreover, it had been designed to be specifically effective against the Legiones Astartes. Through the breaks in the cloud where the dirt-haze thinned to a sickly, sulphurous yellow, Numeon saw his brothers dying. Power armour was little defence against it. The few that had managed to engage their respirators would perhaps last a minute, maybe more, but the rest were dead men. Metal corroded against the cloud's necrotic touch, rubber mouldered and split, flesh and hair burned. More than a hundred of the reconnaissance company collapsed, choking and spitting blood. Dozens more were hacked apart or shot down by resurgent Death Guard attacking in the confusion.

Igataron went to wade in, the cloud still creeping down the slope and less than fifty metres away, but Numeon stopped him.

'We gain nothing by condemning ourselves too,' he said, then voxed to one of the pilots riding strafing runs across the battlefield. 'R'kargan, bring your bird in on our position to blow away some of this filth.'

R'kargan replied with a clipped affirmative before seconds later a throbbing engine sound came into sharp focus above. Several of the reconnaissance company looked up at their salvation as R'kargan brought the gunship low. Turbines burring, the Thunderhawk's downdraught hit the cloud and spread it out, reducing its potency, if not dispersing it completely.

The gunship was rising again, returning to strafing altitude, when a missile caught its left wing and sent it reeling. A whip of black smoke unfurled from its damaged engine, coiling up and then back upon itself as R'kargan was forced to bank. He crashed into the side of the ridge a few moments later, the gunship's fuselage torn up and burning. Scurrying from their holes, the traitors were quick to fall upon it.

There was no time to mourn. R'kargan had made his sacrifice and saved what was left of the reconnaissance company. Now those that yet lived had to make that worth something.

'To your brothers!' roared Vulkan and stormed up the ridge. He let off small gouts of flame from his gauntlet, burning back what pestilence remained to further weaken its effects. The Pyre Guard followed, ploughing into the slowly dissipating cloud, turning the scales back into the Salamanders' favour and breaking their beleaguered company brothers out of the trap.

Many of the 15th didn't wear battle-helms, preferring to be unencumbered for the stealth work at which they excelled. These warriors had suffered the worst. Skin sloughed away by virulent acids, ravaged by pustules and choking on vomit, eyes drowning in pus from the dirty bomb, there was almost nothing left of them but half-armoured carcasses. As he drove hard into the few remaining Death Guard who had attacked inside the cloud, Numeon heard something scraping at his leg. He turned, glaive angled to thrust downwards, expecting to face a desperate enemy, but instead saw a dying Reconnaissance Marine. Blood was trickling freely from the ruin of the legionary's mouth, sticking to his chin and neck in a viscous film. The dying legionary grasped feebly at Numeon's greave. His fingers had been reduced to stumps, the tips of his gauntlets eaten away, and he left ruddy tracks in the metal. He was trying to say something, but his vocal cords were all but liquefied and the sound that came from his mouth was an agonised gurgle.

'I'll grant you peace,' Numeon murmured and thrust with his glaive to end it.

'Such horrors...' said Varrun after he'd just finished off an enemy that was still twitching, and casting around at his plague-eaten battle-brothers. 'Tell me no such weapons exist in our arsenals.'

Vulkan did not answer. Numeon tried not to meet the gaze of either of them.

'We're not done with this yet,' he said, jutting his armoured chin up the slope where a second Death Guard battalion had converged on the weakened reconnaissance company.

Amidst the carnage, several squads, including Nemetor's command section, had become separated from the main battalion and were facing off against a superior force.

Despite his company's mauling, Nemetor was still on his feet. His armour had been badly damaged from the gas attack, entire sections of it eaten through to reveal the seared mesh underneath. It didn't stop him. With thoughts only of revenge, Nemetor and the survivors charged up at the emerging Death Guard.

Numeon and the others were still finishing off the remnants of the ambushers. The Firedrakes were close but would not be able to intervene. Even Vulkan could not reach the vengeful Salamanders in time.

A fire exchange lit up the slope, casting the acid-ravaged dead in grim monochrome. Where the Death Guard unleashed an indiscriminate bolter hail, the Reconnaissance Marines advanced in a staggered pattern, stopping and sighting with their rifles, shooting and then moving again. They were efficient, cohesive, but taking punishment.

A Salamander went down clutching his shattered gorget. Another spun, a gaping cleft in his torso. A third's head jerked back, his battle-helm's eye slit ventilated and a plume of matter bursting out of the back.

One of the oncoming Death Guard took a hit to the shoulder that blew off his pauldron. A second punched through his chest, a third his right leg greave. He grunted, stumbled but kept on coming.

'Blades!' yelled Nemetor, stowing his sniper rifle and drawing a chainsword when he realised they were about to engage hand to hand, and saw his men do the same.

A well-drilled phalanx came down at them, roughly ninety warriors against forty, tugging axes and mauls from their belts. There was enough time to roar a challenge, before the clash. Nemetor barrelled into his first opponent, using his bulk to topple the legionary. A second went down to a heavy blow from the Salamander's chainblade.

A third he head-butted, making his enemy crumple. Even Barbarus-born Death Guard couldn't resist Nemetor's sheer physical strength.

It struck Numeon as he watched that the honorific of 'Tank' was well deserved. But it might also prove the captain's epitaph, as the numerically superior Death Guard had already overrun the smaller reconnaissance company and were attempting to encircle them.

Vulkan single-handedly prevented that, hitting the overlapping warriors and cutting them apart with his flaming sword. Numeon and the Pyre Guard joined him fractionally later and a dense, chaotic melee erupted.

Further Death Guard reinforcements were entering the fray. They were well drilled and led by a hulking warrior in heavy armour. Numeon caught site of the section leader striding down the slope. Thick plates banded the Terminator's shoulders, a rounded warhelm sitting like a bolt between them. A metal skirt of horizontal slats protected the warrior's abdomen and in a gauntleted fist, he clenched a pole arm with an arcing blade at its summit.

His men gave their commander a wide berth, inviting a clutch of Salamanders to attack him. The brute lashed out with the power scythe, and four legionaries fell back with limbs and heads cleaved off. He advanced, an upwards swing bifurcating his next opponent. As he moved on he crushed the stricken Salamander's head underfoot and left a dark smear in his wake.

This was one of Mortarion's chosen, his elite cadre. The Salamanders had encountered them before, during the Great Crusade, in the joint campaign to settle the world of Ibsen. They were the Deathshroud, and had no equals amongst the XIV Legion.

Chainsword snarling, Nemetor met the formidable warrior in single combat.

It was a fight the brave captain was unlikely to win.

'Nemetor!' Numeon roared, pushing to even greater efforts as he fought to reach his brother-captain.

Death Guard and Salamander exchanged blows, the combat already lasting much longer than any previous engagement of Mortarion's chosen warrior. It took eight seconds for the Deathshroud to cut Nemetor down. His scythe blade sheared the Salamander's chainsword in half, the teeth exploding from the still churning belt and embedding in Nemetor's armour. The backswing raked his chest, opening up ceramite and smashing Nemetor off his feet. He was about to be subjected to the same desultory end as his battle-brother with the crushed skull when Vulkan intervened.

The primarch parried the scythe with his sword blade before reaching inside the Deathshroud's guard to land a blow with his gauntlet. One of the warrior's retinal lenses cracked on impact, revealing a bloodshot eye, burning with hate. Half of the legionary's war-helm was badly dented and a dark fluid was leaking out from under his gorget.

He roared, putting his anger into a two-handed swing that Vulkan stepped aside before cutting horizontally with his sword and slicing clean through the Deathshroud's waist. Coughing blood against the interior of his half-crushed helm, the dying legionary reached for a canister mag-locked to his belt. It was another of the dirty bombs that he had unleashed on Nemetor and his company. Vulkan crushed the Deathshroud's fingers under his boot. Sheathing his sword, the primarch wrenched the power scythe from the legionary's grasp and snapped it over his knee in a flurry of agitated sparks.

It was enough to break the spirit of the Death Guard, who were now engaged by assaulting Firedrakes and fell back in good order. The Pyre Guard were putting the others to the blade when Numeon leaned down to rip off the Deathshroud's helmet.

A pallid-skinned, mashed-up face greeted him. To Numeon's surprise the warrior did not spit or curse – he grinned, exposing a raft of broken teeth. Then he began to laugh.

'You're all dead men,' he whispered.

'Not before you,' replied Numeon, and ended him.

He looked up again when he heard screaming. Not from the dying, but savage and guttural war cries. A ruddy smog was sweeping across the battlefield, fashioned from blood-drenched mist and the smoke generated by thousands of fires. Caught in a crosswind, it slashed in from the east and brought with it the brutal challenge of a Legion that revelled in war. It was air to them, sustenance.

World Eaters.

Their brownish-red silhouettes materialised in the smog like phantoms, along with something else.

Something big.

CHAPTER TWENTY
Immortal

'You have a fine mind, John. We should talk, and consider the options available to beings like us.'
 – The Emperor, the Triumph at Pash

WHEN HE HEARD the screaming, Numeon drew his weapon.

It was coming from the infirmary, a gut-wrenching cry of agony that shook the legionary from a dark reverie. He'd heard screaming like that before, on a plain of black sand. And it chilled him, the symmetry he found in the remembrance of one held against the reality of the other.

The cry of agony ceased almost as soon as it began. A noxious stench permeated the air – whether from whatever had just happened in the infirmary or a false sensory remnant from his bleak imaginings, it was hard to be sure. Numeon didn't move. He kept his eyes on the infirmary door, glaive levelled at waist height with the volkite primed.

Behind him, the dying embers of the pyre crackled into extinction. He paid them no heed, his attention fixed. Others arrived onto the manufactorum floor, drawn by the scream. Numeon kept them

back with a warning hand gesture, before nodding in the direction
of the infirmary.

'What was that?' he heard Leodrakk hiss, and caught the sound of
the Pyre Guard's bolter slide being racked.

'Came from in there,' murmured Numeon, maintaining his aggressive posture. 'Who's here, besides Leo?' he asked. He had taken off
his battle-helm; it was sitting by the side of the pyre dappled with
soot. Without it, he had no visibility of his comrades' positions
relative to his own.

'Domadus,' uttered the Iron Hand.

'K'gosi,' said the Salamander, just above the quiet rumble of his
flame-igniter.

'Shen?' asked Numeon, aware of *four* legionaries in total, and
swearing he could make out the growling undertone of the Techmarine's cybernetics.

'He was dead,' said Shen'ra, announcing his presence with his
answer. 'No man could survive those wounds. No man.'

'Then how?' said Leodrakk.

'Because he isn't a man at all,' muttered K'gosi, raising his flame
gauntlet.

'Hold,' Numeon told them all. 'Approach no closer. Out here, at
a distance, we have the advantage over whatever is in that room.
Domadus,' he added, 'get Hriak. No one else enters. Leodrakk,
guard the door.'

Both legionaries did as ordered, leaving Numeon to maintain
watch.

'We wait for the Librarian, find out what we're dealing with.'

'And then, brother-captain?' asked K'gosi.

'Then,' Numeon replied, 'we kill it, if we have to.'

All of them had heard rumours. War stories. Every soldier had
them. They were an oral tradition, a comradely means of passing
on knowledge and experience. What lent these tales credence was

that veteran officers of the Legiones Astartes had attested to *facts* and given them, in detail, in their reports. To falsify an account of a battle or mission-action was no minor infraction in either Legion or Army. All military bodies took such things incredibly seriously. But facts, explainable through scientific means or not, could not accurately and convincingly reference 'abominations' or even 'physical possession' without coming across as suspect. These were the words of vaunted, trusted men. Captains, battalion commanders, even Chapter Masters. Such testimony should have guaranteed veracity and credence.

And yet...

Creatures of Old Night and evil sorcery had been confined to myth. It was written, in ancient books, that they could reshape men and assume their forms. Towards the end of the Great Crusade, evidence that was concealed at the time – but later brought to light – gave claim that such creatures could even turn a legionary's humours against his brothers.

In Numeon's darkest nightmares, the name *Samus* resonated with eerie familiarity. Here, on Ranos, it had visited him more frequently. It had been the same on Viralis. They were not xenos, and he had seen and exterminated enough aliens to know this was the truth. Numeon knew an old word for them, one that if spoken a few years ago would have earned derision, but that now carried a ring of bitter and forbidding truth.

And, if further rumours were to be believed, the patronage of such beings was sought out and courted by the Word Bearers. They had found a different faith, the followers of Lorgar. In his gut, Numeon knew that was why they were here. He *felt* it.

'Something comes!' hissed K'gosi.

The Salamanders aimed weapons as a man-shaped figure staggered through the infirmary to reach the door to the manufactorum. It was dark inside and only a silhouette was visible through the window.

'If it is allowed to speak, it might be the end of us,' said Shen'ra.

'Agreed,' said K'gosi.

'Wait...' said Numeon. For despite those misgivings and the threat of something unknown gnawing at the resolve of every legionary in this war, this felt different.

With a low creak, the door opened and the man they knew as John Grammaticus stepped through its open frame. His hands were raised, and when he was no more than a metre beyond the doorway he stopped.

'Who are you?' Numeon demanded in a belligerent tone.

'John Grammaticus, as I told you.' He seemed calm, almost resigned, despite the fact he faced off against four battle-ready Space Marines.

'You could not have lived,' Shen'ra accused. 'Your wounds... I saw you die on that slab in there. You could not have lived.'

'And yet, here I am.'

'Precisely our problem, Grammaticus,' Numeon told him. 'You live when you should be dead.'

'I am not the only one.'

The slightest pause betrayed Numeon's doubt before he answered. 'Speak plainly,' he warned. 'No more games.'

'I haven't been entirely honest with you,' Grammaticus confessed.

'We should kill him now,' said K'gosi.

Grammaticus sighed. 'It would do no good. It never does. May I put my arms down yet?'

'No,' said Numeon. 'You may talk. If I deem what I hear to be the truth, you may put your arms down. If not, we'll bring you down a different way. Now, how is it you are still alive?'

'I am perpetual. That is to say, immortal. Your primarch is, too.'

Numeon frowned. 'What?'

'Kill him, Numeon,' K'gosi urged, 'or I'll burn him to ash where he stands.'

Numeon put out his hand to ward the Pyroclast off. 'Wait!'

'He's lying, brother,' murmured Leodrakk, edging up beside Numeon.

'I'm not,' Grammaticus told them calmly. 'This is the truth. I cannot die... *Vulkan* cannot die. He lives still, but he needs your help. *I* need your help.'

Shaking his head, Leodrakk said darkly, 'Vulkan is dead. He died on Isstvan with Ska and the others. The dead don't come back. Not unchanged, anyway. Just shells, like on Viralis.'

K'gosi was nodding. 'Fire cleanses this filth, though...' He advanced a step, close to touching Numeon's outstretched hand with his breastplate.

'Stand down.' Numeon saw the Pyroclast in his peripheral vision, the chain mask and scale long-coat lending him the appearance of an executioner. It might yet be his role.

'I want to believe him as much as you do,' said Leodrakk, switching to Nocturnean, 'but how can we? Vulkan alive? How would he even know? We've already lost enough to treachery.'

'We all wish the primarch were still with us,' added K'gosi, 'but he's gone, captain. He fell just like Ferrus Manus. Let this go.'

'And you, Shen?' asked Numeon. 'You have said little. Am I deceived, a fool to believe our lord primarch yet lives?' He risked a side glance and saw the Techmarine's face was pensive.

'I can't say what Vulkan's fate is. I only know we fought hard and bled greatly on Isstvan. If anyone could have survived, it would have been him.'

'Brother...' snarled Leodrakk, unhappy at what he saw as Shen'ra's capitulation.

'It's true,' the Techmarine replied. 'Vulkan could be alive. I don't know. But this man was dead. He was dead, Numeon, and dead men do not speak. You are our captain and we will follow your orders, all of us. But don't trust him.'

Before Numeon could answer, Leodrakk made one last plea. 'It's likely we'll die here. But I won't have us killed because we were too credulous to act against the danger in our midst.'

'*I am not the one who is in danger,*' said Grammaticus, in perfect Nocturnean.

The shock around the legionaries was masked but noticeable.

'How do you know our language?' asked Numeon.

'It's a gift.'

'Like coming back from the dead?'

'Not one of mine, per se, but yes.'

Hriak entered the room. Behind his retinal lenses, lightning streaked the pale sclera of his eyes and formed into a dark tempest.

'Lower your weapons,' he rasped, stepping into Numeon's eye line and in front of him.

No one questioned him. They lowered their weapons.

Domadus came in just after, taking up position at the door. His bolter wasn't aimed at the human but it was in his hand and ready.

'Are you going to try and prise my head open again?' asked Grammaticus, warily eyeing the approaching Librarian.

Hriak regarded the human silently for a beat. 'For a man, you are... *unusual*. And not just for your ability to cling tenaciously to life.'

'Interesting way of putting it. But you're not the first legionary to remark on that,' Grammaticus replied.

Ignoring the attempted wit, Hriak went on. 'I have heard of biomancy that can knit skin, mend bones,' he reached out to touch Grammaticus's healed body, 'but nothing like this. It could not bring men back from the dead.'

'It wasn't me,' answered Grammaticus. 'I serve a higher power who call themselves the Cabal.'

'A higher power?' said K'gosi. 'Do you believe in gods then, human?'

Grammaticus raised his eyebrow. 'Do you not, even after all you've seen?' He continued, 'They gave me eternal life. It's them whom I serve.'

Numeon detected the bitterness in his reply and, coming up alongside Hriak, asked, 'To what end, John Grammaticus? Evidently you are no creature of Old Night, else my brother here would have urged us to destroy you at once. Nor do I think you're an alien. So, if not malfeasance, what is your purpose?'

Grammaticus met the Salamander's gaze. 'To save Vulkan.'

The tension in the manufactorum suddenly went up several notches.

'So you've said,' Numeon replied. 'But I thought he was supposed to be immortal, like you? What need of saving would our primarch have?'

'I said save *him*, not save his life.'

Leodrakk sneered, his displeasure at this exchange obvious, 'And what makes you think you can succeed where we, his Legion, failed?'

Numeon bit back the urge to tell his brother they had not 'failed', and let Grammaticus continue.

'Because of the spear. I need it, the artefact your enemy took from me. They are my enemy, too. With it I can save him.' Grammaticus turned to the Librarian. 'Take a look if you don't believe me. You'll find I'm speaking the truth.'

Hriak gave Numeon an almost imperceptible nod.

Grammaticus saw it too. 'So, help me. We have a common foe in this, as well as a common goal.'

'An alliance?'

'I've been proposing one ever since you captured me.'

'Where is he then?' asked Numeon. 'Where is our primarch that we might save him? And how can a mere human, albeit an immortal one, hope to achieve such a feat? You say you need the spear to do it, but how? What power does it possess?'

'He's far from here, that's all I know. The rest is still a mystery, even to me.'

'Have Hriak tear his skull open,' snapped Leodrakk. 'He'll unlock what he knows.'

'Please… Help me to the spear and off Ranos. I can reach him.'

Numeon considered it but then gestured to Hriak.

'Tells us what he knows,' he said darkly.

The Librarian took a step forwards so he could press the palm of his right hand against the man's forehead.

'Don't do it…' murmured Grammaticus. 'You don't know what–'

He convulsed as the pain of mental intrusion hit him. Then Hriak jerked, and a grunt of agony escaped through his vox-grille.

Numeon reached out to him. 'Brother…?' The Raven Guard warded him off with an outstretched hand.

He couldn't speak. Hriak was breathing hard, the throaty sound affected by exertion as his powers were tested. He fell down to one knee, but maintained eye contact and kept his hand up to show the others he was all right. He let it drop to his gorget, then detached his helmet clamps, releasing a small plume of pressurised gas into the air. Then he lifted the helmet free. Underneath, his skin was pale, almost bone-white. Ravaged by injury, one half of the Raven Guard's face was pulled up in a permanent grimace. His neck bore the scar of a grievous throat wound. It was deep, and looked grey and ugly now that it had healed. Grammaticus balked at the grim apparition. Since Hriak's discomfort had begun, his own pain had visibly eased.

Hriak let him go, relieved no longer to be in contact.

'Do you see now?' said Numeon. 'We have suffered much and have little left to lose, save for our honour,' he told Grammaticus. 'I would have no compunction killing you now or later if you lie to us or obfuscate the truth again.'

'I am not lying. Vulkan lives,' Grammaticus said simply.

'He doesn't know anything else,' rasped Hriak, taking Numeon's arm as it was offered and getting back to his feet. He had yet to put his helmet back on, even though he was clearly uncomfortable with his comrades seeing his damaged face. Breathing was obviously easier without it, though. 'Or at least, not yet. His instructions have been imparted psychically. Some are locked. I cannot reach them.'

'He's preventing you?'

'Someone is.'

'This Cabal, his masters?'

Grammaticus interrupted, 'They guard their knowledge well. No amount of digging around in my skull is going to unearth what you're after.'

'I have to concur,' Hriak conceded, reaching for his helmet.

'Either help me or let me go,' said Grammaticus. 'This stalemate achieves nothing for either of us. Let me save him.'

'How?' asked Numeon, suddenly angry. 'I need to know. I *have* to know.'

Grammaticus sagged, defeated. 'I don't know. How many times must I say it? I only know it concerns the spear.'

Numeon calmed down, but his frustration was still bubbling under the surface. He turned to the others. 'The cleric likely has the spear now,' he said. 'We'll take it from him.'

'From his dead hand,' put in Leodrakk as he saw the chance for petty revenge.

'One way or another,' Numeon replied. He glanced at Grammaticus. 'Bind him. I don't want him trying to escape.'

Domadus nodded and began uncoiling a length of rappelling cable from his belt.

'This is a mistake,' said Grammaticus.

'Maybe. Either way you are not leaving us just yet. I want to see what happens when you are reunited with the spear, see what fresh secrets tumble from your mind. Then I'll have Hriak pry open your skull and extract whatever is hidden within.'

Grammaticus hung his head, let his arms fall by his sides and cursed whatever fates had delivered him to the Salamanders.

EIGHTY METRES FROM the manufactorum, Narek hunched low behind a half-collapsed wall and peered in awe through his scope.

'Impossible…' he breathed, adjusting the focus, enhancing the image through the shattered window-glass.

He saw six legionaries, the guerrilla fighters from before, just as he had predicted. What surprised him was the sight of the man he had killed, the one who could not have survived his wounds and yet stood unscathed in the middle of the manufactorum floor. Standing. Breathing. Alive.

Narek opened the vox to Elias, vaguely aware of his companions around him and knowing the rest were converging from separate angles on the manufactorum.

'Apostle…' he began.

Things were about to change.

DESPITE THE ATTENTIONS of his Apothecary, Elias was in excruciating pain. After a struggle, two legionaries had managed to get him back into his power armour but his burned arm remained unclad. It was black and almost useless. The wounds from the godfire that had seared him seemed unaffected by his enhanced physiology or any healing skill his Legion possessed. Only a rival patron could restore him, and as he sat clenched with agony in his tent, Elias thought bitterly on the failed ritual.

The spear was nearby, lying on a table within reach. It no longer glowed, nor burned. It simply appeared to be a spearhead fashioned from rock and mineral. But that simple shell contained something much more potent.

Elias was considering when to apprise Erebus of his progress, but wanted to be in a clear frame of mind first. His master would have questions, questions Elias wasn't sure he had the answers to just yet. So when the vox crackled to life, his mood was particularly fractious.

'What is it?' he snapped, wincing at the pain in his arm.

It was Narek.

At first Elias was annoyed. How many more times would he have to tell the huntsman what was required of him? It was a simple task, a well-trained dog could do it. He was considering in what manner to sever his ties with Narek when what he heard changed his mind on the subject. The contortion of Elias's face, a grimace of pain and snarl of anger, turned to interest and machination.

Suddenly the pain seemed to diminish, his maiming become less significant.

The ritual had failed. Not because of the spear, or the words. It was the sacrifice that he had got wrong. Now he knew why.

Elias rose from his seat and reached for his battle-helm.

'Bring him to me. Alive, so I can kill him.'

Fate and the Pantheon had not abandoned him after all.

He smiled. Erebus would have to wait.

SOMETHING HAD HAPPENED. Narek could tell from the tone of Elias's voice. He sounded in pain, and the huntsman wondered what Elias had tried to do with the spear. Something foolish, driven by hubris. He put it out of his mind. Amaresh was waiting. He could almost hear the eager rush of blood in the other Word Bearer's veins.

'What are we waiting for?' he growled.

Narek didn't bother making eye contact. He lowered the scope.

'Plan's changed,' he said, relaying his orders across the vox to his men. 'Our orders are to extract the human. Alive.'

'You are not serious,' snarled Amaresh, grabbing for Narek's shoulder guard. In a single movement, the huntsman twisted the other Word Bearer's armoured wrist and smashed him down onto the ground. He did it so quickly that the others had barely noticed. Amaresh went to rise, but found the blade of Narek's knife pressed at his throat. One thrust and it would pierce gorget, neck and bone.

'Deadly serious,' he told him. 'Dagon,' he began after a few seconds, once he was sure that Amaresh would follow orders. 'Maintain eyes on all the exits.'

Dagon gave a clipped affirmative.

'Infrik, come around the front and– Wait, there's something...' Narek had looked up to gauge the relative positions of his men. That was when he saw the smallest glint of metal, reflected from a scope lens. 'Clever...'

Amaresh had only just risen to his feet when the bolt-round entered the back of his battle-helm, into his head, and exited through his left retinal lens in a welter of blood and bone. Even a legionary as gifted as Amaresh couldn't survive that.

Narek hit the deck.

He doubted that the sniper would take another shot, at least not a meaningful one. He knew the shooter. It was the one from the cooling tower, the legionary who had seen him and Dagon before. Amaresh was a jerking corpse as the last dregs of nervous convulsion left him. Narek found himself liking this enemy.

The plan changed again.

He reopened the vox, relaying calmly, 'Full attack.'

CHAPTER
TWENTY-ONE
Torment

'I have seen darkness, witnessed it in my dreams. I am standing at the edge of a chasm. There is no escaping it, I know my fate. For it is the future and nothing can prevent it coming to pass. So I step off and welcome the dark.'
— Konrad Curze, the 'Night Haunter'

I RETURNED FROM the darkness again, only now I possessed the knowledge of how and why. To most men, learning that you are immortal would be the cause of unbridled euphoria. For is it not the ambition of mankind to endure, to live on, to eke out more years? Cryogenics, rejuvenat, cloning, even pacts with fell creatures... Through science or superstition, mankind has always sought to avoid the end. He will cheat it if he can, devoting the resources of his entire existence to just a little *more*.

I cannot be killed. Not by any means known to me, or to my vicious brother. It would not end. Ever.

To know you are immortal is to know that time is meaningless, that every ambition you ever aspired to fulfil could be, one day, within your grasp. You would not age. You could not be maimed or debilitated physically. You would never die.

To know immortality was, for some men, to know the greatest gift.

I knew only despair.

As I came round, the phantom pain in my chest reminded me of the blade my brother had rammed into it. Curze couldn't kill me. He had tried, extremely hard. It begged the question of what he would do next.

The answer to that would not be long in coming.

When I tried to move my arms, I found that I couldn't. Disorientated, I was slow to realise that I was neither chained nor back in the dread chamber where my weakness had consigned so many to death; I was in an entirely different trap.

At first I felt the weight upon my shoulders, heavy and biting. Bolts and nails had been hammered into my flesh, pinning them. The device of my apparent crucifixion was some kind of metal armature, humanoid in shape but armoured in barbs and spikes that both extruded from and intruded upon the wearer. A crude mechanism locked into my jaw and chin, forcing it up. My lips were wired together. My legs and arms were sheathed in metal, the latter ending in a pair of blades. Stooped, I felt the first jerk of my marionette's strings and saw my left leg rise and fall in a single step.

'Hnngg...' I tried to speak but the razor in my mouth muffled any protests.

I was in a corridor, the ceiling low enough that my armoured chassis just scraped it. The metal bulk of the death machine I was wearing filled its width. Ahead of me, partially shrouded by the gloom, I saw their eyes. They were wide, and widened further when they saw me, or what had become of me.

'Run!' a man wearing a dirty and tattered Army uniform said to another. They fled into the dark, and with the sound of my metal skull scraping the ceiling above, I gave chase. My strides were slow at first, but built with a steady, loping momentum. Rounding a corner, I caught sight of the men. They had taken a wrong turn and were trapped at a dead end. I could smell ammonia and realised that one of the troopers had soiled his fatigues. The other was wrenching a pipe off the wall, trying to make an improvised weapon and a last stand.

He swung it experimentally, like a man standing next to a fire who wields a burning torch to fend off a predator. I heard a low *shunk* of metal as a switch was thrown remotely. Harsh light suddenly filled the corridor from the search lamps on my chassis, blinding the two men. I tried to resist but my armoured frame propelled me after them, the serrated blades at the ends of my arms blurring into life with a throaty roar.

I tried to stop it. I heaved and thrashed, but could barely move. A passenger of the machine, I could only watch as I turned the men to offal and listened to their screaming. Mercifully, it ended quickly and the air grew still again. Only the sound of my desperate breathing and the gore dripping off my spattered frame in fat clumps disturbed the quiet.

Something scurried past behind me and my deadly armour turned as if scenting prey. I was moving again, striding down the corridor on the hunt for fresh victims. I struggled, but could not stop or slow the machine. Along the next stretch of tunnel, I saw three figures. More of my brother's slaves. I had been unleashed upon them in this pit, clad in death. Curze was making me kill them.

My lumbering gait turned into a frenzied run, the clanking footfalls like death knells to my ears. Up came the search lamps again, hot and buzzing next to my face, and I saw three men. Unshaven, brawny, they were veterans. As I bore down on them, they grimly held their ground. One had fashioned an axe from a section of plating, a taped-up rag around the narrow end for a handle; another had an improvised club like my last kill; the third just clenched his fists.

Such defiance and insane valour. It would not avail them.

'Come on!' the one with the axe shouted down at me. 'Come on!'

My armoured frame obliged, responding to the goad with chain-blades spinning.

When I passed another corridor that crossed with the one I was in, I realised what the veterans had done. My puppeteer did not.

As I reached the crossroads, heading blindly at the three men who were shouting and jeering a few metres beyond the junction, a second group of prisoners sprung the trap. A spear thrust grazed my ribs and I grimaced. It went on into the metal vambrace encasing my left arm, severing some cabling. Oil and fluid began to vent furiously.

Just as I was turning to face my first attacker, a second axe weighed in and embedded itself in my right hip. It bit into my flank but the armour bore the brunt. My chain-blade tried to lash out but the cabling snapped and the armature fell limp.

A stern-faced legionary looked up at me, pulling his spear back for another thrust. He wore the black and white of the Raven Guard, though his armour and iconography had seen far better days. My still functional right arm whipped around and took off the warrior's head before he could attack again.

As the black, beak-nosed helmet bounced off into the darkness, my search lamps flickered and all of the ambushers attacked me at once. I spun, opening up two of the veteran troopers and spilling them out onto the metal deck. The third stooped to pick up his comrade's fallen club, but my leg snapped out before he could grab it. The impact hit him square in the chest. I heard ribs break and watched him half spiral down the corridor before crumpling in a lifeless heap.

My last opponent struck again, focusing on the damaged arm,

which was spitting sparks and spraying oil. Another legionary loomed into my eye line. My heart sank when I saw the colour of his battle-plate.

Emerald-green.

He was broad-shouldered, the faded insignia of the 15th Company emblazoned on his dented pauldron.

Nemetor…

I had believed he was dead. Curze had saved him. He'd done it so I was the one that butchered him.

Entombed in the machine, I was unrecognisable to my son. Ducking a hopeful swipe of my remaining chainblade, he hacked into my left arm and jolted some of the pins impaled in my nerves loose. Some feeling returned, and I found I could move the arm again. Watching Nemetor's hope turn into horror as the weapon he thought he'd destroyed began to move as I lifted it, I then turned the buzzing chainblade on myself. Momentum from my frenzied machine's attacks drove the saw into my body, first cutting metal, then flesh.

I let it gore me until darkness began to crouch at the edge of my vision, until death, however brief, reclaimed me.

'CLEVER,' I HEARD the voice of my brother say.

I blinked, opening my eyes and saw the death machine had been removed and that I was back in my cell.

'I stand both impressed and disappointed,' he said.

At first I saw armour of cobalt-blue, trimmed with gold; a firm and noble countenance, framed by close-cropped blond hair; a warrior, a statesman, my brother the empire builder.

'Guilliman?' I breathed, hoping, my sense of reality slipping for a moment.

Then I knew, and a scowl crept onto my face.

'No… it's you.'

I was sitting with my back against the wall, looking up murderously at my brother.

Curze laughed when he noticed my expression.

'We're getting close now, aren't we?'

'How long?' I croaked, tasting ash in my mouth and feeling a fresh brand in my back.

'A few hours. It's getting faster.'

I tried to stand, but was still weak. I slumped back.

'How many?'

Curze narrowed his eyes.

I clarified my question, 'How many times have you tried to kill me?'

My brother crouched down opposite, within my reach but betraying no concern about retaliation for what he had done to me, what he continued to do to me. He nodded to the wall behind me.

I turned to see my reflection mirrored in obsidian. I saw Curze too, and Ferrus Manus, now little more than a walking cadaver in his primarch's armour, standing just behind him.

'You see them?' He pointed to the numerous honour scars branded into my back. Some stood out from the others, a clutch of more recent brandings that I had no memory of and could attribute no oath to.

Curze leaned in and whispered into my ear, 'A fresh scar every time, brother...'

There were dozens.

'Every time, you returned to torment me,' he said.

I faced him. 'Torment *you*?'

Curze stood, his armoured form casting a shadow over me from the low light in the cell. He looked almost sad.

'I am at a loss, Vulkan. I don't know what to do with you.'

'Then release me. What is the point of killing me over and over again if I cannot die?'

'Because I enjoy it. Each attempt brings with it the hope you will stay dead, but also the dread that we shall be forever parted.'

'Sentiments of a madman,' I spat.

Curze's eyes were oddly pitying. 'I think, perhaps, not the only one. Is our dead brother with us still? Is Ferrus here?'

At the mention of his name, the cadaver's mouth gaped as if amused. Without eyes or much flesh, it was hard to tell.

I nodded, seeing no point in hiding the fact I saw the undying effigy of Ferrus Manus.

'I thought so,' said Curze, unable to shake his melancholy. 'Our father gave you eternal life. Do you know what he gave me? Nightmares.' His mood darkened further, his face transformed into genuine anguish. For a moment I caught a glimpse of my brother's true self and despite all that he had done or claimed to have done, I pitied him.

'I am plagued by them, Vulkan.' Curze was no longer looking at me. He regarded his reflection in the obsidian instead. It appeared to be something he had done before, and I imagined him then, screaming in the darkness with no one to hear his terror.

The Lord of Fear was afraid. It was an irony I thought Fulgrim would appreciate, twisted as he was.

'How can I escape the dark if the dark is part of what I am?'

'Konrad,' I said. 'Tell me what you see.'

'I am Night Haunter. The death that haunts the darkness...' he answered, though his voice and mind were far away. 'Konrad Curze is dead.'

'He stands before me,' I pressed. 'What do you see?'

'Darkness. Unending and eternal. It's all for nothing, brother. Everything we do, everything that has been done or will be done... It doesn't matter. Nothing matters. I *fear*. I *am* fear. What kind of a knife-edge is that to balance on, I ask?'

'You have a choice,' I said, hoping that some fraternal bond, some vestige of reason still existed in my brother. It would be buried deep, but I could unearth it.

He turned his gaze upon me – so lost, so bereft of hope. Curze was a mangy hound that had been kicked too many times.

'Don't you see, Vulkan? There are no choices. It is determined for us, my fate and yours. So I make the only choice I can. Anarchy and terror.'

I saw it then, what had broken inside my brother. His tactics, his erratic moods, were all caused by this flaw. It had led him to destroy his home world.

Dorn had seen the madness lurking within him. I suppose I had known it was there too, back on Kharaatan.

'Let me help you, Konrad…' I began.

Pale like alabaster, eyes dark like chips of jet with about as much warmth, Curze's face changed. As the thin, viper's smile crawled over his lips, I knew that I had lost him and my chance of appealing to what little humanity still remained.

'You would like that, I think. A chance to prove your nobility. Vulkan, champion of the common man, most grounded of us all. But you're not on the ground, are you, brother? You are far from your beloved earth. Is it colder, here with me in the dark?' he asked, bitterly. 'You are no better than me, Vulkan. You're a killer just the same. Remember Kharaatan?' he goaded.

I remembered, and lowered my head at the memory of what I had done, what I *nearly* did.

'You weren't yourself, brother,' hissed Ferrus, his graveyard breath whistling through skeletal cheeks. 'You had a backbone.'

Curze seemed not to notice.

'Our father's gifts are wasted on you,' he said. 'Eternal life, and what would you do with it? Till a field, raise a crop, build a forge to make ploughshares and hoes. Vulkan the farmer! You sicken me! Guilliman is dull, but at least he has ambition. At least he had an empire.'

'*Had?*'

'Oh,' Curze smiled, 'you don't know, do you?'

'What has happened to Ultramar?'

'It doesn't matter. You'll never see it.'

I suddenly feared for Roboute and all my loyal brothers that fell beneath Curze's notice. If he had done this to me, then what could he have done to the rest of them?

'Nemetor…' I said, as parts of my most recent ordeal came back to me, including the appearance of a son I had thought dead. 'Was he…?'

'Real?' Curze suggested, grinning.

'Did you kill him?' I pressed.

'You're dying to know aren't you, brother?' He held up his hand. 'Sorry, poor choice of words. You'll see him again, before the end.'

'So, this *will* end then?'

'One way or another, Vulkan. Yes, I sincerely hope it will end.'

He left me then, backing off into the shadows. I watched him all the way to the cell door. As it was opened, I saw the slightest shaft of light and wondered how deep my prison went. I also half caught a hurried conversation and got the sense of a commotion outside. Though I didn't hear his muttered words, Curze seemed irritated in his curt responses. Booted footsteps moved quickly, hammering the deck, before they were cut off by the cell door shutting.

Lumen-globes burning in the alcoves in the flanking walls died, darkness returned and with it the faint, mocking laughter of my dead brother.

'Shut up, Ferrus,' I said.

But it only made him laugh louder.

CHAPTER
TWENTY-TWO
Egress

THE NORTH-FACING ASPECT of the manufactorum was a broken ruin. Outside, the dead and injured littered the streets.

Narek had lost eight legionaries in the frontal assault, not including Amaresh, who had been cut down by their sniper. Despite the losses, he appreciated the symmetry of that, one hunter pitched against the other. He decided that he would have a reckoning with this warrior – see how sharp his own edge was and if, despite his grievous injuries, he could still consider himself worthy. It was an honourable contest, not like the bloodbath he had left behind.

Distasteful and profligate as it was, it was also necessary. Discovered in the midst of stealthing to their gate, Narek had no other choice but to push down the throat of the loyalists, knowing full well that they had a track-mounted cannon and a defensible position. Admittedly, he hadn't predicted they would open fire straight away – the bulk of his troops were still vaulting barricades and running stooped-over to the next scrap of cover when the world lit up in actinic blue – but it had served its intended purpose. Dagon, Narlech and Infrik had circled around the rear egress. That left Melach, Saarsk, Vogel and himself skirting the flanks; two on the right, two on the left.

Head down, hugging the edge of the street as the gun battle to the front of the manufactorum raged, Narek hissed down the vox to his elite, 'Close the trap, find the human and bring him to me alive.'

'*And the rest?*' Narlech voxed back.

Narek could already hear the bloodlust in his voice. 'Kill anyone that gets in your way. I don't want prisoners, give me corpses.' He cut the feed.

Nearby he could hear that his enemies had broken out of the back of the building.

'How did they find us?' Leodrakk had to shout to be heard, bolt shells and chips of rockcrete from the manufactorum's slowly disintegrating structure raining all around them.

Numeon shook his head. 'Could've been the pyre smoke or we may have been under watch already.'

'But why come at us like this, straight at us?'

'Pergellen forced their hand.'

'Doesn't make sense. They would have hunkered down, circled us and called in reinforcements.'

Numeon paused, eyeing the gloom beyond the walls. Behind him, he heard Domadus shouting orders between the percussive reports of his heavy bolter. As soon as word came from Pergellen that the XVII had found them, all legionaries inside the manufactorum had formed up into a firing line. Only Numeon, Leodrakk and two in raven's black moved through the back of the building to the manufactorum's rear exit. It was no fortress, and they couldn't stay here, but what Leodrakk was saying made sense. Why not lay siege and wait until they could storm the barricades in force?

'It's a distraction,' he decided. 'Keeping our attention front.'

The rear exit to the manufactorum was a depot strewn with the half-blasted carcasses of freight-haulers. Lots of cover, lots of places to hide.

'You see that?' said Numeon, crouching down by the rear door and gesturing outside.

'There are three of them,' whispered Hriak, his hand firmly gripping the human's shoulder.

'You aren't seriously considering going out there?' asked Grammaticus.

Numeon ignored him. He caught the slight movement again. Whoever they were, they were using the haulers to get close.

'They're after the human,' he said. 'Capture, not kill, this time.'

'How can you be sure?' asked Leodrakk.

'The frontal assault was to flush us out. They knew we'd try and bolt with the human. Because if they *have* been watching us, it's likely they saw what we saw.'

Hriak looked down at Grammaticus. 'Your apotheosis…'

'No explanation was needed,' Grammaticus replied snidely. 'It doesn't matter what I say, does it? You're going to carry on blindly like this, regardless of consequence, aren't you? You've lost your faith in everything.'

Leodrakk snarled. 'We've lost much more than that.'

'Be calm,' Numeon told him, giving Grammaticus a quick glance to shut him up before going on. 'We're wasting time. Get *him* out of here. We can draw these three off.'

He looked at Avus crouching next to him, the foils of his jump pack folded back for now. The legionary had kept his own counsel until that moment.

'I'll have weregeld for Shaka, measured in blood. And when my corvidae hangs in memory of the sacrifice I made, and I become part of the raven's feast, only then shall I know peace,' he vowed. '*Victorus aut Mortis.*'

Hriak bowed his head in solemn respect. *'Victorus aut Mortis,* brother.'

Numeon nodded to all three.

'We'll rendezvous in the tunnels. *All* of us. May the Emperor go with you.'

Elias felt restive, and not only because of the dull agony in his arm. Outside the tent, the sacrificial pit was quiet, though the air still trembled with the urgent fury of the Neverborn. He could sense their anger. It mirrored his own. To be thwarted so close to his goal, and for what? Some human he had let slip through his grasp.

The overeager hand snatches air, where the considered one holds on to substance.

He had heard Erebus use these words before. They echoed mockingly back at him through the years.

Ranos was dead. His Word Bearers had effectively denuded the city of all life and now only these loyalist dregs and their prisoner remained. But still he was denied the prize he so coveted. Weapons, Erebus had told him. Half dead, his face a bloody ruin, he had uttered this truth. Elias was certain that the spearhead was one such weapon of which his master had spoken. It was raw power incarnated in a fulgurite. Any doubts he may have had about that died along with his arm and the seven acolytes that had burned to ash earlier.

Warily he reached out to touch the spear. It was surprisingly cool and certainly inert, whatever past reaction it may have undergone now dormant but not yet spent. It hummed with a faint vibration, and the blade still threw off a lambent light that suggested its godlike provenance.

Monarchia... Yes, Elias remembered it well, too. He had wept that day, first tears of zealous joy as the cathedra had risen to the sky then righteous anger when the XIII had shamed his Legion and his primarch. He scarcely remembered the human dead, and felt the Emperor's snub more keenly. Erebus had counselled him that day. He had counselled many. His master had seemed oddly sanguine, as if he knew some measure of what was going to happen before it had actually transpired. *That* was power. To see fates, to bend and shape them to your will and benefit. Why Erebus had always skulked in the shadows, the power behind the throne instead of its incumbent king, Elias would never understand.

'What does Erebus know that I–'

The thought was interrupted by the activation of his warp-flask.

Even in the eldritch fire of the flask, Erebus looked crooked and broken. He was dressed in dark robes with a deep cowl hiding his face and head.

Elias bowed at once. 'Master... you are recovered?'

'*Evidently not,*' said Erebus, gesturing to his bent-backed form, '*but I am healing.*'

'It is glorious to behold, my lord. When I left you in the apothecarion–'

Erebus interrupted. '*Tell me what is happening on Ranos.*'

'Of course,' said Elias, bowing again so he could unclench his teeth without his anger being seen. He held up the spear. 'The weapon,' he announced proudly, 'is in my possession.'

Erebus looked at him in silent incredulity.

Elias could not hide his confusion and said, 'To win the war. Your last words to me before I left with my warriors.'

'Your *warriors, Elias?*'

'Yours, my lord, humbly appropriated for the task you gave me.'

'*You have nothing but a spear, Elias. I mean* weapons. *That with which we shall win this war for Horus and the Pantheon.*' There was a slight angry tremor in Erebus's voice when he mentioned the Warmaster's name, and Elias briefly wondered what had happened between them. '*Sharpen our own, blunt theirs,*' Erebus told him.

'*Whoever has the most weapons wins. Don't you understand that yet?*'

Elias was confused. He had done all that was asked of him and yet his master was obviously displeased. Erebus had also neglected to mention his injury, as if perhaps he already knew of it...

'I... My lord?' Elias began.

Erebus didn't answer at first. He was muttering something as if speaking to someone Elias could not see, but the image in the flask showed a chamber that was empty save for Erebus.

'*Where is John Grammaticus?*' he said at last.

'Who? The human, you mean?'

'*Where is he, Elias? You need him.*'

'I have men hunting for him as we speak. They are bringing him to me.'

'*No,*' said Erebus. '*Do it yourself. Find John Grammaticus and hold him for me. Do not sully him in any way, that is my only warning to you.*'

Elias raised an eyebrow, and tried to keep the fear out of his voice. 'You are coming here?'

Erebus nodded. '*I have seen the mess you have made on Ranos.*'

Fear turned to anger in Elias. 'I could not have predicted the other legionaries' presence here. Nor can I leave the ritual site. The Neverborn are–'

Erebus cut him off for the third time with a swipe of his hand. Elias noticed that it was a bionic and appended to his master's severed wrist stump. '*As usual you have failed to grasp the subtleties of the warp. No more blood or further entreaties will get you what you want, Elias.*'

'I only serve you, my lord.'

Erebus chuckled. It was an unpleasant, throaty sound, like he was the victim of some pervasive cancer with only hours to live.

'*I have matters to attend to here, but be ready for my coming. Be sure that Grammaticus is in your hands by the time that I arrive, or a fire-blackened limb will be the least of your concerns...*'

The warp flame evaporated as quickly as it had manifested, leaving Elias alone. Despite the pain in his arm, his entire body tensed with barely contained anger.

'I am your disciple...' he gasped at the uncaring air. 'Your follower. I saved you, took you from that chamber where you would have died without my help.' His jaw clenched, so tightly that he could no longer utter words. All that came from Elias's mouth was a spitting, frothing snarl. He fought for calm, found it in the dark pit of his rotten soul.

Elias called out to summon his equerry. 'Jadrekk...'

The warrior appeared at the tent mouth almost immediately, bowing low.

'We are leaving. Gather everyone, but leave two squads to maintain vigil over the pit. We are rejoining Narek and the others.'

Jadrekk bowed again and went to carry out his orders.

Thirty-seven legionaries awaited Elias beyond the confines of his sanctum. Twenty of those would stay behind, whilst the rest would reinforce Narek. It had never been intended as a battle force. It was an honour guard, Elias's own personal cult. Mortals were but lambs to slaughter in the Pantheon's name. Legionaries demanded sterner attention. Elias had thought the loyalists nothing more than an inconvenience, sustenance for the Neverborn when he unleashed them upon this world and forever tainted it for Chaos. Now they stood in the path of his deserved glory. They had proven resourceful so far, but their resistance was at an end. Sheathing the fulgurite spear in his scabbard, he lifted his mace with his good arm. It was heavy, but it felt good to wrap his fist around the skin-bound haft.

It would feel even better when it was cracking skulls, every blow a step towards his eventual apotheosis.

EREBUS SEVERED THE psychic communion to his disciple and staggered. Reaching out, he supported himself against the wall of his cell and exhaled a shuddering breath. Even imbued by the power of the warp, his regeneration was slow. He looked down upon the bare metal of his bionic hand. It was already clenched in a fist, as if his will alone could sustain and restore him. The grimace on Erebus's face was transformed into a smile. He saw it reflected in the metal floor of his sanctum, just as he saw the slow creeping of flesh that had begun to colonise his flayed visage. It was harder, darker than before. Tiny bone nubs protruded from his skull. His eyes took on a visceral cast. It was the favour of the gods, Erebus knew it. Lorgar and Horus might have forsaken him for now, but the Pantheon had not. He could feel their restlessness, however. Despite the Dark Apostle's knowledge and manipulation of the fates, Horus was not the pawn that Erebus had claimed him to be.

In the earliest days, when sedition was muttered in whispers and the warrior lodges were in their infancy, there had been other choices. It need not have been Horus. None of that mattered now. Erebus was, above all, a survivor. His ravaged face and body bore testament to that.

'I am still the architect of this heresy...' he hissed to the darkness, which had been listening eagerly ever since he arrived.

His mistake was at Signus. Had he known, had he caught the slightest inkling of Horus's jealousy... Sanguinius was supposed to have turned and become a Red Angel. Instead, he lived, and neither Horus nor Erebus had got what they wanted. He would be subtler next time. But he needed answers. The Angel and the Warmaster were not his concern now. Erebus's eye had fallen upon another.

It took some effort, but he raised his head to meet the gaze of the other being in the room.

'Can it kill him?' he asked.

The creature manifest in a pall of roiling smoke opposite nodded its feathered heads. Its beaks chattered, incessantly mumbling. Erebus forced his mind to shut out these words, for they were madness and to hear them was to be damned to the same fate.

He bowed as the smoke faded, taking the daemon with it. The great pressure upon Erebus was relieved, and he could straighten his back. He breathed for the first time in a long time without it feeling like a saw was ripping through his chest.

'Then it shall be done, Oracle,' he said to the ghosting smoke, and left the sanctum.

CHAPTER
TWENTY-THREE
Penumbra

HIS BREATHING GAVE my brother away.

'Ferrus, leave me alone…'

Since my last encounter with Curze, I had sunk into a deep melancholy, struggling to put together what was real and what I only imagined. Each time I returned from death, I felt a piece of my mind slip away like a shed scale or flake of ash. And the harder I tried to grasp at it, the more it fragmented. I was breaking – not physically, but mentally. Yet I was not alone in that. Curze too had showed me some of his inner doubt, his pain. Whatever he had witnessed in the visions he described had disturbed an already fragile mind. The sadistic tendencies, his obvious nihilism, were both symptomatic of that. I didn't know if he meant to share his trauma to make me pity him or somehow lull me into trusting him as part of some longer torture, or whether his mask had simply slipped and I had been treated to his true image. Both of us had been reflected in the obsidian glass and neither of us liked what we saw.

'Ferrus is dead, brother,' a voice answered, prompting me to open my eyes.

The cell of volcanic glass hadn't changed. In its walls I beheld my reflection, but could see no other, despite the fact that whoever was in here with me was close enough that I could hear them whisper.

'Who are you?' I demanded, standing. My feet were unsteady but I held my ground. 'Ferrus, if this is some trick–'

'Ferrus died on Isstvan, as I once thought you had done.'

My eyes widened, I dared to hope. I recognised the voice of my unseen companion.

'Corvus?'

From the darkness, I saw a shadow that bled outwards into a silhouette before finally resolving into Corax, my brother. It was as if the Ravenlord were wearing a long cloak that he had suddenly cast off to reveal his presence. Despite the fact that he was standing in front of me, he still portrayed no reflection in the glass, and as I regarded him I found it difficult to pinpoint his exact location in the room. He *was* shadow, always within the penumbra even in the harshest daylight. It was his gift.

I reached out to touch his face and whispered, partly to myself, 'Are you real?'

Corax was clad in black power armour of an avian aspect. With two taloned gauntlets he disengaged the locking clamps that affixed his war-helm to his gorget. The beaked helmet came loose without a sound. Even the Ravenlord's power generator from which sprouted his jump pack's incredible wings functioned almost silently. It was only by the virtue of my primarch's hearing that I could detect the lowest, residual background hum.

'I am as real as you, Vulkan,' he said, lifting the war-helm to reveal a slightly aquiline face framed by long, black hair. There was a quiet wisdom in his eyes that I recognised, as well as the greyish pallor common to inhabitants of Kiavahr. A pelt of raven feathers ringed his waist and there was a large skull that rested above his armoured pelvis from some great prey-bird that he had once stalked and killed.

'It *is* you, Corvus.'

I wanted to embrace him, to embrace hope in the form of my brother, but Corax was not as tactile as Ferrus had been. Like the bird from which he took his name, Corax did not like his feathers to be touched. I saluted him instead, pressing my clenched fist against my bare chest.

Corax saluted in return before replacing his helm.

'How?' I asked. 'We are aboard Curze's ship.'

'I can explain how I found you later.' He clapped me on the shoulder, a rare concession for him, and for the first time in what felt like years I experienced a lost sense of brotherhood and comradeship. 'Now I need you to come with me. We're getting you out of this place.'

As he spoke, my eye was drawn to the half-light spilling into my cell. Through the open door, I saw a dimly lit corridor and a strike team of Raven Guard surrounded by dead Night Lords.

'Can you fight?' Corax asked me, glancing over his shoulder as he led me to freedom.

'Yes,' I replied, and felt some of my faded strength returning. I had been a long time from earth and beaten constantly as I was, my fighting prowess was far from its height. I caught a bolter in mid-flight. It felt good to wrap my hand around the trigger, feel its heft. I racked the slide. It was Corax's own weapon, not his favoured armament but a back-up. I was glad to receive it.

I had questions, many of them, about the war and Horus. But this was not the time.

As my brother reached the doorway, he said something to his Raven Guard in Kiavahran that I didn't understand before unfurling his power whip and letting the three barbed tips crackle with energy as they touched the ground. Four silver claws extended from his other hand, their blades wreathed in actinic fury.

'Our ship is close, but these corridors are swarming with Eighth Legion filth. *We* can bypass them easily enough but we'll need to take a different route with you, brother.'

Corax was about to lead us out when I gripped his forearm.

'I had almost given up hope,' I said quietly.

Corax nodded. 'So had I, of ever finding you alive.' He held my gaze for a second, before turning towards the corridor. 'Follow me, brother.'

He swept out of the cell and though I was close on his heels, I almost immediately lost them in the gloom. The corridor was wide, but low and well enough lit, yet Corax and his kin were hard to locate.

'We cannot wait, Vulkan,' my brother whispered.

'I can barely see you.'

'Make for the end of the corridor. Kravex is there.'

My eyes narrowed and I found the legionary, just as Corax had described, waiting at the end of the corridor. His appearance was a fleeting shadow, for when I reached the point where he had been standing, Kravex was gone again.

It continued like this for what felt like hours, moving unchallenged and unheeded through myriad tunnels, vents and ducts. Sometimes the way led us down or crawling through some narrow conduit or climbing up some claustrophobic shaft. Always Corax was nearby but never close enough to actually feel like he was there. He was a shade, moving through the darkest fog, cleaving to the shadow's edge and never quite stepping into the light.

I followed as best I could, catching glimpses of Kravex or one of the other Raven Guard when my sense of direction faltered and they had to put me back on the path. I think there were five in all, not including Corax, but I could not swear to that. The XIX were experts in subterfuge. Ambuscade and stealth fighting were an art form to the Ravens. I felt woefully under-schooled.

Several times I was stopped suddenly – my brother, though still occluded, hissing a warning to make me pause. Legionaries were looking for us. We heard their booted feet, caught snatches of their passage, through the vents and iron grilles of the vast ship.

Deeper now, into its bowels, we found ourselves in the ship's bilge. Effluence ran in a thick river and the walls were crusted with grime and other matter. It was a vast and cyclopean sewer, wrought of dark metal, crosshatched with girders and hanging chains. Heat from the enginarium decks wafted down through slow-moving turbine fans, churning up the vile stench of the place. The toxic air would have killed lesser men, and I suspected that the uneven floor underfoot was actually bone.

'Through this channel,' said Corax, stepping down into a sloping aqueduct and keeping his voice low as a search team rattled the deck grille far above our heads, 'we can bypass a heavily guarded part of the ship. A hatch at the end leads out to an ancillary deck where we breached.'

'And what if your ship has already been found?' I asked, following my brother and his warriors as they waded into the murky sewer. It was dark in the tunnel, only illuminated by the fizzing glow of phosphor lamps.

'Unlikely,' Corax answered. 'It is masked beyond the means of this vessel's sensorium to detect. Come on.' His warriors were ranging ahead, and I soon lost them in the gloom.

We tramped on through the filth in silence, the disturbed waters only making the fumes more noisome. As above, below it was a labyrinth and I had the distinct feeling we were heading down towards its core. A part of me yearned to find Curze waiting there, so I could inflict upon him every act of retribution I had dreamed about since being incarcerated at my mad brother's pleasure.

It would be so easy... His skull in my hands, the bone cracking as I slowly crushed it.

The long stretch of straight bilge pipe was finally giving way to a sharp bend when I caught the stark muzzle flash in my eye line and heard the grunted accusation of discovery.

Corax was already moving, several metres ahead of me, power whip cracking in his gauntleted fist. 'They have found us!'

I heard one of the Raven Guard fall, but didn't see it. Our vanguard was beyond the bend; so, too, was Corax now, and I could only hear the battle. There was a loud splash and I assumed that the warrior had sunk into the water.

I reached the turn but found only darkness in front of me. Even with the phosphor lamps, spitting and flickering in the rank air, I could see neither friend nor foe.

Another flash set me to purpose, a fleeting pict-capture of monochrome grey lodged in my retina of two legionaries clashing with blades. I roamed towards them, finding sludge under my feet and progress slow. The next section of pipe was equally as long as the first and my allies fought some way down it, far from my aid.

I stopped, trying to ascertain how many enemies we were facing, and where. Without the muzzle flash my sight was hindered again. I set the bolter I had been given under my chin, resting the stock against my cheek as I slowly panned it around the sewer. Weapons fire reverberated off the vaulted ceiling, echoing loudly, making it difficult to pinpoint. I realised the pipe in this part of the sewer was far from straight. Columns supported it, their foundations beneath the rancid waterline. There were alcoves and sub-ducts, maintenance ledges and antechambers. Without a bearing I could quickly lose my way, and my rescuers with it.

Somewhere in the distance, Corax was fighting. I heard the crack of his power whip, and could smell the ozone reek of his lightning claws even above the rancid fluid slowly riming my waist. I broke through the viscous skin that had started to encircle me, wading quickly through the morass as I fought to reach my brother.

In shuddering silhouette I saw another Raven die, his wings bent outwards as a bolt shell tore him open.

'Corax!' I called out, still panning with my bolter, concerned that any snap shot might hit my brother or one of his sons.

I heard the clash of steel, a burst of bolter fire, but got no answer.

'Corax!'

Still nothing. The tunnel yawned in front of me, a diseased and gaping maw, and the darkness closed like a storm. I caught flashes, muzzle fire and the ephemeral flare of power weapons. Nothing more than silhouettes greeted me, the after-image of a blow already struck, a kill already made.

In the foulness sloshing around my waist, I caught a brief sight of an armoured corpse. In the dark, face down, it was hard to discern who it belonged to. I forced my way over to it through the mire, but was too slow. Trapped air escaping from the gaps in its armour, the corpse sank without trace. I plunged my hand into the filth, reaching and grabbing for it. I needed to see it, to touch something undeniably real. Something scraped against the tips of my fingers. Delving deeper, the rank waters lapping at my face, I grasped the object. Bringing it up into the light, I saw a skull. Sewer-filth peeled off bleached bone like a sloughing skin. It grinned, as all skulls do, but I found some familiarity in its macabre visage.

Ferrus Manus's cleaved head stared up at me.

Recoiling, I dropped the skull and was about to reach back down for it when I heard Corax shout out.

'Vulkan!'

A small spherical object, its activation stud flashing, arced overhead. Its parabola took it down into the waters, almost on me.

I turned, taking a sharp breath and closing my eyes as a concussive blast pushed me down into the mire. Skin stinging with the host of shrapnel embedded in my back, I touched the floor of the tunnel, my head and shoulders completely submerged. The spike of a rib, a jutting femur, the ridged line of a spinal column – I scratched at the underwater boneyard in a desperate attempt to gain purchase and rise above the water.

Then I was rising, carried along in the sudden swell caused by the explosion, before breaching the surface. Thrown into the air, chased by a gush of filth, tendrils of it clinging to my body, I hit the wall hard and slid down against it.

I had lost my bolter, the weapon slipping from my grip during the fall. Gagging, coughing up filthy water from my lungs, I heard approaching footsteps splash through the mire.

Dazed, my vision blurring, I looked up and saw a hand proffered towards me.

'It's over,' said Corax.

'I didn't even see them,' I gasped.

'Trust me, brother, they're dead, but more will be coming after that explosion. We have to move.'

With Corax's help, I got to my feet and together we reached the end of the sewer tunnel, where a maintenance ladder led up and out.

'Where are the others?' I asked, not seeing Kravex or any of the other Raven Guard.

'Dead,' Corax replied grimly, and kept his eyes front. 'Here,' he said, gesturing to the ladder. 'I'll go first. Follow me closely.'

I nodded and tried not to think about what my brother was feeling at that moment.

Halfway up the ladder, Corax said, 'They knew the nature of this mission, and accepted its risks.'

I didn't reply, merely followed in silence.

Though thick with fumes emanating from the enginarium decks, the air beyond the sewer was almost cleansing by comparison.

Another large chamber stretched out before us. It was cluttered with machinery and packing crates. Cranes loomed overhead and a gantry overlooked the space on one side. It appeared to be empty.

'Ancillary deck,' Corax explained, breaking into a steady run, 'mainly used for storage and repairs. Relatively small. Difficult to breach.'

'Your ship is close?' I asked, keeping pace.

'This way...'

Corax reached the junction first. As he stopped dead, I knew something was wrong. When I caught up to him, I realised what.

Pressure vented from a tear in the Thunderhawk's fuselage. A jagged hole punched inwards, scorched marks radiating from the breach. It was still seized in its locking clamps, though one of its stanchions was twisted. The glacis plate in the nose cone was shattered, its prow-mounted guns wrecked.

'Looks like your flight will have to be aborted,' a low voice declared from the shadows.

The lumen strips overhead were extinguished with the sharp *thunk* of a thrown switch.

Darkness prevailed for a few moments until twin ovals of crimson light from a warrior's retinal lenses pierced the gloom. He was joined by twenty more, fanning out from alcoves and behind the scuttled gunship where they had been lying in wait, assembling in front of us to block off the deck.

Corax and I stood our ground.

'So few of them...' he remarked to me.

Ten more legionaries clanked into position behind us.

'So very few,' I agreed.

A warrior in Terminator armour, one of the Atramentar, stepped forwards. 'Lay down your arms.'

I recognised his voice as belonging to the one who had addressed us earlier.

'I don't take orders from Nostraman gutter scum dressed as soldiers,' Corax replied.

Behind us, a further ten warriors cut off our escape.

I glanced at them, smirking. 'Only forty? Curze has overestimated your ability to stop us.'

The Atramentar laughed; it sounded dull and grainy through his vox-grille. Spikes protruded from his shoulder guards and painted-on lightning bolts livened up the drab metal of his midnight-blue armour. In one gauntleted fist, he clutched a heavy-looking maul.

'Night Haunter told us to take you alive,' he said. 'He didn't say you were to be left unscathed.'

All around the four Night Lords squads, blades and cudgels were drawn.

'His mistake,' muttered Corax, soaring into a turbine-boosted leap. A shriek ripped past his lips, an avian war cry that stunned the Atramentar for a precious half-second. Steel wings spread, an angel of death's shadow bearing down, Corax impaled the warrior on his lightning claw, and I saw the Atramentar's body slide to the deck where the Night Lord died, gurgling blood.

The Ravenlord lashed out with his whip as he landed, snaring a charging legionary around the waist, yanking him off his feet and smashing him into the wall.

I turned, tearing down a tower of crates that crashed into the path of the warriors behind us. It would hold them for a few seconds, but it was all I needed.

Barrelling into the Night Lords coming at us from the front, I met two legionaries in mid-charge and swept them up off the deck with my sheer bulk and momentum. I hurled one like a discus, my arm around his waist, and saw him pinwheel into three others. The second of them I seized around the head and pile-drove into the floor. The deck bent and split under the impact, several of its rebars impaling my opponent through the back to jut out from his chest.

Panicked, some of the remaining Night Lords drew bolters. I felt a shell score my side, leaving a burn. It barely even slowed me down. I backhanded the shooter, snapping his neck at an awkward angle before hoisting another above my head and bringing him down across my knee, breaking his back.

I seized the generator of a fifth, dragging him towards me and caving in his stomach with my fist. With the blade of my hand, I shattered the clavicle of a sixth. Someone got a sword thrust in and I felt it pierce my midriff with a sudden sawing motion. I snapped the blade off at the hilt, and scooped up my attacker by the chin, gripping his jaw before swinging his flailing body overhead and slamming it into a heavy crate. The legionary's head punched right through it and I left him there, hanging by his neck, dead.

Killing was not akin to revelry for me, but I revelled in this. Every torture I had endured, every injury against my men, I visited back upon the Night Lords. As the barricade broke down behind us, I welcomed my enemies. A host of corpses lay around me. Blades and bolters were within easy reach, but I had no need of them. Clenching and unclenching my hands, I wanted to tear these warriors apart in the most intimate way possible.

'Come unto my anvil,' I challenged, a feral snarl curling my lip.

The fact that the ship was gone, our only means of escape lost with it, didn't even enter my mind. I craved this violence. I desired nothing more than to break these warriors, who would suffer for the deeds of their father.

My fists were like hammers, my fury blazing like forge-fire.

One by one, the Night Lords died and I rejoiced in their destruction.

By the time it was over, I was breathing hard through clenched teeth. Spittle flecked my trembling lip. My entire body quaked with the violence that was slowly bleeding from my every pore. In my mind's eye I beheld an abyss. It was red-raw, the colour of blood and death. I stood upon its edge, looked down into the chasmic black at its nadir. Madness waited there for me. I heard its calling and reached out to touch it...

Corax brought me back.

His hand upon my shoulder. The urgent tone in his voice.

'Are you all right, brother?'

It took me a few seconds to realise he was referring to the sword still impaling me.

I yanked out the blade. A welter of blood came with it to paint the deck, soon lost on an already blood-soaked canvas.

'Believe me, it's nothing,' I said, steadily regaining my composure.

Corax nodded, betraying no sense of what I had shown to him, expressed in the charnel leavings on the deck around me.

'What now?' I asked, the wrecked Thunderhawk before us.

'Delve deeper, penetrate the ship's core. There'll be other vessels we can commandeer.'

It was a small hope at best. I knew Corax realised that, but chose not to say it out loud.

'Failing that, we could fight our way to the bridge,' I replied. 'And take our wrath out on whoever we find enthroned upon it.'

'Agreed.'

Corax jerked his head up, listening.

'More are coming.'

'Let them.'

His cold retinal lenses regarded me. 'Does it end here, or on the bridge with Curze's beating heart clenched in your fist?'

I nodded, though I thought our chances of reaching the bridge and Curze were remote at best. 'The bridge. Lead on, brother.'

Leaving the massacred Night Lords in our wake, Corax took us through several more chambers until we entered a warren of sub-tunnels reached through a service hatch. The confines of the tunnels were close, and my brother was forced to leave his beloved jump pack behind. Despite his efforts at obscuring the trail, our pursuers were always close behind us. Snarled Nostraman curses followed us down vents and pipes, the din of scraping power armour echoed. I imagined Curze's men on their knees and elbows, crawling after us.

But however deep we went, however many the turns we took, the Night Lords stuck to us like our shadows. They knew this ship, its every inch. I felt the trap again, its rusty teeth closing around my neck. Escape or capture, there was no other way for this to end for me. I feared for Corax, though. Curze would not be kind to him for this affront.

After an hour of scurrying through the service tunnels like rats, Corax found another access hatch. Kicking it through, the grate landing with a clatter below, my brother dropped from sight for a moment before calling up to me to follow. I went after him and plunged from the lightless warren into a barren chamber. It was dimly lit, fashioned of dark iron like so much of this desolate place, and I discerned blade marks in the floor. There were bloodstains too, but it was empty. It was strangely familiar, though I had never been here before.

A single archway led further, though it was beyond the weak corona of light cast by the lumen orbs ensconced in the walls, and therefore heavily shadowed.

'See, the way is unobstructed,' Corax hissed, gesturing to the archway and the darkness beyond it. 'I'll make sure we were not followed. Here.' He tossed me his gladius, the last of his secondary weapons. I caught it and nodded, hastening to the archway, but could see and hear no danger.

'There are steps leading down,' I called. 'And I can feel a breeze.'

It was artificial of course, and the air was musty, but it could indicate that we were close to a deck with atmospheric recycling, which almost certainly meant a human presence.

Corax waited under the gaping hatch for a few more seconds before joining me.

'What of your helm sensors?' I asked, knowing that my brother was already cycling through the visual spectra of his retinal lenses.

'Shadows...' he hissed, his tone leaving me slightly unnerved.

If I didn't know my brother better, I would swear he sounded concerned about that.

'Only way is down,' I muttered, levelling my gladius at the darkness as though it were a foe I could engage.

Corax agreed, unsheathing his talons, and together we descended the steps.

At the bottom, the darkness was just as thick and abject. It was like trying to see through pitch. I knew it wasn't an ordinary absence of light. Our eyes would have penetrated that easily and left us in no doubt as to our surroundings. This was different. Viscous and congealing, here the shadows clung to us like tar. As I stared into the oily depths, I saw the vague adumbration of what appeared to be a coliseum. We were standing back to back in its arena. Beneath our feet were sand and earth.

'It's a trap!' I cried, but too late.

Corax was halfway up the steps when a sliding blast door sealed us in. A step behind him, I turned to face the arena as the unnatural darkness bled away through vents in the floor and a chill I hadn't realised was affecting me melted from my body. Flaming torches delineated an eight-sided battleground where the skeletal remains of gladiators and their shattered trappings still lingered like unquiet spirits. I recalled where I had seen the antechamber before. It was in Themis, a city of Nocturnian warrior kings who engaged in gladiatorial contest to prove their prowess and choose their next tribal leader. Before each fight, the combatants would wait in barrack rooms to sharpen their blades or their minds before the upcoming contest. Corax and I had done neither. I suddenly wondered what our gaoler had in mind for us.

'It's a little archaic, I admit,' said Curze, our attention drawn to him. He was standing above us, looking down from the pulpit of an amphitheatre. 'But I think Angron would have appreciated it. A pity he isn't here to see it. Your paths almost crossed on Isstvan, didn't they, brother?'

I arched my neck, meeting Curze's gaze in the highest echelons of the amphitheatre. He was not alone. Thirty of his Atramentar Terminators encircled the arena, the threat of their reaper cannons obvious.

'A pity *ours* did not,' I replied.

'You had your chance on Kharaatan and didn't take it.'

'You will wish I did when this is over.'

Curze smiled thinly. The two Atramentar flanking him proffered arms, a sword and trident.

'On Nostramo, we had no grand theatres like this. Our gutters and hives were our arenas, but offerings of bloodsport were plentiful.'

He tossed the sword down to us. It impaled itself in the ground, up to a third of its blade deep.

'Gang culture ruled our streets and everyone wanted to be a part of the strongest gang.'

The trident followed, striking the earth with enough force to send vibrations all the way down its haft.

'Even murderers and rapists have ritual,' Curze went on. 'Even to scum like them it's important. Opportunities were always limited, often only enough for one. First thing,' he said, looking down at Corax, 'the fight must be fair. Remove your armour, brother. Vulkan stands unequal to it.'

'I didn't think you approved of holding court, Konrad,' I replied, stepping forwards as I challenged him. 'Isn't that why you butchered your world's overlords and spire nobles?'

'They did not lord over me, nor were they noble,' Curze uttered darkly. 'Now, Corax will remove his armour or condemn your own sons to death.'

From the back ranks of the Atramentar, two warriors were brought forwards on opposite sides of the amphitheatre. On one side there was Kravex, my brother's errant son that he had believed dead; on the other was Nemetor.

Both warriors struggled vainly against their captors, not to escape but rather to make clear their defiance.

'Nemetor...' How one wounded son had come to mean so much... Curze had not told me what had become of the rest of my Legion, and I had not the heart to ask him. I believed they still lived, though in what numbers I could not say. Had they perished completely on Isstvan, Curze would not have passed up the opportunity to twist that particular knife. And for all the deception of his trials, Curze had not yet lied to me in anything he had said. The Salamanders yet lived. I yet lived. I had to save Nemetor.

Evidently, Corax had reached the same conclusion and quietly removed his armour until he was standing alongside me in the arena with only the lower mesh of his leggings, greaves and boots. His magnificent war-plate lay discarded on the sand like worthless chaff.

Curze had brought us low, and I felt the gnawing guilt of bringing my brother into this crude pantomime.

'I am sorry, Corvus. For all of this.'

'Put it from your mind, Vulkan. I made my decision free of will, as I know you would have done also.'

'But there is something you don't understand, brother...'

Two gladiatorial helms thrown in our midst interrupted my confession. One was black, fashioned into the likeness of a bird of prey; the other was dark green and draconian. It was obvious what Curze wanted us to do.

'Are we to dance next?' I said, stooping to retrieve the helmet intended for me.

'In a manner of speaking,' Curze replied. 'Put them on.'

The inside of the helmet was rough. It felt heavy.

'*One lives, one dies,*' said Curze, his voice channelled to me through a reedy vox-link inside my armour. '*Gang culture is brutal, brothers. But I wouldn't expect you to understand that yet. You will.*'

I looked up at Nemetor, my son seeming oblivious to his surroundings, then back to Corax, seeing him do the same with Kravex.

I felt the presence of the abyss again, my bare feet teetering on its edge, looking down into hell and darkness. Pain seared my skull from everywhere at once and I realised the helmet was rough because its interior was studded with a host of tiny nails. Curze had just embedded their points in my skull. The abyss throbbed in my mind's eye, urging me to act, to step off and be lost to its heat.

I fought to stay calm, to rein in the madness threatening to turn me raving.

Corax hadn't moved yet, though only a few short seconds had lapsed.

'Survivor goes free, as do his men,' Curze gave his last edict to us out loud. 'For let me say now, I have several more drakes and ravens in my rookery. Now, fight.'

Curze had yet to lie to me. If the game was to have meaning, he would tell the truth here too. But I could not kill Corax. I would sacrifice Nemetor for that, though it would hurt me to do so. I would not bow down to barbarism and become like him. Insanity clawed at the edges of my consciousness but I refused to submit to it. Curze would not win. I would not let him.

Corax would defeat me, Nemetor would die, but at least Corvus would live. I could make that sacrifice, I could do that for my brother.

I reached for the sword.

'*And, Vulkan...*' Curze whispered through the vox-link, a final instruction just for me, '*I lied. Beat Corax, render him unconscious or*

I kill him and his Ravens, letting you watch as I do it.'

I tried to shout out, but a wedge of steel slammed into my open mouth from a device wrought into the helm, muting me.

Corax had yet to move. I wondered if Curze had told him the same thing as me, only the reverse of the scenario I had been presented with.

'Still reluctant to fight?' asked Curze. 'I don't blame you. It's a heavy thing to have to kill your brother to survive. But trust me when I tell you that hungry dogs have no loyalty when the prize is survival. I remember a family on Nostramo. Their bonds were tight and they fought tooth and nail for one another, gutting entire gangs that dared raise a hand against them.

'One winter, one *particularly* bitter and frigid winter, they went to war with a rival gang. Territory and status were the prize. It became about honour, if you can believe that? Such a lofty and costly ideal. It took them far from what they called home. It was war, only much grubbier than you have ever experienced.

'Towards the end, food ran short, when the rats were gone and the litter in the streets bereft of sustenance. Desperation breeds desperate men. The loyal gang, the one whose blood ties were so strong… they fell upon each other. Murdered each other. One side wanted to keep fighting, the other just wanted the war to end. You see, brothers, sometimes the enemy is just the person preventing you from getting home.' Curze stepped forwards, put his hands on the rail in front of him. 'No more delays. Only one of you is getting out of this. Only one gets to go home.'

Corax picked up the trident.

'I am sorry, Vulkan.'

I could give him no answer.

Curze retreated into the shadows again.

'Remember what I said, brother,' he whispered to me.

I had barely wrapped my hand around the sword's hilt when

Corax lunged. His feet left the ground, his leap taking him halfway across the small arena. Dragging the blade free, I rolled and felt the trident punch the earth where I had been standing. A second blow darted past my cheek, tearing it open and flecking the sand with blood. I parried, smashing a third trident thrust aside and landing a heavy punch to Corax's midriff, staggering him back. I had a second's rest but he came at me again, crafting a series of small but piercing jabs against my improvised defence.

I had never fought Corax before, but had seen him in battle often enough. His fighting style was not unlike the avian creature from which he took his honorific. Deft, probing attacks like the snapping of a beak assailed me. He was swift, with an ever-shifting combat posture, attacking my blind side and often moving into peripheral assault patterns.

I turned and blocked, took small cuts on my arms, torso and legs. He was relentless, and had not spent the last few. months or years of his life trapped in a cell. Furthermore, he was willing to kill me. There was a fury to his attacks, something I had not yet embraced for the duel. Since picking up his trident, a change had come over my brother – one that I was unprepared for.

The abyss returned in my mind, beckoning as the hot nails pushed deeper into my skull, stimulating my anger and need for violence.

Was I the monster that Curze had described all those years ago on Kharaatan? When I had burned that eldar child to ash for her part in killing Seriph, was it retribution or had I just used that to justify an act of sadistic self-satisfaction?

I reeled, feeling my sanity unpicking at its already frayed seams.

Corax landed a telling blow, the trident lodged in my left pectoral, digging into muscle and below. I would have screamed were it not for the wedge in my mouth gagging me.

Rage.

I cut a savage wound across Corax's torso as he found his guard compromised with the trident still impaled in my body.

Rage.

I snapped the trident's haft in two, leaving the fork still embedded in my flesh.

Rage.

I threw down my sword and hurled myself at Corax.

I am strong, perhaps the physically strongest of all my father's sons. Corax had claimed as much once. Now he felt it first-hand. With a single blow of my clenched fist I smashed apart his helmet's grille, revealing his anguished mouth beneath, spitting blood. I landed a second punch around his left ear, snapping his head to the side and denting the helm inwards. Corax shrieked like a bird. I wanted to break his wings, fracture that weakling skull. Despite his attempts to fend me off – a knee into my chest, a heavy jab to my exposed kidneys, a throat strike – I overwhelmed him. With sheer bulk, I bore him down to the earth. He grunted as his back hit the ground hard, and I punched the air from his lungs. Like a vice, my hands were around his throat. Straddling him, Corax's arms pinned by my knees, he couldn't move. All he could do now was die.

During the savage assault, his helmet had come apart. I saw his dark eyes staring at me, that quiet wisdom turned to terror.

I squeezed harder, feeling his toughened larynx giving way to my fury as I slowly crushed it. His eyes bulged in their sockets and through blood-rimed teeth he choked two words.

'*Do it…*'

At my side, I felt the presence of Ferrus, his skeletal form hovering in my peripheral vision.

'*Do it…*' he rasped.

Above me in the amphitheatre, held fast but still struggling, I heard Nemetor whisper.

'*Do it…*'

It would be so easy. I had but to tighten my grip a fraction and…

I stopped. Fingertips still clinging to the edge of the abyss, I hauled myself up and rolled away from its burning depths. In that moment, I knew that I would not be granted my freedom. I *wanted* to kill Corax to sate my rage.

'Kill him, Vulkan!' Curze snarled, rushing up to the rail. 'He's finished. Claim your freedom.'

'Return to your Legion,' urged Ferrus. 'It is the only way...'

I released my grip around Corax's throat and let him go. Exhausted, physically and mentally, I rolled off my brother and onto my back.

'No. I won't do it,' I gasped, breathing hard. 'Not like this.'

'Then you have damned yourself,' hissed Ferrus.

Not knowing what had happened, Corax got to his feet, picked up my fallen sword and stabbed me through the heart.

I CAME ROUND screaming. I had returned to my cell, but still lay on my back. The door was intact and there was no evidence of my recent escape. I was strapped down to a metal slab, arms, legs and neck. I couldn't move and there was a metal wedge in my mouth, gagging me. Surrounding me was a coven of human psykers, feral-looking with strange sigils daubed on their bodies and robes.

'Davinites,' Curze explained as he walked into my eye line, before killing every one of the witches in a sudden and violent blur. 'They have served and failed their purpose,' he said when he was done butchering them.

It was all a lie – visions implanted in my mind.

Curze removed the wedge from my mouth.

'Did you expect me to kill him?' I snarled.

My brother looked profoundly unhappy.

'You are not noble. You are no better than me,' he muttered, before killing me again.

CHAPTER
TWENTY-FOUR
Sacrifices

'You have suffered. I know this. You have come to the abyss, and almost surrendered yourselves to it. That changes now. I am father, general, lord and mentor. I shall teach you if I can, and pass on the knowledge I have gained. Honour, self-sacrifice, self-reliance, brotherhood. It is our Promethean creed and all must adhere to it if we are to prosper. Let this be the first lesson...'

— Primarch Vulkan in his inaugural address
on Terra to the survivors of the XVIII Legion

NUMEON DIDN'T KNOW who had survived the battle. He was lying face down, his armour's sensors screaming in a rash of red warning icons. Undoubtably, the fall had saved his life. He hoped it had taken others with him. Groaning, he rolled onto his back and fought to bring the physical trauma under control. Pulse was returning to normal. Breathing also. He waited, in silence and in darkness, for his body to repair and his armour systems to reboot and stabilise.

Someone stirred in the darkness next to him.

Shen'ra's battle-plate was split, gored by blades and shell holes. His cybernetic eye flickered and went dead.

'Lost the half-track...' he croaked.

Numeon managed to nod.

'Lit those traitors up well though, didn't it?' said the old Techmarine, smiling as he passed out. His vital signs were holding; Shen'ra yet lived.

There were others too, some less fortunate than Shen'ra. After Leodrakk and Hriak had escaped with the human, Numeon had returned to the manufactorum. Avus was dead, giving up his life so that his kinsmen could get away. He had saved Numeon in the process, then killed the other Word Bearers into the sacrificial bargain. A melta bomb at close range.

The third legionary, another sniper and probably one of those responsible for the shooting of Helon, Uzak and Shaka, had fallen back before the Raptor's impassioned onslaught. Avus was another kill-notch on his rifle now, the Word Bearer's disengagement from the fight leaving Numeon impotent to enact vengeance or make his own sacrifice.

By the time he got to the others, the fight had spilled out onto the streets. Domadus was down, Pergellen nowhere to be seen. K'gosi and Shen'ra remained, surrounded by the dead and dying. In desperation, the Techmarine set off a seismic charge, hoping to take their enclosing enemies with them. He succeeded in part, but collapsed the manufactorum's already weak foundations.

Numeon remembered the ground coming apart beneath him, the sense of weightlessness akin to the last moments of a drop-pod insertion. Debris was coming down on top of him. A chunk ripped off his right pauldron and sent radial fractures up his arm. He clutched the sigil, Vulkan's sigil, as they touched down in water. A sewer pipe, running fast, carrying them away from the battle, cheating them of the honourable death they had all earned.

Half submerged, the air rank with the stink of effluvia, Numeon stared up at the ceiling as crawling sewer vermin came to inspect the latest offerings from above but found them brittle and tough.

'K'gosi...' he breathed.

'I am here.'

'Can you move?'

'Not yet.'

'Then wait for a time, wait until you can,' said Numeon.

'I'm not going anywhere, Pyre Captain.'

'Good,' Numeon answered, half dazed and drifting in and out of consciousness. 'That's good.'

He still clung to the sigil and lifted the hammer icon into a shaft of light lancing through a crack in the wall to inspect it. It was smeared with grime; Numeon used his thumb to clean the sigil and was reminded of when he saw it last on Isstvan.

Isstvan V

THE CONTEMPTOR LUMBERED through a pall of smoke, blood flecking its blue-and-white paintwork. Numerous blade and shell scars marred its armour, the true laurels of battle by which all warriors were ultimately judged, or so the XII Legion believed.

Ash-fall from the many thousands of fires was turning the sky grey. It baptised a cohort of warriors, clad to various degrees in ancient gladiatorial trappings and wielding ritual caedere weapons. They were the Rampagers, a deadly breed even amongst the Eaters of Worlds, and a throwback to Angron's incarceration as a slavefighter. Bellowing guttural war cries, they charged ahead of the Dreadnought to engage the Salamanders.

Numeon balked at what the battle-maddened World Eaters attempted. He counted no more than thirty men. Just three squads. Yet they charged over a hundred. Several went down to sporadic bolter fire. Some were clipped by shrapnel but kept on coming. Only those too injured to fight, unable to run because of missing limbs or critical wounds were halted. Something urgent and terrible spurred them on. Numeon had read reports of the ferocity of the XII. Even when they were the War Hounds, their reputation in battle, particularly close-quarters, was fearsome. As the reborn World Eaters under Angron, they had become something else. Rumours abounded within the ranks, of arcane devices that manipulated the legionaries' tempers, simulacra of the ones embedded in Angron's skull by his slavers.

Now he saw them, ignoring pain and injury, frothing with frenzy, Numeon believed those stories to be true.

A howling berserker, a falx blade in either hand, leapt at the primarch. Vulkan swatted him aside, but the crazed warrior managed to parry a killing stroke and came up fighting as he landed. A second Rampager whirled a chain with a barbed hook around his head. Lashing out, it snared Atanarius and dragged the swordsman into the World Eater's killing arc.

Numeon had no time to react as he threw himself aside from a massive hammer smashing down at him. Driven by a small rocket-propelled ignition system, it struck the ground with meteoric force and trembled the earth underfoot. Varrun stepped in to engage the warrior but was taken off his feet by the hammer's backswing. Trying to rush to Varrun's aid, Numeon found the falx-armed legionary in his path. The Salamander blocked one swing of a curved blade, barely turning it aside as he felt the hook of the other rake his armoured face. One of the lenses cracked and he lost resolution in it. Ganne bore the frenzied legionary down and pummelled him with his storm shield, whilst Igataron crushed the World Eater's shoulder to disarm him of the falx. The blood-splashed legionary was about to lunge, ignoring the excruciating pain he must be in, when Numeon impaled him through the chest with his glaive.

'They are insane,' growled Ganne.

Numeon nodded, and in the brief respite searched for the rest of his Pyre Guard to see how they were faring.

Varrun was still down but at least moving.

Atanarius was on his knees, butcher's hooks digging into his armour, still snared by the chain. Skatar'var was trying to release him as Leodrakk fought the chain-wielder, but was finding the Rampager's fury hard to counter. He staggered, on the defensive, and would have fallen if Vulkan hadn't lifted the World Eater off his feet and rammed him head first into the ground to silence his screaming.

Another hammer-bearer smashed aside three of Heka'tan's Fireborn, the 14th and Fifth Companies having found a way through the trenches to engage the World Eaters. Gravius's troops were still catching up. Below them, K'gosi and the Pyroclasts held the trenchworks. Elsewhere on the slope, a much larger force of Firedrakes fought Angron's Devourers to a bloody stalemate.

For once, the Lord of the Red Sands was close to his honour guard. Numeon heard him bellow a challenge, heard Vulkan's name amongst the guttural syllables of his native tongue. The ash and smoke were thickening; down to one retinal lens, the other a static-veined mess, it was difficult to get a visual. He caught sight of Vulkan.

The primarch was trading blows with the Contemptor. Though it dwarfed him, the hefty war machine was slowly being taken apart. Vulkan had fought it back and was amongst the Firedrakes in the heart of the battle.

Torn between rejoining the primarch and gathering his brother Pyre Guard, Numeon ran to Varrun, who was still down.

'Get up! This is far from over.'

Varrun muttered something, but did as he was told.

As he hauled his brother to his feet, Numeon found Vulkan again through the throng.

The Contemptor towered over him, twin power claws trailing jagged loops of energy. Its chest plate was badly dented and cables in its neck spat dangerously.

A dense muzzle flare erupted from Vulkan's pistol. It had been a gift from Lord Manus, a gesture the primarch of the Salamanders had reciprocated. Discharged at close range, it severed the servos in the Dreadnought's right arm, rendering one of its weapons limp and useless. Vulkan clambered up the Dreadnought's torso and when he reached the summit rammed his sword downwards into its armoured head. Like a beast felled but still catching up to the realisation that it was slain, the Contemptor sank to one knee. Its dead arm hung loose by its side whilst the other gripped its knee, struggling for purchase.

Numeon rejoiced as the war machine collapsed, triumph turned to anguish when he saw the pair of Rampagers closing on the primarch. Vulkan was pinned, unable to release the weapon he had sunk so deep to kill his enemy. With a savage twist, the primarch snapped the blade and hurled its jagged remains at one of the Rampagers. It struck the savage gladiator in the face, goring out an eye and killing him instantly. Pushing back off the Dreadnought's corpse with his feet, Vulkan dodged the eviscerator meant for his skull. It chewed into the Contemptor's metal chassis instead, grinding metal and spitting sparks before getting stuck.

Yanking at the eviscerator's hilt but unable to release the weapon, the Rampager roared and abandoned it, intending to take Vulkan on with his bare fists. The primarch had drawn *Dawnbringer* and took the Rampager's head off with a desultory swing. Blood was still fountaining from the World Eater's ragged stump of a neck when a shadow loomed on the ridge-line above.

Anointed in blood, partially obscured by scudding clouds of smoke and shimmering heat haze, Angron bellowed.

'Vulkan!' His voice was the like fall of cities, rumbling and booming across the vast battlefield.

Angron jabbed down to his brother with one of the motorised axes he carried. Its blade was burring, roaring for blood. *'I name you high rider!'*

Spittle frothed the red primarch's lips. His oversized musculature, seemingly too tight for his vein-threaded skin, rippled. Thick ropes of sinew stood out on his neck. A scarred and war-beaten face, framed by the nest of cybernetic scalp-locks snaking back across his head, tensed as Angron's eyes widened.

Farther down the slope, Vulkan gripped the haft of his hammer and went to meet his brother's challenge.

Numeon saw it all, and almost urged his primarch to hold.

An arcing missile salvo from one of the traitor gun emplacements forced the Pyre Captain's attention skywards. He tracked the spear-headed missile all the way down, following its trajectory until it struck part of the slope between the two primarchs.

A firestorm lit the hillside, several tonnes of incendiary ordnance expressed in the expansive bloom of conflagration. It swept outwards in a turbulent wave, bathing the lower part of the slope in heat and flame. This was nothing compared to its epicentre. Firedrakes were immolated in that blast, blown apart and burned to ash in their Terminator armour.

A hundred dying sunsets faded from Numeon's sight. Blinking back the savage afterglow he saw Vulkan wreathed in flames, but stepping from the blaze unharmed. The remaining Firedrakes gathered to him, tramping over the dead where they had to.

Badly burned, the Ravagers were still fighting. The Pyre Guard and some of Heka'tan's men finished them before Numeon led the warriors after their lord. Varrun was limping. Atanarius clutched his side, but clung to his blade determinedly with one hand.

'Are we whole, brothers?' Numeon quickly asked.

Atanarius nodded.

Varrun gave a mocking laugh. 'Perhaps we should look to

increasing our ranks when this is over?'

Ganne came to his side, not supporting the veteran but keeping watch.

'Are you my protector, brother?' Varrun asked.

'Not remotely,' snarled Ganne, but didn't leave him.

Igataron said nothing, and merely glowered. His eyes behind his retinal lenses always seemed to burn brighter than his brothers'.

Mauled as they had been by the World Eaters, Numeon knew that his warriors had suffered but would not stop until they were dead or the battle was over. But it was grievously attritional, and he was not ashamed to admit relief when he heard that reinforcements were coming in to make planetfall behind them.

Hundreds of landers and drop-pods choked the already suffocating sky, emblazoned with the iconography of the Alpha Legion, Iron Warriors, Word Bearers and Night Lords. Even the sight of Konrad Curze's Legion gave Numeon hope that the battle could be won and Horus brought to heel at last.

Vulkan had seen the arrival of his brothers and their Legions too, though he gave no outward sign of relief or premature triumph. He merely watched impassively as the manifold shuttles touched down and the loyalists took up position on the edge of the depression. Of Angron, there was no sign. The firestorm had beaten him back, it seemed, and now with the arrival of four more Legions, the Lord of the Red Sands had ordered a retreat.

Grainy static preceded the opening of the vox-link. All the Pyre Guard heard it, too, though it was on Vulkan's channel, the primarch's view that there could be no secrets from his inner circle. Through the choppy return, the Gorgon's voice thundered.

'The enemy is beaten!'

His anger was obvious, his desire for retribution palpable. Lord Manus wanted blood to salve his wounded pride.

'See how they run from us!' he continued, an eager fervour affecting

him. *'Now we push on, let none escape our vengeance!'*

Numeon exchanged a glance with Varrun. The veteran was badly wounded but able to fight on. Atanarius was also struggling, whilst Skatar'var stayed close to his brother Leodrakk on account of his injuries. With reinforcements ready to deploy, it made sense to fall back and consolidate. Pressing the advance now yielded only glory and profligate death.

Vulkan was impassive, betraying none of his thoughts as he allowed Corax to speak up.

'Hold, Ferrus! The victory may yet be ours, but let our allies earn their share of honour in this battle. We have achieved a great victory, but not without cost. My Legion is bloodied and torn, as is Vulkan's...'

Again, the primarch kept his own counsel, as the Ravenlord concluded his speech.

'I cannot imagine yours has not shed a great deal of blood to carry us this far.'

Lord Manus was belligerent. *'We are bloodied, but unbowed.'*

Making the most of the enemy's retreat and the brief cessation in the fighting, Vulkan chose that moment to give voice. 'As are we all. We should take a moment to catch our breath and bind our wounds before again diving headlong into such terrible battle.' The cost of which lay all around, clad in bloody green armour.

'We must consolidate what we have won,' Vulkan suggested, 'and let our newly arrived brothers continue the fight while we regroup.'

But the Gorgon smelled blood and would not relent.

'No! The traitors are beaten and all it will take is one final push to destroy them utterly!'

Corax tried a last attempt at reason.

'Ferrus, do not do anything foolish! We have already won!'

It was to no avail, as the link to the Iron Hands' primarch went dead.

'Our brother has overmuch pride, Corvus,' said Vulkan candidly.

'*He will get himself killed.*'

'He is too tough for that,' Vulkan said, but Numeon heard the lie in his words, the hollow tone of his voice.

'*I won't be dragged in with him, Vulkan. I won't lead my sons into another meatgrinder for the sake of his pride.*'

'Then hope reinforcement reaches him quickly, for he won't be dissuaded by you or I.'

'*I am converging on the dropsite. Will I meet you there?*'

Vulkan paused and it felt like the few seconds stretched into minutes before he gave his answer. Numeon was reminded of their words aboard the *Fireforge*, of Ferrus Manus's wrath being his undoing, of the foreseen distemper in Horus and the profound disquiet about this very battle. They rose up in the Pyre Guard captain, threatening to choke him with their sense of foreboding.

'Aye,' said Vulkan at length. 'We shall consolidate at the dropsite. Perhaps Ferrus will see sense and muster with us.'

'*He won't.*'

'No, you're probably right.' Vulkan ended the transmission. It was as if a mantle of grief lay about his shoulders, heavy with the burden of a fear that had been confirmed in what he'd just heard or felt. Numeon could not explain it.

'Order all companies to fall back to the dropsite,' Vulkan told him.

Numeon voxed down to K'gosi at once. The Pyroclasts had all but cleansed the trenches of the enemy, leaving the route back clear and open.

Whilst the retreat of Horus's rebels was ragged and disorganised, the warriors of the XVIII and XIX Legions fell back in good order. Tanks returned to column, rumbling slowly but steadily back down the slope. The scorched trenches emptied as legionaries filed out in vast hosts, company banners still flying. They were battered but resolute. The dead and injured came with them, dragged or borne aloft by their still standing brothers. It was a great exodus, the black and green ocean of war retreating with the tide to leave the flotsam of their slain enemy behind it.

Most of the fortifications were destroyed. Huge sections of earthworks and spiked embankments lay open like rotting wounds. Bodies were impaled upon them, some clad in dusky white, others in arterial red or lurid purple. It was the evidence of fratricide a thousand times over, and it was this that Vulkan lingered behind to look upon before he quit the field.

'This is not victory,' he murmured. 'It is death. It is bonds broken and bloody. And it shall mark us all for generations.'

On the northern side of the Urgall Depression, a fresh sea made ready to sweep in and carry all of the mortal debris away.

Across from the muster field of the Salamanders, which was little more than a laager of drop-ships, were the Iron Warriors. Armoured in steel-grey with black-and-yellow chevrons, the IV Legion looked stark and stern. They had erected a barricade, the armoured bastions of their own landing craft alloyed together, to bolster the northern face of the slope. Great cannons were raised aloft behind it, their snouts pointing to the ash-smothered sky. A line of battle tanks sat in front, bearing the grim icon of a metal-helmeted skull. And in front of that, Iron Warriors arrayed in their cohorts, thousands strong. They held their silence and their weapons across their bodies, with no more life than automatons.

The drop-zone was flooded with warriors now, as a makeshift camp materialised to serve the injured and secure the bodies of the dead. Tank yards manifested as labour teams of Techmarines and servitors assembled to make standing repairs. Multiple triage stations were being set up in the lee of the larger Stormbirds, whilst the holds of some Thunderhawks acted as emergency infirmaries. The able-bodied looked to their armour and weapons. Quartermasters took stock, replenished ammunition and materiel where they could. Officers reorganised in the face of casualties. Subalterns and equerries gave brief reports to line officers, and standard bearers acted as rally points as the entire Vexillarius was put into motion organising for the second assault.

Not a single legionary about the XVIII stood idle.

Yet the Iron Warriors, the entire muster on the northern slope, neither spoke nor moved beyond what was necessary to assemble.

Chief Apothecary Sen'garees voxed through to the command echelon, including Vulkan and the Pyre Guard, complaining of the lack of reply regarding requests for aid, specifically medical.

Numeon felt a grim silence descend across the whole Urgall Depression like when a storm eclipses the sun, as he saw Captain Ral'stan of the Firedrakes raise his fist in salute to their iron allies.

Not one responded to his hail. Only the wind kicking at their banners gave any sense of animus to the IV Legion throng.

'Why do they ignore us?' asked Leodrakk openly.

Vulkan was staring in the direction of his brother, Perturabo. The Lord of Iron returned the Lord of Drakes' gimlet gaze with one of his own.

'Because we are betrayed...' said Vulkan, disbelieving, horror turning to anger on his face. 'To arms!'

More than ten thousand guns answered, the weapons of their allies turned on them with traitorous intent.

CHAPTER
TWENTY-FIVE
Reunited

'Though the battle had ended and the enemy was far from the reach of our blades, most of us didn't come back from the Urgall Depression. Even those men who escaped, those pitiful few, even they didn't come back. They're still there now. We all are, fighting for our lives.'
— unknown legionary survivor of the Isstvan V massacre

IT LOOKED BAD. There was no other way to describe it. Definitely bad. Nurth was bad, but this was a whole other pit of groxshit that Grammaticus had found himself in. And then there was the alien. Not Slau Dha, or Gahet. Certainly not anyone affiliated with the Cabal. Here was a different player entirely, an eldar whose agenda was as inscrutable as his identity.

And then there was Oll.

But he couldn't worry about that now. He'd done everything he could on that front, and as much as his old friend had clearly resented being reached out to, what other choice did Grammaticus have?

The universe suddenly felt very small, and Grammaticus was somehow at its beating heart and under intense scrutiny from all interested parties. Insects on microscope slides had more privacy. He thought of Anatol Hive, and wished that he had been allowed to die in the Unification Wars.

Fate had other plans for him, though. If asked at the time, he doubted he would have said that that fate included a battered group of legionaries and running for his life down a sewer tunnel. If they knew of his true mission…

His two minders looked tired, and fraught. The one called Leodrakk, the Salamander, had eyed him several times since they had reached what Grammaticus assumed was a rendezvous point. He also assumed that whoever Leodrakk was meant to be rendezvousing with was late. This would be Numeon, his captain and the legionary in charge. It didn't bode well. What boded worse was if Numeon was dead. That left Leodrakk running things, and he looked about ready to charge to his glorious death, killing Grammaticus into the bargain. Not that it would matter, but then his mission would effectively be over. He also feared to imagine what the Word Bearers would do to him.

He didn't know what the Salamanders and their allies in the other broken Legions had intended to achieve here on Traoris. Whatever it was, it had gone awry, and he suspected that he carried some weight of blame in that.

Leodrakk's eyes told him all of this. They spoke of grief and a dangerously fatalistic desire for revenge. Grammaticus had seen men like that in the united armies, when they were fighting Nar-than Dume. He'd never seen it in a Space Marine before, and he wondered just what these warriors had lost to transform them so egregiously.

'What are you staring at?' snarled the Salamander. He was crouching down, and had been looking at his helmet, facing him on his lap.

'I'm wondering what happened to you,' said Grammaticus.

'War happened to us,' he replied curtly.

'You are made for war. There is more to it than that.'

Leodrakk looked into the stinking filth that streamed beneath their feet, but found no answers in the dirty water.

Instead, the Librarian spoke up.

'We were betrayed,' he rasped, 'at Isstvan. It was worse than atrocity. The massacre we endured was only the physical manifestation of our collective trauma. The real pain was to come, and it was a malady of the mind. Not everyone survived it.'

Hriak, the Raven Guard, paused as if trying to see into Grammaticus's mind for the source of his curiosity. It was deeply unsettling, and Grammaticus fought to keep his hand from trembling. Many years ago he believed that a very close friend of his had succumbed to a psyker's mental intrusion. It was all lies, of course. Everything about it had been a lie, one way or another. It had still unnerved him, though, the sheer destructive potential of battle psykers. No wonder the Emperor had removed them from the Legions.

'From the horror of Isstvan, we escaped aboard a drop-ship,' Hriak continued, 'but the horror did not end there. All of us were changed by what we had witnessed, the sight of our brothers slain in droves beside us, our former allies turning their guns on our backs while at the same time known traitors to our fronts opened up with their weapons in vicious concert.'

Grammaticus looked askance at Leodrakk for a reaction as Hriak related their story, and found him to be deeply uncomfortable at the retelling, but content to let it go on.

'Some of the survivors aboard our drop-ship were not themselves,' said Hriak. 'When a man is heightened to a certain point of battle fervour, it can be difficult for him to come down from that. Sometimes, if the experience is particularly traumatic, he can never fully recover and a part of him will always be at war, in that self-same conflict. Such men, blinded by this trauma, have killed in error, believing friends to be foes. It takes a great deal for the Legiones Astartes to succumb to such a trauma. Our minds are much stronger than ordinary mortals, but it is possible.'

And then Grammaticus knew. He knew how Hriak had sustained the wound to his neck, the one that had very nearly slit his throat completely. It wasn't actually on Isstvan that he'd received it, it was on the drop-ship. It was inflicted by–

'That's enough, Hriak,' whispered Leodrakk. 'We don't need to remember that, and he doesn't need to hear it either.'

'My presence here has complicated things for you, hasn't it?' said Grammaticus.

'You have undermined our entire mission.'

Grammaticus shook his head, nonplussed at the mordant Salamander. 'What the fug did you intend to achieve, anyway? What were you, twenty-something men against an entire host, an entire city? I get it that you want payback, but how does throwing yourselves on your enemies' swords get you what you want?'

Leodrakk stood, and for a brief moment looked like he was about to end Grammaticus, but decided against it.

'It is not so simple as revenge. We want to get back into the war, make a difference, for what we do to have meaning. Before we came here, we had been tracking the Word Bearers of this particular cult for a while. We followed them to a small, backwater world called Viralis but were too late to prevent what they unleashed there.'

Grammaticus frowned. 'Unleashed?'

'*Daemons*, John Grammaticus, a subject about which I suspect you are well-versed.'

'I have seen the Acuity,' he admitted.

Leodrakk scowled. 'I won't even ask what that is. A gift from your Cabal, no doubt.'

'It's no gift, it's truth and one I wish I could erase from my mind.'

'Again, not my concern. What does concern me,' he gestured to Hriak too, 'us, our mission, is to prevent what happened on Viralis from happening here. Their leader, the Word Bearers cleric, was supposed to die by our hand. We would slip in unnoticed, find him and execute him. Pergellen was our trigger man, the rest of us would ensure rapid egress in the face of reprisal. Our chances of success were good, our chances of survival less so, but at least we would die knowing Traoris was safe.'

'No world is safe, Salamander,' Grammaticus countered. 'No part of the galaxy, however remote, is going to be spared.'

Leodrakk snarled, angry, but more at the situation than Grammaticus. 'We would spare this world. At least from that.' He backed down, the threat of violence ebbed. 'But now we are discovered and being hunted. Shen and Pergellen should have left you in that warehouse.'

Grammaticus nodded. 'Yes, they should have. But they didn't, and now you have me and know what I know, so what are you going to do with that?'

'Nothing,' said a voice from deeper in the tunnel. It was dark, but even Grammaticus recognised the warrior coming to meet them. He was not alone, either.

'Numeon.' Leodrakk went to greet him. They locked wrists. Hriak merely bowed his head to acknowledge the captain. Leodrakk's good mood soured when he saw who else had come back with Numeon. 'So few?' he asked.

'Their sacrifice will have meaning, brother.'

Of the twenty-three legionaries that had made planetfall on Traoris from the *Fire Ark*, barely thirteen remained. Shen'ra had come back with Numeon, as well as K'gosi. Pergellen lingered at the back of the group, returning a few minutes after having made sure they were not followed. Hriak was the last of the Ravens now, and he muttered a Kiavahran oath for the fallen Avus. The rest were Salamanders.

Grammaticus beheld a broken force. Fate, oh that capricious mistress, had conspired against them. It had delivered him into their grasp and the fulgurite spear to the Word Bearers. The phrase 'fugged beyond all reason' didn't even begin to describe it.

He also noticed that a key figure was missing, as did Leodrakk.

'Where is Domadus?' asked the Salamander.

Numeon sighed, weary. He took off his battle-helm. 'We lost him during the fight. He and several others went out to meet the Seventeenth to stymie their assault. I didn't see him fall, but…' He shook his head.

'So, what now?' asked Shen'ra, hobbling to stand beside his brothers.

Grammaticus answered.

'Let me go. Help me reclaim the spear and get off Traoris. What is there to lose now?'

Numeon ignored him, and went over to Shen'ra. He was badly wounded and struggling.

'I have seen better days, before you ask,' said the Techmarine acerbically. He was slumped against the tunnel wall, a trickle of effluence from the cracked ceiling painting a grubby track down his armour. Numeon kneeled to speak with him.

'You saved us all, you irascible bastard.'

'Lost the track-mount, though. Anyway…' he paused to cough, 'someone had to.'

Numeon laughed, but his humour quickly faded when he saw Shen'ra's injuries.

The Techmarine's bionic eye was only partially functional and he carried a limp, but his cracked breastplate hinted at the real damage. Internal injuries, partial biological shut-down.

Two other Salamanders in the returning party were already coma-
tose as their brutalised bodies tried to repair themselves. Prognosis
did not appear favourable. Three more were dead, shredded by
bolt-rounds, impaled by blades. Not one killing wound, but several
small ones amounting to the same. Attritional deaths. Their brothers had carried them, those that were washed down with them into
the tunnels, just as they had before.

Grammaticus was surprised at the level of humanity they
showed to their dead, and wondered if it was a common Nocturnean trait.

'So, what now?' he asked. 'Are we to hide out in these tunnels
until they find us?'

Numeon finished muttering some words of encouragement to the
Techmarine and rose to his feet.

'We move on. Find another way to achieve our mission.'

Leodrakk approached, noticing Numeon touching the sigil of
Vulkan he had carried ever since they had fled Isstvan.

'What do you think it's for?' he asked.

Numeon glanced down at it. Fashioned into a simple blacksmith's
hammer, it looked unremarkable.

'I think it's a symbol,' he said. 'When I see it, I believe in our primarch, that he is still alive. Beyond that, I don't know.'

'I hope you're right, brother.'

Pergellen, returning from scouting out the tunnel ahead, interrupted them.

'The way on is clear,' he put in. 'This tract ends in an outflow.
It's towards the edge of the city and should give us a good vantage
point to plan our next move.'

Numeon nodded. 'Make sure there are no surprises.'

Taking K'gosi with him, the scout headed back off into the
darkness.

'I hate to echo the human,' said Leodrakk when Pergellen had gone, 'but what *is* our next move?'

Numeon regarded Grammaticus.

'They're after him now. The attack on the manufactorum is proof of that. We might be able to use that. To use him.'

And just like that, fate twisted again and Grammaticus bemoaned that he had ever been 'saved' by the Salamanders.

The outflow ended in a broad sink, a few metres deep. It was raining heavily overhead, causing the dirty sewer run-off in the manmade basin to flow over its rockcrete lip in a rushing cataract that crashed down in an ever-deepening pool below.

At one side of the sink there was a wooden jetty. The bodies of three men laid face down on it. Their attire suggested they were sump-catchers. They had been stabbed to death, and the crude sigil daubed in blood on the jetty suggested it was cult-related. Above them hung a lattice of fishing lines, dead sump rats strung along them by their tiny feet. There were a couple of long pikes, too, and a crumpled-up net stuffed into an empty oil drum. A tarpaulin provided ineffective protection against the elements, covering two thirds of the jetty and suspended on guide poles like a crude tent.

'Don't want to slip in there, human,' muttered Leodrakk as he escorted Grammaticus over a wooden walkway that creaked with the legionary's every step.

Grammaticus looked down into the viscous, grimy soup slowly coagulating in the sink. Foulness practically radiated from it, the water an ugly pale yellow. Carcasses bobbed up and down in it, disturbed by the effluvia running out from the pipe and cascading over the basin edge.

It reminded him of the drainage basin on the outskirts of Anatol Hive when he had been just a child. As he looked down into the sink's murky depths he tried not to picture the corpse-white face of the boy, and found that he had to look away. Instead, he thought about the eldar who had *flected* him in the infirmary. He had offered him a way out, a choice, a truth. Albeit one that had yet to be revealed to him in full. It went against his mission – it might also be a pack of lies, a test by the Cabal to see if he could be trusted. Tired wasn't the word for how he felt now. He was ragged, just like the warriors who were escorting him. Not only that, he was a traitor to his race. His *entire fugging race*! That was something not many could claim, not that he was proud of it. He felt grubby, and not just from the sewer pipe. He wanted to believe what he had seen in the infirmary, he *needed* to. But what if it wasn't real? What if Slau Dha, Gahet and all those other bastards were manipulating him still? All he had was his mission, and even that sickened him.

Thoroughly miserable, Grammaticus winced as a droplet from above splashed his eye.

Numeon lifted up his dripping gauntlet for retinal analysis.

'High acid content,' he said. 'Better give him something to keep off the worst of it.'

'How about we go somewhere other than a fugging sewer,' suggested Grammaticus, 'perhaps indoors and not surrounded by shit and piss?'

'Here.' K'gosi handed him his cloak. It was drake hide, virtually impervious to fire and more than adequate protection against acid-rain.

Grammaticus took it, grudgingly.

'Why not give me one of theirs?' he asked, gesturing to the dead Salamanders being carried out onto the jetty.

'Not mine to give,' said K'gosi.

'They're not going to need them.'

'Doesn't matter,' the Pyroclast replied and went to help secure the outer perimeter.

Pergellen was standing at the edge of the basin, a couple of metres away from the gushing cataract.

'It's sheer, over eighty metres straight down,' he told Numeon, who had just joined him. 'Though the water makes it look shorter than that.'

The dirty torrent from the sewer pipe was coming down so hard that it frothed and foamed below, rising and bubbling in a small but violent tumult. The spray kicked up all the way to the top of the outflow, but Pergellen's gaze had moved skywards, to a high column which comprised part of an aqueduct that flanked the torrent.

'Looks like a good vantage point,' he said.

A walkway led from the jetty, along the side of the outflow pipes, all the way to the aqueduct, and had enough room for men to traverse in file. Beyond the aqueduct, the rest of Ranos was laid open. Numeon could see that since making planetfall they had moved east, towards the edge of the city.

His eyes narrowed.

'Is that...?' he asked.

'The space port? Yes, it is,' said Pergellen.

Numeon looked back over his shoulder to where Grammaticus was huddled up and shivering in K'gosi's cloak.

'This is no place to make a stand, brother.'

'Agreed,' said Pergellen. 'What do you have in mind?'

Numeon watched the lines of dead sump-rats swaying with the foetid breeze.

'Bait,' he said.

NAREK'S GLADIUS SLID from the Salamander's neck with a wet *slurrch*. The legionary was dead before he had cleaned the blade and was moving on to the next. Bodies from both sides littered the street. Of the three squads he had taken to eliminate the loyalists, only a handful remained. It had been bloody, and harder fought than he had expected. The sniper had escaped. Again. This stuck in Narek's craw, and irritated. Approaching the edge of the pit where the manufactorum had collapsed, he thought of the ones who had escaped. An underground river flowed beneath this part of the city, connected to its drainage system. He had no map of those tunnels, no knowledge of their existence or where the outflow would deposit anyone caught in the current, so he let it go.

The loyalists were running out of places to hide. Even if it took him to the edge of the city and the lightning-blasted wastes beyond it, he would track them down. He had sworn, so it would be done. Or he would die in the attempt. Honour about one's duty, he felt, should still mean something.

'Stop,' he said, his boot pressed down on the chest of another half-dead enemy, but Narek was looking at Vogel, who was straddling a Salamander's chest and was about to begin cutting flesh with his ritual knife.

'What?' asked the Word Bearer, head snapping round to regard the huntsman.

'None of that.' Narek left the other dying legionary where he was and walked over to Vogel.

'I honour the Pantheon,' Vogel hissed, evidently displeased.

'You dishonour the deed, your kill,' Narek replied, holding his gladius casually in his off-hand. 'Mutilate the human chaff, by all means, but these were Legion warriors, once our brothers-in-arms. That should still mean something.'

Vogel went to rise, but Narek put the tip of his gladius to his throat and he stopped in a half-crouch.

'You overstep your bounds,' hissed Vogel.

'If I do, it'll mean this blade goes through your neck.'

Vogel didn't look like he wanted to back down just yet.

'Dagon agrees with me,' said Narek.

Vogel followed the huntsman's gaze to the other sniper, who had his rifle trained and ready. The belligerent Word Bearer raised his hands in a placatory gesture and Narek let him step away. When he was certain Vogel was content just to curse him and not retaliate, Narek looked down on the stricken Salamander his comrade had been about to defile.

'Thank... you...' the warrior muttered, close to death.

'It wasn't for you, legionary,' Narek uttered, and plunged the gladius into his heart.

The sound of a turbine engine getting louder and closer made Narek turn. He saw the Stormbird that belonged to Elias, and wondered what had happened to bring him here.

'Gather,' he voxed to the others. 'The Dark Apostle is here.'

ELIAS WAS WOUNDED. He had also been paid a visit by Erebus himself. As he stood before the Dark Apostle in the lee of the landed Stormbird, it suddenly made sense to Narek why his master had come. He had been ordered to.

'Another failure?' asked Elias, surveying the carnage.

'Not entirely,' the huntsman replied. He had removed his battle-helm in the Dark Apostle's presence and held it in the crook of his arm.

They were alone, in so far as the rest of the legionaries were standing guard or rounding up still-living prisoners. Narek wished dearly he'd had the time to give all of them clean deaths. Irritating Vogel was one thing; he wouldn't defy the Dark Apostle.

'Did you kill all of them, and apprehend the human?'

'Not yet.'

'A failure then.'

Narek briefly bowed his head. 'One I shall rectify.'

'No, Narek. Your chance has passed for this glory. Erebus himself comes and has asked me to eliminate our enemies and recapture the human, John Grammaticus.'

'He asked you, did he?'

'Yes,' hissed Elias with more than a hint of anger. 'I am his trusted ally in this.'

'Of course, master,' Narek responded coolly. His eyes strayed to the fulgurite spear scabbarded at Elias's waist.

It still gave off a faint glow, and seemed to make the Dark Apostle uncomfortable to wear it. Narek realised that the spear had somehow burned Elias's arm to all but a scorched mess.

'You are wondering if we were right to worship the Emperor as a god,' Elias said to him, when he noticed Narek looking at the sheathed spear.

'I am.'

'We were, brother. But there are other gods, Narek, who would give us favour.'

'I see no boon in it,' he admitted.

Elias laughed. 'I could have you executed for that, for your lack of belief.'

'I believe, master. That is the problem – I just do not like where that belief is taking us.'

'You will come to like it, huntsman. You will *embrace* it, as we all will. For it is the desire of Lorgar and the Pantheon that we do so. Now,' he added, growing bored of his sermon. 'Where is the man, where is John Grammaticus?'

'He is almost certainly still with the broken Legion survivors. Their trail won't be hard to track.'

Elias dismissed the idea with a desultory wave of his hand.

'It's of no consequence. I can find him through different means.' He eyed one of the legionary prisoners, one yet to be given a clean death, and pulled out his ritual knife.

✠ ✠ ✠

DOMADUS WAS ALIVE, but somehow pinned. Since the battle had ended, they had been raking through the casualties, looking for survivors. He dimly recalled being dragged, and half-heard guttural laughter from one of his captors. Part of his spinal column had been severed. He was paralysed from the waist down. He also had several potentially fatal internal injuries, and was too weak to fight back.

His bionic eye no longer functioned, so he was left blinded in it. His organic one opened, and the view this received was of the ground. At the edge of his reduced vision he thought he saw the open hand of a legionary lying on his back. The gauntlet was emerald-green, the fingers unmoving. A bolter lay a few centimetres away from it grip.

'This one,' he heard a voice say. He sounded cultured, almost urbane.

Firm, armoured fingers seized the Iron Hand's chin and lifted it up so that Domadus could see his oppressors.

Word Bearers. One, standing behind the other, had scripture painting his cheekbones in gold. His black hair was short with a sharp widow's peak. One of his arms was badly burned, and he held it protectively to his body. This was the cleric, it had to be. The other one who was holding Domadus's chin was a veteran, definitely a soldier in the most pugnacious sense of the word. He was flat-nosed, but thin of face, and carried a slight limp.

Through dulled senses, Domadus became aware that his wrists were bound with razor-wire and he was attached to the side of a Word Bearers gunship. His breastplate had been removed, as well as his mesh under-armour, exposing the skin beneath.

'There is no other way?' asked the soldier.

The cleric drew forth a jagged ritual knife and Domadus steeled himself for what he knew was coming next.

'None,' answered the cleric, who traced a long nailed gauntlet across the flesh of the Iron Hand's cheek, before taking up a chant.

CHAPTER
TWENTY-SIX
Enter the labyrinth

'Go forwards, ever forwards and always down. Never left. Never right.'

— from the dramatic play, *Thesion and the Minatar*

FERRUS WAS ALREADY watching me when I rose again from death. I think he was smirking, though he always smirked now with that permanent rictus grin of his.

I clenched my fists and fought down the urge to strike the apparition.

'Amuses you, does it, brother?' I spat. 'To see me like this? Am I weak then? Not as weak as you. Idiot! Fulgrim played you like a twisted harp.'

I paused, and heard my own heavy breathing, the anger growing within. The abyss, red and black, throbbing with hate, pulsed at the edge of my sight.

'No answer?' I challenged. 'Hard to chide without a tongue, brother!'

I stood up, unshackled for once, and advanced on the wordless spectre. If I could have, I believe that I would have wrapped my hands around his throat and choked him as I had almost done to Corax in my mind.

I sagged, gasping, fighting down the thunderous beating of my heart. Feverish sweat lathered my skin, which glistened in the flickering torchlight. Another dank chamber, another black-walled cell. Curze had many of them aboard his ship, it seemed.

'Throne of Terra...' I gasped, collapsing to one knee, my head bowed so I could breathe. 'Father...'

I remembered the words, such a distant memory now. *He* had spoken them to me on Ibsen. After my Legion and I had destroyed the world, turned it into a place of death, I renamed it Caldera. It was to be another adopted world, like Nocturne, and with it the Salamanders would be reforged. That dream ended with the end of the Great Crusade and the beginning of the war.

It pains me, but I will have to leave you all when you need me the most. I'll try to watch over you when I can.

'I need you now, father,' I said to the dark. 'More than ever.'

Ferrus clicking his skeletal jaw made me look up. His hollow gaze met my own and he nodded to the shadows ahead of us where a vast, ornate gateway had begun to appear.

It was taller than the bastion leg of an Imperator Titan and twice as wide. I could not fathom why I hadn't noticed it before.

'Another illusion?' I asked, calling out to the shadows I knew were listening.

The immense gate appeared to be fashioned of bronze, though I could tell by looking at it that the metal was an alloy. I saw the vague blueish tint of osmium, traces of silvery-white palladium and iridium. It was dense, and incredibly strong. The bronze was merely an aesthetic veneer, designed to make it look archaic. A blend of intricate intaglio and detailed embossing wrought upon the gate described a raft of imagery. It was a battle scene, which appeared to represent a conflict of some elder age. Warriors wielded swords and were clad in hauberks of chain, and leather jerkins. Catapults and ballistae flung crude missiles into the air. Fires raged.

But as I looked closer, I began to see the familiar, and realised what my Iron brother had done.

Three armies fought desperately in a narrow gorge, their enemies arrayed on either side, loosing arrows and charging down at them with swords and spears. On a spur of rock, a warlord carrying a serpent banner held the head of a defeated enemy aloft in triumph.

'It's Isstvan V, isn't it?'

'Yes,' said Curze, suddenly standing alongside me, where I realised he had been all along. 'And it is not an illusion, Vulkan. Our brother laboured long over this piece. I think it would offend him to know you thought you had conjured it in your mind.' He almost sounded defeated.

'What's wrong, Konrad? You sound tired.'

He sighed, full of regret.

'We near the end,' he said, and gestured to the gate. 'This is the entrance to the Iron Labyrinth. I had Perturabo make it for me. At its heart, a prize.'

Curze opened his hand and within it was projected a rotating hololith of my hammer, *Dawnbringer*. Surrounding it and hanging from chains were my sons. The projection was weak and grainy, but I managed to recognise Nemetor from earlier. I was ashamed to admit that the other I couldn't identify, but I could see that both were severely injured.

Curze closed his fist, crushing the image of my stricken sons.

'I've bled them thoroughly, brother. They have only days left to live.'

I saw the blackness crowding at the edge of my vision again, and heard the throbbing of my heart in my skull. I felt the heat of the abyss on my face, saw it bathe my skin in visceral red.

With sheer effort of will, I relaxed my gritted teeth.

Curze was watching me.

'What do you see, Vulkan?' he asked. 'What do you see when you stray into the darkness? I would have you tell me.' He almost sounded desperate, pleading.

'Nothing,' I lied. 'There is nothing. You were gone for a while this time, weren't you?'

Curze didn't answer, but his eyes were penetrating.

'I remember some of it. I remember what you tried to get me to do,' I told him. 'Did I disappoint you, brother, by rising above your petty game? Is it lonely in the shadows? Are you in need of some company?'

'Shut up,' he muttered.

'It must burn you to know I beat your moral test, I resisted the urge to kill Corvus. I don't claim to be noble, but I know I am everything you are not.'

'Liar...' he hissed.

'Even though you have me at your mercy, you still cannot manage to drag me down. You can't even kill me.'

Curze looked like he was about to lash out, but reined his anger in and became disturbingly calm.

'You're not special,' he said. 'You were just convenient.' He smiled thinly, and walked around behind me so that I couldn't see him. 'I have enjoyed our game, so much so that when it's over I will go after another of my brothers. And those I cannot kill, I shall break.'

I turned to confront him, to warn him off, but Curze was already gone. He had melted away into the darkness.

The gate yawned open, silently beckoning.

'I will break them, Vulkan,' Curze's disembodied voice declared. 'Just as I am breaking you, piece by fragile piece. And if you're *wondering if there are any monsters in the labyrinth, I can tell you yes, but only one.'*

With Curze gone, I had little choice but to enter the Iron Labyrinth.

CHAPTER
TWENTY-SEVEN
Faith

HIDING AT THE edge of the tunnel outflow, Dagon gave the signal to advance.

Vogel went in first, knife drawn as he closed on his prey.

The earlier battle had hit the loyalists hard and there were fewer warriors than he had expected. Pity, it would mean fewer souls to offer up to the Pantheon. Perhaps he would offer up Narek's soul too if he got in Vogel's way again.

There were four of them, all Salamanders, sitting together with their cloaks wrapped protectively around their bodies. One, a Techmarine judging by his armour and trappings, was talking to the others. They must be discussing tactics. Two more were laid out under a tarpaulin, and squatting next to them, also huddled in drake hide, was the human the Word Bearers were looking for.

Heavy acid-rain was fouling the auspex, but the blademaster didn't need his scanners to tell him the four legionaries with their backs to the tunnel were soon to be dead men.

Foolish to leave the human so lightly guarded, but then Vogel knew that the loyalists had taken a hammering at the manufactorum. He doubted there were many more left. He smiled, showing two rows of pointed teeth he had filed down himself, and remembered how the Dark Apostle's warpcraft had revealed their enemies to him. The tunnels could have led to any one of fifty or more outflows. Vogel was certain that the loyalists would not be expecting an attack so soon.

Unsheathing a second blade, he crept quietly into the open, his footfalls masked by the rain. His fellow assassins were right behind him, but Vogel didn't need them. He was going to kill all of these weaklings by himself.

NUMEON CLUNG TO the side of the cliff, beneath the cascading overflow. Glancing to the right, he saw Leodrakk with his gauntleted fingers dug into the manmade rock face. On the left was Daka'rai, also clinging on. Three of their brothers were hiding on the opposite side of the gushing falls, obscured by the water. K'gosi and three more were submerged beneath the sink itself.

Numeon was blind to whatever was happening above. All he could hear was the roar of the water as it battered against his armour. Even through his helmet respirator, the air was foul and dank.

Soon... he told himself.

It was all up to Shen'ra now. All Numeon and the others had to do was honour his sacrifice.

VOGEL HAD A HUNTER'S stealth but a maniac's urgency. The latter tended to undermine the former, which was why Narek had only wanted him in his squad when he needed killers and could trust less to subterfuge. Had he been allowed to do this with Dagon and possibly Melach, Narek would have gone about it differently. Something about the scene before him, the quiet comradely conversation, the huddled figure of the stock-still human, gave him pause. He could have given voice to it, he could have suggested caution but instead he let Dagon give the all-clear to attack. After that, Vogel had rushed out to be first.

Narek was content to let him and followed on behind with Dagon, Melach and Saarsk.

Elias was amongst the vanguard too, the rest of the Word Bearers waiting in the tunnel if needed. Narek kept the Dark Apostle behind him, irritated that Elias had insisted on joining the kill-squad. Fear of Erebus and a loss of status amongst the XVII was a compelling motivator, it seemed.

Vogel had almost reached the Techmarine when Narek received a horrible premonition. His concerns, abstract at first, became reality and his warning could not then remain unspoken.

'Their eyes...' he hissed urgently over the vox to Dagon.

'What of them?'

'Look!'

The three Salamanders sitting and listening to the Techmarine had dead retinal lenses. Their eyes, normally burning, should have cast a faint light through them.

It meant the eyes were not the only things that were dead, and that in turn meant–

Narek stood up and shouted, 'Vogel! No!'

Too late, the bladesman plunged his dagger into the Techmarine's back. It was a killing stroke, punched right through the legionary's primary heart. Vogel wrenched out the blade. It was covered in blood. He was about to slay another when the dull *thud* of an object hitting the wooden deck drew his eyes downwards.

Blinking red, an incendiary rolled from the Techmarine's open gauntlet. There was a smile etched on Shen'ra's lifeless face as he released the dead man's trigger.

The explosion immolated Vogel, and threw the others off their

NICK KYME

feet. Fire swept across the jetty, igniting a chain of grenades dug into and around the tunnel entrance. They cooked off in seconds, releasing a secondary explosion and effectively sealing the outflow behind a tonne of debris.

Smashed back towards the entrance and then away from it as the second blast hit, Narek was on the ground, stunned but alive. He'd dragged Elias down with him as he sought to keep the Dark Apostle from harm. Hate him he might, but he still had his duty to perform. Peering through smoke and fire, the huntsman saw four legionaries emerging from the sink with bolters raised. He threw his knife, piercing the neck of one before the Salamander had a chance to fire.

Dagon had his rifle up, preparing to execute a second ambusher, when a shot whined out from a distance and struck right through the side of his head. The sniper was dead before he hit the jetty.

Bolt-rounds from the submerged legionaries ripped Melach apart, the Word Bearer with his pistol only half drawn.

Prone, almost underneath Narek, Elias fired off a burst and clipped one of the emerging legionaries, who had now drawn blades and were charging through the water. Narek suspected they were low on – or even out of – ammunition, as a concentrated fusillade would have ended the fight quickly. He wondered what the loyalists might be saving their rounds for.

Six more hauled themselves over the edge of the outflow basin. One advanced ahead of the rest. He was a Salamander, a centurion.

A quick headcount made the odds fairly even, but of the many in the tunnel only a few had got out before the blast hit and sealed in the rest. The loyalists also had a plan and the advantage of surprise.

Elias was on his feet. He fired off a snap shot that took the Salamander officer in the shoulder. He staggered but kept on coming, swinging a hefty-looking glaive.

Narek had other concerns as the two from the sink drove at him. He parried one thrust with his rapidly drawn gladius. A second attack he trapped with his forearm and then dragged the legionary in, crushing his vox-grille with a savage head-butt.

Saarsk had engaged some of the Salamanders who had clambered up over the edge of the sink. He stabbed one and shot another before the sniper ventilated his chest, and the others dragged the Word Bearer down to finish him.

He saw Elias barrelled over as the Salamander officer hurtled into him. The two grappling warriors fell hard against the jetty, which cracked under their weight. A second later and the wooden jetty split, dumping everyone on it down into the filth. It doused the fire still crackling against Narek's armour, and he used the sudden shift in terrain to put a pistol burst point-blank into one of his opponents. Grunting, the Salamander rolled over and sank into the water.

An elbow strike in the second legionary's throat dented his gorget and partially choked him, freeing Narek of immediate enemies. The fall had split Elias and the Salamander officer apart. They were close to the edge of the sink and a long drop into the reservoir of filth below. Ignoring the other legionaries, who had started to regroup after the Word Bearers' fast counter-attack, Narek went straight for Elias.

'What are you doing?' yelled the Dark Apostle.

They were outgunned, with a sniper rifle trained on them at distance. Everyone else in the kill-squad was dead or soon to be, and all their reinforcements were trapped inside the tunnel without any excavation gear.

'Saving our lives,' snapped Narek as he took Elias and himself over the edge of the sink and down towards the foaming tumult below.

NUMEON RUSHED TO the edge of the sink and almost jumped.

Leodrakk stopped him, hauling the captain back by his shoulder guard.

'We've lost enough already,' he said, but leaned over and sighted down his bolter.

'Save your rounds,' Numeon told him, embittered. 'They're gone.'

Putting aside his anger, Leodrakk relented and lowered the bolter. 'We almost had him. That bastard.'

'He'll want revenge for this. We'll see him again.'

'Did you see his arm?' asked Leodrakk. 'He was wounded. Recently.'

'But not by us.'

'Not one of his own?'

'No,' Numeon said, pensive, 'something else.'

After a few seconds of watching the tide of filth still plunging from the outflow and not seeing either Word Bearer snared by the current, they stepped away from the edge.

K'gosi was alive. His breastplate was bloodstained where a Word Bearer had plunged a blade into it, but he was otherwise unharmed. He had long since depleted his reserves of promethium and flexed his left gauntlet irritably. The right he held against Shen'ra's chest.

'We will remember your sacrifice, brother,' he muttered softly, kneeling next to the Techmarine whom he had rolled onto his back in repose. The splinter of jetty Shen'ra rested on was about all there was left of it; the others were still up to their armoured shins in sewage.

The Techmarine was not the only casualty. Daka'rai was also dead, on his back in the filth with a knife jutting from his neck. Ukra'bar had taken a bolt-round point blank and would not rise again. The others all carried minor injuries, and none that would amount to the wounding inflicted by their brothers' deaths.

All present bowed their heads, before Leodrakk spoke up.

'We cannot even burn them.'

'No, we cannot.' Numeon went over to the prone form of the dead human, one of the sump-catchers, and retrieved K'gosi's cloak to give back to him. 'So we must honour them a different way.'

In his left hand he held up the fulgurite spear. During their fight, he had wrested it from the Dark Apostle's scabbard.

Despair turned to hope at the sight of this mundane object, though none who saw it could explain why. It crackled with power, an inner golden glow that spoke of the Emperor's grace and his near-divinity. Stringent steps and sanctions had been taken to refute the idea of the Emperor as a god, but his power had always suggested otherwise, despite the desire to move from superstition to enlightenment. But the past months had begun to challenge that paradigm. For the universe was not the sole province of mortals, be they human or alien – it was the realm of gods, too, and most of them were malign. The Word Bearers believed in them, even courted their foot soldiers for dark favours. They had faith, but what they believed in was horrible.

As he held the spearhead aloft, Numeon knew that he had faith too: faith in the Emperor and his design for the galaxy and humanity, and faith that his primarch was still alive. The power in the fulgurite seemed to ignite that belief; it ignited it in all of them.

He lightly traced his fingers over the sigil at his waist.

'Vulkan lives,' he uttered simply.

Every legionary standing before him replied. First K'gosi and Ikrad.

'Vulkan lives.'

Then G'orrn and B'tarro.

'Vulkan lives.'

And Hur'vak and Kronor.

'Vulkan lives.'

With every new voice, the chorus became louder, until only one remained.

Numeon looked his Pyre brother in the eye, and saw the hurt and pain he held there from when Skatar'var had been lost on Isstvan. If any had cause to doubt, it would be Leodrakk. The memory of

that day and their flight to the drop-ships left a canker of regret in
Numeon's mouth, but he kept his expression neutral as he regarded
Leodrakk.

His gaze moving from Numeon to the spear to the sigil and then
back again, Leodrakk nodded.

'Vulkan lives.'

Together they turned their affirmation into a battle cry, shouting
at the sky in defiance and as one.

'*Vulkan lives!*'

They would hold to this belief, and use it to give their cause much-
needed hope.

For the first time since they had run from Isstvan, beaten and
bloody, Numeon knew what he had to do. Going back to stand at
the edge of the sink, he signalled to Pergellen, with whom he knew
Hriak and John Grammaticus were also waiting.

It was time to talk to the human again.

CHAPTER
TWENTY-EIGHT
Human failings

Kharaatan, during the Great Crusade

NIGHT HAD FALLEN over Khartor City for the last time. Through a combined effort of Imperial Army, both infantry and armoured, Titans from the Legio Ignis and two Space Marine Legions, the world of Kharaatan was at last officially deemed compliant. With the warriors' work now done, the Imperial Administration with its army of logisticians, codifiers, servitors, engineers, manufactors, taxonomers and scriveners could begin the long task of recolonising One-Five-Four Six and repatriating it in the name of the Emperor and the Imperium.

Its old name of Kharaatan, together with the names of all its cities and other important geographical locations, would change. For now simple designations would suffice, such as the signifier it had been given when the war of compliance had been authorised by the War Council. In time, new appellations would be chosen in order to help colonists better adapt and think of the world as their own, as a loyal Imperial world with loyal Imperial citizens.

Kharaatan and all its associated trappings represented rebellion and discord. By changing its names, their power was revoked and supplanted with another's.

Part of this transformation began with the logging and transportation of the entire population of Kharaatan. These men, women and children, be they rebels or innocents, would never see their home again. Some would go to the penal colonies, others would be sent to worlds in need of indentured workers, some would be executed. But in the end, the cultural footprint of the Kharaatan people would disappear forever.

Logistician Murbo thought on none of this as he conducted final checks before the transporters' departure. After what had seemed like days rather than hours of painstaking cataloguing and questioning, the Departmento Munitorum, assisted by Administratum clerks in battalion-strength cohorts, had finally rounded up and divided Khartor's population. This was the last city. It had also been one of the largest. Headache didn't even begin to describe the wretched pounding that was alive in Murbo's skull, so his temper was short as well as his diligence.

As he rattled by the first transport, he didn't notice the smell. He had a gaggle of servitors and a lexmechanic in tow, but they had long since been divested of the burden of olfactory sensation, so didn't raise any question either.

It was dark, and a cold wind was coming in across the desert. Murbo wanted to be back in his lodgings aboard ship, warm and with something warming in his belly too. He'd been saving a bottle for just this occasion.

There were over fifty transports to check, log and verify before he was done, then he had to confirm passenger designation with the pilot and input said data onto his slate, which he now had in his hand. Administratum protocol was to make visual checks also, to ensure that no one was missed. In the chaotic scramble after a successful compliance that began on a war-footing, it was not uncommon for entire swathes of population to be forgotten about.

The first tranche of ex-Khar-tans, the prisoners bound for the penal colonies, had already gone. Murbo's job was to despatch those people who were destined to become Imperial citizens on brave new worlds. He wasn't sure who he pitied more, but his sympathy didn't last. Rebellion reaped its own harsh rewards when it was against the Imperium.

He panned the weak lumen-lamp around the hold, saw the dead-eyed inhabitants contemplating their new lives, and approximated a head count. All seemed fine at first, but when he got to the second transport and was about to move on to the third, he paused.

'Did they seem a little quiet to you?' he asked the lexmechanic.

The hunched clerk seemed perplexed by the question. 'I suspect they are contemplating the folly of rising up against the Imperium.'

No, thought Murbo, that wasn't it.

There was nothing that Murbo wanted more in that moment than to be done with his business and be off to his quarters for the flight up to One-Five-Four Six's atmosphere, but the ex-Khar-tans tended to be more vocal.

Then there was the smell, which, buoyed on the desert breeze, had begun to seem more noisome.

He increased the intensity of the lamp's glow and went back to the first transport.

'Oh Throne...' he gasped, shining the light into the hold again.

Frantically, Murbo ran to the next transport and did the same again. Then he went to the third, the fourth, the fifth. By the time he reached the twelfth, he was violently sick.

Still doubled over, Murbo waved off the lexmechanic who went to help him.

'Don't look in there,' he warned, then asked, 'Who's still planetside?'

Again, the hunched little man looked confused in his drab robes. 'Besides us?'

'Military,' said Murbo, wiping down his chin.

The lexmechanic checked his slate.

'According to the Munitorum's log, all military assets have left the surface...' he paused, holding up a withered-looking hand as he checked further, 'but there are still two Legion transports on the ground.'

'Hail them,' Murbo commanded. 'Do it now.'

VULKAN WAS ALONE standing in the broad expanse of the *Nightrunner's* cargo hold. Ordinarily it would be used for the transportation of weapons, ration packs and the myriad materiel required for war. This night it accommodated the dead. Caskets lined part of the hold's east quarter, but the numbers were mercifully light, thanks to the swift and bloodless resolution of the Khartor siege. How many lives had been used to pay for that mercy... tortured, painful endings to lives... Vulkan knew all too well.

The bloodshed had not concluded with the massacre of Khar-tann City either. The riot during the settling of the Khartor citizenry had resulted in many deaths. And though he suspected his brother's Night Lords had been partly responsible for that, he could not absolve himself of all blame.

Seriph lay before him within her casket. It was plain, unadorned, a simple metallic tube with a cryo-engine built in to retard putrefaction and ensure that the deceased reached their place of final rest unspoiled. The medicaes had cleaned up her wounds, but the bloodstain on her robes remained. Were it not for that and the grim pallor of her skin, then Vulkan might have believed she was merely sleeping.

He wanted to tell her that he was sorry she was dead, that he wished he had heeded her during the burning of Khar-tann and acceded to her request for an interview. His story should be told, he had decided, and Seriph would be the one to do it. But not any more. A corpse could tell no stories.

He bowed his head by way of mute apology.

'Why this one?' a voice asked softly from the shadows.

Vulkan didn't turn, but he raised his head.

'What are you still doing here?' he asked, suddenly stern.

'I came looking for you, brother,' said Curze, coming to stand alongside Vulkan.

'You have found me.'

'I sense a little choler in you.' Curze almost sounded wounded by it. 'Aren't you pleased to see me?'

Now Vulkan looked at him. His eyes were brimming with undisguised vitriol.

'Say what it is you came to say and leave me.'

Curze sniffed, as if amused by it all.

'You didn't answer my question. Of all the mortals who died to make this world compliant for our Imperium, why does this one matter so much?'

Vulkan turned his gaze forwards again.

'I preserve life. I am a protector of humanity.'

'Of course you are, brother. But how you threw yourself in harm's way for her. It was... *inspiring*.' Curze smiled, then the smile became a grin, and unable to maintain the pretence, he began to laugh. 'No, I'm sorry.' He stopped laughing, grew serious. 'I am *baffled* by it. Yours is a bleeding heart, Vulkan. I know how you care for these weaklings, but what made this one so special that you would mourn her passing so?'

Vulkan turned and was about to answer when the vox-bead in his ear crackled. Neither primarch was wearing his battle-helm, but they were still connected to the battle group.

As one primarch's eyes widened, the other's narrowed, and

Vulkan knew that Curze was hearing the self-same message.

Vulkan reached out for his brother, seizing him by his gorget and dragging him close. Curze smiled and did not resist.

'Did you do this?' Vulkan asked. *'Did you do this?'* he bellowed when Curze didn't answer straight away.

The smile thinned and became the dark line of Curze's pale lips.

'Yes,' he hissed, cold eyes staring.

Vulkan let him go, thrusting him back from his sight as he turned away.

'You killed... *all* of them.'

Curze feigned confusion. 'They were our enemies, brother. They took up arms against us, tried to kill us.'

Vulkan faced him again, enraged, almost pleading, abhorred at what Curze had done.

'Not all, Konrad. You murdered the innocent, the weak. How does that serve anything but a sadistic desire for bloodshed?'

Curze seemed genuinely to muse on that. He frowned. 'I'm not sure it does, brother. But how is that any different to what you did to that xenos? She was only a child, no threat to you. The rebels of Kharaatan were afforded a quick death. At least I didn't burn them alive.'

Vulkan had no answer. He had killed the child in anger, out of grief for Seriph and retribution for the damage the rampaging xenos had caused. Perhaps it was also because he hated them, the eldar, for their raiding and the pain they had inflicted on Nocturne.

Curze saw his brother's doubt.

'See,' he said quietly, coming in close to whisper. 'Our humours are similar enough, are they not, brother?'

Vulkan roared and seized the other primarch, throwing him across the hold.

Curze slid, his armour shrieking as it scored the metal deck beneath. He was already on his feet when Vulkan came at him, and succeeded in blocking a wild punch aimed at his face. He jabbed, catching Vulkan in the chest and jarring his ribs even through his armour. Vulkan grunted, pained, but grabbed Curze's head and thrust it down into his rising knee.

Curze rocked back, bloody spittle expelled from his mouth. Vulkan tackled him around the waist, giving his brother no time to recover, and brought him down on his back. A savage punch turned Curze's head and cut open his cheek. He was laughing through blood-rimed teeth. Vulkan hit him again, shuddering his jaw. Curze only laughed louder, but choked a little when his windpipe was being crushed. Vulkan clamped his hands, his iron-hard blacksmiter's hands, around his brother's throat.

'I knew you were no different,' Curze hissed, still trying to laugh. 'A killer. We're all killers, Vulkan.'

Vulkan released him. He sat back, still straddling Curze, and gasped for air, for sanity. He would have killed him if he hadn't stopped. He would have murdered his brother.

A little unsteady still, Vulkan rose to his feet and stepped across Curze's supine body.

'Stay away from me,' he warned, out of breath, and strode from the hold to where his transport was waiting.

Curze stayed down, but turned his head to watch Vulkan go, knowing it was far from over between them.

I KNEW I WAS LOST. I suspected it the moment I stepped through the Iron Labyrinth's gates. This was not a challenge I could overcome, not something I could unravel. Here was a place seemingly infinite and of Firenzian complexity, wrought by a mind equal to my own.

No, that wasn't entirely truthful. My mind was compromised, and so the featureless corridors of brass and iron that stretched before me were beyond my intellect to navigate.

Standing at the hundredth crossroad, each avenue I had chosen on the ninety-nine before it taking me deeper into the labyrinth and yet, at the same time, farther from my goal, I wondered what Curze had promised my brother in return for this gift.

Perhaps Perturabo hated me as much as he did the rest of us, and he had simply decided that hurting one of his brothers was as good as hurting any? Maybe he resented the fact that I had survived his glorious barrage on Isstvan V, and refused to yield to his lines of armour? Whatever the reason, he had crafted this place with one purpose in mind; that whoever entered it would never leave. It suited Perturabo's mindset, I think, to imagine me wandering these halls forever, although he could not have known about my immortality. I believed that Curze needed more immediate closure, however. Patience was not his virtue, nor restraint. In the hammer he had provided me with hope. I suspected that he meant to drive me further into madness with that hope. He did not realise that he had actually provided a realistic means of escaping his dungeon.

Deciding that it mattered little if I couldn't find the heart of the labyrinth, I took the left fork and wandered on.

Unlike my previous trials at my brother's tender claws, there were no traps, no enemies, no obstacles of any kind. I reasoned the labyrinth itself was the trap, the ultimate snare in fact, fashioned by an arch-trapsmith. Once again, I felt the pulse of the abyss nearby, the black and the red, its savage teeth closing around me. It called to a feral part of my psyche, the monster Curze had spoken of.

I shook the sensation off. Somewhere in this accursed place were my sons. I had to find them, and hoped that I would not come across them in the many bodies I had seen so far. Most of the remains were skeletal, though some yet retained their withered flesh. They were Curze's rats, the poor wretches who had tried to conquer the labyrinth before me. All of them had died still clinging to hope, desperate and out of their minds.

I think that was what Curze wanted for me, to be emaciated,

brought low and desperate, a plaything to mock and punish when his own loathsome presence became too much for him to bear.

Ferrus was with me still. He didn't speak any more, he just followed like my shadow. I could hear his armoured footsteps dogging my tread, slow and cumbersome.

'I think we are getting closer, brother,' I said to the spectre lurking a few metres away.

His teeth clacked together in what I took to be mocking laughter.

'Ye of little faith,' I muttered.

I wandered like this for days, possibly even weeks. I did not sleep, nor did I rest and I couldn't eat. Vigour left me and I began to waste and atrophy. Soon I would not be so different from Ferrus, no more than an angry shadow doomed to walk these halls forever.

And then I heard the talons.

It began as the light tapping of metal on metal, a sharp tip rapped against the walls, echoing through the labyrinth towards me. I stopped and listened, sensing a change in Curze's game, a desire to see it ended. The tapping grew louder and transformed into the scraping of claws. I was no longer alone with my slow, creeping madness.

'Curze,' I called out, challenging.

Only the scraping metal answered. I thought it might be coming closer. I began to move, trying to locate the source of the sound, walking at first, then breaking into a run.

'*Vulkan...*' hissed the air in my brother's goading voice.

I ran after it, all the while the scraping and the tapping clawing its way into my skull, setting my teeth on edge.

I rounded a corner, chasing my instincts, but found only another corridor as gloomy and unremarkable as all the others.

'*Vulkan...*'

It came from behind me and I whirled around as something dark and fast slipped by me. I winced, clutching my side. Taking my hand away I saw blood and the shallow cut my brother had delivered.

'Come out!' I bawled, fist clenched and a feral hunch to my shoulders. I barely recognised my own voice, it had grown so animalistic.

Only the scraping answered.

I chased it, a bloodhound on the hunt, but could find no trace of Curze. The line between predator and prey was blurring: at times I gave pursuit; at others, my brother. I reached another junction, another crossroads and tried to get my bearings, but the throbbing in my skull wouldn't allow it.

'Vulkan...' The voice returned, taunting me.

I roared, thundering my fist into the nearest wall. It barely made a dent. I roared again, arching back my neck, calling ferally into the darkness. The monster within was unleashed and it craved blood.

Curze cut me again, unseen in the dark, and drew a line of glittering rubies across my bicep. It drove me on, fuelled my rage. A third cut opened in my chest, the blood flowing in red tears across my pectoral muscle. A fourth slashed my thigh. I almost caught him that time, but it was like grasping smoke.

'Vulkan...' he whispered, ever scraping, ever goading.

I was bleeding from at least a dozen wounds, my vitae running down my legs and pooling between the gaps in my toes so that I left bloody footprints in my wake. It was only when I looked down at the path I was about to take that I stopped and saw the mark of my passage, the smeared but unmistakable impression of my feet.

I sagged, defeated, nothing to do with my anger but turn it inwards. Closing my eyes, I saw the abyss. I was perched on the very edge, staring down.

A sudden lance of pain in my side drew me back snarling.

'Don't worry,' Curze hissed, claws pinching my shoulder as he thrust his knife into my right side. 'This won't kill you.'

I spun around, spitting fury, ready to wrench my brother's head from his shoulders, but Curze was gone, and I was left grasping at air.

Laughter trailed in his wake, together with the by-now ubiquitous scraping of his talons.

A red film laid over my vision, the filter of my wrath. I was about to go after him, sensing subconsciously that this was what he had planned all along, when I stopped.

Barring my path, I saw *him*. He was standing right in front of me, as clear and real as my own hand before my face.

Verace, the remembrancer.

'I have seen you before,' I whispered, holding my hand out towards him as if to gauge how real or spectral the unassuming man was.

Verace nodded. 'On Ibsen, now Caldera,' he said.

'No, not there.' I frowned, trying to remember, but my thoughts were muddled with anger. 'Here...'

'Where?' asked Verace.

He was barely a few metres away when I stopped moving towards him.

'Here,' I repeated, my memory clearing as he stepped towards me instead. 'You were with them, the prisoners Curze had me murder.'

He looked at me quizzically. 'Did you murder them, Vulkan?'

'I couldn't save them. You were at the banquet, too. I remember your face.'

'What else do you remember?'

Verace was scarcely a metre away. I knelt down so we were almost eye to eye. It was the Salamanders' way.

'I am a primarch.' I felt calmer in his presence as the fractured pieces of my mind started to coalesce. 'I am Vulkan.'

'Yes, you are. Can you remember what I said to you once?'

'On Ibsen?'

'No, elsewhere. On Nocturne.'

Tears were welling in my eyes, as I fervently hoped this was not just another apparition, a cruel trick to send me further into madness.

'You said,' I began, my voice choking with emotion, 'you would watch over us when you could.'

'Close your eyes, Vulkan.'

I did, and lowered my head for him to put his hand upon it.

'Be at peace, my son.'

I expected revelation, a flash of light, something. But all that followed was silence. Opening my eyes, I saw that Verace was gone. For a moment I wondered if he had been real, but I felt some strength returning to my limbs and fresh resolve filling me as I stood. The monster within was at bay, firmly shackled. For now at least, my mind was my own again. For how long, I didn't know. Whatever peace I had been given would not endure in this place. I needed to act.

Curze was broken; I think I knew it back on Kharaatan. He had always been that way, without hope, anger turned within and without. I couldn't imagine what it must be like to live with that, but then I thought of all the suffering he had caused, the lives he had taken needlessly to satisfy his sadistic appetites. I remembered Nemetor, and all the others he had tortured and killed all in the name of nothing greater than boredom.

My pity was short-lived, my resolve stiffening by the second.

'You were right,' I called out to the shadows where I knew my brother was listening. 'I do think I am better than you. Only a weakling and a coward fights as you do, Konrad. Our father was right to ignore your mewling and discard you. I suspect it sickened him. Only you know true terror, isn't that right, brother?' I scowled. 'So weak, so pathetic. Nostramo didn't make you the worthless wretch you are, brother. You were languishing in the gutter with the rest of those deviants the moment our father erred in creating you.' I laughed self-indulgently. 'It was inevitable that one of us would be flawed, so rotten with human failing that he cannot bear his own presence or the presence of others. You can't help it, can you? To measure yourself against each of us. How many times have you found yourself wanting after such observation? When was it you realised that blaming your upbringing and your brothers no longer rang true? When did you turn the mirror and see the worthless parody you've become?'

No answer came from the darkness, but I could feel my brother's rising anger as palpably as the iron floor beneath my feet.

'No one fears you, Konrad. A different name won't change who you really are. I'll let you in on a secret... We pity you. All of us. We *tolerate* you, because you are our brother. But none of us are afraid of you. For what is there to fear but a petulant child raging at the dark?'

I expected him to come at me, claws bared, but instead I heard a great engine turning beneath me, under the labyrinth itself. With the grinding of heavy gears, a large portion of the wall retracted into the floor. Then another and another. In seconds, a path was laid before me and at the end of it another gate, etched in the same manner as the Iron Labyrinth's entrance.

I knew I could not have found my way out alone. Once the fog of my feral rage had been lifted, I realised that there was only one way to reach the prize. Curze would have to show me. My brothers and I were made differently from the adopted sons of our Legions. In the process of creating progeny, our father had distilled a portion of his essence and will into all of us. In the Legiones Astartes he fashioned an army of warriors, bred for a single purpose, to unite Terra and then the galaxy. In my brothers and I, he desired generals but also something else; he wanted equals, he wanted sons. Into us he poured his matchless intelligence and peerless ability in bioengineering. We became more than human; every trait, every chromosome was enhanced and brought to its genetic apex. Strength, speed, martial acumen, tactical ability, initiative, endurance, all of it was magnified by the Emperor's miraculous science. But like a lens directed at an old painting, it was impossible to enhance one detail without enhancing all the others at the same time. We were more than human, greater than Space Marines, but while our assets were magnified, so too were our flaws.

It didn't matter at first, not while the Crusade roared on brightly, a comet bringing light to the benighted heavens. Rivalry soon became jealousy, envy; confidence grew into arrogance; wrath turned into homicidal mania. All of us were flawed, because to be human, even enhanced as we were, is to be flawed. A perfect state cannot be rendered from an imperfect design.

Curze was more flawed than most of us. His shortcomings were obvious, his all too human weakness evident in his every word and action. Revenge was in his blood. It clawed at him, a nihilistic desire to turn upon others the hurt that was inflicted upon him. He hated himself and so reflected that hate outwards. But to have the mirror turned back by another, to have one of his hated siblings show to him the self-loathing creature that he already knew he was… that could not go unreckoned. My gaoler had revealed much to me of his inner self during my incarceration. I wondered, in those final days, who in fact was trapped with whom. I had preyed on Curze's weakness and my brother had shown me the way out. He wanted to be released as much as I did.

As I started walking down the path towards it, the gate began to open. Within I saw the heart of the labyrinth and in the centre of the chamber, my hammer, *Dawnbringer*. Around it, I saw as I drew closer to the yawning gate, were my sons.

Here then, was where we would end it. Curze and I. One would be free, the other lost forever to damnation.

CHAPTER
TWENTY-NINE
No more running

ELIAS WAS LYING on his back. He was also alone. Momentary concern turned into anger when he realised that it wasn't only the huntsman he was missing. The fulgurite was gone. Through filth-smeared retinal lenses, he looked up at the roaring cataracts of sewage pouring from the many outflows. Somewhere up there was his enemy. They had the spear. That bastard Salamander, the centurion. He had taken it during the fight before Narek had tackled them both over the edge.

'Narek.'

After a moment, a breathless-sounding huntsman replied over the vox. He was running.

'Our arrangement is concluded,' he said.

'I am lying down in a pool of filth, Narek. How is that a satisfactory conclusion?'

'You have always lain with filth, Dark Apostle. A life for a life, yours for mine. I now have mine back. Our alliance is null and void. I told you

that by turning a blind eye our debt was settled. I've decided to conclude my mission alone. My business is with them now. Be glad I let you live,' he added, before the link was swallowed by static.

Elias didn't bother activating the warp-flask; he suspected Narek had destroyed it. The huntsman wasn't coming back, at least not to him.

A cursory scan informed Elias his armour functions were as normal. Some minor damage had been incurred during the fall, but it was negligible. He got up, struggling with only one hand and one arm, the burned limb cradled close to his chest. It hurt like hell, but he used it to fuel his anger.

Narek's abandonment of his duty would not go unpunished. If he saw him again, Elias would kill the huntsman. Amaresh was supposed to have done it during the attack on the manufactorum, but fate had turned that plan awry. The pleasure of Narek's demise would have to wait. Regaining the spear was paramount. If the loyalists had it and the human then there was but one move left to them.

'Jadrekk,' Elias growled down the vox, knowing that this lapdog would answer its master. Close by he could see the Ranos space port and knew there were docked shuttles capable of launch. Most of the Word Bearers' ships had returned to the station and Elias had instructed a small garrison to guard it.

Jadrekk answered as predicted.

'Lock on to my signal and bring all of our forces to the Ranos space port,' Elias ordered. 'Tell Radek to expect visitors and prepare a welcome party, and by welcome party I mean kill-squad.'

Jadrekk confirmed it would be done and Elias cut the link.

Erebus would be here soon. Elias was determined that both the spear and the human would be in his possession before then. Over to the north, he could see the tempest boiling over the sacrificial pit. Lightning trembled the sky, splitting the night in half. Once

Grammaticus was cut by the spear, one of those jags would open and the Neverborn would spill forth. Elias would be rewarded for his faith and devotion. Trudging through the muck he heard that promise, whispering in sibilant non sequitur. He would be recognised by the Pantheon and ascend. It was his destiny.

'No more running,' Elias muttered, his gaze moving to the dark horizon of the south and the shadow of the space port. 'Only dying.'

CHAPTER THIRTY
Our final hours

Isstvan V

THE BLAST STRUCK with atomic force, or at least it felt that way to the Salamanders within it. They had been following Vulkan up the hill, hard on his heels as he smashed into the disciplined Iron Warriors ranks. He had hit the armour quickly, much more quickly than Numeon had believed possible.

Wrath drove him, that and a sense of injustice. The ignoble actions of his brother primarchs had wounded Vulkan to the core, far deeper and more debilitating than any blade. Vaunted warriors all, the Pyre Guard could scarcely keep up. It was snowing overhead, a squall of white ash descending upon them in their ignited fury. It was thick and strangely peaceful, but there would be no peace, not any more, not now the galaxy was at war. Horus had seen to that.

Battle companies followed in the wake of their lords, captains roaring the attack as thousands of green-armoured warriors chased up the slope to kill the sons of Perturabo. It was relentless, brutal. Withering crossfire from both the north and south faces of the

Urgall Depression cut down hundreds in the first few seconds of deceit. The XVIII Legion were shedding warriors like a snake sheds scales. But still they drove on, determined not to back down. Tenacity was a Salamander's greatest virtue – that refusal to give in. Upon the plains of Isstvan, against all of those guns, it almost ended the Legion.

It was at the crest of the first ridge, a jagged lip of stone studded with tanks, that Numeon first saw the arc of fire. It trailed, long and blazing, into the darkling sky. The tongue of flame climbed and upon reaching the apex of its parabola bent back on itself into the shape of a horseshoe. Rockets screaming, it came down in the midst of the charging Salamanders and broke them apart.

A savage crater was gored into the Urgall hills, like the bite of some gargantuan beast resurrected from old myth and birthed in nucleonic fire. It threw warriors skywards as if they were no more than empty suits of armour, bereft of bone and flesh. As a bell jar shatters when dropped onto rockcrete from a great height, so too did the Legion smash apart. Tanks following after their lord primarch were flung barrel-rolling across the black sand with their hulls on fire. Those vehicles in the mouth of the blast were simply ripped apart; tracks and hatches, chunks of abused metal torn to exploded shrapnel. Legionaries spared death in the initial blast were eviscerated in the frag storm. Super-heavies crumpled like tin boxes crushed by a hammer. Crewmen boiled alive, legionaries cooked down to ash in that furnace. It went deep, right into the beating heart of the Salamanders ranks. Only by virtue of the fact that they were so far ahead were the Pyre Guard spared the worst.

With immense kinetic fury, it threw them apart and smothered their armoured forms in a firestorm. An electro-magnetic pulse wiped out the vox, a threnody of static reigning in place of certain contact. Tactical organisation became untenable. In a single devastating strike, the Lord of Iron had crippled the XVIII Legion, severed its head and sent its body into convulsive spasm.

Retreat was the only viable strategy remaining. Droves fell back to the dropsite, trying to climb aboard ships that were surging desperately into the sky to outreach the terrible storm of betrayal below. It was not a rout, though for any force other than the Legiones Astartes it would have been, faced with such violence. Many were cut down as the traitors threaded the air with enough flak to wither an armada.

Groaning, feeling the extent of every one of his many injuries, and ignoring the urgent cascade of damage reports scrolling down the left side of his one still-functional retinal lens, Numeon staggered to his feet. A piece of armour, one he knew well and had seen before, lay within his grasp. He took the sigil once worn by Vulkan and tucked it into his belt. Leodrakk was with him, but he couldn't see Vulkan or the rest of the Pyre Guard. Through a belt of grimy fog he thought he saw Ganne dragging Varrun by his metal collar – the veteran was on his back, legs shredded but still firing his bolter – but he was too far away to be sure and there was too much death between them to make regrouping an option.

Smoke blanketed the ridge and the ash-fall had intensified. Heat haze from the still-burning fire blurred his vision. He saw the crater – he'd been thrown back from its epicentre – and the hundreds of twisted bodies within. They were incinerated, fused into their armour. Some were still dying. He saw an Apothecary – he couldn't tell who – crawling across the earth with no legs as he tried to perform his duty. No gene-seed would be harvested this day. No one who stayed on Isstvan in the emerald-green of the XVIII would live.

Numeon had to reach a ship, he had to save himself and Leodrakk. As he tried to raise the others and his primarch through the mire of static, he vaguely recalled having been lifted off his feet and punched sideways by the backwash of heat from the explosion. They were far from the crest of the ridge now. They must have slipped into a narrow defile that had carried them back down and shielded their bodies from the fire. Numeon assumed that he had blacked out. There were fragments, pieces that he didn't possess in his eidetic memory of what happened after the missile strike. He remembered Leodrakk calling out his brother's name. But Skatar'var hadn't answered. None of the Pyre Guard were answering.

'Ska!' Leodrakk roared, half delirious with pain and grief. 'Brother!'

He was clinging to Skatar'var's bloody gauntlet. Mercifully, there was no hand or forearm inside it. The glove must have been wrenched off in the blast.

Numeon seized Leodrakk by the wrist.

'He's gone. He's gone. We're leaving, Leo,' he said. 'We're leaving now. Come on!'

The Salamanders were not the only Legion to be punished by Perturabo's ordnance. Iron Warriors, those bearing the brunt of Vulkan's wrath and that of his inner-circle warriors, had also been swept up in the explosion. One, his battered senses returning, went to intervene against Leodrakk and Numeon, but the Pyre Captain cut him down with his glaive before he could open fire on them.

A warrior, one of K'gosi's Pyroclasts, clawed at Numeon's leg. By the time he looked down to help him the warrior was dead, burned from the inside out. A wisp of smoke trailed from his silent screaming mouth, and Numeon turned away again.

'We have to regroup, rally...' Leodrakk was saying.

'There is nothing to rally to, brother.'

'Is he...' Leodrakk gripped Numeon by the shoulder, his eyes pleading. 'Is he...'

Numeon broke his gaze, and looked down to where the guns of the Iron Warriors were scattering the remnants of his once-proud Legion.

'I don't know,' he murmured.

Half blind, they staggered on shoulder to shoulder as the bombs continued to fall, not knowing where to turn or what the fate of Vulkan was. Smoke was spoiling the air, rich with the tang of blood, choking and black. Leodrakk's vox-grille respirator was damaged and he was struggling to breathe. The spear of shrapnel impaling one of his lungs and still jutting from his chest also complicated matters.

The vox in Numeon's ear crackled. He was so surprised by its sudden function that he almost lost his footing. It was an XVIII Legion channel.

'This is Pyre Captain Numeon. We are effecting a full-scale retreat. I repeat, all fall back to the dropsite and secure passage off-world.'

He wanted to go back, return to find Vulkan, but in the carnage of the depression that was impossible. Pragmatism, not emotion, had to rule Numeon's heart at that moment. His primarch had forged him that way, through his teaching and his example; he wasn't about to dishonour that now.

'*Pyre brother…*'

Numeon recognised the voice on the other end of the vox-link immediately. He glanced at Leodrakk, but the warrior was making his way down the ridge towards the dropsite and hadn't noticed Numeon was in communication with someone. It was Skatar'var.

'*Is Leodrakk with you?*'

'I have him. Where are you?' Numeon asked.

'*Can't tell. I can hear screaming. I've lost my weapon, brother.*'

A terrible thought struck Numeon as he paused to end a stricken Iron Warrior with half his chest blown out, struggling to rise.

'What can you see, brother?' he asked, ramming the glaive down and twisting the haft to make sure of the kill.

'*It's dark, brother.*'

Skatar'var was blind. Numeon cast around, but couldn't see him. There was no way of telling where he was or if he was close enough to help. Scraps from other companies were storming back down the

ridge, the Salamanders laying down covering fire as they retreated
back to the dropsite. Numeon waved them on as he continued trying to find his Pyre brother.

'Skatar'var, send out a beacon. We will come for you.'

'No, captain. I'm finished. Get Leodrakk out, save my brother.'

'We might be able to reach you.' Numeon was scouring the
battlefield for any sign, but he couldn't find him.

Death hung in the air like the noisome smoke, palling overhead
from the many fires. Somewhere in the haze, Commander Krysan
crawled from the burning cupola of his battle tank. He was burning too. Salamanders were born in fire, and now Krysan would die
in it. The fuel canisters cooked off and exploded just as Krysan fell
from the turret, rolling, burning down the side of the hull and no
longer in sight. Like their commander, his once-proud armoured
company was no more than a wrecker's yard of flame-scorched
metal carcasses.

'Are you injured, brother?' Numeon asked, increasingly desperate.
'Can you stand?'

'The dead are upon me, Artellus. Their bodies crush my own.'

Looming from the oil-black fog was an Iron Warrior who was
missing his helm and part of his right arm. He raised a bolter to fire
but Numeon's lunge cut short his attack and his life, as he disem-
bowelled the traitor.

'I need more than that, Ska. The dead are everywhere.'

It was like looking out onto a corpse sea.

'It's over for me. Get Leodrakk out.'

'Ska, you must–'

'No, Artellus. Let me go. Get free of this hell and avenge me!'

It was no use. The slope was thronged with retreating warriors now,
and skirmishes between the survivors of both sides were breaking out.

'Someone will come, get you to a ship,' said Numeon, but the
words sounded hollow even to him.

'If they do, I hope we meet again.'

The vox-link went dead and Numeon couldn't raise it again.

Deeper into the valley, smoke was rolling in thick and pooling at the nadir of the basin where the drop-ships were launching in beleaguered flocks. Two, eager to get airborne, collided with one another and both went down in flames. Another achieved loft and was clawing for the upper atmosphere when it was stitched by cannon fire and broke apart, its two burning halves sent earthwards.

Even coming down off the ridge relatively unscathed, escape was far from certain.

Finally reaching the dropsite with Leodrakk, Numeon found visibility was almost zero. Like tar turned into air, the blackness was virtually absolute. Auto-senses were of limited use, but Numeon managed to get as far as a ship. Leodrakk was retching in the vile smoke, so thick it would have killed a lesser man. He clung to Numeon's left shoulder and let the Pyre Captain guide him.

But Numeon was struggling, too. The drop-ship was close enough to touch but the filth besieging them made it impossible to gauge the location of the entrance ramp or if it was even open. Through the rough hull, Numeon felt the tremor from the vessel's engines. They would need to get aboard now or they would have to find another ship.

Hell rained all around them – there would be no other ship. This was it; escape or die.

If it was to be the latter, Numeon avowed he would go down fighting. He would have done so already were it not for Leodrakk.

Out of the darkness, a hand reached for them, and together they stumbled onto the deck of a crowded Stormbird. It was black within the lander; smoke was also filling the hold and the internal lighting was out. Numeon slumped and rolled on his back, his eye burning like someone had thrust a knife into it and twisted the blade. He was more badly wounded than he had at first realised, having taken several hits during the descent as he shielded his Pyre brother from harm. Leodrakk was on his knees, coughing up the wretched smoke from his lungs.

The ramp to the drop-ship was closing. Engine shudder from rapid ignition was rocking the hold as the vessel fought for loft. Then they were airborne, thrusters cranked to full burn to reach escape velocity. The ramp sealed, the blackness became absolute.

Turning onto his side, Numeon saw a single red band of light glowing in the darkness.

'Be still, brother,' a calm and serious voice said.

'Apothecary?'

'No,' the voice replied. 'I am a Morlock of the Iron Hands. Pergellen. Be still...'

Then unconsciousness took him and he was lost to it.

NUMEON OPENED HIS eyes and touched one of his fingers to the wound that had nearly blinded him. It still hurt – the memory of it and what it reminded him of more than the actual pain.

The trek from the aqueduct, after they had met up with Pergellen, Hriak and the human, was a cheerless one. Shen'ra had been a long-standing comrade and, despite his irascible nature, had forged strong allies. Both Iron Hand and Raven Guard had bonded with him in their own way. It was hard to hear of his death, even though they all knew what his sacrifice meant. Daka'rai too would not see another dawn, nor Ukra'bar, and grief for them was worsened by the knowledge that the Salamanders had both been able warriors and that their small company had dwindled still further.

When Numeon had told Grammaticus of their decision to finally aid him, the human had greeted the news with a grim resolve, as if he knew this would happen or perhaps resented what would have to come next.

'What made you change your mind?' he had asked.

'Hope, faith… this.' Numeon had presented Grammaticus with the spear, but only shown it to him. 'It stays with me until we can get you off-world,' he had said, sheathing it in his scabbard. 'And where will you go?'

'I don't know yet. Those instructions won't be given until I'm safely off Traoris.'

The conversation had ended there, as Numeon had gone to consult with Pergellen on how they would approach an assault on a heavily guarded space port.

Using the *Fire Ark* was immediately discounted. Since the commencement of the bizarre storm that kept Ranos smothered in darkness and filled the sky with variegated lightning, there had been no communication with the ship. For all they knew, it was already destroyed. Several amongst the surviving legionaries had suggested as much until Numeon had silenced them.

He had lied to Grammaticus. It wasn't hope that drove them, nor was it faith. It was defiance and a refusal to give in when the possibility of achieving something of meaning still existed, even if that thing were merely vengeance. With his last words, Skatar'var had sworn him to that promise and Numeon meant to keep it. They all did.

Away from the heart of the urban sprawl, the city thinned out and became less of a warren. Tall stacks gave way to smaller, blister-like habs and outpost stations. Here were the stormwatchers, the men and women charged with the dangerous duty of watching the lightning fields and the ash wastes that kept each of the eight cities apart. Even across the grey deserts surrounding Ranos, the lightning had changed. It struck more fiercely, with greater frequency, carving scorched-black rifts in the earth as if nature itself were being wounded by the Word Bearers' ritual.

The space port squatted on a flat plateau, raised a few hundred metres above the cityscape itself. From the outflow and the aqueduct in the valley beneath, the legionaries and their human cargo had headed towards the port, hoping to find a route off the planet for Grammaticus. They had skirted the edge of the plateau, neglecting the roads, for they were well watched. They had come low, through the tributaries spat out from the sewers, and found themselves arriving close to the space port's borders and looking up at its iron-grey towers and desolate landing apron. Like the gnarled creatures of childhood myth, Numeon and his shattered company crouched beneath a large, partially collapsed bridge, the manmade ditch it spanned dry and dead.

On the bridge and beyond it, the strip of Ranos roadway was dead to all forms of traffic. A civilian half-track and a couple of heavier freight loaders cut forbidding skeletons with their chassis burned out and black. Smoke had long ceased rising from their metal carcasses. Here, at the space port, the Word Bearers' wrath had fallen first and fallen hardest. No vessel could be allowed to escape and raise alarm. The XVII Legion had massacred everyone and everything, including vehicles.

Numeon was hidden by shadows and the ignorance of his enemies as he surveyed through his scope. On a slab beside him were his weapons, the rest of his ammunition and the sigil.

He heard Leodrakk approach and saw him pick up the hammer icon that had once belonged to their primarch and would, perhaps, again.

'Do you believe it?' Numeon asked, putting the scope down.

Around him, dispersed along the underside of the bridge and concealed by its overhang, the last of his shattered company made ready for their final hours. All remaining weapons and ammunition had been collected and redistributed to ensure every legionary could fight to his maximum efficacy. At one time it would have been Domadus's task, but the Iron Hand was gone and so K'gosi had taken on his mantle as quartermaster. They had lost Shen'ra too and many others who should have seen a better end. Numeon owned that, all of it. He would carry that to his pyre.

'That Vulkan lives?' Numeon clarified.

'I said the words, did I not?' said Leodrakk, handing back the sigil. 'Still trying to fathom its mysteries, Artellus?'

Numeon glanced at the hammer, at the gemstone fashioned into the cross section. 'Ever since I took it from the battlefield. But I am at a loss, I'm afraid. Much of Vulkan's craft is beyond my understanding. It is a device of some kind, not merely ornamental. I had hoped it might yield a message or some piece of knowledge to guide us...' He shook his head, 'I don't know. I always just saw it as a symbol, something to give us hope in our darkest hour.'

'And this is it then, our darkest hour?'

'It might prove to be, but you didn't answer my question. Do you believe that Vulkan lives? Saying it is not believing it.'

Leodrakk's gaze strayed to where John Grammaticus was hunched down and muttering to himself, arms wrapped around his knees, head bowed as he tried to stay warm. Hriak was nearby, ostensibly keeping an eye on the human. He had shielded him psychically from the cleric's warpcraft, thrown the soul-flare of Grammaticus's essence outwards like a ventriloquist throws his voice, drawing the Word Bearers into the trap at the outflow. It hadn't been a pleasant experience for the human, but the Librarian noticed that little and cared even less.

'I see something in the spear that kindles hope that has only been the barest embers for so long,' Leodrakk admitted, gesturing to the fulgurite sitting snugly in Numeon's scabbard. 'I have resisted because to hope for one is to hope for another.'

'Ska,' Numeon correctly assumed.

'He could yet live.'

'As may all of our Pyre brothers, but I have my doubts.'

'We know he did not die in the blast,' Leodrakk tried, but couldn't keep the bite from his tone.

Only later, when their drop-ship was aloft and had broken through the traitors' pickets surrounding Isstvan, did Numeon tell Leodrakk that Skatar'var had contacted him. He knew Leodrakk would have wanted to go back, that he wouldn't heed his brother's wishes as Numeon had. He hadn't raged or struck out at the Pyre Captain as Numeon supposed was his right. He had simply darkened as a flame does when slowly starved of oxygen.

'I forgave you that moment on the ship when you told me,' Leodrakk said.

'Your forgiveness is irrelevant, Leo. I either saved our lives or went back for Skatar'var and signed all our death warrants. I made the pragmatic decision, the only one I could in the circumstances.'

Leodrakk looked away, out past the bridge and towards the space port. Even from this distance, the patrols were visible.

'Why tell me this now, brother?' asked Numeon.

'Because I wanted you to know there wasn't any bad blood between us for this. I would have wanted to go back, and I know all three of us would have died. It doesn't make it any easier, though. There will always be a part of me that wonders if we could have found him, if he had survived and we passed him by, only metres away.'

'I have had the self-same doubts regarding Vulkan, but I stand by my decision and know if presented with it all over again that I would not waver from the course I have already taken. History cannot be unwritten and scribed anew. It is done, and all we can hope for is that we perform our duty until death, irrespective of the destiny we crave for ourselves.'

Pergellen interrupted on the vox.

'Speak, brother,' said Numeon, reacting to the Iron Hand's comm request as he activated the bead embedded in his ear.

'*I have eyes on our former cousins.*'

'How many?'

'*More than you or I should like.*'

'Then these are our final hours.'

'*So it would seem, brother,*' the Iron Hand replied. There was no regret, no sorrow in his voice. It served no purpose. There was but one duty left to perform now.

Numeon thanked the scout and cut the link.

'Get them ready,' he said.

Leodrakk was turning to carry out the order when Numeon clutched his Pyre brother's arm. 'I know, Artellus,' Leodrakk told him, clapping the Pyre Captain on the shoulder. 'For Shen, for Ska, for all of them.'

Numeon nodded, and let him go.

'It's actually quite stunning when you look at it from this distance,' Numeon said once Leodrakk had gone. He was watching the lightning flashes over the ash wastes.

'The word that springs to my mind is *deadly,*' Grammaticus replied. He was on his feet and standing next to the Pyre Captain.

'Most beautiful things in nature are, John Grammaticus.'

'I didn't have you pegged as philosophical, captain.'

'When you've seen the fury of the earth up close, watched mountains spit fire and the sky redden to the hue of embers, reflecting its hot breath against the ash clouds overhead, you learn to appreciate the beauty in it. Otherwise, what's left but tragedy?'

'It's all about the earth,' Grammaticus muttered.

Numeon looked sidelong at him. 'What?'

'Nothing. You are doing the right thing.'

'I don't need you to tell me that.' The Salamander turned to regard Grammaticus. Towering over the human, his face was unreadable. 'Betray me, and I'll find a way to kill you. Failing that, I'll take you back to Nocturne and show you those fire mountains I mentioned.'

'I get the impression I won't see their beauty like you do, Salamander.'

Numeon's eyes seemed to burn cold. 'No, you won't.'

Behind him, the human became aware of another's presence. Numeon nodded to him.

'Hriak, all is ready?'

'Everything is in place, the plan is formed,' he rasped.

Grammaticus raised an eyebrow. 'What plan?'

Numeon smiled. He could see that it unnerved the human.

'I'm afraid you're not going to like it.'

CHAPTER THIRTY-ONE
Dawnbringer

I NAMED IT *Dawnbringer* for a very specific reason.

Names are important for weapons, they attribute meaning and substance to what might otherwise be merely tools for war. Curze never paid much attention to that. His concerns are less senti- mental, bloodier. To my benighted brother, a spar of sharpened metal is as good as the master craftsman's finest blade if it kills the same. This was his oversight, this was why I had fashioned the hammer as I had. *Dawnbringer* was different. It would literally bring the light.

And now it was before me at the heart of Perturabo's labyrinth, but the hammer was not what my eye was drawn to first.

Both of them were dead. I knew it before I crossed the threshold but I still grieved for them upon sight of their bloodless bodies.

'Were they dead before I even entered this place?' I asked.

To my surprise, Curze answered.

'Before you came aboard my ship.'

His voice was disembodied, but it came from somewhere in the heart chamber.

Nemetor, of course. It would have to be him. He was the last of my sons I ever set eyes upon. Curze knew that would breed a special blend of pain for me. The other one brought me a different kind of grief, for he was part of a brotherhood I had long considered my council.

'Skatar'var…' I whispered the name as I raised my hand to touch his skeletal body, but fell just short of making contact.

Averting my gaze from my dead sons, I resisted the urge to cut them down from where they hung like meat and instead focused on *Dawnbringer*.

The hammer was exactly as I remembered. It looked innocuous enough resting on an iron plinth, though I can humbly say it is the finest weapon I have ever crafted. It shone in a place that was drab and ugly by comparison.

The heart of the Iron Labyrinth was an octagonal chamber, supported by eight thick columns. The dark metal seemed to drink the light, absorb it like obsidian into its facets. But it was merely iron, the walls, the ceiling, the floor. It was heavy and dense with little in the way of ornamentation… or so I at first believed.

As I lingered, I started to discern shapes wrought into the metal. They were faces, screaming, locked forever in moments of pure agony. Beneath each of the arches to which the columns abutted hung a grotesque and malformed statue. They were monstrous things, ripped from a madman's fever dream and trapped in this iron form. No two were alike. Some had horns, others wings or bestial hooves, feathers, talons, a hooked beak, a swollen maw. They were wretched and repellent, and I could not imagine what had compelled my brother to sculpt them.

If this was a heart, it was a blackened, cancerous organ whose slow beat was as the chime of death.

Seeing no other recourse, I walked up to the plinth and reached for the hammer. Some kind of energy field impeded me, giving out an actinic flash of light as I touched it and making me recoil.

'You didn't think I'd just let you take it, did you?' Curze's voice rang out, everywhere and nowhere as it was before.

I backed away from the plinth, the gate by which I had entered the heart closing behind me as I warily eyed the shadows. I had no intention of leaving. There was no escape that way. The end of this torment was in here with my brother. With the entrance now sealed, darkness reigned fully. There were no lumen orbs, braziers nor lanterns of any kind. I touched the energy field again, prompting a flare of light briefly to encase the hammer before dying again like a candle flame. The flash gave me little to see with, though I turned as I thought I saw one of the statues start to move.

'These fear tactics might work on mortals but I am a primarch, Konrad,' I declared, grateful to my father for gifting me these last moments of lucidity. I would need them to fight my brother now. 'One worthy of the name.'

'You think me unworthy, do you, Vulkan?'

His voice came from behind me, but I knew it to be a trick and resisted the temptation to face it.

'It doesn't matter what I think, Konrad. Nor what the rest of us think. You behold your reflection, brother. Is that not what you see?'

'You won't goad me, Vulkan. We've come too far, you and I, for that.'

'Did you think there would be no mirrors in the darkness, nothing to reflect your worthless self? Is that why you cower there, Konrad?'

I began to turn, sensing my brother's closeness, if not his actual presence. He was gifted, despite my taunts suggesting the contrary, not so unlike Corvus, though his methodology was far removed from that of the Ravenlord.

'Do you seek me, Vulkan? Do you wish to have your chance again, like you did at Kharaatan?'

'Why would I want that? You are beneath me, Konrad. In every way. You always have been. The Lord of Fear has no land, no subjects but the corpses he makes. You have nothing, you are nothing.'

'I am Night Haunter!'

And at last Curze gave in to his self-hatred, his pathological denial, and revealed himself to me.

One of the statues hanging down from an archway, a chiropteran creature I mistook to be a carved gargoyle, slowly unfurled its wings and dropped to the ground. It was him, and he brandished a long serrated blade.

'We are both such savage weapons, Vulkan,' he told me. 'Let me show you.'

Curze lunged, laughing. 'Never gets old,' he said, hacking into my body again and carving a deep wound.

I cried out but kept my senses long enough to hammer a punch into his neck. Even his armour was no protection against my blacksmiter's fists. I had bent metal, grasped burning coals. I was as inviolable as the hard onyx of my skin and I let my brother feel every ounce of that strength.

He staggered, slashing wildly and catching me just above the left eye as I advanced. A jab aimed for his exposed throat missed and fractured Curze's right cheek instead. In return, he skewered my left leg, ripping the blade and some flesh out before I could trap it. Now I stumbled and Curze wove round my clumsy right hook to bring his sword down onto my clavicle. I threw up my forearm just in time and felt the weapon's teeth bite bone. Then I charged in with my shoulder, trying to ignore the agony igniting down my arm. I heard him grunt as my body connected, smashing into his torso.

Curze tried to laugh it off, but his fractured cheek was paining him and I'd just punched most of the air from his lungs.

Out of the corner of my eye, I could see Ferrus watching the uneven duel. He was no longer the cadaverous ghoul I had made him. The Gorgon had become as he was, as I wanted to remember him. No longer berating me, I sensed in him a willing urge for me to triumph instead.

'Let me tell you a secret, brother,' I said, breathless.

We were a few handspans apart, battered but regrouping for another round. Amused, Curze bade me continue.

'Of all of us, father made me the strongest. Physically, I have no equal amongst my siblings. In the sparring cages I used to hold back... especially against you, Konrad.'

All the mirth drained away from Curze's already pallid face.

'I am Night Haunter,' he hissed.

'What was your boon, Konrad?' I asked, backing up as he advanced with sword held low.

'I am the death that haunts the darkness,' he said, angling the blade so it would cut across my stomach and spill my viscera.

'Always the weakest, Konrad. I *was* afraid, I admit that. But it was from the fear of breaking you. I don't need to hold back, though, any more,' I said, smiling in the face of my brother's rising hatred. 'Now I can show you how much better than you I am.'

Possessed by a sudden rage, Curze threw down the blade and came at me with his bare hands. I knew it was coming and had shifted my stance just slightly so I was ready for it. I let him land the first blow. It was vicious and tore a hunk of flesh off my cheek. He reached for my throat, talons poised to rip it out, teeth bared in a savage snarl... before I clamped my fist around his forearm, falling back and using his momentum to carry him up and over me.

In the forge, the hammer swing is everything. Shaping metal, bending it to my will, it is the blacksmiter's art. By its nature, metal is unyielding. It breaks stone, sunders flesh. Strength is not enough.

It takes skill, and timing. Judgement of when the hammer has reached its apex, when the strike is purest, that is what I knew. It was ingrained in me by my Nocturnean father, N'bel.

I used his lessons in that moment, I lifted my brother like the smiter lifts the fuller and brought him down upon the iron plinth, my anvil. A sharp crack and a light surge that painted the chamber in blueish monochrome preceded the collapse of the energy shield. Curze broke it with his back, his body. As he rebounded hard off the iron floor, the energy coursed over him, setting fire to nerve endings and burning hair and scalp. He rolled with the last of his momentum, smoke exuding from the plates of his armour.

I stooped and picked up the fallen hammer. It felt good to have *Dawnbringer* in my grasp again and I ran my thumb along the activation stud I had put on the grip.

'You should not have led me here, Konrad,' I told him. My brother was still curled up and shaking with the energy spikes from the shield. At first I thought he was sobbing, his shame and self-loathing having reduced my poor brother to melancholy again, but I was wrong.

Curze was laughing once more.

'I know, Vulkan,' he said, having recovered some of his composure. 'Your beacon won't work. This chamber is teleport-shielded. Nothing goes in or out except through that gate behind you.' Still trembling with the aftershocks of absorbing the energy shield, Curze managed to stand. 'Did you think you had broken me, brother? Did you believe you had tricked me into letting you escape?' He grinned. 'Hope is cruel, isn't it? Yours was false, Vulkan.'

Before I could prevent it, he twisted something on his vambrace, activating some system slaved to his armour.

Hearing the churn of gears, I braced myself. I expected another death trap, a long plunge into a still deeper dungeon. Instead, I saw the floor retreat beneath my feet, leaving a sturdy mesh that supported our weight and that I could see through.

There was another chamber below the heart of the labyrinth, but it was nothing more than a dank cell. No, not a cell, a *tomb*. Weak lumen strips flickered in this hidden undercroft, and their combined light and shadow revealed hundreds of bodies. Humans and legionaries, prisoners of the Prince of the Crows, languished in the gloom. They were dead, but before they had died they had been tortured and brutalised.

'This is my true work of art,' Curze revealed, gesturing to the slain as a painter would his finished canvas, 'and you, Vulkan, the immortal king presiding over the anguished dead, are my crowning piece.'

'You're a monster,' I breathed, eyes wide with the horror of it.

'Tell me something I don't know,' he hissed.

Meeting his madman's gaze, I decided to oblige him.

'You're right,' I conceded, holding up *Dawnbringer* so he could see it. 'I fashioned it as a teleporter, a means to escape even a prison such as this. I counted on you leading me here, on you *needing* to face me one last time. It seems I was fooled into thinking you hadn't planned for this.' I lowered the weapon and let the weight of its head pull the haft down until my hand was wrapped around the very end of the grip. 'But you're forgetting one thing...'

Curze leaned in, as if eager to hear my words. He believed that he had me, that I would never escape his trap.

He was wrong.

'What's that, brother?'

'It's also a hammer.'

The blow caught him across the chin, a savage upswing that took Curze off his feet and put him on the ground again with the sheer force of the impact. He got to one knee before I hit him again, this time across his left shoulder blade where I split his pauldron in half. I jabbed into his stomach before swinging a second blow that put him on his feet.

Curze almost fell again when I drove into him, pressing the hammer's haft against his throat and pushing him back until he slammed up against the wall. His gorget had broken apart and was hanging loose, so I kept the haft across his trachea and pushed against it, one hand on the pommel and the other on the hammer head, and slowly began to crush bone.

Blood and saliva flecked Curze's armour, spat from his still grinning mouth.

'Yes...' he choked at me. 'Yes...'

So wretched, I wanted to kill him, to end his suffering and take some measure of vengeance for all the suffering he had caused me and my sons.

'Come on...' Curze's eyes were pleading, and I realised he *wanted* this. Ever since Kharaatan, he had wanted this. Not every chink of weakness I had seen in this place was feigned. Curze truly did loathe himself, so much so that he wanted it to end. If I killed him he would have everything he wanted, death and a means of bringing me down to his despicable level.

'I am damned, Vulkan...' he gasped. 'End it now!'

The abyss was pulsing at the edge of thought, black and red, the monster crawling up from its depths to claim me. So many dead, I could almost hear the corpses willing me to do it, to avenge them.

And then I saw Ferrus, his proud and noble face looking down upon me, the beloved older brother.

'Do it...' Curze was urging. 'I will only kill again, take another for my amusement. Corax, Dorn, Guilliman... Perhaps I'll bait the Lion when we reach Thramas. You can't risk letting me live.'

I released him, and he fell clutching at his throat, choking the air back into his lungs. From beneath the lank strands of his hair, he glared at me, eyes filled with murderous intent. I had scorned him; worst of all I had let him live when I had every reason not to, and proved that he was alone in his depravity.

'You can't escape,' he spat. 'I'll never let you go.'

I looked down at him, pitying. 'You're wrong about that too. No craft you possess can hold me here now, Konrad.' I brandished the hammer, held it aloft like it was my standard. 'Your dampeners are useless. I could have left as soon as I took the hammer from your cage, but I chose to stay behind. I wanted to hurt you, but most of all I wanted to know I could spare you. We *are* alike, Konrad, but not like that. Never like that. But if I see you again, I will kill you.' I spoke these last words through clenched teeth, my sanity hanging by the barest thread as the grace Verace had given me finally faded. Or perhaps it was my own resolve that had preserved my mind, one last herculean effort to stave off madness? I would never know.

Pressing the stud upon *Dawnbringer*'s haft, I closed my eyes and let the flare of teleportation take me.

CHAPTER
THIRTY-TWO
Lightning fields

K'GOSI WAS DEAD. The last burst had punched straight through his plastron and taken most of his upper torso with it.

'Brother...' Leodrakk snarled, firing back through the darkness and accumulated gun smoke. 'Vulkan lives!' he shouted, trying to be heard above the roar of automatic weapons. The remnants of his company were pinned. Blistering fire exploded overhead, showering the hunkered warriors with sparks and shrapnel from their slowly disintegrating cover.

A sub-entrance had got them this far, past the first patrols and through the outer gate. The space port was based on three concentric rings, each one diminishing towards the centre where the main landing apron resided. All the ships from the outskirts of the facility had been scuppered, leaving only those in the core.

Unfortunately, this area had proven to be the most heavily guarded, and the sub-entrance a lure to draw the shattered company inwards. A few hundred metres away, three shuttles as well as the Word Bearers' own vessels stood ready for take-off.

Despite his defiance, Leodrakk knew they would never reach them. According to his retinal display, only six legionaries were still standing. The rest were down, or dead.

Firing off a snap-shot, he bellowed into the vox, 'Ikrad, move your men up. The rest of you, covering fire!'

Three Salamanders advanced, inching along a corridor section overlooked by gantries that led onto the landing apron. G'orrn went down before he reached the next scrap of cover, a buttressed alcove with scarcely enough room for Ikrad and B'tarro.

Even with auto-senses it was hard to tell how many they were facing. Between bursts Leodrakk tried to count the power-armoured silhouettes jamming up the end of the corridor, but every time he did more were added to the horde.

The Word Bearers were holding and showed no signs of allowing the Salamanders to break through. Leodrakk emerged from cover for a second look. A shell whined near his head, the sound of it glancing off his helmet amplified by his auto-senses. Warning sigils cascaded across his failing retinal display. A close call, but his head was still attached. For now.

Ikrad's voice crackled over the vox, 'I can't see the cleric.'

'I can't see much of anything,' snapped Hur'vak.

'It doesn't matter,' Leodrakk replied. 'Keep their attention focused on us. Hold them here.'

'That may prove problematic, brother,' said Kronor, gesturing behind them to where a second force of Word Bearers could be heard moving into position.

Beneath his faceplate, Leodrakk smiled. His ammo count was low. He suspected that his brothers' were the same. Bolter fire was raining in from the end of the corridor now, accented by the occasional flash of a volkite. It chipped at the iron buttresses and the columns where the Salamanders were taking cover. Soon it would stitch them from either side and that would be an end to it.

Muttering an oath for Skatar'var, Leodrakk addressed what was left of his men.

'How do Salamanders meet their enemies?' he asked.

'Eye-to-eye,' came the response in unison.

'And tooth-to-tooth,' Leodrakk concluded, drawing his blade. He roared, and rose up. The others shouted after him, determined to die with their weapons in their hands and their wounds to the front. It was a glorious but short-lived charge.

'Vulkan lives!'

JAGS OF LIGHTNING were dancing hard and fast across the desert. Buried under Numeon's drake cloak, Grammaticus eyed them warily.

'You'll kill us all out here,' he said, voice muffled through his rebreather. It was the one from the dig site, the only part of his original equipment he still carried, if not the persona they had formerly belonged to. As well as the lightning, which cracked the sky in a circulatory system of veins and arcing tributaries, ash storms raked the wastelands. The grit and mineral flecks were as abrasive as glass, and deadly when whipped up close to hurricane speeds. No barrier to an armoured legionary, they could prove fatal to a mortal.

Hriak warded off the worst of it with a psychic kine-shield he had thrown up and was taking painstaking effort to maintain in front of them. It was taxing the Librarian, and he hadn't spoken since the three of them had entered the lightning fields.

'*Out here* is what's keeping us alive, John Grammaticus,' Numeon replied.

Like Hriak, his armour was taking a battering out in the storm. Already, much of its green paintwork had been abraded by the gritty ash winds. Since planetfall the storms had worsened. Their initial march to the city proper was much less treacherous. There was but one small mercy – they had, as of yet, avoided the lightning. A bolt struck nearby, throwing up a gout of crystallised sand.

'All evidence to the contrary,' said Grammaticus, seeing the dark scar left in the wake of the lightning. 'I think I would have preferred to be with our comrades at the space port.'

'No you wouldn't,' said Numeon darkly, and that was an end to it. 'The ship isn't far. And besides,' he added, glancing away to the dunes rising far off on their right, 'we aren't unprotected.'

PERGELLEN KNEW IT grated at Numeon to leave the others behind. In the end, it was Leodrakk who had volunteered to lead the rest of the company into the space port so that the Pyre Captain and Raven Guard could reach an alternate means of escape. Assaulting the space port had never been viable. It was dismissed before being mooted, but their enemy didn't know that. Intent on killing the interlopers who had interfered with their plans, the Word Bearers had concentrated their entire force on the team attacking the space port. No one would see the three lonely travellers insanely braving the lightning fields. At least, that was the theory. Pergellen would have stayed with the diversion group, too, were it not for the fact that further insurance in getting the human off-planet was deemed prudent. His scope would watch them and track the ash wastes for errant legionaries who had scented the ruse and decided to come hunting.

He was lying flat, the scouring ash wind raking his power generator and shoulders as he propped his rifle beneath his chin. His eye had not left the scope since he had found his position on the dune. It was a good vantage, high enough to allow for decent coverage but low so that he didn't stick out. It was solid too, a ridge of bedrock sitting under all that ash.

He first tracked Hriak, then Numeon, and finally Grammaticus, allowing the crosshairs of his targeter to settle on the human's hooded head. Then he moved the scope back across the wastes to see if they were being followed.

So far, so good…

By his reckoning, the landing site wasn't far, and once there they would find the gunship they had secreted upon planetfall. The other operational vessel didn't matter now. It was far from their reach, but Pergellen had plotted a return route to it in case an emergency exfiltration was still possible.

A brief blizzard of ash squalled across him, muddying the lens of the Iron Hand's scope. He maintained position, but as he peered through the now occluded scope he thought he caught sight of three large humanoid shapes moving against the storm. Visibility was already poor, but it was made worse by the dirty lens. Pergellen considered raising the alarm but decided against it in case vox-traffic was being monitored in any way. He doubted it was Leodrakk or any of his men, but had to be sure if he was going to make a kill. Lifting his body up onto his elbows, he went to clear the lens when he heard the faintest crunch of displaced sand behind him.

'Stand and turn, I won't shoot you in the back,' ordered a gruff voice. It was the first time he had heard it, but Pergellen knew instinctively who it belonged to. With that information in mind, he relaxed the grip on the bolt pistol strapped to his hip.

'Honour?' queried Pergellen, rising. 'I understood that the Seventeenth had long abandoned such scruples.'

'I serve my own code. Now turn.'

Pergellen did so and saw a warrior armoured in red and black. His trappings were battered and stained. He remembered him from the ambush site, the attack on the manufactorum and the skirmish at the outflow. Seemed the Word Bearer remembered him too.

'You are the scout,' he said, nodding.

Pergellen wondered if he'd done it out of respect.

'And you the huntsman.'

The warrior nodded again.

'Barthusa Narek.'

'Verud Pergellen.'

'Your skill is impressive, Pergellen,' Narek admitted.

'I don't think we're here to compare notes, though, are we?'

'Correct. I would have preferred to match myself against you rifle to rifle, but there is no time for that now.' He sounded almost regretful. 'Instead, we are left with bolt pistol or blade.'

Upon first sight of him, Pergellen had logged and gauged the threat of each of the huntsman's weapons. They seemed to consist mainly of blades, but he also had a bolt pistol and the sniper rifle currently aimed at the Iron Hand's heart.

'Are you agreeable to these terms?' Narek asked.

'Why are you doing this?'

'I assume you're not asking about the acts of my Legion, or my fealty to that Legion. If what I think you're asking is why did I not just execute you where you lay and why now am I allowing you a chance to kill me, the answer is simple. I need to know... who is the better?' Crouching down, his eyes never leaving Pergellen for a second, he unhooked the rifle's strap from over his shoulder and set it down on the ridge in front of him. Then he stood. 'Now we are even, so I shall repeat, bolt pistol or blade?'

The ash wind was howling and the grit lashing around the two legionaries facing one another across the dune. Pergellen estimated there was little more than four metres between them. He had to end it quickly. Enemies were converging on Numeon and the others. If nothing else, he had to issue a warning, but not before he dealt with this. He made up his mind.

'A fair offer,' said Pergellen. 'Blades?'

'Very well.'

Each legionary grabbed for his pistol, knowing that the other would do the same. A single shot rang out. Narek was faster.

✠ ✠ ✠

NUMEON LOOKED OVER to the ridge, tracking the report of a pistol heard even above the storm. A lightning bolt cracked the earth in front of him and sent the Pyre Captain crashing down onto his back, armour drooling smoke.

In the same instant he turned and saw the warriors behind them. He counted three, and they were moving swiftly through the churning ash. They flickered, like a mirage shimmer, first distant, then closer, and closer still. It was warp-craft.

'Hriak!' he bellowed, slow to rise. On the far ridge, the one where Pergellen was meant to be keeping watch, he saw a slumped shadow and another, this one standing, disappearing into the storm as it backed away.

'Prepare yourself,' the Librarian hissed at Grammaticus. Then he was running, but not to Numeon's aid. He passed the Pyre Captain without a second glance, having sensed the psyker in their midst. 'It's the cleric,' he shouted. 'I'm sorry, Artellus, he must have followed my psychic spoor into the wastes.'

Numeon was back on his feet and rushing over to Grammaticus, who was struggling through the storm. Without the kine-shield he was being battered, and only the drake hide was keeping him alive.

'Where is your fugging ship?' he snapped, irritated, from inside the cloak.

'Close.'

'You hid a ship out here?' asked Grammaticus.

'Not I – my brother Ravens,' said Numeon. 'It was undetectable.' He turned his attention to Hriak, who had begun to describe arcane patterns in the air before him. 'Brother?' Numeon called out. He blink-clicked a proximity icon that had recently flashed up on the part of his retinal display that was still working, and gestured into the storm.

Looking in the direction that Numeon had pointed, Grammaticus noticed a bulky silhouette looming through the ash-haze.

Hidden in plain sight, using the storm as cover, thought Grammaticus. *How like the XIX.*

'Go, get him out,' said Hriak. 'I'll deal with this. The raven's feast has been long overdue for me. *Victorus aut Mortis.*'

Numeon turned back to the human. 'Are you all right, are you–'

Grammaticus aimed his fist at him. Something sparkled on the ring he wore.

'Better than you, I'm afraid.'

The las-beam stabbed into Numeon's retinal lens, burning out his eye and searing his face beneath. He cried out, clutching his eye, the trauma of it putting him on his knees. The bolt had struck him, and split part of his armour. It wasn't clotting properly, Numeon's enhanced physiology undone by something in the storm, something the cleric had incepted. It made the eye burn all the more painfully.

Half blind, he snatched for the human, meaning to crush him this time.

Grammaticus had hit him with a potent charge. Whilst the legionaries were plotting their assault on the space port and this cunning feint to get him to another ship, he had been altering the tech in his ring. The blast had exhausted it. The digital weapon was done and wouldn't charge again, but it pierced the legionary's defences and put him down long enough to scurry from the warrior's grasp.

He snatched the fulgurite from Numeon's scabbard, deftly avoiding the Salamander's grab.

'I'm sorry,' said Grammaticus, his voice growing more distant the farther away he ran, 'but you were in my way.'

Running hard against the storm, he reached the ship. The gentle throb of turbine engines was obvious up close. Now he was alongside the ship, he could see it more clearly. He looked back for any sign of his captors.

Lightning crackled in the distance that was not caused by the storm. It illuminated three figures, armoured in legionary battle-plate. One other, the Raven, opposed them. Numeon was still down but rising.

He could pilot this vessel without the Salamanders help, but Grammaticus knew he didn't have long to get aboard and get away. Moving around to the rear access ramp, he paused.

There was something dripping through the rear access hatch, as if someone had released a valve and filled the hold with water. It was dark, murky and reeked of stagnation. There was something *wrong* about this place, this city. Grammaticus had felt it ever since he had made planetfall with Varteh and the others. He had no weapon – the ring was useless, and so he could only rely upon his own wits. At that precise moment they seemed more than a little fragile.

Hammering the hatch release icon, Grammaticus braced himself for what was within. He had wanted to leap up and onto the gunship's still descending ramp, to rush to the cockpit and quit Traoris for good, but the figure standing before him was blocking his path.

Trapped for so long in the drainage basin, all those years... The water had not been kind. Grammaticus couldn't remember his name, but the thing glaring at him through the strands of lank hair hanging down over its sunken face *knew* Grammaticus.

Instinctively, he backed away, his ankle throbbing where the five tiny weals still showed on his flesh.

'You aren't...' he began, but how could he be sure? All the things he had seen, all the deeds he had done...

The drowned boy advanced towards Grammaticus, his gait shuffling and unsteady, leaving a trail of drain water behind him.

A childhood trauma, one from his first life; why did this horror eclipse all the others?

Grammaticus recoiled and found unyielding war-plate preventing further retreat. He turned to face his attacker, knowing the game had ended at last.

'You're headed the wrong way if you want to escape,' said Numeon, one eye ablaze through his retinal lens.

Glancing back, Grammaticus saw that the drowned boy was gone. But the delay had cost him dearly.

'Is this when you kill me?' he asked, still a little shaken but shoring up his composure with each passing second.

'I should have killed you when I saw you. Tell me this. Is what you said true, does Vulkan still live?'

'As far as I know–' Grammaticus's answer was cut by the report of a bolt pistol.

In front of him, Numeon convulsed as the shell struck him in the torso and punched the Salamander off his feet.

'You have proven remarkably elusive, John Grammaticus,' said a cultured, yet terrifying voice. The dull click of a bolt pistol being primed to fire again froze Grammaticus in place. He turned, having made it halfway up the ramp, and saw the Word Bearers cleric drawing down on him. 'But then you are quite remarkable, aren't you?'

'So I'm told,' he said, fulgurite still in hand.

'Give the spear to me,' the Dark Apostle ordered. 'Throw it onto the ground.'

Numeon was still down and not looking like he was going to get up. Grammaticus obeyed.

'What now?'

'Now you will come with me and I shall show you the true meaning of the warp.'

'I'll pass if that's all the same to you.'

'I didn't say you had a choice, mortal.' Elias wagged the pistol's muzzle, gesturing for Grammaticus to step down from the ramp and out of the gunship's waiting hold.

He hesitated. 'I'll be shredded out there.'

Elias briefly looked at the athame dagger sheathed at his belt.

'You won't be out here long enough for that. The shredding comes later, though.'

Grammaticus was taking his first steps back down the ramp, trying desperately to think of a way out of this, when a charge trembled the air. It wasn't from the lightning field, it was nothing to do with the storm at all. Elias felt it, too, and began to turn.

Something was coming.

NUMEON WAS DYING. He didn't need the failing biometric data relayed by his armour to tell him that. Red warning icons were flashing across his vision, a sputtering, static-crazed feed that did more to impede his senses than enhance them.

He discharged the locking clamps on his helmet and tore it off.

The Word Bearer, the cleric they had been seeking, who had undoubtably killed Hriak, paid him no heed. As he gazed into the storm, Numeon detected a change in the air. He felt heat, and imagined the trembling of atoms as the veil of reality was parting and being rewritten.

He reached out, ostensibly for a weapon, perhaps his pistol, as the glaive was now too far to grasp, but found himself clutching the sigil.

Vulkan's sigil.

For his legionaries it had become an enigmatic symbol of hope, but for the primarch it held no such mystery. He had crafted it, imbued it with technologies beyond even his Legiones Astartes sons.

It was a beacon, a light to bring a stricken ship to shore or a lost traveller home.

For a few brief seconds the storm abated to a murmur, the last jag of lightning seemingly frozen in place and becoming a tear in reality that exuded light.

Gazing into that light, Numeon saw a figure limned in godlike power.

'Vulkan lives...' he breathed, emotion and blood both swelling up into his throat to choke him.

Elias holstered his pistol, realising it would have little effect on whatever was about to emerge into reality. He was reaching for his athame, intent on flight, when he recognised the figure that appeared before him.

'My master,' he murmured and fell to one knee, bowing his head before Erebus.

Erebus ignored him. Instead he regarded John Grammaticus, who was still standing on the ramp of the gunship, transfixed by what he had just witnessed.

THE TRAVELLER WAS hooded. His dark robes swathed a power-armoured frame. There was no face beneath the cowl, only a silver mask fashioned to resemble one. In one hand Erebus held a ritual knife which he secreted back beneath his robes; the other was bionic, yet to be re-fleshed, and reached to retrieve the fulgurite.

'Rise,' he said to Elias, though he was looking at Grammaticus. His voice sounded old, but bitter and filled with the resonance of true power.

'You have arrived at an auspicious moment–' Elias began, before Erebus lashed out with the fulgurite and slit the other Dark Apostle's throat.

'Indeed I have,' he said, allowing the blood fountaining from Elias's ruptured arteries to paint the front of his robes.

Dying, unable to staunch the wound from a god-weapon, Elias was reduced to clawing at his former master. He managed to grasp the silver mask and tear it from his master's face before Erebus seized his flailing hands and threw him back.

Grammaticus recoiled as Erebus faced him. Something akin to a daemon regarded him, one with a hideous flayed skull, blood-red and patched by scar tissue that wasn't healing as ordinary flesh and skin. It was darker, incarnadine, and shimmered with an unearthly lustre. Several small horns protruded from his pate, little nubs of sharpened bone.

At Erebus's feet, Elias was gasping like a fish without water. He was dying. His desperation seemed to draw Erebus's attention, and Grammaticus was glad those hellish eyes were no longer focused on him.

Crouched down, Erebus addressed his former disciple.

'You are as stupid as you are short-sighted, Valdrekk.' He showed him the fulgurite, still glowing slightly, clenched in Erebus's bionic hand. 'This does not win wars, mere chunks of wood and metal cannot do that. It was never the weapon you were looking for. The *primarchs*, the god-born, are the weapons. Sharpen our own, blunt our enemy's.'

Erebus leaned down and clamped his flesh hand over Elias's gaping mouth. The struggle was brief and uneventful.

'He goes to the Neverborn as a reward for trying to betray me.'

It took Grammaticus a couple of seconds to realise that Erebus was talking to him. He looked down and saw the fulgurite brandished towards him.

'Take it,' Erebus said. 'No one will stop you.' Now he looked up and there was terrible knowledge in his eyes. 'Go to your task, John Grammaticus.'

Warily, Grammaticus took the spear. He then walked back up the ramp and pressed the icon to close it. When he looked back, both Erebus and Elias were gone.

Although he was no legionary, he could fly the ship. His abilities as a pilot were exemplary and there weren't many vessels, human or xenos, that he couldn't fly. Heading across the troop hold, Grammaticus opened the door that would allow him access to the cockpit. It was large, built to accommodate a legionary, but he managed well enough. It took him a few minutes but he got the ship's systems online for atmospheric flight, and the engine turbines were already warmed up.

Through the glacis plate he noticed the sky over Ranos was changing. There were shapes in the storm clouds now, looming large and too distinct to be merely shadows. Erebus had done more than end the life of a rival when he had killed Elias. Grammaticus wasn't about to stick around and find out what that was.

Engine ignition sent tremors through the ship as Grammaticus boosted forwards and then started to gain loft. A quick check of the sensor array revealed a path through the scattering of vessels in orbit. None of them were suitable; he'd need to find another space port and gain passage aboard a cruiser, preferably non-military.

It would be guarded, he knew that. But if he got there before Polux, he'd have a much better chance of slipping through their security nets.

Dark sky gave way to desolate, black void as the gunship streaked through the upper atmosphere and beyond.

A reflection in the glacis made Grammaticus start at first, the memory of the drowned boy still all too fresh, but he masked his sudden panic well. The eldar regarded him sternly.

'You were successful, John Grammaticus?' asked Slau Dha.

'Yes, the fulgurite is in my possession.'

'And you know what you must do?'

'You still doubt my conviction?'

'Just answer the question.'

Grammaticus sighed, deep and world-weary. 'Yes, I know what must be done. Although killing a primarch won't be easy.'

'This has ever been your mission.'

'I know, but even so...'

'His grace is bound to the earth. Separated from it, he will be weak and can be slain like any of the others.'

'Why him? Why not the Lion or that bastard Curze? Why does it have to be him?'

'Because he is important and because he must not live to become the keeper of the gate. Do this and your pact with the Cabal is ended.'

'I somehow doubt that.'

'It doesn't matter what you believe, *mon-keigh*. All that matters is what you do next.'

'Don't worry, I know my mission and will carry it out as ordered.'

'When you reach Macragge,' said the autarch, threatening even though he was only *flecting*, 'find him. He has been there some time already.'

'Shouldn't be too difficult.'

'It will be harder than you think. He is not himself any more. You'll need help.'

'Another primarch, yes, I know. I suspect few will be lining up to be his executioner, however.'

'You would be surprised.'

'Your kind are full of them.'

Slau Dha ignored the slight, deeming it beneath his concern.

'And then,' he asked instead, 'when the fulgurite is delivered?'

A sudden star flare forced Grammaticus to dim the glacis, effectively ending the *flect*, but he answered anyway.

'Then, Vulkan dies.'

Falling from grace...

BURNING. ENDLESSLY BURNING.

I awoke to heat and the stench of my own scorched flesh. My body was wreathed in flame. I didn't need to look to know it, my every nerve ending screamed it.

Falling.

I thought I had succumbed to another of my brother's death traps, some pit or chasm of fire.

But I had descended for too long and too weightlessly for it to be that.

I opened my eyes and in the few seconds I had before their vitreous humours boiled and then evaporated in their sockets, I saw a vast orb below me through the blazing heat haze.

It was a grey – almost pallid world – wreathed with white cloud. I was far above it, breaching its upper atmosphere without a ship or even the protection of my armour.

Skin burned away. Flesh too, then muscle.

My head wrenched back, my mouth agape in a silent scream as I experienced agony on a scale without measure.

Stars and nebulae flashed before me but I had not the facility to see them.

As my brain rebelled against what my body was telling it, I witnessed my own destruction through my mind's eye.

Vulkan, his body an inferno...

...skin shrivelling like parchment, his meat-fat spitting...

...his flesh sloughing away and disintegrating.

Vulkan, rendered down to blackened bone.

His withered skeleton breaches the upper atmosphere until finally...

Vulkan dies.

ACKNOWLEDGEMENTS

A FEW THANKS need sharing around to some dedicated and very special folks without whom this novel would not have been possible, my editors Christian Dunn, Lindsey Priestley, Laurie Goulding and Graeme Lyon. Also, the legendary Neil Roberts for the fantastic cover. To Dan Abnett, whose advice and support has been utterly invaluable. Last, but not least, my wonderful other half, Stef, whose patience, understanding and encouragement got me through the tough times.

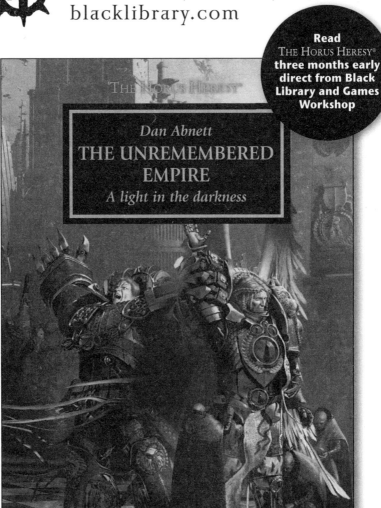

An extract from
The Unremembered Empire
by Dan Abnett

THE PEOPLE OF the farming community did not hold the Pharos in any particular awe. It was simply part of their world. They often used its obsidian apertures as caves to shelter them and their herds from storms. They had also, long ago, discovered the extraordinary acoustic qualities of the linked chambers and halls, and had taken to playing their pipes and horns and psalteries in the deep caves, creating music of unparalleled beauty and mystery.

From the first moment that he arrived to inspect the Pharos, Dantioch had understood that the interlinking chambers had not been intended as occupation spaces, at least not for any creatures of humanoid dimensions. There were often places of near impossible access between chambers: deep, polished drops; smooth sheer curves; untenable slopes. There were no stairs, no measured walkways. In one particular instance, a vast tri-lobed chamber, shaped almost like a stomach, plunged away into a polished tube seven hundred metres deep, which opened in the ceiling of another vast, semi-spherical hall a hundred metres high.

A long, slow process of construction had been undertaken over the years, establishing self-levelling, pre-fabricated walkways of STC design to provide platforms, ladders, stairs and bridges that would allow humans to traverse and explore the almost endless interior of the Pharos.

Dantioch and his Ultramarines escort descended on just such a walkway. The Imperial equipment, solid and steady, locked into place over the rolling, polished curves of the Pharos's chambers, seemed crude by comparison: treated, unpainted metal, cold-pressed from a standard template, stamped with the Imperial aquila, echoing to their footsteps with leaden clatters. When they walked upon the polished black, they made only the softest tapping sounds. The walkways, stairs and platforms were also dwarfed by the gloomy chambers they threaded through, and seemed frail by comparison to the sheened black curves and cliffs.

Arkus and his Scouts patiently led the crippled warsmith to the abyssal plain of Primary Location Alpha. Twice on the journey they passed farmworkers eating supper and playing their instruments. Oberdeii, one of the Scouts, and the youngest of the entire company, shooed them away. The Pharos had been officially out of bounds ever since Dantioch had brought the quantum-pulse engines, deep in the mountain's core, online. They could all hear, or at least feel, the infrasonic throb of the vast and ancient devices.

Dantioch had stood in Primary Location Alpha, and nodded to his escort to withdraw. He had been fairly confident that he understood the function of the Pharos even from the data he had studied before his arrival on Sotha. Guilliman had deduced it too. Primary Location Alpha was, he was sure, the centre of the entire mechanism. Dantioch found himself referring to it in his notes as the 'tuning stage' or the 'sounding board'. It was a vast cave of polished black, with a domed ceiling and an almost flat floor.

Ghosts walked here, images of things light years away, drawn into the Pharos by its quantum processes. They were often fleeting, but always real. It had taken Dantioch two weeks and immense astronomical calculations to tune the Pharos as he wanted it.

As he walked onto the tuning floor, Dantioch saw Guilliman appear before him, as if in the flesh.

He had finally tuned the xenos device to far distant Macragge.

'It is as you speculated, my lord,' Dantioch said. 'The Pharos is part of an ancient interstellar navigation system. It is both a beacon and a route-finder. And, as we just saw, it also permits instantaneous communication across unimaginable distances.'

'You say I speculated, Dantioch,' said Guilliman's image, 'but I never had the slightest clue what manner of technology it was.'

'It is not fully understood by me either, lord,' replied the warsmith. 'It certainly involves a principle of quantum entanglement. But I believe that, unlike our warp technology that uses the immaterium to by-pass realspace, this quantum function once allowed for site-to-site teleportation, perhaps through a network of gateways. I also believe its fundamental function lies not with psychic energy, but with empathic power. It is an empathic system, adjusted to the needs of the user, not the will. I will provide fuller findings later.'

'But it is a navigational beacon?' asked Guilliman.

'In many ways.'

'You said it was part of a network?'

Dantioch nodded.

'I believe other stations like the Pharos must exist, or once existed, on other worlds throughout the galaxy.'

Guilliman paused.

'So it is not one, single beacon, like the Astronomican?'

'No, lord. In two ways. I believe the Pharos and other stations like it once used to create a network of navigational pathways between stars, as opposed to a single, range-finding point the way the Astronomican does. Or did.'

'Go on.'

'It is more like a lantern than a beacon, lord. You tune it. You point it, and illuminate a site or location for the benefit of range-finding. Now I have tuned to Macragge, I can, I believe, light up Macragge as a bright spot that will be visible throughout real-space and the warp, despite the Ruinstorm.'

'Just as I see Sotha as a new star in the sky?'

'Yes, my lord.'

Guilliman looked at him.

'I am loath to use xenos technology, but the light of the Astronomican is lost to us because of the Ruinstorm. To hold Ultramar together, to rebuild the Five Hundred Worlds, we must restore communication and travel links. We must navigate and reposition. We must pierce and banish this age of darkness. This is the first step towards our survival. This is how we fight back and overthrow Horus and his daemon allies. Dantioch, I applaud you and thank you for the peerless work you have done, and the labours you are yet to undertake.'

'My lord.'

Dantioch, with difficulty, bowed.

'Warsmith?'

'Yes, my lord?'

'Illuminate Macragge.'